T0354945

J. T. O'Brien

Black Snow

iUniverse, Inc.
Bloomington

This is a work of fiction. All of the characters, names, incidents, organizations, and dialogue in this novel are either the products of the author's imagination or are used fictitiously.

iUniverse books may be ordered through booksellers or by contacting:

iUniverse
1663 Liberty Drive
Bloomington, IN 47403
www.iuniverse.com
1-800-Authors (1-800-288-4677)

Because of the dynamic nature of the Internet, any Web addresses or links contained in this book may have changed since publication and may no longer be valid. The views expressed in this work are solely those of the author and do not necessarily reflect the views of the publisher, and the publisher hereby disclaims any responsibility for them.

Any people depicted in stock imagery provided by Thinkstock are models, and such images are being used for illustrative purposes only.

Certain stock imagery © Thinkstock.

ISBN: 978-1-4502-8294-9 (sc)
ISBN: 978-1-4502-8297-0 (hc)
ISBN: 978-1-4502-8296-3 (ebook)

Printed in the United States of America

iUniverse rev. date: 12/31/2010

This book is dedicated to my three sons;
Timothy, John and Steven,
J. T. O'Brien

My special thanks to Carl Park for his cover art work
and valued advice.

Chapter One

Sunday Night.

Jack Kelly spotted an unusual hump laying in the fresh snow just a couple of doors down from the Tavern. Snow flakes the size of quarters had been blowing on a gale wind for about twenty minutes. A sudden squall line had roared down across the western prairie and lightning strikes flashed frequently emphasizing the intensity of the storm. The resultant thunder rumbled continuously, not in pulsing impacts, but incessantly echoing back and forth across the dark cloudy skies in an intense low roar. It was an unusual sound and signified a very bad night indeed. It was weather such as this that made life extremely unpleasant for a Chicago Cop. Walking a Beat in the freezing cold of December was bad enough, but pushing through snow and against that wind was cumulatively exhausting.

For an hour and half since coming on duty he had been going through the same old boring routine of shaking doorknobs and peering into the dim interiors of the businesses. Then twenty minutes ago things went from unpleasant to miserable as he fought his way through the weather. That he had seen the figure lying there by the curb in this blizzard was primarily due to a red neon sign in the window of Becker's Furniture Store. He had glanced toward the street and noticed a dark red shadow. In weather such as this one tends to concentrate on the immediate task at hand and shielding your face from the wind tends to limit your breadth of vision. Jack was so preoccupied with checking out the doors that it was entirely possible that he could have missed the body lying on the wide sidewalk.

At first sight Jack figured it was probably just another drunk, someone that had slipped on the ice and had passed out in the new snow. As he approached the body he considered the distinct possibility that it may have been a pedestrian that had been struck by an automobile or perhaps hit by a streetcar. Stranger things had happened along this street on stormy nights. Had the body been there for very long, somebody, a passerby or a bar patron should have noticed, but then again it was just after midnight and due to the storm and to the fact that it was a Sunday night the streets were almost devoid of traffic. Jack was very surprised when he recognized the man, it was Myron Howard. It was good old Myron, alias "Hymie," and the poor soul was laying flat on his back in the fresh snow. There was a surprised expression on his face and two very large bullet holes in his chest. A patina of snow had dusted the dead man's apparel. Jack could reasonably conclude that the body hadn't been lying there for very long. After a quick moment spent in appraising the overall scene for the killer or killers and finding no apparent threat Jack reached down and checked for a pulse. The flesh was cold to the touch, but inside the coat there was still a faint warmth. There was no discernable pulse. The bullet holes in the coat were surrounded by the powder burns indicating close contact with the barrel of the gun. So Mister Howard had been shot at extremely close range, taking two quick ones in the chest. No wonder he appeared to be surprised. Jack stood up again and looked around the area. There were no fresh tracks leading too or away from the crime scene and therefore he could conclude that the shooting had to have occurred at least fifteen to twenty minutes ago, or at least before the heavy new snow began falling. Off to the side, up against the wall, he saw two cartridges and he picked up the two spent forty-five caliber shells. So it seemed safe to conclude that Mister Howard had been shot with a forty-five caliber semi-automatic pistol.

Based upon the position of the body and the location of the shell casings, Jack surmised that the Shooter had stood about here. About four feet away from the victim and then the Killer, man or woman, had simply reached up and placed the weapon next to Hymies' chest and coolly and with great malice pulled the trigger. Old Hymie with a faint smile on his face and who was evidently not expecting a problem, had been slammed on his back on the sidewalk as if he had been hit by a truck. There was no rolling or writhing of the body because the poor guy was probably dead before he hit the ground. In a way it was very professional.

He had always liked Hymie Howard. Sure the guy was something of a flake and a hustler, but he was an amiable flake. For the most part Hymie was a quiet and unassuming sort of guy and not a trouble maker. Jack liked guys that could go about their business peaceably, whether it was straight or dishonest, just as long as they didn't hurt anybody. "Hymie" was of course a derogatory nickname indicating Mister Myron Howard's Jewish ancestry, but oddly enough there seemed to be no insult intended and to Hymie it was just a nickname known only to a few of his close acquaintances from the Depot Tavern. He usually responded to the nickname with a sardonic smile.

For his last big performance Hymie was dressed very well. He looked much as a banker might. He wore a very nice camel hair coat, which was now marred by two very neat, slightly singed bullet holes, but still, Hymie looked very good, very professional. That is he looked very good taking his present condition into account. The old boy had evidently been going first class and the big diamond ring that he had always worn and constantly flashed to the suckers was still on his finger, which would sort of rule out the possibility of a mugging gone wrong. The inescapable conclusion was that this was cold blooded murder.

Once again Jack looked left and right for as far as he could see in this mess of weather and the street was empty. There were no shadowy figures lurking about. Jack believed that Hymie was too wise an old fox to have allowed some punk approach him at night. So what did that say about the killer? The people that knew the dangers of the street always looked around carefully and sized up the conditions before they barged blindly out into traffic. This was a jungle and if you weren't a predator you learned to move carefully.

Across the street to the south of where he stood were the steps leading up to the entrance to the Englewood Train Station, which was just east of the wide viaduct that shaded the street and accommodated the four or five tracks of the Wabash and Mono Railroads. It was usually quiet here at this time of night and at this time of the year. During the summer the street would still be roaring even on a Sunday night, but not in the depths of winter.

There were no cabs waiting at the station, because the last commuter train for the night had left long ago and it would be a couple of hours before the locals began pulling into the station again. No cabbies, no red caps, nobody waiting for a street car. That meant that there probably weren't any witnesses to the shooting. A streetcar rattled by, its bell clanging out a warning in the blinding swirl. There were no passengers on board the car and apparently no one was waiting at the stop in front of the tavern, therefore the Motorman didn't even bother to slow down. Jack wondered if someone in a passing streetcar could have witnessed the shooting, but that was unlikely given the steamed up windows and blowing snow. Jack bent down again and moved the body slightly. There was no fresh snow beneath his legs, but then whatever had been there could have melted due to body heat. He removed the diamond ring and searched inside for Hymie's wallet. Then he checked the pockets and put everything that he found in his big coat pocket. Satisfied that he had seen all that there was to see he checked his location in reference to the nearest Police Call Box. Pat McDonald's Depot Tavern was still open and as much as Jack hated to leave the scene he had to make contact. It was at least half a block or more to the next call box and so he opted for the shorter distance and walked down to the bar and went inside.

There were four men in the bar. Pat McDonald was behind the bar and Barney and Joe, who were two of the regulars, sat in their usual positions down at the far end. Jack nodded to the aging drunks. He had busted both of them on occasion and they always went along peacefully, which was good for everybody. A tall, broad shouldered stranger was having a shot and beer and all of them looked up in a startled fashion as Jack entered the room.

McDonald shouted out rather gleefully, "Well, well, Officer Kelly, what brings you in here on this terrible night?"

4

"I need to use your phone." Kelly moved closer to the bar and removed his night stick from its keeper. "You guys see anything unusual or hear any noises outside about twenty minutes ago?"

The pair at the end shook their heads and went back to their drinks. Pat replied that he hadn't heard or seen a thing. Only the stranger remained silent, but he was watching Kelly in the back bar mirror.

Kelly stepped up to a point directly behind the man. "How about you mister, did you see anything?" Kelly asked.

The man shook his head no, but didn't turn around.

Kelly jerked the man off of the bar stool and slammed him back up against the bar. "Don't move, don't do anything stupid. Spread your legs and lean your hands against the bar."

"Hey, what the fuck are you doing?" The man shouted belligerently. "You can't do this to me! Goddamn Chicago Cops, think they can do anything that they want to! My lawyer will hear about this."

Jack ignored the complaints and rapidly searched the man, keeping one hand in the middle of the guys back. "Don't try to kid me. The only lawyer you ever knew was the prosecuting attorney. You got any ID?"

"I don't have to put up with this bullshit! Why don't you search the other guys?"

Jack leaned forward and whispered in the man's ear. "Because, I know the other guys, asshole, and you're the one I'm interested in. Now, give me your wallet, or I'll take it from your unconscious body."

"Jesus Christ! This is the last time I'll ever come into this joint." He protested in a loud whining tone, but he prudently produced the wallet.

"What are you doing out here on the south side, Mister Bill Sweeny? This license says that you live on the North side."

The burley man tried to turn around, but Jack wouldn't let him and pushed him back up against the bar. "I told you not to do anything stupid," Jack warned.

"If it's any of your business I'm visiting a relative."

Jack looked up at McDonald. "Do you know this flake, Pat?"

McDonald shrugged exaggeratedly. "Oh yeah, we're old pals, Jack."

Jack was suspicious. "How long has this guy been in here Pat?" "Aw hell, we've all been here for a couple of hours or so, Kelly. Why do you ask?"

"I'm just curious. Patrick, you wouldn't be covering for this guy would you?"

"No, no we were just having a little chat. He's an old friend."

Jack didn't believe a word of it. "When did Hymie leave?" Jack asked.

"Hymie Howard? Hell I ain't seen him. In fact I ain't seen him for several days."

Kelly decided that was another lie, then he noted that McDonald was sweating slightly, which was unusual for such a chill night. Nevertheless, he nodded pushed the big man back into his seat and went to the phone. He warned the man. "Stay there and keep quiet." Then he called. "Operator, this is an emergency call. Give me Englewood Police Department." There was a long pause, during which Kelly fidgeted impatiently. "Sergeant Polansky, this is Patrolman Kelly, I have a homicide on the north side of Sixty-Third Street, just a few steps east of the Depot Tavern. We'll need the Coroner's wagon, and the Homicide Squad. I'll be at the scene waiting."

Kelly listened impatiently for a moment and then said loudly. "Because the poor bastard has two forty five bullet holes in his chest. Now, I know that you think that I'm still just a new guy, Sarg, but I think that qualifies as a homicide don't you."

Kelly listened intently for a couple of minutes. "Yes, Sergeant, the guy is dead. No, Sergeant Polansky, we don't need an ambulance, yes Sergeant Polansky, we will need the Coroner. I'll be out there watching for the units." There was a pause as Kelly listened, "Because, Sergeant, this bar is a lot closer than the call box and it's a hell of lot warmer in here. Yes I'll be out there waiting." Kelly hung up the phone and walked to the door. He experienced an impulse to take Sweeny along with him, but other than a hunch and some indication

Black Snow

that the guy was an ex con there was really nothing to tie the guy to the shooting. "Stick around for a while Pat, the Detectives will want to talk to all of you. That includes you Mister Sweeny!" Kelly shouted a goodbye as he buttoned his coat and went back out into the cold. He hated to go back out because his feet were just beginning to warm up. He wasn't surprised to find that the street was still deserted and that his old friend Hymie Howard was still lying there as peacefully as ever. The snow was a little deeper now. Jack concluded that a train must have passed over the viaduct because now the new fallen snow was black with soot. He probably hadn't noticed the passing of the train, because he had been too interested in Mr. Sweeny.

This guy Sweeny was big and kind of ugly looking. Jack concluded that he may have been mob muscle. The guy had the look of an ex-con; he had jail house tattoos on his knuckles, which meant that he had been in the can and that he was dumb enough to mark himself. Furthermore, emphasizing Sweeny's jail house experience, no matter what was said he would never meet Kelly's eyes directly. Cons didn't try to stare down the jailors or cops; it was a learned trait, like shuffling their feet slightly due to chain restraints. Mister Sweeny was Jack's number one suspect, but he hadn't been carrying a weapon, not that it mattered much, because the piece could be anywhere. It could be in the men's john in the trash or behind the bar, or the guy could have passed it to Pat for safe keeping. Not that any of this speculation would matter much because the Detectives weren't apt to listen to the opinions of a new beat cop. Of course, Jack wasn't exactly new, he had been on duty nights for six years now, but these days they weren't doing much hiring and so he was still the 'New' guy.

As he expected, the first thing that happened was that the Coroner's guys walked all over the area for a few minutes totally screwing up what little evidence existed, which meant that his notes of the pristine scene were the only basis for the investigation.

Sergeant Monaghan of the Homicide Squad looked down at the corpse and asked the name.

"Myron Howard," Jack responded, "he is one of the local flakes. Because I had to leave the body here I had to take this ring," Jack

7

gave the ring to the Sergeant, "and his wallet and I cleared his pockets of the larger items including these car keys." Jack had looked up from his notes to inform the Homicide Detective.

Dick Monaghan was a quiet, brainy old guy, with years of experience, but his side kick, was an obnoxious and ambitious moron named Auggie Schmidt, whose uncle ran the Chicago Sanitation Department, which in Chicago, explained how anyone as dumb as Schmidt could get on the PD.

"What are you doing, Officer Kelly?" Schmidt bellowed.

"I'm making a copy of my notes for Sergeant Monaghan."

"You won't need any copies! Give the fucking notes to the Sergeant."

Kelly looked up momentarily and then went back to copying his notes.

"Did you hear what I said, asshole?"

Kelly smiled at the bellicose detective and went back to his notes.

Schmidt snatched at the copybook and Kelly deftly turned away. "Keep your hands to yourself Schmidt, or you'll be riding to the hospital with Hymie."

Schmidt barked a loud laugh. "You really think you're tough don't you Kelly. One of these days I'll kick your ass till your fucking ears ring."

"Leave him alone, Schmidt," Monaghan said quietly. "We are here to conduct a homicide investigation not to wrestle around in the snow." He turned to the uniformed officer, "What else have we got Jack?"

He dutifully handed a copy and a rough sketch of the scene over to Sergeant Monaghan. Jack Kelly briefly went over his arrival at the scene and handed the Sergeant the two empty shell casings. "Then I went down to the bar to make the call to the station. The owner and two regulars were in there, plus this guy named Sweeny. I shook Sweeny down, but he didn't have a weapon on him. Unless I miss my bet this Sweeny is an ex con and just might be the shooter. I didn't have the time or the man power to lock down the activities in the bar and still watch over Hymie, but we ought to go back there and check things out."

"Auggie go down to the Depot Tavern and check on this guy Sweeny."

"Why don't you send the new guy?"

"Cause, I'm sending you."

"Yeah, well okay, Boss." Auggie walked off grumbling about the injustice of a Detective choosing a Beat Cop to converse with rather than another Detective.

Monaghan glanced at Auggie and said irritably," Ignore that obnoxious asshole."

A few minutes later Auggie was back. "There wasn't anybody named Sweeny in there."

Monaghan nodded absently as if he wasn't surprised by this news and went back to talking to Jack Kelly.

"Did they say which way he went?" Jack asked.

Auggie imitated a female voice, "No, they didn't say a fucking thing about that Detective Kelly."

Monaghan glanced sharply at Auggie and the big man looked away from the Sergeant's angry stare. "How did Mister Howard get here?" Monaghan asked.

Jack shrugged, "I would imagine that he drove. The car keys are to a Ford. There are lots of Fords around here."

"So he drove to this rendezvous?"

Jack looked around and shrugged. "I have no clue," he said.

It was well after one thirty when they got back to Pat's Tavern. The owner was waiting impatiently to lock up. Everybody had a drink to ward off the chill and the drinks were on the house of course. The regulars were still sitting there happily sharing the late hours, but Mister Sweeny had long ago left the scene.

"I told the guy to wait," Jack complained.

"He said some things about you that weren't very complementary and suggested that if you didn't like it, you could stick your badge up your ass," Pat smiled broadly. "Mind you, I didn't say that Jack, he did."

Kelly laughed, "I think you're enjoying giving me that message, Patrick. He didn't leave anything with you did he?"

Patrick shook his head emphatically. "Such as?" Pat asked and then he caught the implication, "Oh hell no, no, no nothing at all."

"You say that he came in here a couple of hours before the shooting?"

Pat wasn't to be fooled. "I don't know what time the shooting took place, Jack, but he was here for quite a while."

Kelly nodded, "I have feeling that you aren't being completely truthful with me, Patrick."

"Jesus Christ, Kelly, you fuckers come in here and drink my whisky and then call me a liar. What the hell kind of friends are those?"

"Calm down, McDonald!" Dick Monaghan ordered. "This is a murder investigation and we don't want to be investigating your demise. If you know anything you had better tell us before this asshole comes back looking for you."

McDonald folded his arms belligerently across his chest and said nothing.

As the Officers left the bar Monaghan turned to Kelly. "What do you think, Jack?"

"I think that he's lying and that he is scared. Pat is usually mellow."

"Yeah, well he's a buddy of the Captain's, so we got to take it kind of easy."

"Buddy of the Captain's? Hell, I didn't know that."

"Yeah, he gives the Captain a big prime rib at Christmas and a turkey at Thanksgiving."

Jack was impressed. "Well, tomorrow is my day off. I can kind of stop by and have a drink or two and ask a few questions."

"This is an official investigation, Patrolman Kelly," Schmidt said. "Keep your fucking nose out of it."

Monaghan frowned at Schmidt, shook his head in disgust and then turned to Jack. "You've done a good job of this Jack, why don't you stop by and check on Pat tomorrow. Maybe he'll be feeling more like talking. By the way Jack when you come in off duty I want you to look through the mug books to see if we can ID this clown Sweeny."

When they went back outside the thunder and lightning was moving further away toward the East and the wind had diminished, but the snow had increased. It was quieter now as the falling snow muffled all of the normal street sounds. Jack watched the attendants load old Hymie in the ambulance and then after the photographer took pictures of the mess in the bloody black snow, the Officers departed the scene. By that time they were all shivering and stomping their feet to keep warm. Now he was alone again in the deserted street. The excitement was over for the night. He looked around the street and then bundled his coat tightly about his chest, His intent was to continue on this beat and go back to shaking the door knobs. As he passed the bar he could see Pat and the two regulars jabbering excitedly about the night's events. Then he noticed the only set of fresh set of half covered tracks that had exited from the side door leading away toward the viaduct. That great detective Auggie might have noticed something as obvious as the tracks, Jack thought, but he hadn't or hadn't thought to follow them. In another half hour you'd never see these tracks, because with the snow and all, the surface would be smooth. Of course the snow only extended a few feet inward under the railroad bridge that extended over the street, but he followed along under the big structure and picked up a single set of tracks leading out to the west. There was a side street adjacent to and parallel to the railroad bridge and it was on this rarely used street that he found the car. The tracks led straight to it and then led away toward the next streetcar stop. Jack couldn't see down to the car stop in this blizzard and he didn't want to walk down there, at least not yet, but he had to check. There was no one waiting there, although there were some tracks and some cigarette butts on top of the snow. Mister Sweeny evidently couldn't start his car and had decided to take public transportation. Jack walked back and checked and recorded the license. He suspected that the car had been stolen specifically for transportation to this murder. The driver's door was partially open and the keys were in the ignition. The car hadn't been hot-wired so maybe it wasn't stolen. A quick check of the glove compartment revealed that this 1937 Packard Sedan belonged to a Mr. Steven Kaplan, who lived up in Oak Dale, which was a North side community. Well, Kelly thought, if it was stolen then Mr. Kaplan had just lucked out, because he got his car back in one piece. There was a Police Call Box at the corner and Jack called in to report the stolen vehicle. He asked for Detective Monaghan and waited for a few minutes. So this Sweeny character had parked around the corner well away from the bar.

As Jack waited he wondered why Mister Sweeny would kill a guy like Hymie Howard. Could it be a Jew-Gentile thing? He didn't think so. Hymie was too smart to antagonize a guy like Sweeny. Sweeny might have killed him in a bar fight, but Pat had not described any such argument taking place or if there had been such an altercation, he had conveniently forgotten about it. There was no doubt in Kelly's mind that a guy like Sweeny would be capable of spontaneous murder, but this didn't have the marks of a bar argument, what with the car parked unobtrusively on a side street and all, it had the look of premeditated murder. Obviously the question was why?

Monaghan came on the line and Kelly explained the tracks and the stolen car.

"I think you've nailed it, Jack. Good work. We'll be out to look at the car as soon as we can get there." He paused for a moment, "Is there anything else, Jack?"

"If this guy is the killer as I suspect, then Pat was lying in his teeth."

"Yeah," Monaghan agreed. "This guy Sweeny, or whatever his name is, probably intimidated everybody in the bar to tell the same story. Well, we'll look up Mister McDonald in the morning. Meanwhile the fingerprint guys can go over the car. Take care Jack, it's dangerous out there on nights such as this."

"Sarg, just a minute please, my point is that this guy didn't have any weapon on him. It's got to be in the bar. I don't think he would take a chance of walking out of Pat's with a weapon when the Cops were right outside."

"Are they still in there?" Monaghan asked.

"They were when I walked by, but I think I saw Pat's car driving down the street."

"So you think we better check Pat's place when it opens in the morning?"

"That might be the prudent thing to do."

"Take care Jack, I'll see you in a couple of hours. Be at Pat's bar when it opens. By the way when does it open?"

"Calvin usually starts swamping it out and restocking the bar around five-thirty in the morning so that they can open for the first commuters. I occasionally stop in there around then for a cup of coffee."

"Be careful, it's a dangerous place out there."

Jack laughed, "Hell Sarg, it's always dangerous out here."

"Hold on, Jack the Desk Sergeant wants to talk to you."

"Yeah," Jack responded to the Sergeant's shout.

"Where in the hell are you?" The Sergeant wanted to know.

"I'm at a Call Box at Sixty-Third and Lowe. I've been checking out this stolen car."

"Listen there Hawkshaw, who in the hell do you think you are Sherlock Holmes? Get your ass back on the job and leave the investigations to the Dicks."

"Jesus thanks Sarg, for a minute there I thought I was a police officer."

"Never mind your smart college boy bullshit! Wait a minute! A disturbance call just came in at Sixty-first and Lowe. That is just two blocks away. It's at sixty-one-twenty-six to be exact. It's an apartment building. Get down there and see what's going on."

"Okay," Jack replied. "I'm on my way, but it will take me a while to get there."

Jack closed the Call Box and shivered at the chill wind. Two blocks to walk in the black snow, he thought. The snow was beginning to build up and he went out to walk down the center of the street where the snow was compacted.

As he trudged along he thought about the murder. It was true that Hymie had a shady reputation and had been known to have

13

played a little fast and loose with other people's money. The good side was that Howard had never used a gun, nor had he ever done hard time as far as Jack knew. He had believed that the little guy was too smart for that. Unfortunately, for Hymie there were guys in Chicago that had mean tempers. They were the type of people that had been known to get violently irate about people taking their money. So perhaps Hymie had inadvertently made the final mistake and had chosen the wrong mark?

When Jack finally arrived at the scene of the disturbance there were several people standing on the front porch in their night clothes. Whatever in the hell was going on it had to be threatening for people to be outside dressed like that on a night such as this. "What's going on here?" Jack shouted and everyone tried to respond at once.

"He's killed a dozen people!" A woman shouted.

"He's got a shotgun! And he's using it," cried another female.

"Who has a shotgun?" Jack demanded.

"That crazy drunken Dago that lives up on the third floor."

"You say he has shot some one?"

One man nodded vigorously. "I'm the Super. That's why I'm out here! Why the hell else would I be standing half naked in this goddamn blizzard in the middle of the night. He's been raising hell for at least an hour and then he started shooting. We called the Goddamn Police Station a dozen times and they finally send one Cop. Who in the hell are you, Superman?"

Jack glared at the loud mouth and the guy shut up and turned way from him. "You say he's on the third floor?" Jack asked.

"He was until he started shooting. I don't know where he is now, Officer"

That's better, Jack thought, on impulse Jack removed his overcoat. He wanted to be able to move fast and the big coat was inhibiting. He wrapped the overcoat around the shoulders of an elderly lady.

She thanked him profusely.

Jack shrugged and went inside. In here, without the wind noise and the murmurs of the crowd it was very quiet and Jack found that ominous. He would have preferred to hear someone raising hell so that he would know where his enemy might be. It was also very hot and stuffy and the odors of the various suppers were still floating on the atmosphere, He could detect boiled cabbage and roast beef, but that's the best he could do. He loosened his revolver in its holster and started up the stairs. Small dim bulbs lighted the passageways and the stairways, except that on the second floor landing it was dark. It was on the second floor landing that he found the body of a man who had suffered a cluster of chest and stomach wounds. Jack recognized the pattern. Double-ought buckshot, eight, thirty-two caliber rounds fired in one quick explosion from the barrel of a twelve gauge shotgun. A charge of this sort had been designed to take down a large animal. It was a deadly force, but it didn't scatter like birdshot would. At this range the shooter would either hit or miss. Half way up the stairs to the third landing there was another body and above him, on the third level he could hear a faint movement and a moaning. There was no helping that first poor devil on the second landing and so Jack moved to the next victim, which was that of a woman. She evidently had been fleeing for she had caught the full force of the buck shot in the back and the mangled body had been thrown forward and down and had slid about half way down the stairs. Her nightgown had evidently been hoisted up, presumably so that she could run. Her plump little legs, scarred by varicose veins were pointed upward toward the third floor. Her thick black hair was rolled up in ringlets and held in place with bobby pins. She still had a nice, slightly plump figure and looked okay, but for the mangled back. From the look of her she too may have been dead before she hit the floor. Jack moved to the wall side of the stairs to reduce the possibility that the steps would squeak and he removed his hat, laying it on the floor well away from the blood pools. He moved upward tentatively until just his eyes were above the floor level. There was another body near the head of the stairs and it was this poor guy that was moaning. At the far end of the hall a man was leaning back against the wall and he had a shotgun in his hands. His head was down and he was shaking it to and fro.

Jack removed his revolver from its holster and cocked it. The sound seemed to reverberate through the silent hall. The man's head came up instantly and he stared at the stairwell, but he didn't move.

Jack reasoned that there wasn't much light coming up from below and that he was still in the shadows. The man probably couldn't see him.

"Put down the gun," Jack said calmly.

"Who are you?" The man shouted.

Maintaining a steady tone of voice Jack said. "I'm Police Officer Kelly, put down the gun."

"So, you fuckers finally got here, huh?" The man was alert now and was moving slowly toward the stairs. Obviously he was not awed by the arrival of the police. "Where are you, you Mick sonofabitch?"

Down below the front door banged open and Jack could feel a cold blast of air and could hear Auggie Schmidt shouting. "Jack where in the hell are you?"

Once again Jack calmly ordered the man to lay the gun on the floor.

The killer raised the weapon and fired two rounds in quick succession. As the man had raised the weapon Jack had ducked down and threw himself down upon the stairs. As the two shots went overhead and impacted the wall behind him he raised up. Now the man had opened the breech and held the shotgun in his left hand and was plucking out the two used cartridges from the chambers and dropping them to the floor. As Jack cleared the top of the stairs the man was fumbling in his pocket, presumably for more ammunition. Jack rushed across the intervening space in a second as he ran toward the man. The guy inserted the first round and made the mistake of reaching for a second round. Jack's thirty-eight came down with tremendous force squarely between the man's eyes and he dropped to floor as if he had been struck by lightning.

Auggie and Monaghan were running up the steps as Jack stepped to one side to lean against the wall to gather his wits for a moment. It had been a very near thing. His hands were shaking as he leaned back. Then he reached down and picked up the shotgun and cleared the weapon. As he did so he called out. "It's okay. I got him. He's disarmed." Then Jack reached down, leaned the shotgun against the wall and cuffed the unconscious killer.

Auggie had stopped on the second floor as Monaghan had continued racing up the rest of the stairs to the third floor.

"You're having quite a night of it Jack," Monaghan laughed, as he bent down next to the bloody form of the moaning victim that lay at the head of the stairs.

"Ain't that the truth?"

Monaghan looked up from the wounded man and looked at Jack and shook his head. His expression said that this one wasn't going to make it. "Did you kill that miserable bastard?" Monaghan calmly inquired.

"No. Er, that is, I don't think so. But I did hit him awfully hard."

Monaghan kneeled down and checked the pulse of the killer. "Too bad, he's still breathing."

The killer stirred and moaned.

"It does appear that he's still alive," Monaghan said. Then he returned to the stairwell. "You can come up here now Auggie, it is all over."

"Aw for Christ's sake, Monaghan, I was just checking out these casualties," Auggie explained in an aggrieved tone of voice.

"They're dead, Auggie. Leave them for the Coroner."

Monaghan and Kelly exchanged momentary glances and the sergeant grimaced and nodded.

The moaning of the wounded man at the head of the stairs stopped in a series of gasps. Monaghan had knelt to check the victim on the floor and he looked up and shook his head, "Three dead," he said.

The people were allowed back into their apartments, but the scene from the second floor up was barred and so the folks on the lower floors had to accommodate guests for a while, but at least they were all in the from the cold and Jack had retrieved his overcoat.

The old lady thanked him again and again. He had trouble getting away from her.

The story that slowly unraveled was that Mr. Di Angelo had been making a night of it, which evidently was not all that unusual. He got home around two a.m. and the nightly fight had started.

Then the neighbors had begun loudly complaining and what with the booze and the wife and neighbors all raising hell with him, Di Angelo evidently decided to kill a few of them, which is what he promptly did. Monaghan listened patiently to their stories as Jack completed his report of the incident. Then they all went back out on the street. Auggie was unusually and curiously silent throughout the investigation.

"Four homicides in one night," Auggie muttered. "That's the worse in a while."

It was just a little after three-thirty when the bodies were removed and the scene investigation was completed. Jack caught a ride back to the Sixty-Third Street Call Box with the Detectives and then he called in.

"I'm going to lunch, Sarg. I'm starving."

"Okay, Hawkshaw, but the Sergeant from homicide wants you down at the Depot at five thirty, so finish your lunch and make a quick round of the area."

"Sarg, on this night there is no such thing as a quick round."

"All right, all right, just do your best and for Christ's sake, don't get in any more trouble."

Jack Kelly thought that was funny. He had been on this beat since he got out of the Academy six years ago and though he normally bitched about boredom, on this particular night he had run into four homicides and had come close to getting his ass shot off. That was all the excitement that he needed.

He took the streetcar down to Halstead where there was a restaurant on the corner. He stood there for a minute looking around, checking out the shadows in the doorways for any unexplainable movement. Then he checked out the cars along the curb and looked through the steamy windows at the few people scattered about the restaurant. None of the cars parked there were on the want list. He took one last cautious look around and then he went in and took his usual seat. This was always way in the back, where the lights were dim and where he could watch everyone. He didn't like bright lights or seats that would place him with his back to the doors. Jack took off his heavy coat and muffler and laid his hat on the table.

The waitresses saw him come in and began whispering.

"There's that handsome beast and that's my table." Sally said.

Lucy shrugged her shoulders as if she didn't care to argue. "I don't think he's so handsome. Look at those pale blue eyes. Angelo the cook says that those are the eyes of a killer."

"I didn't say he was pretty, as a movie star might be. He is kind of roughed up in places. He's got a broken nose and there are those scars over the eyes. Those are from fighting. I know that because my cousin Bernie is a boxer. Bernie has the same kind of scars."

Lucy chuckled, "I'd like to get that big rascal in a bed. I'll bet that I could tame him."

"You're a married woman, Lucy, watch what you wish for." Sally smiled, "With that dark red hair and pale blue eyes, he is special. And on top of that he's a decent kind of guy, for a cop that is. I'd better get moving that big ape looks as though he's hungry."

Jack normally had a couple of cups of coffee and a hot sandwich, for which he always paid cash. He teased Sally and waved at Lucy, who always blew him a kiss. Then he settled down to relax a bit. By all estimations it had been an eventful evening. It wasn't often that he came across a corpse, much less four of them. He finished the sandwich, which had been excellent and filling and then he toyed with his coffee killing time as he thought about the events of the night. His hands weren't shaking anymore, but he was still as nervous as a cat. If that drunk hadn't been concentrating on reloading that shot gun, if he had slammed the breech close with that single round in the chamber he may have been able to nail Jack as he charged up the stairs. He rubbed his face with his hand. Jesus, he thought, that had been a close call.

Damn it. It is time to go back out into the cold and to make another round of the area. He dreaded that thought, but it had to be done and so he started to get up. Sally hurried to the table and poured him another refill of coffee and Jack settled back down. Well, he equivocated, maybe in another minute or two.

The problems in the Diner had started out simply enough; one drunk inadvertently spilled his coffee on another drunk. The movement caught Jack's attention and he was watching the action as the second drunk retaliated by pouring his coffee over the other guys head. Despite his impulse to laugh, Jack groaned and put on his cap. As he moved toward the altercation the first drunk took umbrage and sliced at the second guy with a steak knife. The second guy reached for his back pocket and Jack, who had been moving up slowly, suddenly knew he had trouble. Jack was reaching for his holstered thirty-eight when the second drunk managed to get a pistol out of his back pocket and fired three rounds at point blank range into his antagonist. Startled customers were diving for the floor or at least as close to the floor as they could get. The waitresses and counter guy were heading for the back.

The second drunk sensed that Jack was behind him, or perhaps he had caught the looks of darting fear in the eyes of the cook and waitresses. He spun about pointing the weapon at Jack and fired twice, both rounds went wide of the mark. Jack returned fire and shot the drunk twice through the upper body. The man staggered back and then tried to lift his weapon and fired again. Jack saw the life leaving the eyes of his opponent even as the man fired that last shot. This last round ricocheted off the deck and slammed into Jack's thigh. Jack took aim and fired again, putting this round directly through the man's head. It was a deliberate kill shot. He wanted to make damn sure that there would be no more shooting. The man was dead even as he fell backwards to the floor. Jack's hands were shaking as if he had palsy. He tentatively lowered his thirty-eight into its holster. It had all happened so incredibly fast. To cover his own fear he mustered his deepest masculine voice and told everybody to remain seated and had the waitress call for the homicide team. He checked the bodies for life and determined that they were both out of it. By now the women were screaming and crying. Jack tried to reassure them that it was over and then because he had to have something to do, he took out his notebook and began recording the names of the witnesses. He dropped his pencil twice and grimaced as his hands were still shaking. He had never before shot a man at point blank range. Even as he tried to disguise his fear he realized that it could just as easily have been him lying there dead on the floor of the diner. Had he been a fraction of a second slower, or if his opponent had been a shade more accurate, it could have gone the other way.

It was one of the girls that had noticed that the big cop was bleeding and Lucy tied a bandage around his thigh. It had felt to Jack as if someone had hit him on the leg with a hammer, but other than that he wasn't aware that he had been hit by a bullet. He stared down at his leg. "Jesus Christ! Do you see that?"

"Are you in much pain Jack?"

"Pain hell, do you see that hole in my trousers? Do you have any idea how much these Goddamn uniforms cost? Look at that, there's blood and all, Christ that stuff will never come out." It was a brave effort to disguise his fear, but he wasn't entirely successful and he began to shake again.

When Monaghan arrived he stood there and looked at Kelly for a long time before saying anything. "Jesus, Jack, have you got some kind of a bug up your ass? What the hell is going on tonight? Then he saw the bloody wrap on the thigh. "For Christ sake, Jack, sit down, we've got to get you to a hospital."

The witnesses were of one accord, the big young cop had done what he had to do. Things had happened so fast that most of the customers were still confused. A few weren't sure where had the cop come from? The ladies all thought that he was exceptionally handsome. Some people remembered seeing him come in. The waitresses were fawning over him and now he was certain that some of the sexual offers were quite sincere and though he was somewhat preoccupied he was flattered.

"Auggie, take this crazy bastard over to the hospital. "Come on, come on," Monaghan shouted, "get on with it."

At the hospital they wanted to cut his trousers away from the wound. He absolutely refused and insisted on taking off his trousers and as he did so he explained to the amused doctor that uniforms cost money.

"Can I cut the long johns, officer?" The Doctor asked.

"Oh yeah, we can sew those up."

The Doctor was chatting as he worked on the wound. "You know, son, I never had a guy that was shot worrying about the cost of his uniform before." He inserted a needle into Jack's swollen leg.

Jack watched the operation with irritation as he tried to explain. "I just got on the job six years ago. I don't make a hell of a lot of money. I live in a hotel alone. My mom can sew up the long johns when I get time to go out to her house, or we can just throw them away, but those uniforms are expensive. I hope I can get it fixed."

The Doctor was grinning as he probed the wound in Jack's thigh and the shattered bullet was removed. The wound had been more of a surface tear than it has a deep puncture. "Never saw one like that before. Did it hit something else first?"

Jack looked at the projectile. "Yeah it hit the floor first and then went up into my leg. I felt a punch, but I didn't think it was a bullet."

"I'm no expert but it looks like a twenty-five caliber. You're lucky it bounced first."

"It was a bullet from a little toy back up gun, something that you can carry in your back pocket." Jack handed the bullet to Auggie. "You can keep that as a souvenir, or as evidence, whichever you prefer."

Auggie stood there looking at the shattered round.

The Doctor took fifteen stitches to sew up the wound. "It's fairly clean, Jack. As I say you're lucky that the round lost a lot of energy when it hit the floor. Otherwise, you might be spending a couple of days here. Keep it clean. Come by tomorrow and we'll change the bandage for you. Take it easy for a couple of days or at least until it heals up a little, you can take aspirin for the pain or maybe a couple of shots of something."

Jack nodded his thanks and acknowledged the instructions.

A nurse came up to him with his trousers. "We washed the blood out of them, Jack. I'm sure that they can be repaired as good as new. If you want to come by my place later, I can do that for you."

Jack looked her up and down and smiled broadly, "I'd really appreciate your help, by the way what's your name?"

"My name is Alice Williams and I'll give you my address."

The Doctor was grinning broadly, "Good luck, Jack and take care of your self. Miss Williams we have patients waiting."

Alice smiled and gave Jack a note then she turned and hurried after the Doctor.

Auggie helped Jack out to the car and drove over to the station. Officer Kelly sat quietly in the right seat not saying anything.

"You okay, Jack?" Auggie asked.

Jack looked up, "Yeah, Auggie, I was just sitting here thinking that I shot that little bastard twice with this thirty-eight and he was still shooting. If he hadn't wasted three rounds on that other guy he just might have put a couple into me."

"Christ," was all that Auggie could think to say.

Once back at the station Jack changed into civilian clothes. He was to be rewarded with a couple of days off for taking a round in the leg. The Lieutenant, who was Watch Commander, was very happy with Jack's conduct at all three incidents and Jack was to be rewarded with a decoration for the action at the apartment building and at the restaurant and a commendation for the wound. Two medals for heroism in one night after six years of boredom.

Monaghan came into the locker room and asked, "Are you up to taking a walk with me? It's almost five thirty and I'd like to go up stairs and check the mug shots, we got to identify this suspect."

Jack followed Sergeant Monaghan upstairs. It bothered his leg but what the hell, it had to be done.

He spent another hour and half browsing through the photos and picked out three possibilities. The problem was with the angles and the lighting. Some of the photos in those books were so old that they had faded around the edges, but these new ones were reasonably sharp. He finally settled on a guy named Russell Crouse. The height and the weight matched. Russell had done time at the Illinois State Penitentiary for armed robbery. He had been out on probation for about a year. Before that Russell had done time for car theft, and before that for shop lifting, and before that for mugging drunks. This guy Russell was a classic.

Monaghan made some calls to the Probation Office and then sent the north side cops out to find Mister Crouse. "With any luck they'll find him in bed." Monaghan said. Then he told Jack that he had also asked the officers to contact Mister Kaplan, who was the guy that owned the car.

Jack and Sergeant Monaghan finally went down stairs. They were going to McDonald's Depot Tavern to check the place out, but now it was closer to seven than it was to five-thirty. Monaghan explained. "You know those guys better than I do. I could charge in and pressure them, but I prefer to take the easy course."

Jack grinned. He was carrying his torn long johns and uniform trousers in a paper bag. "Sure let's go. Then I got to go see a pert little nurse. She wants to take care of me and I'm going to let her. I'm driving my personal car. So I'll meet you over at Pat's."

Chapter Two

Jack and Monaghan met outside the bar. The sun was just coming up and the traffic was beginning to move. Cabs were pulling up in front of the Railroad Station. The first commuter train would be coming in soon and one of the passenger trains heading south for New Orleans was also soon due. The Red Caps were out in front of the station helping the passengers with their luggage. A freight train was lumbering off to the south and the entire bridge and all the nearby buildings were reverberating from the weight of the cars. The engine bell was clanging out a warning and the shrill whistle was shrieking repeatedly and it was enough to deafen a man. It occurred to Jack that the kids that usually collected the coal that fell from the trains along the railroad tracks were probably running back and forth in front of the train. Below the viaduct commuters were cursing the snow drifts and the slush and ignoring the clanging bells of the streetcars and the horns of the motorists. They were hurrying over to Pat's to grab a couple of quick drinks before their trains came in.

Monaghan seemed bemused by all this action. "Who are the main characters in there?" He asked.

"Calvin Smith is the part time swamper and full time bookie. They call him Nigger, for obvious reasons. He's a little dark complexioned. The day time bartender is an old white guy, called Red, whose name is also Smith," Jack chuckled, "The guys call them the Smith Brothers, but Red is no apparent relation to Calvin. That's it. The regulars are a few retired guys that are supposed to be out on their morning walks and the rest are Commuters that are grabbing a last fast shot and laying down their bets for the day."

"You wouldn't think that the old guys would be out walking in this blizzard," Monaghan laughed.

"You wouldn't think that the commuters would be running across that street full of ice and snow dodging streetcars and cabs just for a quickie drink, but they do."

Monaghan watched the traffic for a minute. "How's the leg?"

"Sore, it's stiffening up. Maybe a drink would be good for me."

Monaghan grinned. "Maybe it would at that."

They went in and took seats at the bar and ordered whisky with beer chasers. Calvin waved a cheery hand to Jack and came over to chat.

"Morning, Mister Jack, how you all doing today?"

"Hi Calvin, meet my buddy Sergeant Monaghan."

"Ooh shit," Calvin muttered.

"Not to worry Calvin, we're off duty."

Calvin smiled, "Well in that case, How you doing Sarg?"

"I'm doing pretty good, Calvin. Say Calvin, are you aware of what went on here last night?"

Calvin's blank stare told the story before he opened his mouth, but he rarely answered a direct question with a direct answer. "Like what, Sergeant Monaghan?"

"Well, there was shooting outside the bar last night."

"No," Calvin replied slowly drawling out the no. "Who did what to whom?"

It was Jack that replied, "Hymie Howard got it last night, Calvin."

Calvin frowned, "Oh my, I'm sorry to hear about that. Mister Howard was a good guy."

"You haven't heard from Pat or he didn't leave a note or nothing?"

Calvin shook his head. "Naw, Mister Jack he doesn't usually call till about noon."

A man came in the bar and began shouting. "Hey Nigger, I'm in a hurry, what have you got running at Bay Meadows today?"

"Shoosh man, oh shit, ignore that fool, Mister Jack."

"Go see what he wants, Calvin, I'm not working vice."

Calvin went over and grabbed the man by the collar and dragged him behind a partition.

Monaghan and Jack exchanged grins. "Calvin's all right," Jack laughed, "he just plays it a little loose."

Monaghan reached into his coat and removed a cigar. "Would you like a Cuban cigar Jack? My brother gets them from Miami every once in a while."

"Smoke a cigar at six o'clock in the morning?" Jack laughed. "That's a tough act, but no thanks Sarg, I don't smoke."

Monaghan bit off the end of the cigar. "This is my pre-supper cigar. Just as this is my pre-supper drink."

Jack nodded. "That's right, I forgot, our days do get turned around don't they? I always think of it as if the second part of my day is starting." Jack explained. "Until last June, I used to go to class during the day, which is probably why my grades were so low." He stood up and stiffly moved his injured leg, "I'm going to check out the toilets to see if our friend Sweeny left us any presents in the water tanks."

Monaghan nodded, lit the cigar and sipped at his drink. Out of professional curiosity he was keeping an eye on Calvin and his friends. As Calvin's customers came in the door, he motioned to them to come into the back room. Monaghan was amused. This guy Calvin was about as subtle as a kick in the ass.

Jack took a quick sip of his drink and limped stiffly to the men's room. With some difficulty he stood up on top of the stool and reached above the water tank. There was nothing there. He searched under the sink and then he went into the Ladies room. He hadn't expected to meet an occupant in there, but one of the local girls, Sadie Malone was coming out of one of the stalls.

"Oh hullo Jack, what are you doing in here?" Her voice was perfectly calm as if she expected male guests in here and this was all perfectly usual and normal.

Jack knew her both by reputation and by occasional contact. Sadie was about thirty years old and was regarded as a regular in Pat's and probably could correctly be classified as a semi-professional. She didn't walk the streets and had a regular job, but she wasn't beyond selling a little of her ass to boost the economy. "Sorry to bother you Sadie, but I'm looking for something."

"Well hell, go right ahead don't let me stop you."

Jack stood up on the stools and checked the tanks. In the second stall his hand encountered a forty-five caliber pistol. He climbed down and taking a piece of toilet paper released the magazine and laid it on the little dressing table. Then using another piece of paper he pulled the slide to the rear and ejected a round. He laid the weapon down and gathered up the ejected round from the floor.

Sadie was standing there flabbergasted. "Jesus Christ! Who would have thought?"

"Hymie Howard got killed last night. I think we just found the weapon."

Sadie appeared shocked for a brief moment. The news of some one's sudden demise was not all that unusual along Sixty-Third Street. "Aw that's a shame. I always liked Myron, he was kind of a nice guy and there aren't too many of those around any more." She stared at the weapon. "Did a woman shoot him? I always figured that some broad would catch up with the crazy little bastard some day."

"Why do you say that? I thought you said he was okay?"

Sadie laughed, "The truth is that he always had three or four broads trying to get him to marry them. You have to give him credit he could con you right out of your skivvies."

Jack laughed, "Did he ever con you out of yours?"

"I'll never tell," she giggled.

Jack put the weapon in his pocket. "You wouldn't know where he worked would you Sadie?"

"They were running a racket. He told me it was called factoring or something like that."

"Factoring is an honest business," Jack paused, "Well," he equivocated, "reasonably honest. They buy up bad loans and try to collect them."

"That's not the way these guys played it. They collected but never paid off. Hymie was laughing about it one night when he had a few too many drinks."

"You wouldn't know where all this was going on, would you?"

"No, and I'm going to forget everything I ever knew about it."

"Smart girl! Thanks Sadie, say you wouldn't know where we can find any of Myron's ex-girl friends would you?"

Sadie put her hands to her face for a minute as if thinking deeply, "There was one girl, a blond, well to be truthful she was kind of grayish, she is about fifty, I'd say. Her name, now what in the hell was her name? Silvia, that was it Silvia, Silvia Goldberg, she wears a little silver Star of David pendant around her neck, but I don't think she's ever been in a synagogue. Well, maybe she did when she was a kid. Myron and she were kind of tight, she hangs out down at the Normal Avenue Bar."

"Thanks Sadie, you're a great gal."

"Are you sure that's all you want Jack?"

Jack nodded. "That's all for now."

"You know I don't sell information, Jack. I gave that to you for free. Come to think of it you big handsome devil, I just might give you anything else you want for free too."

Jack smiled and kissed her on the cheek, "Thanks for the offer."

Jack called to Red Smith and asked if Red might have a paper bag behind the bar. He did and Jack surreptitiously wrapped the weapon in the bag and handed the weapon to Monaghan. "I'll bet that we've found your murder weapon, Sarg. Maybe we can take some prints off of it?"

Monaghan looked into the bag and smiled.

"Do you suppose that Mister Crouse will come back for this?" Jack asked.

"I doubt it. The guys in the last war brought hundreds of these things back from France. It's probably a throw away. The big problem is that Pat and the two other guys knew that Crouse was lying. They can identify him. If the guys I sent up north don't find him I think we'd better find all of the witnesses and put them some where safe."

"I can identify him."

Monaghan nodded, "Which is probably the only thing that takes the heat off of our friends. I think that when Mister Crouse consults with wiser heads, that is to say the guys that hired him, they will suggest that he move to the west coast for a few years. Or" Monaghan paused, "they will eliminate Mister Crouse for being stupid and rid themselves of a problem."

"What in the hell could have ever prompted this guy to come into this place."

"He's probably a boozer and he needed a drink," Monaghan said. "He had just killed a man in cold blood and there aren't very many guys cold enough to calmly walk way from a thing such as that."

"It was a stupid thing to do. By coming in here he identified himself." Kelly said. "But then if I hadn't been on duty when my shooting occurred I too could have used a drink, or a couple of drinks." He looked away for a moment. "I was shaking like a leaf afterwards."

"Were you frightened?" Monaghan asked.

"Nah not while it was going on, but later, after it was over, when I had time to think about it I was shaking like a leaf in a wind storm."

Monaghan nodded, "That make sense. I have been on the force for twenty years and I only pulled a gun once and then I only wounded the guy." Monaghan sipped his drink and then changed the subject. "The difference between you and this guy, Crouse is that you were in the heat of face to face combat with that creep in the diner. That's a hell of lot different than cold blooded murder. But you're right about Crouse. It was indeed arrogant and stupid of him to come in here." Monaghan paused, "on the other hand how could he possibly anticipate that a cop would follow him in?" Monaghan finished his drink and pushed it away from him and laid a dollar on the bar. "That should cover it. Don't you think?"

Jack nodded, "Yeah, that's very generous as a matter of fact." Jack paused for a moment, "Tell me did we ever find Hymie's car?"

"The day shift will pick it up if they have to test every Ford in the neighborhood."

"Aw it can't be too far away," Jack said.

"You know I've seen you around the PD, Jack, but we've never worked together have we?"

"No, I went to school during the days, winter and summer. I have been working my ass off for the last six years. I made a deal with the Captain that I don't get over time and I've been offered promotions a couple of times but I had to turn down the opportunities because of the schooling."

"What did you study?"

"Engineering at first, but then I switched to law. I passed the Bar examination in September." Jack chuckled, "My Dad says that I'll be the only lawyer in Chicago that understands math."

"So now you go into defense work and spring guys like Crouse?" Monaghan asked with an abrupt laugh.

Jack shook his head, "I don't know what to do. I've got to think about it for a while. I've been working so hard for so long that I don't know how in the hell to stop. "

"Have you ever thought of applying for the Detective's test, Kelly?"

"I took it three weeks ago. I studied for a few weeks to prepare."

"What made you join the police force?" Monaghan asked.

"I joined the Marines right out of High School in twenty-nine. I had applied for Annapolis. My Dad's a lawyer, but he really took a bath in the market. Hell we lost everything. Dad didn't have enough political pull after the financial crash. The old man used to be able to call the Senator or one of the Congressmen and get a rapid reply, but not after the money went away, which of course says something about friendship with politicians. Anyhow, I couldn't afford college, because the depression was screwing everything up. I finished my four year hitch in the Corps in nineteen-thirty-three. That had been a piece of luck. The Marines, I mean. I enlisted right here in Chicago and they had a very small quota at the time and I was told that I was lucky to have been selected. I really joined because I had heard that the Services received appointments from the Service Academies, but that plan didn't work either. Then I served three years in China and the Philippines, which was also very lucky, because some guys never get out of the states. Then I was back in town looking for a job and wanting to go to school. Jobs were really tough to find in Thirty-three. I could have reenlisted, but like most guys I wanted out of the regimentation. I won this position after excelling at a battery of tests involving physical agility and intelligence." Jack laughed in self deprecation, "But I really got it thanks to an Uncle with political clout who works in the City Recorders Office. You don't get on the Fire Department or on the PD these days without some sort of influence." Jack gestured with both hands in a vague manner. "Now I'm ten years older than I was when I left home and I'm still wearing a uniform, but what the hell, I'm twenty-eight and I'm working and eating regular and there are still a lot of guys that I went to school with that still can't make that claim."

"Couldn't your Dad help you with the school tuition after you got out?"

Jack grinned, "Naw, he wanted too, but I got two little sisters coming up that also needed an education."

"So for you it's just a job, right. No ambitions to change the world and wipe out crime?"

"Nope. I don't fantasize. "

"Take it easy Jack. You've got a couple of days off according to the Wounded Officer Policy. Stay out of trouble. By the way if you want to know how we're doing with Crouse come by the office tonight after you rest up today. I'll see if I can find McDonald and the other two guys."

Jack drove back to his hotel room and disrobed and then went down the hall to the toilet and shower. One reason he liked his shift was that he was off when everybody else was working and the water was always hot and the bath was rarely occupied. After cleaning up Jack went downstairs to the phone and called Alice Williams. She was delighted to hear from him and invited him over for breakfast.

Alice met him at the door and was wearing a frilly little housedress. She made a fuss over him and made a nice breakfast and then she faithfully repaired the uniform trousers and they chatted happily for a while and then he took his like-new trousers and thanked her and offered to take her to a nice dinner.

She was standing close to him and reached up and touched his cheek. You've shaved. You didn't get any water in that wound did you?"

"Well I showered, but I don't think I got it too wet."

"Or for Christ's sake, you men, come over here and sit down. Wait you want to take off your trousers first."

"Take off my trousers?"

"I'm going to clean and dress that wound again."

"Aw hell, that ain't necessary."

"No," she agreed, "Not unless you want gangrene to set in."

Jack understood that term he had seen men with gangrene. He removed his coat and started to remove his trousers, but hesitated.

"Don't tell me you're shy. I'm a nurse remember. I've seen more naked men than I care to think about."

Jack removed his trousers and folded them on the back of a chair. He was wondering what in the hell was going on in her mind.

Alice brought a wash basin and some bandages to the table and then set about removing the old bandage washing the wound and reapplying a better bandage. "The swelling has gone down, so we're able to put a neater bandage on and now the wound is clean." She rubbed his leg suggestively. "You are a very muscular man, Jack."

Jack self consciously put his trousers back on as soon as he could and oddly enough felt better about getting dressed. It wasn't that he was shy; it was just awkward, although he wouldn't have minded tussling in a bed with her, but he believed that she was a nice girl and he didn't want to offend her with some immoral offer.

She even allowed him to kiss her good bye at the door and that too had left him wondering. They agreed that he would call tomorrow and maybe get his bandage changed again. He had to admit that he was a bit jumpy and weary at the same time and so he went back to the hotel to get some sleep. It was only about ten o'clock, but he was tired. He was as happy as a clam when he first lay down. The bed seemed positively luxurious, but that wasn't what pleased him, for the first time in six years he had met a very pretty and a very nice girl. Oh he had run into his fair share of waitresses and Sadie types, and some of those goofy communist college broads peddling free love, but they were not what he would classify as really nice girls. This Alice was a little sweet heart and on top of that she had a nice ass and great little tits. He drifted away from that thought; he had received a wound in the line of duty and was going to get a medal or something. Then just before he closed his eyes he thought about the man that he had killed. Who was the guy? Why was he carrying a gun? Why in the hell did he react as he had? Why didn't he drop the weapon when he saw a uniformed police officer in front of him? Did he have a family? That thought really bugged him. Was there some poor distraught woman and a couple of kids out there somewhere that had lost a dad? He thought about that look in the man's eyes as he died. It was as if the lights were going out. It was different when you were up close and personal. He had nailed a Chinese Sniper one day. Actually it had taken him three days to find the guy, but that had been at six hundred yards and you didn't see anything except the body tossing up into the air as if it were a rabbit or something. He too tossed and turned for a while and then his leg began to hurt and he fell asleep.

It was his aching leg that woke him. The sun was going down, but it was only four thirty or so. He peaked out the window and noted that the snow had stopped and that the sky was clearing. He sat on the edge of his bed unconsciously massaging the area around the wound. It was beginning to itch. He usually stayed awake until mid afternoon or so after class and then went to sleep. Then when he woke, he would shower shave and go to work. His daily routine was all upset. This was like a day off, when he really got all turned around. What the hell could he do? If he slept the day away he'd be up all night. That damned leg really stung. Then he thought about the guy that shot at him. If it had been under any other circumstances he and the bad guy would have been trading shots and that could be real bad. The thirty-eight just didn't have enough punch. Maybe he ought to go shopping? He remembered an old Marine Gunny Sergeant telling him that when they got hit with a forty-five they usually didn't shoot back. It occurred to him that if he was going to be in the shooting business that he had damned well better get the best weapon available. It also stood to reason that he had better get some more practice. That resolved, he would go out this afternoon and drop his trousers off by the cleaners and buy a forty-five semi-automatic pistol. That would take a chunk out of his budget. Then he remembered that he wasn't on that budget any longer. Buying a better weapon seemed the prudent thing to do.

Jack left the room and decided to walk to exercise the leg a bit. He didn't want it to stiffen up on him. The snow had been cleared from the walks in most of the areas and along the main avenue. It was cold and crisp and the wind was ripping in off the lake. He thought that it was refreshing and the air was clean and sweet when compared to the stench along Sixty-Third Street or when the wind came out of the west and over the stockyards. Actually the stench wasn't from the yards so much as it was from that damned glue factory.

The Pawn Shop Owner gave Jack an excellent price on the weapon and threw in a box of ammo, and a holster and two magazines. The deal was done and Jack went out of the shop with a forty-five hanging on his left shoulder. For a while he felt as though everyone was looking at him, but then realized that he was walking down the street with a deadly weapon under his arm and no one seemed to be aware of it. Perhaps the truth was that most people didn't expect to see a man carrying a concealed gun in public. He had personally learned to spot such things before he left the Academy, but the average citizen didn't have the slightest idea. Those guys that did know and who cared about such things would spot the bulge instantly.

Next stop was Pat's Tavern and Pat should have been on duty behind the bar, but he wasn't. Bernie Matson was tending bar and he was busy with the commuters, most of them were on their way home.

Jack waited patiently until Bernie could spare a minute. "Where's Pat?" Jack asked.

Bernie shrugged. "I don't know where he went. He said he had to leave town in hurry, a sick relative or something, and he wanted me to take up the slack."

"Do you have any idea where Barney Lawrence or Joe Murphy live?"

Bernie shook his head slowly as if trying to think. "Lawrence lives down on Lowe, I think, and Murphy lives over on Union, but I'm not sure where. Hell, I can't keep track of those guys."

"Have they been in?"

Bernie's eyes widened. "No, jeez, I hadn't thought about it, but they're usually here about this time."

Jack thanked the man, "Maybe I'll sit here for a bit and wait for them. Give me another beer please."

Sadie sidled up and slid onto the seat beside him. "Oh Jack, you big darling you look so dashing in civilian clothes. How's the leg?"

Jack was surprised. "You heard?"

"Oh hell yes, you're quite a hero. It's even in the papers." She flashed a copy of the Trib, which had a picture of the wounded officer of the front page. The headline squawked "Police Officer Wounded in Shoot Out with Assailant."

"I didn't even know they had taken that picture," Jack said.

"It says here that you killed the guy. Did you?"

Jack shrugged and grinned sheepishly, "Say, have you seen Pat? I hear a rumor that he might be out of town for a while?"

Sadie smiled conspiratorially. "He's making himself scarce. Maggie called and told me they were going down to her parent's place in southern Illinois."

Jack laughed. "He told me that he hated that place."

Sadie giggled. "They're all hard shelled Baptists down there. They won't have booze in the house. Pat has to keep his stuff in the cellar. He told me that he takes a lawn chair and sits out on the lawn. He wraps a newspaper around his beer. Then he wraps a blanket around himself and sits out there on the snow covered lawn drinking beer and reading porno magazines."

"They must love that," Jack was chuckling at the description.

Sadie laughed aloud, "Yeah, and then one day his uncle or something comes out and stands there staring at Pat and he says - "Patrick," in this real serious voice, "are you giving ten percent of your earnings to the Lord?"

Jack and Sadie shared a laugh. "And what was Pat's reply to that."

Sadie could barely contain herself. "He says," she stuttered stifling a laugh, "he says - If the good Lord wants to come down and get it he can have it, but I ain't giving anything to any of his agents." Off she went in a gale of unrestrained laughter.

Jack smiled. He thought that it must be great to have a friend such as Sadie helping you when you are trying to make yourself scarce. "You don't have any idea where they will be staying do you?"

Sadie got up from her stool and went behind the edge of the Bar. Bernie frowned at her but didn't say anything. She retrieved a couple of envelopes and went back to Jack. She pointed out a return address on a letter. "This is her mother's place."

Jack wrote down the address, Decatur, Illinois was about a hundred and forty miles or so south of the city. It was maybe about a three or four hour drive, maybe more in this weather. He took the envelopes and gave them to Bernie. "Put these away in a drawer and don't let anybody have them but Pat. You got that, Bernie?"

"Yeah, yeah, I wondered what that goofy broad was up to coming behind my bar."

Jack walked back and sincerely thanked Sadie. Then he left the bar and took a streetcar ride over to the Station. When he entered the Squad room he got the usual amount of rough joshing. The Desk Sergeant wanted him to go to work.

"Thank God you showed up Hawkshaw. I'm really shorthanded. I've got five guys out with the flu."

"You're still short handed, I'm on sick leave," Jack replied and as he went into the booking office he added. "I've been badly wounded."

Polansky shouted something insulting and obscene.

Jack shut the door and looked up the booking information on Hymie's old file, minor stuff, book making, a few small time swindles. There was nothing about Hymie getting physical or any records of glaring crime. He was just a small time con man going through life with his hand in his neighbor's pocket. Jack wrote down the address. He figured that being the sort of guy that he was Hymie didn't move around too much. Maybe it was a good address, then again maybe not.

Jack left a note with Pat's address in Decatur and the photos of Hymie on Monaghan's desk and suggested the need for copies of Myron's photos. Then he started to go out to get something to eat. He assumed it would be ten-thirty or so before Dick Monaghan came in and Jack intended to call later and check in with the Detective. Much to Jack's surprise they met on the station steps. Monaghan grabbed Jack's arm and turned him around, "Come on Jack we got things to do."

Jack was tempted to tell the Sergeant that he was off duty, but thought that he had better not.

"I got a compliment for you from the Chief. You're one of those rare guys that can fall into shit and come up smelling like a rose. That guy you shot in the Diner was a real piece of work. He was wanted by the Feds for robbing banks. According to them he was supposedly one of the original Dillinger Mob, but you can't believe everything the Goddamn Fed's say. Hell, they way they got it, half the guys in town were in Dillinger's mob. The guy you nailed was reputed to have been a crack shot. You're one lucky son of a bitch, Jack. You got in a couple of lucky ones before he got you."

"That wasn't luck, Sarg. I'm a damn good shot. When he lifted that weapon and cranked off that first round I intended to stop him."

Monaghan looked up at him for a moment. "Good to know that, Jack. Well, lucky or not you did alright." Monaghan thought for a minute. "The only thing that they kind of balked at was the head shot. The inference was that you were deliberately trying to kill him.

"You couldn't be more right, but that was the last round."

Monaghan frowned and made a shaky gesture with his hand. "That's not good. It's okay with me and I believe me I understand, but don't take any more head shots. The do gooders don't like the idea that we're killing criminals." He paused. "You told me you were in the Corps right?"

Jack nodded hesitatingly. "Right," he replied.

"What did they have you doing?"

"Oh, a little of this, and a little of that, you know they don't keep you in one place for long. A little intelligence work here and there, mostly in China and the Philippines. Mostly it was a quiet tour, but things can get a little hostile in some of those places."

"Yeah," Monaghan said. "I'll bet they can at that. Well you came out smelling like a rose on that one in the diner. It's getting so the District Attorney is getting a little pissy about police shootings. Monaghan touched Jack's left side, "Your carrying some professional heat there Jack."

Jack explained his thinking.

Monaghan nodded. "Yeah, but they won't let you carry it on duty. The Chief wants everybody in his little army to be dressed and armed the same. The theory at the moment is that the weapon is for self-defense. Theoretically, a police officer doesn't need a heavy caliber weapon. And assholes like that fat bastard at the desk downstairs agree with them, because either through good luck or brainwork, he's managed to avoid trouble for his entire career."

"I got a hunch it was through luck," Jack said.

Monaghan chuckled. "Yeah, I think you're right."

They went into Monaghan's office and he read the note that Jack had left. "You know Jack; you do good work for a rookie."

Jack just smiled.

"Oh okay, you ain't really a rookie, but hell you've only been at this for six years, Now I have been --." He looked down at Jack and caught the young man's bored expression. "You've heard all this before I take it."

Jack nodded.

"You passed your exam for detective. Come with me," Monaghan commanded. He led Jack to the Lieutenant's office and pointed to a seat outside the door. Monaghan went in and left the door just slightly ajar. "Lieutenant Crowley, I been talking to the Captain about my Homicide Squad. I'm really short handed. Kennedy is sick and so is Schultz. I think they got pneumonia. I need some help and I found out that Kelly has passed his test for Detective and is in the top three percent. I think the guy has a lot of promise. I asked the Captain if we could use him on my Squad till the rest of the guys get back on duty and he said it was up to you. What do you say?"

"Jesus, Monaghan, I kind of agree that the kid has promise, but we usually move the guys up to burglary, not to homicide."

"Well it's just for a temporary kind of thing," Monaghan pleaded.

"Polanski is short handed too. I guess there's some kind of bug going round."

"Polanski is always short handed. He could have a thousand men downstairs and he'd still be bitching."

"Careful Monaghan, you might grow up to be a Desk Sergeant yourself some day."

"Come on Lieutenant. I need help. It'll just be for a short while."

"What the hell Monaghan, are you this guy's rabbi, or something?"

"No, but the guy did a hell of job on the Howard case. He's got the brains and guts to work alone, which more than I can say for a couple of those clods I got working for me."

"Aw okay, but don't get the idea that this is permanent. I'll give you two weeks, well maybe three weeks." The Lieutenant picked up the telephone. "Stick around, I got to tell Polanski."

Monaghan rushed out and grabbed Jack's arm. "Come on we got to get the hell out of here. Polanski will have a fit." Before he left he called in to one of the officers in his office, "Canaday, I need copies of those mug shots. Find out what we know about the prints and ballistics on that weapon we picked up this morning."

Jack followed along obediently and was excited that a new assignment was awaiting him.

"Can you work with that bum leg?"

"You bet, Sarg! I ain't going to be moving too fast with this leg, but I ain't supposed to be running any foot races, or walking any beats. I can get around. Say, I want to thank you for the chance to get some experience on your squad."

"Save it, you may regret having anything to do with it. It is boring, sometimes, frustrating work. It is three times as bad as the Patrol and you thought that was boring. Well, wait till you work a couple of stake outs for a while. On top of that the goddamn paper work keeps climbing higher and higher until you think it will fall over and bury you. By the way can you type? We really need someone that can type. That Goddamn Auggie can't even print much less spell."

"Yeah Sergeant, I took a course in high school and I've made good use of it. They had this good looking gal as a teacher. I don't know where the hell she came from, but all the guys took typing that year."

"Great. Somehow I knew that, I had a good hunch. You'll work with that flake, Auggie."

Kelly frowned but said nothing. The Sergeant was right, there were drawbacks.

"Just keep an eye on him so that he doesn't go completely off track."

"Right," Christ, Jack thought, now I'm a baby sitter. Jack remembered an old adage in the Marine Corps, "They said cheer up things could be worse, so I cheered up and sure as shit things got worse." "You had supper yet?" Monaghan asked.

"No."

"Any suggestions?"

Jack nodded. "Yeah there's a Chinese joint down from the theater, it's called the China Clipper."

Monaghan shrugged. "What the hell it will be something different. Let's go figure out what we're going to do about Mister Crouse." He opened the right side door to the car. "You drive. I hate icy streets."

Jack drove along and concentrated on the road as Monaghan described Jack's new duties and the requirements of the job. "You learn to work long hours, if you got something hot you got to stay with it. So we do get a little over time, but mostly the Captain insists that we take commensurate time off, cause he doesn't want a high payroll. The City just can't afford it right now. But the work continues and never slows down. Fortunately, most of the cases are fairly simple. He shoots her, she shoots him. The father shoots the son. The son shoots the father. We even get a poisoning once in a while, but mostly those are uptown cases. On the south side it's either a knife or a gun, or maybe even a baseball bat. Most of it is mindless crap. Does the overtime bother you?" Monaghan asked.

"Not particularly, as long as it doesn't get too far out of proportion." Jack pulled into a red no parking zone in front of the China Clipper.

"Your learning fast," Monaghan laughed.

They were escorted to a table and the girl smiled at Jack and swayed her hips exaggeratedly as she led the way.

"They know you around here, huh?"

Jack grinned. "I like Chinese food, but I really like the Chop Suey that they make here. It is really great. Strangely enough Chop Suey was first prepared by a Mick named Sullivan or O'Brien or something like that up in San Francisco. I can recommend it if you've never had it."

Monaghan nodded, "Sounds okay, Chinese food prepared by an Irishman."

The manger came to the table and bowed to Jack. He spoke in Chinese and the two men conversed briefly. Then the Manager bowed and left.

"You speak Chinese?" Monaghan asked.

"Yeah, mostly just Mandarin, I told you I spent a couple of years over there."

"What else did you do?"

"There was a war going on between the Communists and the Nationalists. I accompanied a Marine Major, who was an Intelligence Officer. I drove for the guy and he did all the work, but I had to take a special snap shooting course from an Old Gunny Sergeant. The guy could put six rounds inside of a silver dollar at fifteen feet in the blink of an eye." Jack laughed, "It was hell of an education. I thought I was good till I saw this guy shoot. The lesson stuck, there is always somebody a little better than you are."

Monaghan made a face. "I'm impressed. What's the Gunny doing now?"

"A Chinese sniper nailed him from about six hundred yards."

"Too bad, we could have used him here."

Jack nodded, "Yeah, it was too bad. He was a damned good Marine."

"Did you guys get the sniper?"

"Yeah."

"So you've been in a couple of little wars, huh?"

"Well nothing formal with real giant armies. Like the Great War, but potentially just as deadly on a slightly smaller scale."

During dinner they discussed what to do about Mr. Crouse and Monaghan explained that the Police that tried to track him down didn't have any luck. Monaghan decided that, since they had an address to start with, that Jack and Auggie could go hunting for him. "Check in with the local PD, let them know that you're in town, they may have a finger on this guy. The address is probably a bummer, but the locals might know him. He's a boozer, hit a couple of the local bars, he might be saucing it up."

Jack nodded acknowledging the instructions. "I also got Myron's address while I was looking up the regulars. Maybe we ought to stop by and check things out. I'm kind of curious who his friends might be."

"I didn't know he had a record. I had never heard of the guy. I asked Auggie to check, but I guess that like most things that Auggie is supposed to do that didn't happen. Yeah, that's a good idea; we'll go check him out. I was going try and look up something on the guy when I came in tonight, but I sort of got side tracked."

"According to the record he used to live over on Sixty-sixth and Union, it is just a minute away."

"Okay, we'll go over there."

"Did they ever find Myron's car?"

"Yeah, it was parked over by that Italian Grocery on Parnell."

"I remember that place." Jack laughed. "There used to be a big yellow cat that would sit up on the cabbages and sun himself."

"Did you know why that goofy Dago kept that cat?" Monaghan asked.

He had never thought of Tony as being a goofy Dago. Jack grinned, "No, I never knew why."

"Well Tony used to put down new saw dust on the floors every day and the old ladies would come in with their little lap dogs and the dogs would shit in the saw dust. Then some other old broad would step in it and begin raising hell. So Tony got this big tom cat that hated dogs. When the old gals came in with their little dogs that cat would jump off the cabbages and plant all four feet and all the claws in the backs of the little dogs."

Jack was laughing, "God I'll bet the ladies must have loved that stuff."

Monaghan shrugged, "It worked. Pretty soon they didn't bring their dogs in anymore and Tony was happy and the cat was happy."

Jack was still chuckling at the story. "I never heard that one but I heard the other part."

"What other part?"

"Well, old Tony was over in Pat's place bragging about how tough his cat was and he runs into this lunatic Mick named Sullivan who had a Pit Bull. They got to arguing and betting that the cat would scare hell out of the pit bull. I think Tony knew better, but it was the booze talking. Anyway, this nut Sullivan brings in this big pit bull in one day and sure enough the stupid cat jumps off the cabbages and in the resultant carnage there was blood scattered all over the place, so Tony calls the cops. The dog latches on to the cop's leg and the cop shoots him, then he was going to shoot Sullivan too. All the time the women were screaming and raising hell." Jack laughed again, "They still talk about it down at the bar."

When they finished eating Monaghan paid the bill. "Great chow," He declared. "Let's go see what we can find out about Mister Howard."

As they left the staff of the restaurant bowed politely to Jack and Monaghan was once again impressed. "These guys treat you with a lot of respect."

"Aw there were a couple of local mopes leaning on the manager and I straightened them out."

They drove south on Union until they came to the house. It was a private residence sitting well back from the street. The snow plows hadn't been along this way as yet and the base of the road was compacted snow and ice. Out here away from the railroad the snow was pure white and it would be for a week or so until the wind changed and then the snow would be dusted with increasing amounts of soot until it gradually turned black. Actually it wasn't all due to the railroad, every house in the area used coal fueled furnaces. Just a few were beginning to change over to oil, because it was cheaper than coal and less trouble to manage.

At the moment the house looked as if it were the classic winter scene taken from a Christmas card. The place sat back under an elm tree and the snow weighed heavily on the branches. The snow along the walk way that led to the house was about three feet deep. Out on the street it was heaped up on either side of the driving area. Snow and icicles hung down from the eves on the houses. It was all very scenic. They had trouble parking the car because the snow was still piled so high along the street.

It was silent out here away from the main drag and there was not so much as a breath of wind. Both of them stood there by the car for a long minute looking around. Their exhaled breathes hanging visibly and heavy in the still air. These houses were so well insulated that not a sound escaped to mar the lovely night. It was quiet, except that is for the lonely whistle of a distant steam engine far out on the prairie.

"They say that you can hear those engines for a hundred miles on a cold still night," Jack thought it an almost magical setting and had stopped to listen to the whistle.

Monaghan nodded "It is kind of pretty, isn't it? Haunting, is what my mother called it."

The man of the house checked the badges offered as ID and invited the officers into the house. Monaghan asked if Mister Howard still lived there and the owner affirmed that.

"We haven't seen him for about three days or so. Myron has lived here with us for years."

"I hate to give you this news, without a warning of some sort, but Mister Howard is dead and we are investigating the circumstances of his unfortunate demise."

"May I ask how did he die?"

Monaghan frowned and then figured, what could it hurt? "Mister Howard was shot to death last night."

"Lord have mercy," Said the old woman who was seated near the fireplace.

"Aw shit," the old man said. He had a sad expression on his face.

"May we see his room?" Monaghan asked.

"Yeah, sure, I knew that little Heeb would get his ass shot off some day."

"What made you think so?" Monaghan asked as the man led the way upstairs.

"Aw don't get me wrong Myron was okay, but he was always chasing women and playing the horses."

"Playing the horses?" Monaghan asked.

"For years and years, but he always paid his rent on time and he was quiet and considerate, hell you can't ask for any more than that. I don't know where we're going to get any body as nice as Myron." The old man shook his head in despair and opened the door to Mister Howard's room.

Monaghan walked in and stood there in the center of the room absorbing everything that he saw. A bed covered by a beautiful and thick comforter. A chest of drawers, slippers under bed, it appeared to be a comfortable well kept room. Jack opened a closet and checked the clothes hanging there. Several suits hung in a color oriented order. Monaghan thanked the man and dismissed him closing the door as the owner was left standing in the hallway.

"Nice room," Monaghan said. "It looks warm and comfortable."

As Jack started going through the chest of drawers, Monaghan was going through the small desk that sat in a corner. Whatever else he may have been, Hymie was a pro and the first cursory search yielded very little information. "I got some business cards here," Monaghan said. He read the card, "Mr. Myron Howard, financial advisor and broker, Atlanta Finance Inc, 590 South Michigan Boulevard, suite 506, phone number Harvard 6400. It's kind of a fancy card and a fancy address."

The Jack began pulling out the drawers and sorting through them without messing them out. He checked the bottoms and backs and then stacked them carefully on the floor in the proper order. Then he looked under the chest and carefully examined the inside. He found a key taped to the underside of the top. It was set far too the back where it couldn't be seen by a careless searcher. He held the key up in a gesture of triumph. There was a number on the key and the name of the manufacturer, but that was all. Then he replaced the drawers in their proper order.

"Where did you learn to search like that?" Monaghan asked.

"I told you I was involved in some intelligence work. Sometimes we didn't want them to know that we had been searching. You have to put everything back just as you found it. What do you suppose this key unlocks?"

The Sergeant examined the key. "Hard telling, but I suppose it might be to a safe deposit box. There's an outfit in Cleveland that makes them specially."

Jack put the key in an evidence envelope and put it in his pocket.

There was nothing else of value in the room. Jack had checked under bed and the between the mattress and springs, but there was nothing there. "The old man said that Hymie lived here for years, but he didn't leave much of a mark. It won't take long for them to clean up after him."

"Yeah," Monaghan agreed. "You say he had some girl friends, maybe we can find a couple and check them out?"

"Sadie knew of one, a gal named Sylvia. This broad allegedly hangs out down at the Normal Tavern. According to Sadie I just might find out about a few more."

They thanked the old couple and left the house. Nothing had changed outside and as they drove away the lights started to go out in the house and they had the impression that Hymie had sort of come and gone through life without leaving much of a trace.

After a bit Monaghan made a decision. "Look Jack, scratch that trip with Auggie tonight. I want you to go home and get a good night's sleep because tomorrow I want you to go from bank to bank until you find out where that key comes from. It may be downtown, or out here locally, but somebody will recognize it. Once we find out where it came from we'll have to get a court order to open the box. I doubt that he would have used his real name, but you never know. We got some close up photos of Howard lying in the snow. They're on my desk. Take the best one with you for ID. They may not know him by name. I'll send Auggie and Frawley up to the north side because that will take hours. I want you to get a good night's sleep, because it will be a long day for you tomorrow."

Jack shrugged; he hadn't been too enthusiastic about going to the north side with Auggie.

Monaghan was clicking off his thoughts in his mind. "I'll make arrangements for you to pick up a car tomorrow at the station. When do you want to come in?"

"Early, I guess. The banks open at nine or ten. Are we going to check on the regulars tonight?"

"No, I've got to get back to the station. You can check on those guys if you wish, but you don't have too. If you do, you'll have to take a marked car."

Jack shrugged again, it didn't matter to him what kind of car he was driving. "By the way Sarg, what did they find in Hymies car?"

"Nothing," Monaghan said. "There was a figure of a Saint on the dash, and a Rosary was hanging from the mirror, but that was it."

"A figure of a Saint and a Rosary?" Jack asked incredulously. "So what's a nice Jewish boy like Myron doing with a Rosary?"

Monaghan laughed and shrugged. "So, who knows? This is Chicago."

They returned to the station and Monaghan went to work and Jack checked a car out for his little tour. Sergeant Polansky was having a fit, "Turncoat!" He shouted. "What in the hell do you mean by going behind my back to request a new job? Do you know how short handed I am? You're one of the best men I've got and you stab me in the back!"

"You never told me I was one of your best men."

Polansky blushed and began to stutter and bluster, "Well - well, what the hell has that got to do with it."

"Maybe if you had told me how vital I am, I'd have refused the reassignment."

"Bullshit!" Polansky shouted, "You are trying to bullshit an old beat cop and you can't do it! Get your traitorous ass out of here Kelly!"

Jack was laughing as he left as were most of the other officers. He drove around to the addresses, but both men had long since either moved, either of their own volition or they had been thrown out for lack of payment of the rent. He drove back to the PD and dropped off the car and took the streetcar back to his neighborhood. A short walk to his hotel gave him time to think about the case. Pat had told him that Hymie hadn't been in the bar. Maybe that meant that Crouse had been waiting outside. Okay that made sense, and if that were true maybe he didn't need a drink to calm his nerves so much as he needed to warm up, but he sure as hell hadn't been waiting there on the off chance that Hymie would show up at midnight in the middle of a blizzard. So Hymie had probably made an appointment to be there, but to meet who? What in the hell could have been so important that Hymie would come out at midnight during a snow storm? Perhaps more importantly who could have persuaded him to do that? The old guy at the house said that he hadn't seen Hymie for about three days. If the old man was telling the truth, Hymie had come from somewhere else and if they had summoned him, they, whoever they might be, knew the other telephone number. He'd have to verify that by checking with the old man. Maybe the call had slipped the old guy's mind. Well, what the hell, that sort of thing happened with old guys from time to time. Maybe this gal Silvia was important.

When he got to the hotel he found a note under his door. Sometimes the superintendent took calls for the guests and stuck them under the doors. This note was from Alice Williams. The note read - "I'll be home at eight a.m. come by and I'll change your dressing." Now there was a promise for a decent breakfast and a little pleasant chatter. She really seemed to be a nice gentle girl. Jack believed her to be the kind of lady that you take home to mom. He cleaned up and hit the sack, his leg was really sore from all the activity and he tossed and turned for about an hour, but as he finally dozed off it occurred to him that he didn't remember giving Alice his telephone number.

Chapter Three

Tuesday

Jack swung out of the sack early and hurried to the shower to get ready for his visit to Alice. Now he remembered why he preferred working nights, the shower went cold about midway through and he was freezing by the time he finished. He shaved in his room and even used a little perfumed after shave. After a couple of cups of coffee at the little diner on the corner, he caught a streetcar and went to the station. The weather was clouding up again and the wind was picking up. What the hell, it was late December in Chicago and the weather could change from bad to worse in a matter of minutes. Rather than going into the warmth of the passenger compartment on the streetcar he stood on the back platform and enjoyed the fresh air. The heat from the interior of the street car had turned the snow and ice on the platform to slush, which was a gruesome mixture of slush and tobacco spit. One guy that looked to be a little unsteady on his feet was reaching into his pocket to get some change and was also simultaneously hanging on to the steel bar that stood in front of the Conductor's position. Up ahead a vehicle suddenly pulled from the curb and the motorman of the streetcar slammed on his brakes. The unfortunate passenger lost his footing and fell on his rear end in the awful slush. This man was in a rage when he got to his feet and he struck the Conductor a mighty blow that dropped the Conductor on his rear end into the same mess. The Conductor, holding his swelling jaw, complained. "What in the hell did you hit me for? I ain't running this damned thing."

"You were the closest one," the man explained angrily.

"I'm going to call a cop and have him throw your ass in jail. You can't go around punching people."

The Conductor was still complaining when Jack and the irate man got off the car.

Jack just smiled and went his way. He was kind of glad that he hadn't been in uniform this morning. When he got to the station house, Monaghan was still there. It seemed that Auggie didn't have much luck with the Crouse address and had hit several saloons looking for the fugitive. Unfortunately, both Auggie and his sidekick Frawley had at least one drink in each place that they had visited. Pretty soon they had forgotten all about Crouse and concentrated on having a good time. As a result of all this imbibed exuberance Auggie had fallen asleep behind the wheel on the way back to the station and had run into the rear end of a Streetcar. Not only was a car smashed up, but Detective Frawley was in the hospital and Auggie was on his way back to patrol. Both Monaghan and Sergeant Polanski were in a fury.

"How did that stupid thick headed Kraut sonofabitch ever get on the PD? He's gone," Monaghan shouted. "He's out of here!"

Jack puttered around the desk and picked up a photograph of the dead Mister Howard and a mug shot of Crouse. That was all the evidence they had at the moment so he took the photos with him.

Polansky was complaining just as loudly to the Lieutenant that he didn't want any cast offs from the Dick Squad screwing up his patrol. In frustration the lieutenant went into his office and slammed the door.

Jack checked out a car, with the remonstrations of Polansky ringing in his ears. "Don't be screwing up that car, we're running out of vehicles. You bastards are breaking them up faster than we can fix them." Jack, who was only half listening, took note that he was suddenly considered to be one of them bastards, as opposed to being a patrol asshole. And it occurred to him that now with Auggie back on the street he just might have a permanent position with homicide. As he drove over to Alice's place he was wondering just what in the hell kind of day this was turning out to be?

She met him at the door and she was wearing a blue silk wrap that went barely down to her hips. It was obvious that she wore no bra and he was mildly amazed and pleased at her appearance. She kissed him lingeringly at the door and led him into her front room. "Remove your trousers please," she said as she hurried into the kitchen to get her basin and bandages. Her black lace panties were peaking from beneath the blue silk. Jack thought it was all quite charming and inviting, but surmised that his intended courtship of the nice girl was just about over. She wasn't quite the person that he had thought her to be. Then he tried to reason it out. What the hell she isn't eighteen years old. She's been around for a while just as he had been around. He wasn't a virgin, why should he expect her to be? Maybe she was just a healthy young girl with a bit of a hunger. In truth he ought to be flattered. Still he was surprised at the situation and though he recognized an invitation when he saw one, he continued to play it cool. He removed his coat and tie and shoes and laid his folded trousers on a chair.

She came back in and sat down on the floor before him, her wrap had opened slightly and her breasts were clearly and pertly visible. Alice removed the bandage and cleaned the wound and redressed it. Then she stood up and slid into his lap and he kissed her tentatively and then she responded passionately. In fact she responded with considerable enthusiasm and he picked her up and carried her to her bed room.

As he disrobed she exclaimed in surprise. "Jack you have hair on your chest, and it's red hair. Oh that's gorgeous. Come to me my big bear."

He was pleased and simultaneously dismayed by her expertise at sex. She enjoyed giving him oral sex and went from one position to another with all of the practiced skill of an acrobat. Unfortunately she was bouncing up and down on his bad leg. Despite the pain he declined to mention the discomfort. She seemed to most enjoy being on top and she rode him for a series of climaxes as she would a horse. Alice would bring herself to the very edge and then slow down, only to bring herself up to the crest again. Then she lay against his chest, breathing deeply but still moving subtly until she began a definite rhythm that once again brought her upright and lunging at him. Then they lay there resting and touching one another. There was no talk of love or affection. It was all animal hunger.

"You're all muscle, Jack. How did you get so strong?"

"Luck, well maybe it was walking. I do a lot of walking," he replied. His dream of a very nice girl was gone, but on the other hand she was one tremendous piece of ass. Later as they had a quick breakfast, he was still wondering just what in the hell kind of day this was going to be? First came all of the fighting and all the hell-raising on the streetcar and then this the absolute greatest surprise of recent months and what in the hell could possibly top this? He was half convinced that everything had to go downhill from here.

"Shall we go back to bed?"

"I wish I could, but I've got to go to work."

She frowned and pouted. "Oh Jackie baby, but I'm still hungry."

"I've got a new job as a Detective, Alice, and I can't take the first day off as much as I want to."

"Detective," she said cheering visibly, "Why that's just great. That means you can come back later tonight right?"

He forced a smile, "Right, just as soon as I visit a few banks."

"Oh Jack, please tell me about it."

Jack briefly described the case as he dressed.

"That's so exciting. You will come back later, won't you?" She implored.

"Sure."

"When? Can we have supper?"

"I'll be here at seven," he promised. "I probably won't be working tonight."

"I'll call in sick and be waiting." She promised, and as he kissed her goodbye she curled a leg about his and rubbed suggestively against him.

He kissed her again and took his leave of her. He was slightly exhausted this sweet little home girl had ridden him to a frazzle.

Jack was completely at ease that day and was even comfortable with the fact that he had visited every bank in the immediate neighborhood with no results. The keys to all of the Security boxes were somewhat similar, but the folks at the local banks didn't recognize the key for Howard's box or the photo.

It was around two p.m. when he finally got downtown and he drove around for a while and then checked out the street address on Hymie's business card he found that it was an impressive building. He didn't want to go inside and attract too much attention as yet, so he just checked out the lobby. Down here the streets had been cleared and even the wide sidewalks were devoid of snow and ice which made the footing secure. So if you had to walk around with a gimp leg this was the place to do it. He finally mapped out a little route to follow around the down town area and parked the car. He didn't have much luck with these banks and he was beginning to despair of ever finding the correct one. It could be damned near anywhere, except that he didn't believe that Hymie would walk long distances if he didn't have to. So Jack had hit all the closest banks first. Then he finally came to the fanciest sounding establishment and figured that this has got to be it. Sure enough they recognized the key, but not the name. They did however identify the photograph as being Mr. Mangram, who did have an account and a safe deposit box here at the back. As suspected it would take a court order to open the box and Jack called in the information to the PD.

Jack called the PD thinking that he could expedite the preparation of a warrant, but he didn't get much cooperation. He was still muttering to himself about bureaucratic incompetents when he got into his car and began the long drive through the icy streets out to the south side. It was snowing again. He hadn't even noticed it when he came out of the bank. This wasn't a blizzard such as that of the other night. It was just a gentle dusting. It was just enough snow to make the street car tracks slippery and the walkways treacherous.

It was getting on toward supper and he cut over to the Depot to have a beer and a sandwich and see what was going on. It was close to four-thirty p.m. and the winter sun was already setting. Bernie was on duty behind the bar. He was looking haggard and a bit apprehensive.

"Where's Red, didn't he come to work today?" Jack asked.

Bernie came over and leaned across the bar. He was excited and Jack could see that he was extremely agitated. "They told me that some big guy came in about noon and he started beating on Nigger, then when he didn't get what he wanted from Nigger he started beating on Red."

"It was kind of a bad day for the Smith brothers, huh?" Jack chuckled at his joke and then when Bernie appeared shocked at this callous disregard, he changed his expression. "What did the guy want?" Jack asked.

Bernie shrugged. "I don't know. Red and Calvin were on their way to the hospital when I got here. Sadie was too."

"Sadie? The guy hurt little Sadie?"

"Yeah, I guess she was in here having a drink and after the guy got done with Nigger and Red he slapped her around a little."

"Did the guy find Pat's address?"

Bernie shrugged and looked around as if the question had never occurred to him.

"Which hospital are they in?" Jack asked.

"St Bernard's Hospital, it's over of Sixty-Fifth and Elm."

"I know where it is. Thanks Bernie, you can relax that big guy probably won't be back."

"Oh, hell, that sort of stuff don't bother me, I can handle myself."

"Right," Jack laughed and headed out the door for his car.

Red was still in the hospital ward. His arm was broken and a couple of ribs were cracked, which is tough for a guy in his seventies. Red wasn't sure whether he glad to see Jack or not and his expression was easy to read. "Are you here as a Cop or as a buddy?"

"Both."

Red laughed feebly, "Never the twain shall meet."

"I want to know about this guy that was thumping on you?"

"Big, ugly, and very unpleasant to say the least."

Jack produced a mug shot of Crouse, "Is this the guy?"

Red was hesitant and then nodded. "Yeah that's him. The guy came behind the bar and was searching through the drawers. He wanted Pat's address. Hell, I don't know his address; I'm an employee not a friend." Red winced as he changed position. "Then the guy beat hell out Calvin. He was looking for something that he had left in the ladies john and accused Calvin of taking it."

"Where's Calvin?"

"He went home. I think that one of his kids came and got him. He said there was nothing that they could do for him here that he couldn't do at home."

Jack nodded, once the immediate repairs were made that was probably true.

"I understand he slapped Sadie around too?"

"Yeah, he hit with a forty-five a couple of times. He took a big chunk out of her cheek; she's going to need some delicate repairs there. I understand she has a concussion and her face was bleeding."

"Where is she?"

"I don't know."

"Do you know where she lives?"

"Naw, Sadie, took on guy once in a while, but she always took them to a little flea bag hotel, never to her home."

"Do you know where Calvin lives?"

"Yeah, I was there once for Christmas dinner. His wife is a fine woman and great cook."

"Where is it, Red?"

"Thirty fifth and Emerald, It's a big three story Brownstone right on the northwest corner. It's a rough neighborhood Jack. If I were you I wouldn't go down there without a couple of cops to back me up."

"You evidently got along okay."

"That's because I had Calvin with me. He's a boss down there."

"Take care Red. I hope you come out of this okay."

"Yeah, thanks for coming by Jack, I'll be alright in a couple of days. If you catch that guy beat hell out of him for me and Calvin will you"

It was five-thirty when he got out of the hospital and the snow was coming down harder. Jack knew the neighborhood in which Calvin lived. Back a few years ago it had been white. That was before the big bankers and the guys that owned the Stockyards and the Rail Roads started importing the poor Colored guys from the agricultural south to break the Union strikes. The newcomers had been disliked by the Whites as much as they had been disliked by the older established Colored families. These poor ignorant devils had to live somewhere and they been yanked from the farms and thrust into a world they didn't understand. Many of them had never seen a flush toilet before and they didn't understood indoor plumbing, which made for some rude jokes. The Unions put a bounty on the heads of the Coloreds, ten dollars apiece for proof of a dead man. All that was bad enough, but they couldn't tell the difference between the older residents and the newcomers, so this Union lunacy exacerbated the racial problems, because as far as the Coloreds were concerned it was the Whites hunting the Blacks. Those feelings had not dissipated in the least in the four years that Jack had been away and in his opinion, it just might be a long time before it did.

He found Calvin's house and was impressed. The walks were clear and the structure appeared to be in good shape, which wasn't true of most of the houses along that street. Shortly after he got out of his car two Colored men came up to him and asked what he was doing down there?

Jack replied that he had come to see Calvin.

"Why?" Was the next question and it was set in a belligerent tone.

"Because he is a friend of mine," Jack replied with equal truculence.

"Don't I know you?" One man asked.

"I'm Jack Kelly."

"Yeah," the man smiled, "You was a short stop, and a good one too. I'm Willy Hicks. I was on the Halstead Street Tigers."

Jack smiled and offered his hand. "Forgive me Willy, I should have recognized you."

"Well hell, it's kind of dark out here and I ain't exactly a ray of sunshine."

"Maybe not, but you were a hell of a second baseman."

"Yep," Willy grinned, "That's me. What are you doing now, Jack?"

"I'm a Cop."

The smile vanished and there was a palpable change in the mood.

"Don't get me wrong, Willy. I'm not here to give Calvin any grief. I want to nail the bastard that beat on him."

Willy wasn't all that sure, but he and his friend escorted Jack up to the door. Calvin's wife met them and a shout came from inside the house, "Hey Mister Jack, come on in."

The smile came back to Willy's face. "Good to see you again, Jack. We'll care of your car for you."

Jack shook hands with Willy again and went inside. Calvin looked like hell. Both of his eyes were black and there was a deep gash in his cheek. Crouse had kicked him in the ribs several times and Willy had a compress on his side. "I got to turn the light on Calvin, okay."

"Okay," Calvin groaned, but reluctantly agreed.

Calvin looked a lot worse with the light on and Jack could hear a gasp from Calvin's wife. "Sorry about that Mrs. Smith, but I got to show Calvin this picture."

"Calvin," She admonished, "Don't you go getting involved with no White Cops."

"Bullshit woman, I want this sonofabitch in jail where I can get at him!"

Jack produced the picture. "Is this him?"

"That's the guy, Jack. So, what do you do next?"

"I catch his ass and slam him into jail and then we fry him for Hymie's murder."

Calvin smiled, "Yeah, I like the sound of that. It sounds like a great plan."

"Get well, Calvin. Take good care of him Mrs. Smith."

Calvin's wife was clearly happy to see Jack leave.

Willy and his friend were no where in sight, but Jack waved a friendly good bye as he stepped into his car.

The snow was really coming down hard as he turned southward on State Street and it was almost seven o'clock. Well, unfortunately, he was going to be late for the date and he still had some work left to do. Crouse had been looking for Pat's address. It was likely that he had found it, which meant that he had probably gone to Pat's house here in Chicago. Once he found the house deserted he would go looking for some indication of where Pat had gone. If he found the address in Decatur he just might have gone down there. If he found Pat, it might not matter to him whether Pat had the weapon or not. Pat was really the only sober witness to establish the approximate time frame. At the moment all that Jack could prove was assault and battery. Jack had to think about that one.

Oddly enough it was that time of night when things were quiet at the precinct. Jack found the forms required for the request of a court order and typed up the data. Then he obtained the reference to the police report concerning the beating of Red, Calvin and Sylvia and appended a note listing Russell Crouse as being the person identified by the victims as being the perpetrator. He left that on Monaghan's desk and took the court order into the Day shift Lieutenant's office.

"I hate to bother you, Lieutenant, but I have a couple of problems that need some immediate attention."

The Lieutenant frowned and laid his crossword puzzle aside. "Look, Jack, the sergeant will be in about ten-thirty. We can't be jumping around willy-nilly at every little imagined emergency." Then he reconsidered, "Well okay, Jack, since you're brand new so to speak, maybe I can give you a little guidance, what is it?"

Jack laid the court order on the desk. "This just might be a routine matter, though I think it's important to the investigation to get this court order signed tonight. What is definitely important is the distinct possibility that our suspected murderer is on his way to Decatur to kill Pat McDonald."

The Lieutenant was looking at the court order. "Did you type this Officer Kelly?"

"Yes sir."

"Jesus, why didn't you tell me that you could type like that?"

"The murderer, Lieutenant," Jack reminded him.

"What murderer? Say that again Jack?"

Jack repeated the comment concerning McDonald's peril and added the word imminent.

"Imminent danger you say?"

"Yes sir."

"What would you suggest?"

"Perhaps we could call the Decatur PD and alert them to the possible presence of a murderer in their town."

The lieutenant had gone back to looking at the court order. "Jesus, Jack, this is really good typing."

"The murderer, sir?" Jack prompted.

"Yeah, that," He shouted out the door to his assistant. "Billy, get the Decatur PD on the line and have Jack talk to them." He laid the Court Order down. "You're a great typist, Jack. I didn't know that. Say Jack, I really need somebody in this office that can type like that. There are no mistakes on this thing. That's incredible, shit my guys make all kinds of mistakes and when they're done the damn thing looks as though it went through a grinder. You wouldn't consider moving into the administrative end would you?"

Jack didn't want to burst the Lieutenant's bubble. "Well sir, that's always a possibility. Do we get that order signed tonight?"

"Hey Jack," Billy called, "Decatur PD is on the line."

Jack spoke with the Watch Commander in Decatur and explained the circumstances. Much to his surprise this guy sounded alert and on the ball. He promised to cover the residence of Pat's relatives for as long as he could.

Jack described Russell Crouse and added that he had beat hell out a couple of innocent bystanders. "The guy is a murderer and we got his prints on the weapon, which was a forty-five. Tell your Officers to be very careful with this one."

"Yes sir." The guy replied. Then the watch commander asked who was calling and Jack couldn't imagine him cooperating with a rookie who was one step away from being a clerk typist. "This is Captain Kelly."

"Yes sir, Captain we're on it."

Jack passed the phone back to Billy.

"How are you going to explain that, Captain, bullshit, Patrolman Kelly, and I don't recall seeing anything about finding prints on that weapon?"

Jack shrugged. "It was a bad connection."

"Hey Jack," the Lieutenant shouted. "Take this over to Judge Marvin at the night court. He'll sign it. If he has any questions you can give him the answers."

"Yes sir."

It was seven thirty and Jack had to call Alice it was the only fair thing to do. He apologized and explained that the case was getting away from him.

She was so angry she was crying. "I've waited for you all day. I let you make love to me and then you let me down like this. That's cruel, Jack, terribly cruel."

"I've been working on the case and I'm still working. I haven't eaten lunch or supper and I still have to go to night court."

"Say you love me, Jack."

Jack hesitated, well maybe he sort of loved her and then again maybe he didn't. "Yeah, Alice, I love you."

"You act as though you aren't sure. I love you, Jack. I love your rock hard body. You are absolutely the best that I've ever had."

Christ, he thought, the best I've ever had. How many had she had? Maybe he didn't want to know. Am I back in high school again or what?

"Tell me you love me!" She shrieked.

"Jesus Christ, take it easy, Yes, I love you. Calm down a little."

"Come and love me Jack, come as soon as you can, I'll be waiting in my bed." Then she hung up.

He hung up the phone and shook his head in bewilderment. What in the hell had he stepped into? Could that goofy broad be a nympho? No, that didn't seem likely."

He drove over to the court and managed to get in just as the Bailiff was closing the door. The Judge had a few questions concerning the case. "What is it that you are hoping to find in this safety deposit box?" the Judge asked.

"Mister Howard was the victim of a premeditated murder. We want the name of the person that dispatched the killer to the scene. Someone had to have set this up. We figure that this shooting was probably part of the overall conspiracy to defraud the customers of this bogus factoring operation. The evidence that we need to identify the killer might be in this safety deposit box. If it isn't and if the material isn't pertinent we will secure it and return it to the rightful owners."

The Judge listened and then thanked Jack for a very lucid explanation. He signed the order in triplicate.

When he stepped out of the Court he observed that the snow had stopped. Jeez, he thought, where does the time go? It was nine o'clock and he still had to drop off the car.

"When he returned to the station he was told that the Lieutenant wanted to see him."

Sergeant Monaghan and the Lieutenant were waiting.

"Did you get the court order signed?" Monaghan inquired.

"Yes sir, if you wish, we'll get on it first thing in the morning."

"Yeah, I do wish! In fact you and I will go down there together, but we've got some good news Decatur has Crouse in custody and want to know what Captain Kelly wants to do with him?"

Jack blushed red and started to stammer.

Both Monaghan and the Lieutenant were laughing. "Gas up the car in the morning, Captain, we'll go down to Decatur to get him after we clear that deposit box. You can pick me up at my house. I'll give you the address. In the meantime get some sleep. I'll meet you at about nine. You got any questions Captain?"

"No sir," Jack smiled, they were ribbing him and that meant it was alright.

"And Captain Jack," the lieutenant laughed, "we did get the prints and ballistics off of that weapon. Crouse is as good as convicted."

Now that was good news. He called Alice and told her that he'd be there in half an hour.

She met him at the door. He had no more than knocked and the door sprang open and she stood there naked. There were no polite preliminaries. She led him into the bedroom and helped him disrobe. He found this haste a little inhibiting, but managed to demonstrate his excitement at what he considered a rather bizarre approach to passion. She forced him gently back on the bed and began kissing and licking him all over. And when he was properly excited she mounted him again and began her passionate ride. Once again she was pummeling his bad leg, but he gritted his teeth and held on. Then he couldn't remember whether they had closed the door or not. Much later, when they had found a quiet moment, he asked her what would have happened had there some one else at the door?

For the first time in their relationship she laughed in a low sexy tone. "Then you'd never have gotten in that door."

The woman was practically insatiable and every time Jack dozed off to sleep she was back on him again. Her repeated requests for him to assure her that he loved her were driving him nuts. He imagined that it was normal for a woman to seek some reassurance of her man's love, but he found that this incessant repetition was incredibly distracting. As much as he appreciated all the attention he was getting from her, he was growing a little weary of the hectic pace she set. In his wildest dreams he could never have imagined that he would grow weary of having sex with this sweet looking little blond. Later, that next morning, as he drove over to Sergeant Monaghan's home he was thinking that tonight he would go back to the hotel and get some sleep.

Monaghan was fresh and alert having slept through the night and it was Jack that was operating at some much lower level of activity. Despite his fatigue Jack was as anxious as Monaghan to see what was in the mysterious Deposit box. Would this give them the answer to who had contracted Crouse? Hell, Jack thought, they could have this case wrapped up in a few hours. Then they could go down and get Crouse and get his confession on the books and that would be that. Then they could pick up the guy that had hired Crouse and wrap it up. He suggested this procedure to Monaghan, who looked at him and had laughed heartily.

"You're dreaming there, Captain Jack. It would be nice if it worked that way, but I'll bet you a steak dinner that's not the way it goes."

"What could go wrong?"

"Everything!" Monaghan predicted.

The banker was waiting for Jack and the Sergeant when they arrived. They went straight to the Deposit and removed the box. The Bank Officer stood nearby to observe the proceedings. Jack offered Monaghan the key, but the Sergeant declined. Jack opened the box. It contained money, lots of money and a note book. Jack counted out the money and the passed it to Monaghan. "There is seventy-six-thousand, five-hundred and seventy bucks in the box." Monaghan agreed with the total passed it to the banker and asked him to count it. The black book contained the phone numbers of dozens of names. At the back of the book were the names and numbers of the other members of the Atlanta Finance, Inc.

Monaghan glanced through the book. "There is a list of players here in the front and our friend Mr. Steven Kaplan the owner of the Packard is the President of Atlanta Financial."

"That's really a surprise," Jack said. "This should wrap it up, sir. Shall we go back to the PD, or should we check out this Atlanta outfit and nail Kaplan?"

"We go back to the PD. Seventy six grand is a lot of dough to be carting around." Monaghan thanked the banker and signed the various forms taking custody of the contents of the box.

About the time they arrived at the office they got a call from Decatur PD. Crouse had killed a police officer and had escaped with a weapon and a car. One of the precinct officers took the call and relayed the data. "Crouse was being transferred from the City to the County Jail. They don't know how it happened yet, but he's gone and they got a guy dead. There is an all points bulletin out and they think that they can get him before he gets to Chicago."

The news was disturbing. Monaghan slammed his fist angrily on the desk. "Sonofabitch, those goddamn hillbillies let that bastard get away and if they catch him they'll probably kill him."

Jack took it in stride. "I would under the circumstances. To hell with him, we don't need him. We got the proof that he did it. We've got the weapon, the ballistics, the prints, to hell with Crouse, he's probably on his way to Mexico or to hell. Shall we go look into the affairs of Steven Kaplan? Can we get a warrant to search his place?" Jack asked.

Monaghan thought for a second, "No, all we got is Howard's business card and the fact that Kaplan's car was used for transportation. We can surmise that this guy Kaplan is possibly involved in the murder, but that isn't hard evidence. Now with this book we've got another connection and that is reason enough to haul Kaplan in as a possible accomplice." The Sergeant thought about that fact. "Let's sit down here and read the book that he left for us before we go off half cocked. First, let's see what we can make of the connections."

Jack nodded, it all made sense to him.

An officer came to Monaghan's office and announced the arrival of three Federal Agents and Two State of Illinois Agents. Monaghan and Jack were going over the book and were surprised when the spokesman indicated that they wanted all of the evidence gathered concerning Atlanta Financial.

The Senior Federal Agent was a man named Walt Albright. He was a tall man, nearly six foot six inches tall and large in every other direction and respect. Even though he was speaking in what he considered to be a normal tone of voice his tones boomed across the small office. "We have been conducting a long term investigation into interstate fraud and one of our guys just happened to read in the newspaper where one of our suspects was killed the other night. Now that perturbs me because we put a request out about two weeks ago to all the PDs in the Chicago area to find and keep track of this guy Myron Howard." He turned to the two state agents, "That's right isn't it guys?"

One agent began to hem and haw a bit, "Well sir, we sort of reconsidered that directive. We didn't want to bring any attention down on our inside guy."

"Stop right there!" Walt shouted. He took a few deep breaths to control himself. "We are not prepared to share all of the intricacies of our investigation with an outside agency." He turned to Monaghan and Jack, "Forget what you just heard. It is highly classified information and privy to our investigation."

Monaghan was amused. "Okay, since we can't read your minds, there was no reason for us to assume that the murder of Myron Howard was anything other than the result of a simple robbery and therefore we had no reason to notify anyone. Until we got access to that safety deposit box we didn't have any reason to suspect that the Feds or the State, would even be interested."

Walt drew himself up to his full height. "The case that you are working is a murder and has no connection to the information that you have unwittingly gained access to, which is clearly not in the jurisdiction nor is it of concern of Englewood Station. You might make a case for Chicago PD to have an interest, but the State and Federal investigations will take precedence. Therefore you can safely turn the contents of that box over to us."

Monaghan was getting a little annoyed. "That's not true. We have a murder case that takes precedence. It was just this morning that we found out what was in Mister Howard's Deposit Box and we are still in the process of reconsidering the ramifications of the case. Whatever the other consequences may be, we are still looking for the motive for the murder and the conspiracy of the murderers. If there is a conspiracy we have an obligation to apprehend all of those directly or indirectly involved."

"How many inside guys to you have?" Jack asked innocently.

"What the hell has that got to do with you?" Walt demanded to know.

Jack grinned disarmingly, "Well, we are still charged with finding Mister Howard's murderer and by all indications Mister Howard's murder was clearly premeditated, which means that someone other than Crouse and his boss are involved. At the moment I have to wonder what in the world, or perhaps to put it a little better, who in the world could have drawn the victim out at midnight on a stormy night to meet his killer."

Walt and his men stood silently taking in what Jack was saying.

"You see, gentlemen," Jack continued, "Myron was all dressed up, as though he was going to meet somebody important, which means that this meeting was probably not a spur of the moment type of arrangement. I think that you will agree that this act of meeting in the middle of the night in a blizzard, late on a Sunday night, infers a sense of prior planning. Not the blizzard part so much, but certainly the place and time. So the question is: who could have summoned Myron Howard out at this time of night and have simultaneously advised Crouse to meet him."

There was a murmur from the agents.

"Bear with me for a second," Jack demanded. "This guy wouldn't have met any of his partners on a lonely street at midnight. He probably didn't trust them that much. So who would he trust under those circumstances? Who would he dress up for?" Jack looked around the group. "Which one of you guys called him out that night?"

That really started the uproar. Denials flashed across the room, and all the while Monaghan was laughing uproariously.

"You people are an embarrassment!" Monaghan shouted.

Walt was in a tizzy. "Goddamn it, we didn't come down here to be insulted!"

"It is a viable question! Answer it!" Monaghan said loudly over the noise.

Walt really got loud. "No one on my staff would have had anything to do with the murder of an informant."

"How can you know that?" Jack shouted. Then he smiled broadly and said calmly. "Somebody did it. Somebody set him up. We think that somebody called his girlfriend's house and lured Myron out into the cold. Your staff members are the logical suspects. Perhaps none of the people in this room did it, but somebody on your staff let this guy Kaplan know that Howard was going to meet him at midnight near a train depot. At the moment it appears that Mister Kaplan sent Russell Crouse, who is a known killer, to intercept Mister Howard and murder him. But before all that happened somebody had to know about the meet. Who was the case officer?"

Walt Albright was quiet and he sat down on a nearby chair. His brother agents stood silently and respectfully away from him. He looked at Jack for a long minute, "What you say makes sense of a sort. What do you do next?"

"We intend to arrest Kaplan and sweat the truth out of him," Monaghan stated.

"How do you know about this Kaplan fellow?" Walt asked.

"Crouse used Kaplan's car to get to the murder scene. Kaplan was the first tie that we had to the scheme. At first we thought that the car had been stolen, but apparently that is not the case. Maybe they didn't trust public transportation, who knows why a man would lend his car to a murderer? Then, when we found Kaplan's name in the book taken from Mister Howard's safety deposit box. Two and two rapidly added to four. Right now we've got enough evidence to implicate Kaplan in a murder conspiracy." Jack shrugged. "When we find Kaplan we will find the person that set it all up."

Walt considered this. "And what does this suggest to you?" He asked Monaghan.

"That they may be experts at swindling money, but that they are novices when it comes to conspiracy and murder," Monaghan said.

"I can't believe that," Walt said, "these guys are professionals."

"They are bullshitters!" Jack said forcefully. "They are accustomed to acting out parts. They give the impression of competence, because that is their profession, they're actors, but they are really no smarter than the next guy when it comes to a subject that they aren't familiar with."

Walt appeared to be examining his manicured finger nails. "How do you see this?" He addressed his question to Jack.

Jack thought for a second. "Howard probably came in to you or your people and offered to turn states evidence for a light sentence. He may have suspected that the Feds were on to them and wanted to bail out. You guys convinced him to hang in there just a little while longer. Perhaps it all started innocently enough. Maybe one of your people was acting as a warning bell for the gang in the event that you started looking at their antics. One can almost hear Kaplan suggest to someone in your office that a confidential warning call would be worth a great deal of money. Whatever, the arrangement may have been this guy got wind of Howard's offer and knew that he had to be stopped or else the house would crumble and the money would go away." Jack paused for a moment.

Walt exploded. "Not one of my agents would betray the agency! Maybe one of the State guys ..." He didn't finish the statement because the State Agents leaped to their feet and started shouting.

"Quiet, Goddamn it!" Monaghan shouted. "We're theorizing. We don't know for certain that you have been penetrated, but everything certainly points to it. Some insider spilled the beans to the gang. Maybe it was an accident, maybe one of your guys was talking in a bar. Shit, who knows how it went down?"

Walt winced visibly momentarily, but quickly regained his aplomb.

Jack scoffed. "The only way it could have gone down is that your control, the guy that was playing connection for Myron got wind that Myron was bailing out on the gang and he lured Myron out."

"That theory assumes that the agent assigned to Howard, was also the mole. That's a long stretch."

Jack shrugged, "I've heard of stranger coincidence."

They all settled down, but the State agents were still glaring at Walt and the older of the two wasn't having any part of Walt's put down of State Agents. "It was probably one of your semi cops, an accountant or a shyster bragging to his goddamn girl friends," A State Officer sneered.

Walt waved away the insult.

Jack continued. "What had you all on the line was that Howard claimed to have the evidence that would sink the boat and if that was true then this guy Kaplan had to get his hands on it to destroy it. So they arranged the meet, but Howard was probably too smart to bring the stuff with him and that idiot Crouse. The clown that Kaplan sent to do the job killed the golden goose."

"That's so much, fanciful nonsense." Walt declared. "We don't know how this guy Kaplan fits in to the murder. For all I know he's the janitor not the boss."

"If he's the janitor, he's driving a new Packard. It's just a theory at the moment," Jack laughed sarcastically. "Perhaps it is just one of many possible explanations for the sequence of events."

"Perhaps," Walt said sarcastically, "but it is fanciful and it is full of ifs and maybes."

"What was it that brought you guys down here?" Monaghan asked.

"We got a call from our agent at the bank and found out that you people had gained access to a Mister Mangram's Safety Deposit Box. You flashed Howard's picture. We knew that he had a box there, but we couldn't identify it. He was Mister Mangram to the bankers. We intend to confiscate the material that you found in that box as being pertinent to an investigation into Interstate Fraud, which is a Federal offense."

Monaghan shrugged, "We'll cooperate fully and have photo copies of the book made. The money that we have is in the bank is legitimate and not phony and there is no reason that you will have to have the actual cash. Howard had seventy-six, thousand, five-hundred and some change, rat holed for himself. But you don't need it, at least not right now." Monaghan turned to one of his investigators. "Canaday take this book over and get photos made of each page as soon as possible. Wait there for the book and for the copies."

"That's going to take hours," Walt grumbled.

"You've waited this long, so another hour or two won't screw up your case."

"We want the original book. Our lab guys can examine it."

"I'll send you the pictures." Monaghan said.

Walt frowned; Monaghan's answer did not make him happy. "I think I can get J. Edgar Hoover to talk to the Chief of the PD and get the sort of cooperation we need."

"Go ahead," Monaghan said, "But don't screw this up or your name and that of old J. Edgar's will be on the front page of every newspaper in the county."

Walt settled back in his chair, "Look. As foolish as that threat is, there is no reason that we can't get along. Send the photos, if we need more we will request it through channels. Now," he sat up in his chair and leaned forward, "what's your next step."

Monaghan shrugged, "I told you we're going to grab Kaplan and sweat him a little."

"That should effectively tip them off to the investigation," Walt remarked sourly.

"Tough shit! I have a murder to solve and that is far more important to me than any little con game," Monaghan said.

Jack suggested an alternative situation, "Consider the possibility that there was no inside guy and that they found out that Hymie was skimming off the cream. They know they killed him and if somebody doesn't follow up with an investigation, that lack of a follow up might tip them off that something else is going on. Kaplan knows that his car was found, one of our detectives called to inform him. So he's probably been waiting for the next step. If he hasn't left town we'll find him. The only flaw in that theory is the question of who they used to lure Hymie to the scene, which is what convinces me that there was an insider."

"Who in the hell are you?" Walt asked.

"This is Detective Jack Kelly of the Homicide Squad." Sergeant Monaghan introduced Jack, but said nothing about temporary or rookie.

Walt stood up, "Okay, when you get the pictures send them to us, here's my card."

The entourage left the office and Monaghan and Jack sat there looking at one another in bewilderment. "Who in the hell was that masked man." Jack asked with a laugh.

"It took five guys to come down here to try to intimidate us?" Monaghan was incredulous.

"I get hungry when I'm scared. Let's go to lunch," Jack suggested.

Monaghan agreed. "Then we'll go find Mister Kaplan. It's time he found out that he was in trouble."

By the time they finished lunch it was two o'clock, by the time they fought their way to the north side address through the ice and snow it was close to four. The winter sun was setting and it was going to be a cold clear night. The Kaplan residence was in an upper middle class neighborhood. The officers that had first interrogated Mister Kaplan on the phone had remarked in their report that Kaplan had denied knowing anything about this guy Crouse, but that he had not reported his car stolen, because he didn't know it was stolen. He hadn't locked the car the night before, because such things didn't happen in their neighborhood. After all this wasn't the South Side.

The path from the street to the house had been cleared as had the path from the Kaplan driveway to the house. Monaghan walked up the walkway as Jack strolled up the driveway. Monaghan knocked at the door as Jack continued down toward the rear of the house. He didn't anticipate Kaplan beating it out the back door, but then one could never predict such things. Jack stood at the garage and noticed that there were fresh footprints in the snow that went out toward the alleyway behind the garage and then returned. Jack opened the garage door and there was the Packard looking powerful and sleek. He closed the door and finding nothing else of significance he turned and went back to the front.

Monaghan was still standing on the front porch, Jack joined him.

"No answer? The car's here," Jack said.

"We'll try again," Monaghan said.

Jack leaned out over the metal porch railing and peered in a window. There was a frost covered storm window that impaired his vision, but he could see a body lying on the floor in the living room. "We've got a body in there," Jack said.

Monaghan tried the door and found that it was open.

The two officers loudly announced their intrusion and identified themselves several times as being Detectives from the Chicago Police Department. There was no other sound in the house. It was cool in here, but not uncomfortably so. The missing Russell Crouse was lying dead in a pool of blood near the archway to the living room. Another body, presumably that of Mister Kaplan was lying on the floor in front of the desk. This was the body that Jack had seen from the window.

Monaghan carefully circled the scene. "It appears that they've shot each other. We might as well call the locals. It's their jurisdiction it will be their trouble. Our murder is solved."

"No hurry, right?" Jack suggested. "I mean since they are dead an all. So there's no rush."

Monaghan frowned, "We follow procedures, Jack. In this case we have no choice."

"Right, boss, but we can take a look see can't we?"

"We definitely can, until the locals get here. Don't touch anything."

Jack peered down at Mister Kaplan's body. "Nicely dressed, a vest and tie, but he wasn't wearing a coat. His shoes are shined and his hair is combed. Two bullet holes, look to be from a forty-five, which is Mister Crouse's favorite weapon, the holes are close together, which either means damn good shooting, considering the distance between them or they were standing a hell of lot closer when the shooting started. As I said there are no powder burns. There's a thirty-eight revolver in Kaplan's right hand and a forty-five in Crouse's fist."

Monaghan was checking out Crouse's body and made a similar report. "Three holes in this one's gut, probably thirty-eights. The group isn't tight, but it wasn't bad shooting."

"So we're supposed to believe that these two up standing members of society gunned one another down," Jack suggested.

"It would appear so," Monaghan replied.

"That's really convenient for someone. It would have been a spontaneous thing, I guess," Jack said.

"I'll call the cops." Monaghan said with a laugh.

Jack was peering closer, careful to avoid stepping on any potential evidence. "This guy has a wrist watch on his right hand."

"Which means that he was probably left handed," Monaghan commented.

"Yeah, that was great shooting for a left handed guy using his right hand." Jack looked at the desk. The pen that Kaplan used was on the right side of the paper work, which could mean anything. "So this left handed guy," Jack continued talking even as he looked around the room, "this left handed guy grabbed a weapon in his right hand and fired three shots into the gut of a guy that was standing ten feet away and who was presumably firing a forty-five at him."

Monaghan was giving the Precinct Desk Sergeant directions to the house. As he laid the phone down he said, "That's not impossible, you know."

Jack grinned. "Either of the rounds that entered Kaplan's body would have killed him instantly and driven his body backwards. So we are to believe that even as he died he fired three rounds into Crouse. That sounds like a fairy tale to me."

Jack had walked around to Crouse's body, "I think Crouse shot Kaplan up close and personal and then somebody else shot Crouse."

"Why up close and personal?"

"Primarily because that's what Crouse liked, that's the way he shot Hymie."

Monaghan scoffed, "And then, while he stood there with a forty five in his fist, this dead guy shoots him three times, huh? Well that doesn't figure. Crouse was an animal, if someone threatened him, he'd be spraying bullets all over this place."

"Maybe, Crouse had finished with Kaplan and had put his weapon away."

"Look at the blood trace," Monaghan instructed.

Jack looked at the blood around Crouse's body. He had evidently been shot and staggered backwards to where he finally fell. There was a blood splatter on the wall behind his body. There were faint traces of powder on his shirt and coat.

"So it wasn't a ten foot shot. The shooter was maybe three feet away. There's a bruise on Crouse's left cheek bone." Jack looked at the scene again. "Kaplan was probably dying as he hit the floor or he had already died. The shots were too close to the heart area for anyone to have endured the shock of the impact and then begin shooting. The holes in Crouse wouldn't have killed him, not immediately, he would have been in great pain, but looking at the blood pool he appears to have to bled to death. So Kaplan who probably died almost instantly couldn't possibly have shot Crouse. On the other hand Crouse could have shot Kaplan, shortly after Kaplan had stated shooting at him. Then as Kaplan died Crouse could have stumbled backward mortally wounded."

Monaghan spoke up. "May I suggest that Kaplan first wounded Crouse and that Crouse retaliated."

"The location of the bodies seems to refute that possibility." Jack stood there, trying to reason out the sequence of events. As he did so he pointed an imaginary forty-five at Kaplan and looked around the room. The shell casings were under a couch that had a skirt around the bottom fringe. Then he noticed cigar ashes in the ashtray at the end of the couch. He bent down and smelled Kaplan's hands and his coat. Then he went over to Crouse and moved his coat back slightly to reveal his left breast shirt pocket in which there was a pack of cigarettes. "Neither of these guys were smoking cigars. So we may have had a third person in the room." Jack looked closer at Crouse's body. The bullet holes went into the gut but came out the right side, so they had been fired at an angle from Crouse's left. Jack pointed this out to his sergeant. "Crouse killed Kaplan and then someone else shot Crouse. Then the perpetrator planted the gun in Kaplan's fist." Jack grimaced, "but he chose the wrong hand."

Monaghan nodded. The theory seemed reasonable and logical to him. When the local Detectives arrived Monaghan offered that theory and the officers followed through the scene nodding slowly in agreement. Lt. Dekker of the Cook County Sheriff's Department, which handed the law enforcement for Oak Dale, complimented Sergeant Monaghan on his theory. Monaghan pointed out that it was Jack that had come up with the reasoning, but once again Monaghan didn't mention the word rookie or temporary.

As the officer's and the Coroner's people worked at the investigation, Jack walked out to the hall closet. There were three hats on the shelves, one was Homburg. There were three overcoats hanging in the closet. Two were hanging in the center of the closet and a single empty hanger was there between the two coats. A third coat, a fancy camel hair overcoat was pushed back against the wall. All of the other hangers were behind the camel hair coat. This certainly wasn't definitive, but it appeared that three coats had once hung in the center of the closet. Two still hung there.

He tried on the Homburg and checked his image in the hall mirror. The hat was too small for him. Then he closed the closet and walked outside. It was dark and cold, but there was no wind. He was troubled by something. It seemed to him that there was something missing. It was comparatively warm when one first walked into the house, but after you had been inside for a while you would realize that the house was actually slightly chill when compared to the normal temperature. It wasn't cold, just a bit chill. Maybe Mister Kaplan didn't believe in really heating the place up. Then why was he in his shirt sleeves? Why not a sweater? Maybe he was just hot blooded? Jack walked back up the driveway and out past the garage. He was careful to make a set of tracks apart from those which had already been there. When he reached the back alley he followed the tracks to a trash can and opening the can found a suit jacket that matched Kaplan's trousers. There were two holes and powder burns on the jacket, which explained why there were no powder burns on the vest.

When he reached the deep snow he roughly measured the size of the foot print. It was smaller than his foot, but admittedly he had big feet. It would be smaller than that of a tall man. Perhaps a size ten shoe.

Jack walked back to the house and gave the jacket to Lt. Dekker. "It was a double murder, Lieutenant. There's the evidence."

Dekker looked at Jack quizzically.

Jack explained where he got the jacket and then repeated the theory. "This proves that Kaplan was shot up close and personal and that means that Crouse was shot later. How much later, or by whom we don't know, but the guy probably smokes cigars and wears a size ten shoe. I'd check with the neighbors to see if they spotted any other cars in the area? By the way the foot prints in the snow are out by the garage. The guy was probably five ten or so, maybe a little smaller. Your guys will probably want to measure the length of the shoe."

The Lieutenant stood there with the jacket in his hand. "That's great Detective Kelly, you just gave me a giant problem, you wouldn't care to stick around and help us solve this case would you?"

Monaghan laughed. "We've got problems of our own Lieutenant."

"Yeah, well, I've got one for you guys. The dead guy by the desk is carrying an ID, which says that he is a thirty-five year old white male accountant, named, Martin Warner."

Monaghan frowned and speculated, "Maybe this guy Kaplan killed both of them?"

"Kaplan's car is in the garage," Jack said softly. "He couldn't have gone far."

"Let's check the house," Jack suggested.

"My men will handle that," Dekker said. "We've already gone through the place once."

An all points bulletin was put out by the Sheriff's men for Mr. Kaplan.

Dekker grimaced, "I'll send someone around the neighbors to see if there's a Missus Werner."

It was late when Jack and Monaghan got back on the south side and after checking in at the PD, Jack drove Monaghan out to his house.

"Keep the car until morning, Jack. Turn it in so that they can use it and then take the day off. We'll be back on our regular schedule, come in around ten p.m. or so."

"What about Kaplan?"

Monaghan shrugged, "We'll have to run him down or we'll let the Sheriff's and the Fed's chase him. Maybe If I can spare you I'll send you around looking for him, but our case is ostensibly solved. Crouse is dead. So the only question left to us is did Kaplan kill this guy Werner and Crouse, or maybe just Crouse? How in the hell can we make a case on Kaplan participating in the murder of Howard? Our only witness the only connection was Crouse and he's dead. Personally I don't care who killed Crouse. Could there be prints on the thirty-eight? Yeah maybe," Monaghan shrugged at his own question and then answered it. "Collusion to commit murder is the best we can do with Kaplan and proving it is chancy unless Kaplan admits that he was involved. To hell with it, let the Sheriffs fight with the Feds."

'The only problem left is to determine who set Hymie up."

Monaghan nodded and then shook his head, "Right now, I don't care who set him up. Let the Feds find their problem child."

Jack was glad that he didn't have to go back to the PD tonight. He was really tired. He stopped and grabbed a late snack and then went to his hotel. He opened the door and heard something move; he reached for his forty five and switched on the light. Alice was in his bed. She threw back the covers for a moment and she was naked.

"It's cold in here, hurry up Jack."

Jack groaned and turned out the light.

Chapter Four

Thursday

Jack recalled that when he was a very horny young man in the service, he had often dreamt about a woman such as Alice. He really wasn't that much older now, but the third night in a row was in his opinion, pushing things a tad. One could enthusiastically put on an Olympic quality sexual performance night after night as long as one could occasionally catch a little shut eye. What the hell, he thought philosophically, he could sleep tomorrow. Alice didn't complain at all and in fact she apparently rather enjoyed the night. He asked her how she had found his apartment. The answer was that Detective Auggie Schmidt had volunteered the information. The manager had obligingly allowed her into his room when she confidentially explained that they were lovers. Jack made a mental note to thank both the manager and Auggie. Alice had also explained that their last night together was so exhausting that she had slept all day. The irony of that didn't escape him. He did his absolute best to hold up his reputation through the night and she seemed pleased, if not sated.

The next morning he cleaned up and then took her to breakfast and after that took her home. She said that she could sleep till noon. Jack sort of sympathized. He dropped off the car at the PD and stopped in at the office, just to check on what was going on. Photos from the Howard book were lying on Monaghan's desk and Jack sat down and browsed through them. Martin Werner's name was there just below that of Myron Howard. The case was over as far as Englewood PD was concerned. Hymie Howard was dead, God

Bless him, and Crouse was dead, this guy Werner was also dead and Kaplan was in the wind. Kaplan's involvement in the first murder was almost certainty as a conspirator and possibly as the perpetrator in the second set of murders. The whys and wherefores or motives of the killers didn't matter. Except that somewhere out there was a guy that had a hand in the killing of three people and he ought to be made to pay for that crime. Screw it, Jack thought, let the Sheriff handle it Englewood was off the hook.

"Hey there, Cap'n Jack," Billy said, "We're really short handed today and Lieutenant wants to know if you'd take that book and photos and a check downtown to the Feds? The Captain says we don't need them anymore since our case is closed. The murderer is dead."

"Hell, Bill, I'm working tonight."

"Take your time, Jack, no hurry, the lieutenant says he'll fix it up with the Captain so that you can come in tomorrow."

"Right," Jack muttered. Oh well, he thought, let's get it over with.

He checked out the car again and ignored the sarcastic comments of the Desk Sergeant.

"Why don't you just take the fucking thing with you and put your name on it."

"Talk to the Lieutenant. I'll be glad to let someone else have it."

"Go on get out of here." The Desk Sergeant snarled.

Jack drove back to the hotel and managed to grab a little sleep, not much but a little. When he woke up he felt restless and worn out, it was almost as if he had a hangover, but he hadn't had so much as a single drink. Between Alice and the case he was exhausted. His leg hurt, his head hurt, it was a very bad day. Then he took all the material that they had gathered downtown to the Federal Building. Walt Albright's office was on the seventh floor and he was listed on the door as being the Special Agent in Charge.

Jack announced himself and his mission to a very trim, pretty little secretary. She asked him to wait. On her desk was a little tab that announced that she was Marcy Mason. As he sat half asleep his mind was beginning to wander. Miss Marcy began primping her hair and fussing about with her clothing. He as a male understood the signal. It had long ago occurred to him that men must emanate some sort of subliminal signal to women. Perhaps it was some odor or some facial characteristic that the female unconsciously read. It was some signal that indicated that the male standing or sitting before them had recently been in the clutches of another female. Over the years Jack had come to believe that women sensed this state of satisfaction and depending on those secret signals they behaved quite differently when first meeting a man. He had never been able to determine whether this feminine response was due to curiosity or jealousy.

She soon asked him to follow her and she swayed provocatively as she led the way. He appreciated her attention, but he just wasn't interested. He had all the Alice that he needed for a while. The location and size of this office accommodation loudly announced that Walt the boss. The desk was big and the master sat behind it ensconced in a throne like chair. A single rather uncomfortable chair was placed directly in front of the desk to accommodate the visitor.

"Mr. Albright, this is Detective Kelly."

Walt thanked her and gestured Jack to the chair. There was a folder sitting directly before Walt on the desk and though he appeared relaxed his fingers drummed silently on the folder.

Jack placed his folder containing the check and the pictures on Walt's desk and then sat down. "The book and the photos are both included as is a check for the funds found in the Deposit Box. Our part in this case is over. It's all yours. If you give me a receipt I'll be on my way."

"I'd like to have a little chat with you Officer Kelly, if I may?"

Jack shrugged, "You may." He noted that he was Officer Kelly not Detective Kelly.

Walt leaned back in his chair. "I have been thinking about our conversation yesterday and it occurs to me that you have a unique way of thinking and of expressing your opinions."

"I apologize if I offended you. That was not my intent."

Walt waved that thought away, "No, no, no offense taken, it has just occurred to me that you were thinking and that in my experience is a unique talent. And may I say, without any intent of antagonizing you that it is seldom that I encounter that sort of thing in the local PD's. I have examined a copy of your personnel files." Walt opened the folder. "A high school graduate, you went into the Marine Corps, scored extremely well on your IQ test. You speak Mandarin Chinese fluently, you have a third degree Black Belt in Ju Jitsu, whatever that is, and you're also an expert with pistol and rifle. You were trained in intelligence and participated in several classified intelligence missions. You were decorated twice for unidentified actions in China and made Corporal before you got out. Subsequent to your career in the Corps you enrolled at the University of Chicago and received a B.A. in three years. Last spring you were presented with your Law Degree. In September you passed the Illinois Bar on the first time around. You also took several classes in English, History and Psychology specializing in Criminal behavior." Walt looked up, "So you worked nights at the PD and went to school in the daytime for six solid years. That's a tough schedule, Mister Kelly."

Jack nodded, "It certainly can be."

"Why Law?"

"Engineering was my initial preference, but it was too tough a schedule. There was too much extra work on various projects. I decided to shoot for something achievable, plus my father is an attorney."

"That's reasonable," Walt said.

"Why the investigation," Jack asked. "You wouldn't be trying to intimidate me are you?"

Walt appeared shocked. "Oh no, no, quite the contrary, I'm interested because your approach to the crimes seemed to indicate a grasp of the situation, which I have found to be unusual. Then I found that you were in fact a patrol officer and not a detective, so to speak, and that is even more amazing. I am offering you a chance to work with the FBI, because you know this case so well and I think that you can be of use to us. If you were to decide to accept our offer this will constitute a transfer to us for an extended length of time." Walt paused, "Actually, until we resolve this case. Or," here he paused for effect. "You can permanently come to work for us at three times your present salary. I suppose you are aware that we normally hire Lawyers, Accountants or people with degrees in Chemistry. You have the desired prerequisites and also have practical law enforcement experience which makes you valuable to us."

The term 'experienced' tickled Jack. Yesterday he was a six year rookie. "And what would I be expected to do for this interim period?"

"Initially your work would be with our experienced operatives in resolving the murders and this fraud case. Actually, I'm inclined to assign you to the task of solving the murders and discovering if there is in fact a leak within our organization. It occurs to me that you might be uniquely talented in identifying that individual."

"So you want to use me as a lure? Is that it?"

Walt grinned broadly, "You do have a talent for cutting through to the chase. You may have forty eight hours to consider this offer."

Jack sat there with his hands folded in his lap. He was thinking about the six years of effort and struggle to achieve a goal and then when all of that work was completed he discovered that the goal had been the achievement itself. He had no other real goal. The task had been accomplished. Suddenly the dream was over and he was still living in a cheap hotel room. Six years of his life had disappeared as if they had evaporated. Then, as if to make matters worse, he was given a half assed promotion not because the upper brass thought that he had done a good job, but because a decent guy needed a little help. "Okay, I'll take the job."

Walt gestured with his hand, "No, Jack you ought to think about this."

"I have, when do I start?"

"How about tomorrow?"

"Okay! I'll be in about eight."

"Make it nine. Here is an ID card that I had made out for you. Take it down to the third floor and they'll take a picture of you and seal the card. You'll have to fill out the usual forms, but that shouldn't take you too long."

"What do I tell my former boss at the PD?"

"Tell him to call the Chief's office for confirmation. I'll contact our liaison over there."

Jack took the card and paperwork, shook hands with Walt and left. He was as surprised at the offer as he was at his acceptance. This experience reminded him of that time in China, when Major Wade had asked him to volunteer for special duty. The alternative was either doing the same boring thing everyday, or getting into something new and exciting. This time, Walt had struck the right chimes when he offered an increase in salary and slightly more civilized working hours. You were expected to stay with the case and work seven days a week if necessary, but that was rare. The Department had been a life saver at the time and the night work had enabled him to attend school, but he felt no deep debt of gratitude. He had been paid and had done a good responsible job for them. Now that drudgery was behind him. What the hell he thought if it doesn't work out I can always go into law.

The Lieutenant was pissed. He said that he felt betrayed and asked if Jack had no loyalty to the department?

The answer as far as Jack was concerned was yes and no. Yes he was grateful, but there was little or no future with the Department that he could visualize. There had to be something better than sitting behind a desk in a dusty, foul smelling old Police Station doing crossword puzzles.

Monaghan shrugged philosophically, "I wondered how long you'd stay. Good luck, Jack, I'm kind of envious, if I were twenty eight years old again I'd be going along with you."

Jack turned in the car and went back to his hotel to get his own car. He packed his belongings and checked out claiming that the manager had jeopardized him by allowing that strange woman into his quarters. He didn't get his rent back, but it was worth the try. Then he went back to the PD to clean out his locker. As he walked through the squad room he encountered the usual horse play.

"Hey there, Cap'n Jack, I saw your unit parked out in front of Alice Williams' house the other day. She gives great blow jobs right?"

Another guy suggested that Alice really liked to take it in the ass, but that hadn't been Jack's experience with her. Maybe she would, he thought, and then again maybe not. He ignored them. They might really know everything about her habits and preferences or might be guessing. If she had a rep, and he wouldn't be surprised if she did, it really didn't matter. He intended to cut off the so-called romance anyway.

Auggie was there and feeling unwanted. "Hello ass kisser, taking your uniforms home?"

Jack ignored him, but Auggie didn't want to be ignored. He was going to show the other officers just how tough he was. He grabbed Jack by the arm and ended up on his ass in the corner of the room. Auggie couldn't quite remember what had happened so he decided to try again. Jack was waiting for him and this time Auggie landed flat on his back on the floor and the breath went out of him with a loud woof.

"Now Auggie, you just better lay there until I get done here or I'm going to put you in a hospital."

"What did you do to me?" Auggie asked plaintively.

Monaghan came into the room and looked at Auggie and then at Jack. "Stop fucking around Auggie, you're back on Dicks, let's go." Monaghan grinned at Jack and waved goodbye.

Jack drove to the north side and found a little hotel that was set back on a quiet side street away from the street traffic. They had a residence plan and the rooms were much larger and brighter than the room that he had before and there was even a little kitchenette, a phone and a private shower in the room. This was positive luxury when compared to that hovel on the south side; of course the big difference was that now he wasn't trying to save to pay for college courses. He arranged his gear as best he could and then went out and grabbed some food. Jack had some misgivings about the abrupt change of arrangements, because he actually harbored some very fond memories of the PD, but Monaghan had made it a lot easier than it might have been. He thought about calling Alice, but wasn't in the mood for histrionics. He had a hunch she might miss him for almost an entire day or two. A bit later Jack lay down and slept soundly and without stirring until early the next morning.

He rose up feeling completely refreshed and ready for the day. It was an incredible pleasure to take a hot shower and to leisurely stroll naked about the room in no big hurry to get dressed and not to endure the ignominy of the next guest banging impatiently on the shower door. It was as if he had somehow slipped from the Nineteenth and into the Twentieth Century. Before he left his room he positioned a small thread across the bottom of the door. It was a paranoid ploy that he had learned in China back in the days when knowing whether or not someone had been in your room was important. He felt awkward about it, but he didn't like surprises and being a Federal Agent was a lot different than being a Cop on a beat. He would never have thought that anyone could have found his old hotel room, but thanks to a brother officer, Alice had.

Marcy. That was the name of Walt's secretary; Marcy courteously fetched a cup of coffee for Jack and then proceeded to ignore him until Walt showed up. Jack had time to consider his theory of the subtle emanations transmitted between the sexes. He was not exactly hungry for a woman again, in fact he was still quite comfortable, but he asked himself whether Marcy could sense that he hadn't experienced sex for an entire twenty four hours? He decided to use Marcy as a barometer. It was an interesting experiment, but that ruled her out as a potential contributor to a healthy life. As he sipped the coffee and watched her he considered that this too, might be a mistake.

Walt cleaned up his messages and then took Jack around to introduce him to the other agents. Unlike Walt twelve of these guys inhabited a single large office containing twelve desks. At the head of the room sat a single desk and this belonged to the Evidence Custodial Officer who supposedly would also see to all of Jack's administrative needs. The man smiled, said hello, and then pointedly ignored Jack. Almost to a man the other agents looked at Jack as if they might examine a creature straight from darkest Africa. Jack attributed this to the fact that he was the new guy again. He could almost hear the thought's racing through their minds, a former police officer? What in the hell were they going to do with a police officer? Jack was told that on the floor below there was a secretarial pool that did all the typing and monitored the teletype machines. He was told that there were about sixty agents in the offices and they were all busy and coming and going constantly.

That was it. He was introduced. No cheery hello, or welcome aboard. Just a courteous nice to meet you and then back to work. He was assigned a desk that even had a private telephone on it. He had never had his own desk or telephone before and he sat there staring at the barren desk top. At first Jack examined the drawers thinking that he might find a piece of paper or a pencil, but the desk was clean as a whistle. He sat back and glanced up at Walt. "Okay what next?"

"The Cook County Sheriff's office hasn't moved very far on that double murder case. Suppose you go over there and start poking around? See this guy Dekker."

"Can I read Howard's log book first? I ought to know the players by heart, because one of them just might be the killer."

Walt nodded and went back to his office and fetched the photos. "These will have to do for the moment. We're holding the actual log as evidence."

Jack nodded, bid Walt a good morning and went to work. Another agent grudgingly offered Jack a single piece of paper and a pencil. Jack sat there examining the photos of the pages and making occasional notes. He was well aware of the curious stares of his coworkers, but ignored them. It seemed to him that there was an invisible wall existing between the old guys and the newcomer. Having been in the Marine Corps and thus having been previously exposed to some rather unique human behavior Jack readily endured the treatment. Some guys might develop some sense of inferiority at this sort of relationship, but Jack rather enjoyed the seclusion. What few friendships he had developed over the years had always taken time.

At one point he sat back and looked at his fellow workers. There was a slightly over weight guy in the far corner smoking a cigar.

Big deal, lots of guys smoked cigars. The guy looked more like a bookie than he did a cop. Fifty percent of them were going bald; Jack decided that these must have been the accountants. Many of them wore glasses and all of them appeared to be busy. How do they do that he asked himself? How in the hell does a guy make himself look busy? It must be an acquired talent, or perhaps there was some special training program that offered a unique government course entitled 'How to deceive your supervisors.'

Later on Jack obtained a set of car keys and was offered a thirty-eight caliber weapon. He declined saying that he had a weapon of his own that he much preferred. At this point he was corrected. J. Edgar, much as had the Chicago Chief of Police, wanted all of his officers to carry thirty-eights. That was 'The preferred' weapon." Evidently there was no room in the FBI for individuality. J. Edgar had also demanded dark suits, preferably dark blue or black, and dark unobtrusive ties, properly trimmed hair and shined shoes. Everyone wore a fedora of course, gentlemen wore hats. What the hell, Jack thought, this is just like the Corps and he was back in another uniform. It also occurred to him that unlike the detective staff on the PD none of these guys were really grossly overweight. Wine and martini drinkers, he told himself, pâté and finger sandwiches, versus the Polish sausages, rye bread and the beer and whisky preferred by the City Cops.

He left the office by a door separate from that of the front office. It turned out that the agents had their own door and rarely went into Walt's office area. Unfortunately, he wouldn't get to see much of Marcy at this rate. As he reached the big hallway Walt thundered out of his office and flagged him down. "Wait Jack, wait! I want to introduce you to Michael Caine, he is one of our field supervisors and he is going with you."

Jack stood there patiently waiting. He had no idea what this was about, but assumed it was routine. He didn't like Michael Caine from the moment he saw the man. This guy was about five foot eight, he wore bifocals, was completely bald, but for a fringe of hair about his ears, he wore high collar shirts, which had been made popular around the turn of the century. Such garments were extremely uncomfortable for any man with a normal sized neck. Michael had a very thin neck and he did not seem to be in the least discomfited. Pencil neck, was the term that came to Jack's mind. He wore the standard dark blue suit and black shoes with rubber over shoes. Jack thought that these last items were suitable for downtown wear, where the sidewalks were cleared, but were a complete waste of time out in the suburbs, where the snow would cover his entire shoe.

Jack preferred to wear Wellington boots which were dressy looking and reached calf high, should the snow get any deeper than that nothing would help. In Jack's opinion these rubbers said something about Mister Caine; the man was an office pinkie. A pencil necked office pinkie. He was obviously a lot more comfortable sitting behind a desk than he would be out in the field. The collar also said something, Mister Caine was old fashioned and he liked it that way. Jack didn't really care if the guy wore a clown suit as long as he stayed out of the way, but something told Jack that was not to be.

Walt was saying something. "Mister Caine, will ensure that you do not violate any Bureau regulations or protocols." He then looked at Caine, "You are to allow Mister Kelly full freedom to move about as he chooses and to follow the leads as need be." Then Walt stepped back and addressed both of them. "Gentlemen this is a vitally important case. Do not, I emphasize that word, do not! Do not do anything that will embarrass the Bureau."

Jack wanted to remind Walt that 'do not' are two words, but held his tongue.

Michael clicked his heels and nodded his head sharply as if he were taking orders from the Czar or a Nazi, rather than from a supervisor. Jack wondered, where in the hell this guy came from? Then he wondered if they had a special locker where they stored these guys.

"Is that clear Agent Kelly?"

"Perfectly clear."

Jack offered his hand, Michael ignored the gesture.

"You will give me the car keys, I shall drive." Michael said.

Jack shrugged, and handed over the keys.

"Where are we going?" Michael asked.

Jack was tempted to say, "You're in charge, Mister Supervisor, you figure it out." But he reminded himself that this was his first day on the job. "We're going to the Oak Dale office's of the Cook County Sheriff. We will meet there with a Lieutenant Dekker and see what we can do to assist him in his investigation of the double murder of a man named Crouse and a man named Werner. Do you have any questions about that?"

"When did this murder occur?" Michael asked.

"We found the bodies Wednesday."

Michael and Jack rode down in the elevator to a basement level and then searched about until they found the proper car. Jack opened the passenger side door and got in.

"Here, here," said Michael in a loud chastising tone. "In the Bureau we inspect the vehicle first to ascertain whether it is in proper shape. Didn't you do that in the PD?"

"If we had, we'd never take the car," Jack replied.

"You have a tendency to be flippant, please get that under control. I am your superior officer. Please join with me in an inspection tour of the vehicle."

Jack obediently followed Michael around the vehicle and it became apparent to Jack that Michael was not mechanically inclined.

"It seems to be in tip top shape." Michael announced.

"The radiator is leaking," Jack said.

Michael ignored him.

It was an excruciatingly long trip out to Oak Dale. The car overheated twice and they had to pull into a gas station and pour water in the radiator. At one point Michael appropriated the hose and wet down the engine thoroughly. It was his intent to cool the engine. Jack could almost swear that he could hear the engine block cracking. They had to call for a replacement vehicle, which took nearly an hour. Now, not only was the water leaking out freely, but in addition there was also a steady stream of oil. Then the mechanic inquired loudly as to the identity of the horse's ass that had wet down the engine?

Much to Jack's surprise, Michael stepped forward and took the blame. Thereupon there was a lengthy scene during which the mechanic threatened Michael with bodily harm should he ever again get behind the wheel of an agency vehicle. Since Jack signed for the vehicle he was to have charge of it and Michael, the mechanic said, was to keep his mouth shut.

Jack thought the mechanics' treatment of Michael was a bit overdone, until that gentleman explained that this sort of thing had happened before. Once behind the wheel of the vehicle Jack drove at a speed considerably over the speed limit. He explained to Michael that the local Police took into consideration the fact that Federal Agents were not strictly bound by the local traffic regulations. This was, of course, a blatant lie, but the technique did accelerate their arrival in Oak Dale.

"I am a CPA and graduated Magna Cum Laude," Michael suddenly stated.

"How nice," Jack replied.

"I am not, shall we say, mechanically oriented."

"I noticed," Jack replied. "I believe the mechanic said that you didn't know your ass from third base about cars."

Michael frowned and changed the subject. "What are we going to do here at the police Station?"

"We are going to try to get permission to search Kaplan's house."

"Why? I mean we are Federal Agents. Don't we have precedence?"

"It is a matter of courtesy to the Sheriff. It is his crime scene. Right now I want to know more about the background of Mister Kaplan and his friends."

"And why is that?"

Jack mentally questioned as to whether he ought to tell his new partner about his theory that there was a leak within the unit, but reconsidered. "Because everything is interconnected and we will soon come full round back to the murders."

Michael sat there in silence evidently thinking about what Jack had said.

Lieutenant Dekker seemed pleased to see Jack and was amazed that Jack had quit the PD for the Feds. "Before we begin this will you give me one good reason for your choice to leave the Department?"

"Money," Jack explained.

Dekker nodded, "A commendable choice," he said, "and perfectly reasonable in these times."

Jack introduced Michael as a Special Agent.

Dekker and Michael shook hands and Dekker noted that Michael was writing down his name in a notebook.

"Dekker with two Ks. One K is German, two Ks is Dutch." He grinned, "If you ain't Dutch you ain't much." Dekker then opened a folder. "We obtained ballistics on the weapons and matched the fatal rounds, we took fingerprints off of the thirty-eight and they matched up with Mister Werner, except for two distinct prints on the cylinder of an unknown person."

"Perhaps Crouse's real killer," Jack said. Then he glanced at Michael who was sitting there being attentive.

"Precisely," Dekker agreed. "We found the overcoats of both victims in the hall closet. We checked out the kitchen and found that someone had made coffee and that three cups were in the sink, which could be a subtle mistake on the part of the killer. The prints on cups 'A' and 'B' were matched to the bodies and the prints on the third cup are still unknown, but matched the prints on the cylinder of the thirty-eight. We considered that the third set of prints were those of the missing Mister Kaplan. However the only cigar ashes in the house were those near the couch. So it is safe to assume that there was another person. There was no evidence that either of these people actually lived there, oh, I forgot to mention that there were three coats in the closet, but a forth hanger that was next to the other two coats. The rest of the hangers in that closet had been pushed back against the wall and were behind the third coat, which was apparently unused that day."

"More evidence of the third person," Jack said.

"Right," agreed Dekker. "The guy hung up his coat and then when he left he took his coat with him, hence the empty hanger. We have an all points bulletin out for Mister Steven Kaplan and early yesterday I visited the Offices of Atlanta Finance." Dekker was watching Jack for some sort of reaction, but there was nothing in Jack's face or demeanor that would indicate the significance of the Atlanta Finance Inc., but Jack's companion, Michael Caine seemed to come awake as if startled by the name. "Does Atlanta Finance mean something to you Mister Caine?"

"Ah, no, no, nothing at all."

Jack smiled. "Confidentially, Lieutenant we are looking into their activities, but that information must not leave this office."

Dekker nodded. He had mentally classified Michael as being a clumsy liar and Jack as probably being a good poker player. "Okay Jack, I appreciate that. There is no information in the outer office indicating the nature of their business. There is however a splendidly beautiful secretary, named Lisa. She was also very professional and according to her Mister Kaplan is out of town on business and there was no one else that that we could talk to. In short they stalled us."

"They are in the business of factoring debts."

Michael started to interrupt.

Jack held up a warning hand, "We do not lie to our friends, Mister Caine, or we shall soon run out of friends. We do not tell them everything we know, because we are bound by regulation, but suffice it to say that we are aware of the activities of this group."

"What in the hell is factoring?" Dekker asked.

"The Factor usually agrees to collect a bad debt for a significant portion of what is owed. It is a high pressure business."

Dekker thought for moment. "It sounds a little shady, but it isn't against the law."

Jack grinned, "It all depends on how they handle their business."

Dekker grinned, "Yeah, yeah, I can see that. Well, I'll be damned." He glanced at Michael and then back to Jack. "Okay, Jack, Kaplan's in the wind and may even have an excuse that will let him out. What's on your menu?"

"I want to examine his house."

Dekker frowned. "You've been reasonably straight with me Jack; let's go look the house over, maybe we can find something that we didn't see the first time."

Jack drove and this time Michael got into the back seat.

"You should never have told him about Atlanta Financial," Michael said.

"I didn't. I gave him the definition of factoring."

"You told him we are interested in that company."

"And you think that's some sort of mystery? What in the hell else would the Feds be bugging the Lieutenant for? He's not interested in our help. As a matter of fact we are probably diverting him from something that he would rather be doing. The man is doing us a little favor in hopes that we can help him with his case. It is to our mutual advantage to be cooperative, what part of cooperation didn't you learn at Brown?"

"Don't take that insolent tone of voice with a superior agent."

"The word is not superior, Mister Caine, it is senior. Your position in this is instance is to caution me with regard to Bureau regulations, not to inhibit my activities."

"We shall see Agent Kelly."

"Indeed we shall, Field Supervisor Caine."

Jack would have left the little pain in the ass in the car if he could have, but there was no getting away from the man. The house smelled musty and the fire in the furnace had gone out. It wouldn't be long before the pipes froze up and burst. That realization brought Jack to the obvious question. Who was supposed to be baby sitting this hole? He went down to the cellar with the intent of starting a fire. The odor struck him instantly and he looked around for the spot that a body might be hidden. Aw well, body or no body, he thought, they need some heat in this place. As he descended down into the basement he had been surprised that the place was so clean. There was none of the usual junk that tends to gather in basements. He removed his coat and hung it on a nail and began shoveling coal from the bin into the furnace it was then that he discovered a corpse buried under the coal. He stopped and called to Lieutenant Dekker.

"I have another surprise for you Dekker."

Jack went back down and threw some fire wood into furnace and started a small blaze.

Dekker was grumbling about the injustice of it all and was visibly annoyed when he viewed the body. "Christ, what the hell did they do, kill everybody in the company?" He turned to Jack, "who to do think this one is?"

Jack shrugged, "Maybe this is the missing Mister Kaplan?"

"We'll find out. Shovel some more coal away from the body would you?"

Jack obliged, being very careful to remove only the coal.

Dekker bent down and examined the remains. "Three thirty-eight caliber wounds in the stomach. That would have made for a very painful death. It looks as though they took careful aim. The holes are all fairly close together. Powder burns and all." Dekker rolled the body over and removed a blood soaked wallet. He pieced carefully through the packet trying to avoid the blood. "His name is, well, well, it seems that we've found the missing Mister Steven Kaplan."

Jack shoveled some more coal on the fire and closed the door. "Where's my albatross?"

"Albatross?" Dekker inquired.

Jack laughed, "Yeah, remember from school, The Rhyme of the Ancient Mariner, Well my boss hung Mister Caine around my neck this morning. So I think of him as being my albatross."

"Very funny!" Michael said with scathing sarcasm from the staircase.

Dekker was chuckling. "I see what you mean."

"And you, Sheriff, your men did a lousy job of searching the house. I found the body of female in a bed room on the third floor."

"Sweet Jesus," Jack muttered as he leaned on the shovel. He reopened the furnace door and began shoveling in more fuel. "Hell, we're apt to be here for hours."

"Don't you want to see the woman?" Michael asked.

"She ain't going no where," Dekker grumbled. "Man, this is a Goddamn Friday afternoon and I don't know why in the hell I ever let you two guys into my office."

"Hell, Mike, this place doesn't have three stories."

"Oh yes it does Mister Kelly, and my name is Special Agent Caine, not Michael and certainly not Mike."

Dekker stood up and looked down at the corpse. "No marks on the body other than the wounds. What do you think, Jack?"

"I think that they had dug sort of a hole in the mound of coal during everyday use and all the killer did was lay the body out on the ground and pull the rest of the mound down over him."

Dekker nodded. "It's kind of obvious when you point that out, but my guys saw the mound and it never occurred to them that it was perfectly symmetrical when it should have displayed use."

"It is easy to miss the obvious."

"Such as the door to the third floor," Michael said sarcastically.

"Okay Mike," Dekker said, "Come on Jack, Mike wants to show us his find."

"I shall be addressed as Mister Caine," Michael said petulantly.

Dekker led the way, "What the hell is wrong with this guy?"

"He has some sort of fixation on his name," Jack replied. "Perhaps we should make it Mister Michael Caine, Field Supervisor, Federal Bureau of Investigation?"

"Fuck him, let's ignore him."

They left Michael standing in the basement staring at the corpse.

Michael was correct there was a door that led to two small attic rooms. It appeared to be a closet door rather than a portal providing access to the third story. There was an ever so faint trail of bare foot prints in the dust leading from the bathroom to this door. As they ascended to the third story along a narrow stair case Jack could see that the bare feet prints in the dust led the way. Then they came to a narrow landing and a door that looked as though it had been kicked off its hinges. The body of a nude female was lying on the floor. She was very pretty, or rather when she had been young she had been very pretty, but she wasn't young any more. Jack tried to open a window to dispel the odor, but the storm window prevented further ventilation other than a small vent, which didn't help much. That option being closed Jack went over to the floor vent and closed it.

Rather unnecessarily, Dekker pronounced the woman dead. "She has collected a round through the head up close and personal. These killings are execution like, don't you think?"

Jack nodded. "Maybe we'd better get your homicide team out here, Lieutenant, before we find any more of them."

Dekker agreed. "I'll go down and call. Don't move anything, Jack."

"I wouldn't think of it."

Then Jack looked around the room, it was empty but for a dust covered dresser. There were smears in the dust where the woman had presumably written the name McGruder.

When Dekker came back up the stairs Jack showed him the message.

Dekker looked at it. "What does it mean? Who is McGruder?""

"Beats me, but from the looks of it she was the one that wrote the name."

"Then we assume that it was one last attempt to identify the killer?"

Jack shrugged. "What's the albatross doing?"

"He was puking his guts out in the downstairs bathroom."

"The guy needs field experience and perhaps some counseling," Jack laughed.

"Right." Dekker agreed.

Jack walked down the stairs and found a bath towel lying on the floor next to the bathroom door. He hadn't noticed it before even though it was out of place. This house was generally well kept and the towel was the sort of thing that was easily overlooked. Then he walked into the main bathroom. The tub was full and ice was forming on the surface. The toilet seat was down and a towel had been placed over the seat.

"What are you thinking, Jack?"

"Try this for size, Lieutenant?" Jack gestured to the bath. "The lady is taking a bath."

"A bubble bath," Dekker said as he held up a container.

Jack grinned, "Right a bubble bath. She doesn't worry about closing the door because it's just her and Steve Kaplan in the house and then she hears the door bell ring and a man's voice. She goes out to the stairs, perhaps out of curiosity and sees this guy McGruder. No big deal, she thinks, so she goes back to painting her nails," He pointed to the pink toe nail paint, "She isn't done yet, but then the men start arguing, maybe this would have been the time when she looks down the stairs, and that was also about the time that McGruder took Kaplan down to the basement. McGruder probably didn't know that she was in the house and so he left the basement door open. She heard the shots and decided that she had better make herself scarce. So she runs out with just a towel draped around her ass and in her panic she drops it. She hears the guy walking around the house and she runs upstairs and locks the door.

This McGruder character decides to check out the house. He doesn't want any witnesses so he comes upstairs and he sees the wet foot prints on the floor or maybe spots the towel. He goes up the stairs, kicks in the door and puts the fourth round in the lady's head."

"And then?" Michael, looking rather pale, was standing in the door way listening.

Jack continued, "And then he ejects the shells and reloads. Then he goes back down stairs and checks out the rest of the house. He finds the coffee perking in the kitchen and being a cold hearted bastard, he helps himself to a cup." Jack began looking around on the floor and found four spent shell casings. He picked them up very carefully with a pencil and laid them in Dekker's hand.

"Why would he reload up here?" Michael asked.

"Because he knew that he had expended four rounds and wanted to be ready should the need arise to do some more shooting."

Dekker agreed and added, "He is a very cold calculating customer and accustomed to murder, this guy has killed before."

Jack nodded, "Then Crouse and Werner show up. This McGruder invites them in and he hangs their gear up in the closet. I checked it out that night that we were here. There were four hangers in the closet, three of them had a coats hanging on them and there were three hats on the shelf, and I didn't think anything about it at the time, but the fourth hanger, the empty hanger that was also centered in the closet, becomes significant. I should have tumbled to the fact that the third coat might have belonged to Kaplan. This guy McGruder was welcomed and treated accordingly. Maybe he was here to meet with the other two. Obviously, he was very unhappy with Mister Kaplan and he took the guy downstairs and put three in his gut. Perhaps a measure of just how cold and calculating the guy can be is illustrated by the fact that Kaplan wasn't dead when McGruder buried him under the coal. He may even have been moaning at the time. Then McGruder starts searching through the house and finds the naked lady. So he dispatches her to eternity. Then something happens and Crouse kills Werner. Perhaps these guys were all arguing about something. Then McGruder kills Crouse. What ever happened to cause the fallout between them is part of the mystery."

Dekker picked up the tale of reconstruction of events. "Then McGruder removes Werner's coat and puts the gun in Werner's hand, cleans up the dishes. The he takes Werner's coat outside to the trash, and then puts on his own coat, which explains the empty hanger and leaves the place closing but not locking the door." Dekker looked around the house and shaking his head as he did so. "This guy McGruder knows something about police procedures. He has killed three people, assuming that Crouse killed Werner, and then the mystery man vanishes into the night."

"Into the afternoon," Jack corrected. He grinned sheepishly, "I never thought about it, because it was kind of your problem at the time. But how in the hell did they get to the house? Did they come with McGruder? There was no other car outside and the Packard was in the garage."

"You two people have very active imaginations," Michael said sarcastically, "You're speculating."

Dekker looked at Michael and asked, "Mister Caine, have you ever been involved in a murder investigation before?"

Michael shook his head in the negative. "We rarely handle murder investigations."

'Then allow me to provide just a small amount of education for you," The Lieutenant said. "We speculate, trying to put the events into some semblance of order so that they make some sense. That system doesn't always work, because the person that commits murder is usually in a highly emotional state and is also usually intoxicated. It is rare that we see a rational, cold, business like approach to murder. In this case they seem to be professionals, but they are making some amateurish mistakes, which is perplexing. It is the contradictions that we are trying to resolve." Dekker moved closer to Michael. "So, Mister Caine, if you don't have anything to contribute, kindly keep your mouth shut."

"I meant no offense," Michael stammered.

Dekker turned to Jack, "If he says another word I will exclude him from the crime scene."

"I don't care if you take him out and shoot him," Jack said with a laugh.

Michael backed away from the door jamb and went meekly down the stairs. About that time there was a hammering at the door and Michael opened it up to allow the Coroners team and the Homicide people to enter the house.

Dekker gave directions and sent officers out to canvas the neighborhood checking for anyone that had seen anything. He turned to Jack, "We'll call the Cab Companies and check on how the victims got here. Do you recognize this guy McGruder's name in any of the correspondence that you have access to?"

"No, but I'll check again and keep you advised. Did you guys ever check this guy Werner's home?"

"I sent a couple of guys to notify the widow, if there was one, but no one answered the door. Werner lived in an apartment. I have the keys and a warrant in the car, but I didn't have enough guys to check it out, so I kind of let it slide a little. Do you want to check it out?"

"Yeah, under the circumstances it has to be done."

"We share what you find right?"

Jack pretended to be hurt, "Have I ever..?"

Dekker just shook his head and led the way out to the car. "You're going to take the albatross with you, right?"

"Right."

"For Christ's sake, Jack, don't find any more bodies. I haven't got enough men to cover the carnage."

Jack offered his hand and Dekker accepted.

"Be careful," Dekker warned, "this guy might be a cop or an ex cop."

"He thinks kind a like a cop, but he's making mistakes that are not Cop like."

"Such as?"

"Such as forgetting to wipe his prints off the cylinder, maybe he got rattled, or got in a hurry, or maybe it never occurred to him. He thought that we would read the Crouse killing as having been committed by Werner, but he underestimated us. Maybe he is some kind of semi cop?"

"Like the albatross?"

Jack nodded, "Yeah, maybe something like that, or maybe like a lawyer."

Jack herded Michael into the car and started off towards Werner's address. It was growing bitterly cold and one could hear the tires crackling on the frozen snow. Jack shuddered and drew his collar closer about his neck. The heater in the car was striving vainly to ward off the chill.

"Are we going back to the office?" Michael asked. "This is Friday night, my wife and I normally go to dinner about seven."

"This is a murder investigation, Mister Caine and such things have a habit of getting out of hand. We often find ourselves following leads that can take us no where or to the heart of the matter, we never know which it will be, but we must follow them up in an expedient manner."

"You can refer to me as Michael."

"Thank you, Michael."

"I'm very hungry," Michael stated.

"I am too, with any luck we'll be able to eat in an hour or two."

"We've got to check in with Special Agent Albright."

"Great idea," Jack spotted a diner on a corner and pulled in. "Maybe we can stave off starvation and simultaneously call the boss."

Jack was munching on a sandwich by the time that Michael got off the phone.

"Special Agent Albright is thinking that we ought to take the gang down. His thoughts presently are that we can gather the evidence at the scene, but he is somewhat ambivalent about the timing."

Jack nodded, "Yeah, if the press ever gets wind that we are just watching these guys as they reduce the population, they just won't understand our thinking."

Michael began to ingest his sandwich with a single minded determination.

"Don't bite your fingers Michael."

Michael frowned at Jack and kept munching furiously.

"What were the boss's thoughts concerning the additional deaths? Does he recognize the name of this guy McGruder?" Jack watched his partner munching furiously. "For Christ's sake, Michael, put that sandwich down for a minute, nobody is going to take it away from you."

"I told you, I'm hungry."

"I asked you what the boss thought."

"He never heard of McGruder. He is concerned and wants a full report on his desk by tomorrow."

"What time tomorrow?"

Michael was munching again and he was trying to talk past the food, "He didn't say."

"Jesus," Jack muttered, "I've seen cannibals with better table manners."

"I told you I am hungry!" Michael blurted out in a loud voice.

"Let's get out of here, Michael you're an embarrassment to the Bureau."

It was snowing again and the sun was going down as they hurried out to the car. Michael sat in the right front and he was in a bad mood again. Werner's apartment building was in newer well kept neighborhood. Now Michael was complaining that he had to go to the bathroom. Jack felt as though he was taking a kid along with him. They knocked at the door and received no reply. Michael was fidgeting as would a five year old. Jack shrugged and produced the key. They had no more than got in Werner's apartment than Michael made a beeline for the bathroom. Jack loosened his thirty-eight in its holster and slowly began clearing the rooms. A door slammed at the rear of the apartment and Jack headed in that direction. He got to the rear door in time to see a stocky, white haired man scurrying down the back stairs and then take the walkway that led toward the alley. Jack opened the back door and the man turned and fired two shots, one of which hit the wall and the other shattered the window in the next apartment. A woman screamed inside that apartment. Jack didn't return fire because he couldn't see the target clearly. The garage structures along the alley got in the way as the man scurried along using the buildings as a shield.

Could this be McGruder? Jack wondered. What was this guy looking for? Jack went over to the other apartment.

"Is everyone okay in there?" He shouted. "'I'm from the police, are you alright?"

There was no answer from within and Jack looked in the broken window. It was the scream that perturbed him. He asked himself if it could that some poor innocent woman been wounded by a stray round? Jack intended to rattle the door knob, but to his surprise the door swung open. "I'm a Police Officer," he shouted. There was no reply. Then he saw her, she was standing with her back to the hallway wall as if she were terrified. "I'm a police officer," he said gently and searched for his badge. "Please don't be alarmed."

She stepped away from the wall and then he saw that she had a revolver and it was pointed directly at him.

"For Christ's sake lady, I'm a police officer. Look, if you're okay, I'll go back outside."

It was at this point that Michael came bursting out the back door of the next apartment. He was waving his pistol and had slipped on the icy porch, as he lost his footing his legs went out from under him and he landed on his rear end in the snow. As he did so the gun discharged and the round ricocheted off the porch roof, striking a collection of empty flower pots. Michael was sliding toward the railing and flailing about trying desperately to stop. As he did so he was simultaneously waving the revolver in the air. Michael had put his right hand down to brace himself and the weapon discharged again.

"Mother of Christ!" Jack exclaimed.

People were standing out on their porches by this time watching this display of professionalism with some confusion and amusement.

Jack stepped outside and took the weapon from Michael's hand and unloaded it, "For Christ's sake, Michael, what are you doing?"

"I thought you were in trouble," Michael explained lamely.

"Yeah, well I wasn't until you started shooting. For Christ's sake be careful with that weapon. Goddamn it, Mike. Don't ever load that son of a bitch again without my permission."

"What are you people, the Keystone Kops?" The woman inside the apartment asked.

Jack looked up at the woman and discovered that she was laughing uncontrollably.

"Sweet Jesus, you guys have got to be Chicago Cops, no one else is that screwed up."

Jack was embarrassed and defensive, "He doesn't get a chance to use his weapon very often."

"I'll bet," the woman responded and started laughing again. Tears were streaming down her cheeks and she was holding on to her stomach as if in pain. She sank into a chair and laid her head down on the table. "Oh get the hell out of here, I can't stand it."

Jack left and kicked at Michael, "Get up off the goddamn floor, Michael."

Jack went back inside the Werner apartment and started chuckling to himself as he pictured the scene. It had to have been funny. He hadn't thought so at the time, but upon review it did sort of tickle him. That gal had a great sense of humor.

Michael came inside and was trying to regain his composure. "Some one shot at you?"

Jack nodded. "They did indeed. You shot at me twice and the other guy shot twice."

"Aw come on I didn't shoot at you. Who was it?"

"I have no idea. Why don't you go next door and ask that lady if she saw anything?"

"She's still laughing. I think she's hysterical. I am never going to ask her anything." Michael protested.

"Well then start a methodical search room by room and I'll talk to the lady."

"What am I looking for?"

"Jesus, Michael, haven't you ever conducted a search?"

"Well," Michael sort of stammered, "No not exactly. Usually they give us the books or financial documents and we do the rest."

"Michael, we'll start the search in the bedrooms and then go from room to room. Each room will be searched thoroughly before we move on to the next." Jack led the way into what had obviously been the only occupied bedroom. First, he took an overall appraisal of the room brushing through the closet space.

"No woman's clothes, but half the space is vacant. So we can surmise that if there was a woman living here then she apparently has left. So we have a single male living here. There is a picture on the dresser of a couple, so maybe this is the wife or girl friend." There was a long low dressing table and the drawers were apparently empty. "I think she is gone. But check this table anyway." Then he went to the man's dresser and demonstrated the search technique by slowly, efficiently checking the drawers. Then he looked at the backs, the bottoms, and inside the frame structure of the cabinets. "Don't make a mess. Put everything back in order, it is a good habit to develop."

Once he was certain that he had Michael going properly. He went to the back door and stepped out on the porch. She was there in her kitchen trying to install piece of cardboard into the gap of the broken window.

"I apologize for all the excitement." Jack said, as he smiled.

"And I apologize for laughing so hard," She replied. "I think I was sort of over reacting out of relief. I was really frightened there for a minute or two. I heard the door slam and somebody running down the stairs then I heard the shot and the window smashed and I ran to get my pistol. I heard your shouts, but I was still scared."

He was looking at her as if seeing her for the first time, of course the first view that he had of her was concentrated upon the revolver in her hand. She was a well proportioned brunette in her late twenties, her hair was raven like black and she had a complexion like cream. Her big blue eyes appraised him calmly and he found her to be very attractive, she wore a loose fitting house dress and a little old lady sweater and very comfortable looking Indian slippers. She appeared to be a perfectly normal, friendly human being with a pleasant attitude. Jack helped her with the cardboard and had her call a glazier.

"We'll pay for the repairs. It is the least we can do."

"But it wasn't your fault."

"Yeah, but my friend wounded some of your flower pots."

She began to giggle, "That was funny."

"Well please apologize to your husband for any inconvenience that we may have caused."

"Oh, I'm not married. I live here alone and I teach fifth grade at a local Elementary school. I just got home a little bit ago." She held out her dress, "I always slip into something comfortable, make some hot chocolate and settle down by the fire place. I find that refreshing after a week in the zoo."

Jack smiled at this little recital of her day. "May I ask if you've seen anything suspicious going on in the next apartment? "

"Mister and Mrs. Werner? No, I've met him a time or two, but he is usually very quiet and his wife is a very nice lady. They are good neighbors, but not very friendly."

"You didn't associate much, I take it?"

"No, I just saw them occasionally."

"Well, I hate to tell you this Eunice, but Mister Werner was killed the other day."

She stared at him for a minute. "And so you are here investigating?"

"That's about it."

"Was it a car accident?" She caught herself, "No it had to be something violent, or the police wouldn't be here."

"Did you see the wife yesterday?"

"May I see your identification again please?"

Jack produced his card.

"Jack Kelly, Federal Bureau of Investigation, Special Agent," she read aloud. "Oh my, I've never met a G-Man before. Who are you chasing, Mr. Kelly?"

"Well, Mister Werner was one of them."

There was a clatter in the front hall and she led the way to the door. Three Chicago Police Officers were banging on the Werner's door.

Jack thanked the school teacher and sent her back inside. Then he took the officers into the Werner's apartment and explained the circumstances. They had all heard about the murders and were impressed. Jack thanked them for coming by and after a bit they all left. Then Jack and Michael went through the rest of the apartment, but found nothing. As they were finishing up the door bell rang and school teacher stood there with a platter of cookies and a carafe of coffee. Jack and Eunice sat in the kitchen drinking coffee while Michael called in and reported that they would soon be on they're way to the office. Then he had to call his wife. Michael hadn't realized that it was close to seven p.m. and that he had missed a supper appointment.

Jack explained to Eunice that they hadn't found anything and she asked if they had checked the basement storage space. Jack didn't know that such an arrangement even existed; he admitted that he should have, but hadn't thought about it. Eunice said that she had seen Mister Werner down there every once in a while. It seemed that Eunice kept some of her school files in a file cabinet in her basement space and so she was down there frequently. Though, she said, that she hated to go down there alone in the winter when it was dark.

While Michael explained to his wife, why investigators had to work nights, Jack and Eunice went down to the basement. Jack found several boxes of files and carried them out to the car. A subdued Michael eventually joined them and assisted in carting out the boxes.

Jack thanked Eunice effusively. She was, he thought, a very nice lady and he asked if he could take her out for dinner and dancing.

She smiled and replied that would be nice.

It was still snowing when he got to his apartment and the snow was nearly a foot deep. He poured himself a shot of scotch and sat there thinking about the day. On an impulse he called Alice. He thought that he owed her that much. She was distraught and extremely annoyed with him. She had been to his room and was startled to find that he had moved away. The manager wasn't very nice to her. Then she went to the PD and they really gave her a run around. "Did you meet Auggie there?" Jack asked.

"Well yes, I did meet him. It was he that gave me your number," she said.

"Well Alice, I'm surprised that you didn't know. Auggie is your secret admirer. He is that big, strong, strapping detective, a man of great sexual potential. He has always cherished you from afar but has been too shy to say hello," Jack gave her Auggies home number, and asked that she not mention his name, and he then explained that he had to leave town, but hoped that Alice and Auggie could be happy together. He said goodbye and before she could begin her usual histrionics he hung up.

Chapter Five

Saturday

Jack was in early and went back out of the office and downstairs to the coffee shop and bought some coffee and a couple of donuts. By the time he got back upstairs Marcy was there making coffee in the big office pot. He shared his donuts with her.

She was friendly and asked how he liked his new job?

Marcy was single and had recently broken up with her boyfriend. She asked if he was single and he replied in the affirmative. They exchanged smiles and she went back to her office as he poured some more coffee and went to work.

At precisely eight A.M. Clarence opened the security locker and Jack pulled the cart and boxes out to his desk. It was Michael that almost literally saved the day. Jack was about to open a box when Michael came into the office.

"Wait a minute!" Michael almost shouted. "We have to get permission to do that?"

"From who?" Jack asked.

"Well," Michael hesitated, "From Chief Special Agent Albright."

"Why?"

"We didn't have a search warrant. We've got to get a judge to give us permission to open these files."

Jack leaned on the boxes and thought about what was being said. Technically, Michael was right. He couldn't remember if the sheriffs had obtained a search warrant that would cover the basement storage. "I'll call the Sheriff's office."

110

"I'll get Mister Albright," Michael announced.

Walt came in and was furious. "We can't remove property from a premise's without permission. What were you thinking?"

"I was thinking that if I didn't take it they would." Then Jack informed Walt that the Sheriff did have a warrant and that they were covered.

"What will we do with it?" Walt asked.

"Let's find out what we've got. If it is financial data, we'll turn Michael loose on it. If it's meaningless, I'll give it back to the sheriffs. If it is pertinent to the pursuit of the case I'll categorize and log it."

"That sounds like a plan, what about Atlanta Financial?"

"If I were you," Jack said, "I'd prepare the warrants and bust that place this afternoon before they kill all the participants."

Walt chuckled and nodded, "I think that you are right on the mark. I'll get the Judge to give us a warrant for Monday. Now, what do we do about the murders, or rather, what do we do about the murderers?"

"Let's let the Sheriff's worry about those guys for the moment. Uh, Mr. Albright I think that we had better hit them today. That guy that took a shot at me was probably looking for this material and he can assume that we have it. Were I them, I would have left town last night."

"Yes well, we have to coordinate the seizure of the assets. An effort of this sort requires pre-planning. This isn't a simple act of driving over there and busting down the door, we must coordinate with the local Police agencies. I think Monday will be just fine."

Jack had stated his opinion and was overruled he had experienced that sort of thing in the Corps and knew better than to press his opinion. Once the leadership had made up their mind that was it, to quarrel with that decision was akin to shoveling excrement against the tide. He shrugged philosophically and went back to his work. Jack and Michael went through the boxes, most of which were files concerning the individual customers. These files detailed the amount of money of the original loan to the subject person. Then it detailed the outstanding amount remaining and the amount of the contract payable to Atlanta Financial for the recovery of sums. Michael went to work totaling those amounts.

"The internal revenue service will be mightily interested in these files," Michael said.

"Maybe a lot of people will be going to jail, huh?"

"No, they don't want people in jail they want people to pay the bills. This material will keep them busy for a long time." The numbers that Michael totaled were impressive, but there was an element of frustration, because the files rarely balanced. "These people aren't accountants, and some of them can't even add and subtract."

"I'll bet that all the mistakes are in their favor," Jack said. "They're dumb, but not that dumb."

Jack was compiling names and as he did so he kept searching for a Mister Warren McGruder, but the name was never mentioned nor did the name of Steve Kaplan or that of Martin Werner appear. The telephone personnel were there, these were the shills that drummed up the business, and Myron's name was there several times. It seemed that Myron was really a go getter when it came to finding businesses in trouble. Myron had also done some traveling to other cities for some level of coordination. Crossing state lines to promote a criminal business definitely involved the Bureau.

It was a long day and it was long after the normal quitting time when Jack called Eunice. He asked if she would care to go out for supper. Then he went home and showered and shaved and made reservations for two at a fancy restaurant. He dressed in a dark suit and even left his weapon at home. He met her at seven and she looked beautiful. She wore a dark fur coat and a fur hat and her lovely pale complexion provided stark contrast to those garments and the absolute best part, from Jack's perspective was that she was ready when he rang the bell. It to be a gay evening with no thought of work. They chatted about her school work, but only briefly and only in the vaguest of terms. She told Jack that she had been born in Indianapolis. She had been married to a Navy pilot who had crashed as he attempted to land on a carrier. That had been three years ago. His buddies had written to her and one even came to call to give her the details of the accident. At the time she didn't want to think about it, but since then she admitted that she would take out his letters from time to time and read them.

Jack was caught off guard. He really didn't know what he had expected, but it wasn't this. She was dwelling on the memories of a dead husband rather than moving on with her life.

"Have you had sweethearts?" She asked. "Oh. Of course you have. You're handsome, virile and obviously intelligent. You'd be quite a catch for some girl."

She was lovely, well, he thought, maybe we can save this evening after all.

The band played some of the new Jazz and Jack and Eunice danced away the hours. At one point, during a slow number, she laid her head on his chest and whispered "Chuck."

At first he wanted to pull away, but resisted the impulse. What the hell, he thought, give the girl her memories, what can it hurt for this one night? In the main he felt that the evening was worth it, but he was wondering if there couldn't be someone somewhere out there between all the Alice's and Eunice's that was perfectly normal?

As they walked up the steps to the apartment he took her hand in his to brace her against the weather. Now the wind was blowing at about thirty knots. Typical Chicago, the wind was growing in velocity even as they stood there on the stoop. She was laughing gaily as they finally pushed open the door. At her apartment door she asked him to come in for a while, she promised to make a little coffee. His first impulse was to refuse, but he didn't want to hurt her feelings. He sat at the dining room table; his overcoat was unbuttoned and open. He hoped that the signal was clear that he wanted to leave.

"Jack please stay the night. I have a pull out bed that's quite comfortable. I'm really afraid for your safety. That weather is potentially very dangerous."

Ah well, he thought, maybe she's right. It is bad out there. "Well if it is no big inconvenience maybe I will take you up on that offer."

She smiled. "Good Jack, I'll get some pajamas for you."

"Ah don't bother, Eunice," he laughed, "I wouldn't know what to do with them."

She grinned and started to say something, but thought better of it.

He could almost imagine what she was going to say, something like, well Chuck never liked them either.

Eunice pulled out the bed and put some sheets, two pillows and a blanket down. They drank the coffee and made their trips to the bathroom and she said goodnight and went into her room. Jack undressed down to his tee shirt and shorts and lay down. He had reconsidered and thought it had been a nice evening despite a couple of minor little flaws. She was lovely and he thought that she was fundamentally a nice person. The bed was sort of comfortable and he turned off the lights and stretched out. It had been a long day.

She came to his bed naked and slid in beside him. She kissed him and urged him to remove his clothes. It didn't take much urging. She caressed his manhood and then took him in her mouth. This was different than Alice. Alice had been frantic and urging, Eunice was caressing and gentle. He thought that either mode was perfectly acceptable. Eunice chose to be on her back and wrapped her legs about him urging him into her and then after they had climaxed she kept moving asking for more. This went on for several times and then she told him that she wanted him to shower with her. She climbed out of bed and he could hear the shower running. God, this was different, there had been no loud moaning or screaming. No scratching or biting. He was beginning to think that despite her one or two little trivial idiosyncrasies, such as moaning softly of her love to Chuck, that she was normal enough.

In the shower she washed him and he washed her, then she went down on him again. After that they dried each other and then went back to the bed. This time she was lunging and clawing, pulling at him. She was an animal then she kissed him passionately again and again.

They lay there in silence and he could hear her deep breathing. After a bit she got up and pulled her robe around her. "I think that you had better go home now, Chuck." Then she went into her room and closed the door.

Chuck? Go home now? His mind was racing. In that Goddamn blizzard? Where in the hell is all the concern for my safety? He dressed slowly, thinking that she might reconsider if he stalled long enough. Then he grew angry. She can get down on her Goddamn hands and knees and I won't stay even if I'm doomed to freeze to death on her door step. Goddamn women! He had worn dancing shoes, a fat lot of help they would be in this weather disaster. He drove home. It took nearly an hour to go a short distance and the heater never did warm up the car. When he finally got into the building it was first time in an hour that he began to feel his fingers. His feet were soaking wet, half frozen and he was literally freezing. As he wearily climbed the stairs, he wondered what time it was.

He started to put his key in the apartment door and then drew back his hand. The small piece of thread that he had put across the top of the door was gone. He had left the weapons in the apartment. Ah shit! He thought. He was really in no mood or condition for this crap. He gently eased the door open, maybe they had gone to sleep? He smelled the faint odor of cigar smoke. Jack didn't smoke at all. He moved the door ever so quietly and gently. The apartment was vacant, but someone had been there waiting for him. Eunice, for all of her lunacy, just might have saved his life. He vowed to never ever leave his weapons at home no matter where he was going. Jack reached under his dresser and removed the forty five. He felt a lot better now. Let them come.

Then he found the thirty-eight still hidden far back under the sink where it was taped into a holster of sorts. He locked the door and looked out the window. There had been a car parked across the street, the vacant space was covered with a thinner layer of snow than that of the surrounding area. So it had been that close. Why? That was a good question. Was it his inquiry into the gang of con men, or into his attempt to find the murderer? Or, what was perhaps more likely, was it his attempt to find the Mole within the Bureau? What ever it was the old ingrained habit of placing a hair or a small piece of string across the door jamb could have saved his life. He could clearly remember Major Wade drilling the idea into his thick head that it would be prudent to know if someone was waiting within, or if your door had been opened. The problem was that the other guys knew about the technique and thus it might be meaningless. The neat thing about the technique was that the locals around here hadn't caught on yet. Ever since Alice had surprised him at the hotel he had decided to go back to the old defensive habit.

He made some coffee and sat down at the table to relax a bit. Jack sipped his coffee, He was mentally and physically exhausted, and his feet were still cold, even in the warm slippers. He needed to go to bed, but he was still hyper at the thought of somebody being there in his apartment waiting for him. He got up and checked out the easy chair. The guy had moved it slightly so that it faced the door. There were faint traces of cigar ashes in the saucer that Jack had used for his coffee cup this morning. So the Killer had cleaned up after himself and but for the absence of a small piece of thread and the faint odor of cigar smoke, Jack would probably never have known how close he had been to death. Maybe Mister McGruder had been waiting for him. Even if he had been armed, when he walked in that door, he would never have had a chance to respond.

This killer was pretty good, but he was making a couple of tiny, but definitely significant mistakes. Could it be McGruder? How could McGruder have found out about him? The indications of the man's presence were certainly there. If it were McGruder then this was about the murders. Why would they bother? He wasn't the only man on the case. They would have had to have followed him when he left work. That was possible Jack hadn't been watching for a tail. Jack poured one more cup of coffee. He had filled out the original applications and forms before he had a new address. He had noted on the application that he would probably be moving and later he had given his change of address to Marcy, so at that precise point, which was Friday morning, she was the only one that knew about this place. Maybe she would have informed Walt, but then again maybe not. He checked his ID Badge and it still had the old hotel address. No one knew about this place but Marcy. So was she the culprit? Or had they been watching him closer than he thought?

Had they decided to come after him just yesterday morning? Marcy wouldn't have memorized the address if she wasn't involved, but they could have gone downstairs and checked with the clerical people. He wasn't sure how that worked so he would have to check it out Monday.

In the meantime he would get some sleep. He hit the sack and tucked the forty-five under his pillow. He thought about Eunice as he was dozing off. That poor devastated kid had better see a psychiatrist or a priest. Personally, he would have preferred talking to a priest. If she didn't seek them out soon, some day she would probably decide to swallow that pistol of hers one round at a time. Or maybe she just might keep enlisting stand in replacements until she finally forgot about Chucky. He wished her well, but mentally scratched her off his list of nice girls.

He awoke about noon. The first thing he did was go to the window. There was no car there or anywhere along the street that he could see. This bastard McGruder was making him as nervous as a cat. The snow was piled to what he would later learn was a record depth. It had been dangerous out there last night in more ways than one. He showered and shaved and put on his off duty clothes which consisted of slacks and leather jacket and an old navy watch cap. The cap was warm and you could pull it down over your ears if you had too. One good thing about Chicago was that after a snow storm, it was usually warmer, that is if you can consider five below as being warm. Jack had packed the forty-five under his arm, He didn't give a damn what J. Edgar wanted, J. Edgar wasn't out here with his ass on the line. He replaced his magic thread as he left. It was impossible to get his car out of the snow without a shovel and he figured that the damned thing probably wouldn't start anyway, so he walked down two blocks to the streetcar stop. No one was following him that he could see. Jack decided that he would take a long ride down to Goldsman's Diner for breakfast and then he would visit Pat McDonald's place for a beer or two and a little chat.

Pat smiled and waved as Jack entered and then Pat signaled the bartender that the drinks were on his tab. Jack stopped to gossip with the usual crew and then sat down next to Pat.

Pat, I got to ask you a question and I hope you don't mind?"

Pat shrugged, "After what you guys did for me ask away."

"That night that Crouse shot Hymie, did he bring a brief case in here with him? I never thought to ask that night, but it might be pertinent."

Pat nodded, "Yeah, I been reading the papers. Somebody shot that shit head Crouse right?"

"Right." Jack responded.

"Thank God! Well, let me think. Did Crouse have a brief case," Pat shook his head. "Gosh, Jack, I don't remember, let's ask one of the boys."

Pat returned after a bit. "Joe says that Crouse came in with a brief case and laid it over on the seat in the booth and then he took it with him when he left." Pat paused for a moment or two, and then he said, "Joe is the kind of guy that notices things like that. Like where you lay down your packages and things."

Jack understood.

One of the local girls came up behind him and began to massage Jack's neck. Jack cringed when she first touched him, but he forced himself to settle down. "Gee Jack, you're all tensed up."

Jack turned and smiled. "It's probably due to a lack of loving."

Margot leaned close, "Come with me honey, I'll give you something you've never had before."

"Christ," Pat laughed, "What's she got leprosy?"

It was a rude old joke, but still kind of funny, Margot hit Jack on the back and walked away.

"Hit him, not me," Jack laughed. "He's the guy that said it."

"Assholes," Margot said indignantly.

One more stiff drink of scotch and Jack got on a street car. It was a long ride back to the north side and Jack had plenty of time to think, but not a hell of lot to think about. The Christmas Santa's were out ringing their bells and the stores were all spiffed up. Even the street lights were decorated with wreathes and things. Right at Sixty-third and Halstead the stores were pumping Christmas music out over the intersection. He really liked the carols and the ringing of the bells.

The sun was going down now and you could see the Christmas trees all lit up in the windows of the houses. Jack liked this time of year. There was always so much hustle and bustle and people hurrying about. Their breath blowing visibly in the cold air, faces flushed with effort. A few even occasionally smiled at one another. As big as it was, Chicago had always been a friendly town. It was too bad that there were so many idiots running around loose screwing things up for everyone else.

Jack got off the street car a block early and strolled nonchalantly down the street looking for some indication of surveillance. Since he hadn't taken his car and wasn't home they would have to assume that either he had never come home or that someone else was doing the driving.

He couldn't spot any sort of a reception team and so he continued down the street. His car was one of the few still covered with snow. Most of the guys were making ready for going to work tomorrow and had cleared away the snow and ice. His first inclination was to walk over and clear some of that stuff away, but he thought twice about that. He just might have someone watching from a window. God damn it, he was getting paranoid, but better paranoid than dead. He went in through the back of his hotel and took the rear stairs to the floor. Then he checked his door carefully. The string was missing. He removed the forty-five and pulled the hammer back from the half cock position. He turned the knob and pushed the door open. Then he waited. There was no sound. He stepped into the doorway and just as quickly stepped away to his left. The man fired three times. Jack leaned out to his right and fired twice. Another round ripped through the door jamb near his head as he ducked again. He had scored, his opponent had missed. He chanced a quick look and the figure of a man was sprawled on the floor. Up and down the corridor people were tentatively opening doors; heads peeked out and then rapidly jerked back inside. Jack moved cautiously into the room. One shooter, face down on the floor with two forty-five caliber rounds in his chest. Jack closed the door and called the police.

Jack holstered his weapon and went to the window. There was no action outside. Then Jack walked over to the kitchenette. The guy had been sitting in his chair and smoking cigarettes. This wasn't the same guy that had been here last night. Jack packed his bags with clothes and the thirty-eight; he unloaded his forty-five and placed it on the bar. He wouldn't be able to stay here.

The manager was tapping faintly on the door and Jack opened it.

"Anything wrong, sir." The guy looked at the body on the floor and backed away.

"I've called the police. I evidently had a burglar. He is deceased."

"Uh sir, we can't have this sort of thing going on here."

"What sort of thing?" Jack asked.

"Uh well, shooting people."

"You mean to tell me that I'm not allowed to shoot people in my own room?" Jack said in mock outrage and then he started laughing as the manager backed away in confusion.

When the first officers on the scene arrived Jack identified himself.

"Why did you shoot him, sir?" The Patrolman asked.

"Because he was obviously intent upon shooting me."

"That seems reasonable enough. Was there any particular reason for him shooting at you?"

Jack smiled, "I don't think he liked cops."

It was the Patrolman's turn to smile. "That's a real pity. Have you touched the body?"

"No, I figured you guys would want to do that."

"Right. Where's your weapon?"

"It's on the counter and it is unloaded."

The officer checked. "Right, nicely done."

When the Homicide Lieutenant arrived he checked the body. "Two rounds in chest, maybe an inch and a half apart." Then he walked to the doorway and raised and imaginary pistol. "Damn good shooting Agent Kelly. Those forty-five's do it every time don't they? By the way, Mister Kelly, since when do the Feds carry cannons?"

"They don't, but I do. I guess I spent too much time on the PD looking at the bodies of officers that had exchanged shots with some idiot. I would prefer not to exchange shots."

The Lieutenant nodded and opened his coat. He was carrying a forty-five. "I couldn't agree more. Based upon the holes in the door I assume that this guy was waiting for you? Who is this idiot?"

"I have no idea," Jack filled them in on the story.

The Lieutenant had heard about this series of murders and scribbled the data down in his notes. "So this guy was an assassin and you were next on the list of those to go?"

"Right," Jack replied succinctly, "But I'm not quite ready yet."

They checked the man's pockets and produced an ID. No one recognized him and based on the fact that the guy was allegedly from Detroit, one officer suggested that the guy was probably rented muscle. They all looked at Jack with new respect. It wasn't often that the mob imported shooters.

"He's got a hotel key here, Lieutenant. Looks like the Sheraton. The asshole was traveling first class."

The Lieutenant examined the weapon, checked out carefully and gave it back to Jack, "You'll probably need this. If this guy missed they'll probably try again, they usually do."

Jack nodded; The Lieutenant had a point they would probably try again.

The lieutenant said, "We're going over to the Sheraton to check this guy's room for evidence, want to come along?"

"Yeah, that's an idea," Jack picked up his bags and followed the Lieutenant.

The search of the room at the Sheraton revealed very little other than conformation of the man's out of town address. No notes. The only possible evidence of any meaning was the cigar ashes in the ashtray. The Lieutenant bent down and smelled the ashes, "Cuban," he announced. "Good stuff; these guys live high on the hog."

McGruder Jack thought. Jack checked into the Sheraton, and asked for the room next to that of the 'would be' killer. He felt that he could afford a couple of nights, which would give him time to set up housekeeping somewhere else. He also asked that he be advised if anybody asked to see or call the deceased or if they asked for the room key to the deceased's room. Mister McGruder was making things increasingly expensive and more difficult.

Chapter Six

Monday

As usual Jack was in early. A newspaper lay on Marcy's desk. His picture was plastered all over the front page. "Policeman kills gunman in self defense." The story was irresponsible journalism at its best. "In less than a week Officer Jack Kelly of Chicago PD kills a second man in alleged self defense."

Great stuff, Jack thought. They put two and two together and come up with five. Fortunately they hadn't mentioned that he had changed his job. He wondered what the laws were with regard to killing photographers and newsmen. Surely there was some sort of special quota or category for hunting news idiots. He picked up the paper and read the lead and dropped it back on the desk. They had his name, which was probably given to them by some ass kissing cop.

Marcy was watching him. "Are you okay, Jack?"

"Yes thank you, I'm just fine."

"It says here that someone tried to kill you."

Jack nodded, "That's right, but they missed."

"Oh my," she muttered.

"Marcy when I gave you my address Friday, what happened to it then?"

"Why, I sent it down to the admin section with the other internal office mail."

"That's the one on the fourth floor?"

"Yes sir," she replied.

She had never called him sir before. Evidently his getting shot at added some degree of status in her mind.

"Did you give a copy to Walt?"

She shook her head. "No Sir, he doesn't like to be bothered with little details."

"What happens to it when it goes to admin?"

She indicated that he should follow her as she went to make coffee. "Well they make changes to the originals then they send it down to the people that do the background checks, those are mostly the new agents. Those are the guys that are on probation. You're the only new guy that we've ever had in this department."

He helped her by pouring water into the coffee urn and she thanked him.

"Was it scary, Jack?"

Jack smiled, "Yeah it was a little bit scary, it always is."

"You've been shot at before?"

"Yeah, a time or two."

"Oh my goodness, I should certainly think it would be terrifying."

Now that Marcy, he thought as he headed for his office, she's really a very nice girl.

Walt arrived he had some paper work in his hand, "We've got the warrants. Gather up all the guys, Marcy and tell them we're going over to Atlanta Financial." He looked at Jack again. "What the hell is this about you're getting shot at?"

Jack shrugged, "I got shot at."

"Why didn't you notify me immediately?"

"How was I supposed to do that, the office was closed."

"There is always a duty officer here," Walt was obviously angered. "We have a protocol; we must notify the Bureau within six hours of any shooting. Now I have to explain to the Director why this office didn't report. God dammit, Jack, you're supposed to read the protocols."

"What protocols?"

"Marcy get those protocols out for Jack and have him read them and initial each of them."

Marcy walked around her desk in a little circle, "Uh sir, which do I do first?"

Walt threw his hands up in a gesture of frustration. "Get the men ready and then get the stuff for Jack.

Jack poured a cup of coffee and sat down on the waiting room couch.

Walt came running out, "What the hell are you doing? Didn't I tell you that we're going to Atlanta Financial?"

"You told me the read the protocols. I thought that you were excluding me until I got educated."

Walt waved his arms again. "Stop fucking with me Kelly. Are you armed? Of course you are. You always are. What did I tell you about carrying a thirty-eight? The paper says you nailed that guy twice with a forty-five." Walt hurried out the door and several agents were waiting in the outer hall. "Come on guys, I don't think that there will be any rough stuff, but be sure you're weapons are ready. Now Kelly," they were hurrying down toward the elevators, "You stick with me and no shooting unless we have too."

When they finally arrived at Atlanta Financial the office was completely empty. Nothing, not so much as a single scrap of paper remained on the floor. Behind the secretary's desk there was a door leading to the telephone switchboard and the offices and these too had been stripped only the telephone lines remained. The instruments and the switchboard had been removed. Jack walked around looking for something, anything, but nothing remained. This wasn't an impromptu exodus, but a well planned, time consuming movement. Jack went out and down to the building manager's office. A secretary escorted the grim faced Federal Officer into her boss's office. Mister Carter was a well dressed finicky sort of person that would periodically pretend to wipe a non existent piece of lent from his lapel. The man wore black trousers, a cutaway coat, a gleaming white shirt and a bow tie. Jack read him instantly and flashed his badge. The Jack demanded to know when the people at Atlanta Financial had moved. He was met with a blank stare. This man was trying to convince Jack that he knew nothing whatsoever about the move or of their plans to move. Jack arrested him on the spot for Obstruction of Justice and collusion with regard to Interstate Crime. He wasn't sure that he could make either charge stick, but having brought his cuffs along in anticipation of arresting the people upstairs he clamped the cuffs on the man and started to drag him from the office.

"Wait, wait, my God what do you think you are doing?"

"I'm going to slap your arrogant ass in jail for a week or two until you decide to cooperate with me."

"Wait! You can't do that. I want my lawyer."

"I'll get him for you in a couple of days."

"I refuse to answer your questions."

Jack laughed and started dragging the man from the office. "Keep that in mind when some gorilla sticks his dick up your ass."

"Wait! Goddamn it! They said that you wouldn't do anything."

"The protocols have changed the Department is tired of fucking around with scum like you!"

"Wait, wait!" Mister Carter's voice had gone up an octave or two. "For Christ's sake, I'm not a criminal. They started moving out Friday evening. I ordered the trucks for them Friday night to arrive Saturday morning and they paid me three times the normal fee to keep quiet and I don't know what they paid the drivers and the laborers for working Saturday and Sunday."

"When did they finally clear out of here?"

"Last night, about eight."

"Where were they going?"

"I don't know."

Jack grabbed the cuffs and pulled Carter around his desk. "You're lying you little asshole."

"Wait! Goddamn it! I'm not lying. I ordered the trucks from South Chicago Trucking. They should know where they went. Ask them," he finished rather lamely.

Jack looked at Carter for a long minute and then removed the cuffs. "If you're lying to me, and I find out about it you'll never stop regretting your mistake."

Walt walked into the office, "Jack what's going on here, have you questioned this gentlemen?"

"South Chicago Trucking moved the company," Jack said. "They started moving shortly after that guy shot at me Friday afternoon."

Mister Carter was sitting behind his desk and trembling slightly. His collar was askew and his tie was off to one side.

"Are you alright sir," Walt asked solicitously.

Carter pointed a trembling finger at Jack. "Is that man a Federal Officer?"

"No," Walt responded promptly, "He's on loan from Chicago Police Department."

"I knew it! I knew it. Goddamn Chicago PD." Carter shouted. "I want to lodge a complaint!"

"Call the Chief of Police," Walt told him.

The two men walked out of Carter's office.

"You lied to that poor man." Jack said accusingly.

"What the hell did you do to him?" Walt demanded.

"I just leaned on him a little."

"I think that I may have made a real serious recruiting mistake." Walt confessed. "Christ you're beating up innocent citizens and shooting people. What the hell else have you been doing?"

"I didn't beat on him."

"Tell me about the shooting?" Walt asked

Jack described the Sunday morning sequence, omitting any mention of Eunice. The man that had invaded his apartment had obviously been waiting there for Jack and had been smoking a cigar.

"What the hell does the cigar have to do with it?"

Jack explained that he man that had killed four people at Kaplan's house had been smoking a cigar. Jack didn't mention the warning thread that he had left on the door. Then last night a second assassin had waited for him.

Walt asked how he had known that the man was in there.

Jack lied, saying that the killer had been moving around inside his apartment. It was, Jack explained, the merest of chances that he had survived the encounter. Then Jack asked, "How do you suppose they got my address?"

Walt actually blushed. "The Mole?" He asked in a shocked tone.

Jack shrugged, "Maybe the Mole, maybe McGruder followed me."

"Where are you staying now?"

"I'd prefer not to say."

"Do you think I'm the one?"

"No, Walt, but at this stage of events, I don't trust anybody."

"How can I get a hold of you, if I need you?"

"I'll call in."

"Hourly."

"Yeah," Jack said resignedly, "hourly."

"Bullshit," Walt said. "You won't do that, will you?"

"I'll try."

"What next?" Walt asked.

"South Chicago Trucking. These guys have got a twenty-four hour lead."

"They won't tell you where they took them."

"Assisting criminals to evade the law by crossing a state border is interstate crime, collusion and involves making false statements to a Federal Officer."

"This won't even get them a slap on the wrist."

"I'll talk to them."

"Goddamn it Jack you're going to get us both fired. This is white collar crime."

Jack laughed harshly again, "It was until they killed Myron and four other people and made the attempt on my life, not to mention the attempt on Pat McDonald and his family. These guys are dangerous and that's sort of an understatement."

"I want you to read those protocols," Walt said.

"Maybe later," Jack replied. "I'll need a car, and I ain't taking the albatross with me."

"What albatross?" Walt asked confusedly.

"Michael Caine. The poor man's Sherlock Holmes."

Walt laughed, "The hell you're not! If you are going out chasing this chimera, you're taking Michael with you. You bastards aren't going to get me fired." Walt was standing there tapping the unused warrant against his leg.

"Let me have that will you. I may need it."

Walt threw his hands up in the air, "There goes twenty years of effort."

Michael had purchased new boots and a parka. He had no intention of ruining his good shoes on these adventures with Jack out in the boondocks. When he was informed that they were leaving the office, he began to fuss about gathering his gear. He even had to strap on his thirty-eight, which he left in his desk most of the time. Jack was brooding when he finally got Michael in the car and got under way. Of course Michael had insisted upon a proper pre-drive inspection even though he had no idea of what he was supposed to be checking.

The first stop was South Chicago Trucking and Transfer, which was located on a big lot on 74th and Wentworth. Marty Sullivan, a driver for South Chicago Trucking, intercepted the Officers when they stopped in front of the manager's office. He asked what they wanted and then went into Lou Kowalski's office and informed Kowalski that a couple of college boy Federal cops were out on the lot and wanted to see him. "One," Marty said, "is a big Mick kid and the other is some kind of a Pansy."

Lou removed a cigar from his mouth and grunted. He had half expected something like this but he hadn't thought that it would be so soon. "Tell them I'm busy and that they can make an appointment for next week with my secretary."

Marty laughed and went outside. He relayed the message to Jack and then Jack started to go by him and into the office. Marty put up a restraining hand and ended up on his knees in sudden and intense pain.

"You don't ever again lay your grimy paws on a Federal Officer," Jack advised him calmly.

Three truck drivers that were watching this little show took offense and moved in on Jack and Michael. One man struck Michael behind the ear and drove him to the ground. The other two attempted to grab Jack, which was a mistake. He first broke Marty's arm with a sudden twist and then turned toward the other two. Marty squealed in pain and dropped to the floor. One man punched at Jack with a round house right, which Jack easily ducked and delivered a sharp stunning blow the fellow's adam's apple. This man was choking and clawing at his throat. The second man caught Jack around the waist and Jack brought both hands down in a rabbit punch that dropped his assailant to the ground. In the mean time Michael's opponent had struck Michael directly between the eyes and driven him back up against the wall.

Several other drivers had noted the confrontation and not knowing who was who, charged in to help their buddies. Michael had regained his senses and drew his weapon. He cocked it and pointed it at the leader of the charging crew. Michael had also produced a badge. "I'll shoot the next man that attempts to stop us!" He shouted. "We are Federal Agents."

The crowd stood back in shock.

Jack picked up a short length of lead pipe and went into the office. The secretaries scattered in terror when he entered and broke the glass on the door that led to Kowalski's office.

Kowalski shouted in alarm, "What in the hell do you think you're doing?"

"You're under arrest for the assault of a Federal Officer!" For emphasis Jack slammed the pipe down on Kowalski's desk, which had a glass top. The glass shattered and the items on the desk went in every direction. Jack slammed it down again and Kowalski cringed back against the wall.

"For Christ's sake, take it easy! I didn't tell them guys to stop you! Hell, you guys are always welcome here. How can I help you officer. I'm a law abiding citizen."

"Sure you are," Jack said derisively. "I'm going to ask one time and one time only. Where did you ship that gear from Atlanta Financial?"

"Jesus, is that all you want? Why sure, here let me get the address." Kowalski fumbled about on the floor for a minute in the spilled ink and broken glass and came up with a set of directions. "Here you can have it, officer. This is their lading bill. There were three trucks. My driver's said it was delivered to an old warehouse. Is there anything else I can help you with?"

Jack read the bill of lading. They had driven the stuff to an address in Gary Indiana. "I'm in a hurry," Jack said, "Or I'd lock up every swinging dick on that lot and you with them. If I find out that you have called ahead to warn these guys you're going to be doing hard time in a Federal Pen. So you had better decide whose side you're going to be on. If I have to come back here, I'll close this operation down so tight you'll never get it open again."

"I got lawyers," Kowalski said defiantly.

Michael had entered the office. "I've got a thousand lawyers, most of whom don't have anything to do. They'd love to tie up your money and grind this place into the sand."

Kowalski was impressed. "Who is the Raccoon?"

"What Raccoon?" Jack asked. Then he turned and looked at Michael who was sporting two very large black eyes. He had to suppress a laugh and took Michael's arm and led him outside. "We're going to Gary Indiana, Michael, are you feeling alright?"

"Yeah, I'm okay, but my eyes are kind of swelling up. That guy I hit me awful hard."

"You should have shot the son of a bitch."

"I couldn't, you took the bullets and told me not to reload, remember?"

Jack looked into Michaels eyes and began laughing, "You were standing out there with an empty weapon?" What the hell would you have done if they charged?"

"I'd have run," Michael said.

Jack chuckled, "That makes perfect sense to me,"

They got into the car and drove to the nearest drug store where Jack bought some gauze and some bottled pure water to provide some soothing bandages for Michael's eyes. He also purchased a pair of sun glasses. "Michael maybe we had better take you back to the office so you can go home and lie down."

"What are you talking about?" Michael asked and then he looked into the rear view mirror. "Son of a bitch! Do you see what that guy did to me? Let's go back and I'll kill him."

"Can't."

"What do you mean, I can't?"

"You could have shot him during the assault, when emotions were running high, but you can't just go back and kill him in cold blood."

"Jesus, is there no justice?" Michael asked. He poured the water on the bandages and leaned his head back on the car seat. "Will this stuff clear this up?"

"It's just water, but your eyes will be alright in a week or so."

"Let's keep going Jack, maybe I'll take tomorrow off."

"Hell of an idea, Mike."

"Don't call me, Mike."

"Right. Load that weapon, Mike."

There had been a warming trend in the weather as they drove south and by midday the ice and snow had begun to melt, now as the sun began to settle in the west this slush was freezing up again and the roads were extremely slippery and treacherous. They had no trouble finding the warehouse. It appeared to be deserted and they found that the place was empty. The marks in the dust on the floor indicated a great deal of moving about. It appeared that the gear had been unloaded here, but it had been moved again within hours. Due to the weather change Jack could see that there had been several vehicles moving in and out during the time of the thaw. So they had unloaded Saturday and Sunday and moved it again today.

Jack was reluctant to leave Gary without tracking down Atlanta Finance and he checked in with Walt, while Michael called the owner of the warehouse. Michael found out that the owner had made no arrangements to rent out the facility, but would have been glad to do so had anyone inquired. Jack reported that news and then speculated on their next move. He was instructed to check in with the local office for any help that he might need and was asked to keep Walt informed.

Jack decided to go to the Federal Offices and check in with the locals. He thanked the local officers for their help and then he and Michael went downtown. The FBI office was closing, but for several officers that were working the evening shift. Jack and Michael were able to relax for a while and had some sandwiches delivered. Both men were starved.

"What next?" Michael asked as he chewed on a roast beef special.

"You shouldn't talk with your mouth full. Didn't you mother ever tell you that?"

"You are presuming to correct me?" Michael said in surprise. "You, a person with the vocabulary of a long shore man, are correcting my table manners."

"Can the bullshit, Mike. We've got a problem here that requires a solution."

Michael shook his head in mock disgust and continued to munch happily on his sandwich.

An agent sat at his desk nearby and he was idly listening to their conversation and watching Michael with undisguised amusement. "I'm Tom Alexander, may I point out that if they need telephones, they'll have to make special arrangements with the phone company. There are problems with getting new phone lines in some sections of the city."

Jack looked up and nodded. "Yeah, you're right. Communications might be the key. In addition they're going to have to get new business cards printed. So they've got to solve all of their communications problems before they can open the doors."

"Let's call the telephone company?' The agent offered, "I've got a friend over there that might be able to help."

"Now there is a man that knows what the hell is going on," Jack offered his hand. "Jack Kelly is the name. This guy feeding his face is Michael Caine."

"Glad to meet you guys. Michael there is a rather uninhibited eater."

Jack laughed. "Hell, I'll bet that there are probably people that would pay to watch him eat."

"Screw both of you." Michael said between bites.

Tom called the telephone company and asked if they had received any unusual requests that day for dedicated phone lines. The answer was in the affirmative. Yes they had been asked to provide extra lines for an organization by the name of Security Financial Services. The office was located at 1247 Easton Boulevard, Suite 444. Then they gave Tom a list of telephone numbers.

Tom had copied all the information down faithfully and passed it to Jack. "Now what?" He asked.

"I think that we ought to go over there and check it out."

"We'll need a warrant," Tom said.

Jack produced the warrant from that morning, "I shall type a new warrant. Do we have a Judge available?"

Tom nodded, "Type it up and we'll see if we can get Judge Lester to sign it."

They went to the office structure because he wanted to check the building plan and check the fire escapes and alternative entrances. Tom parked across the street from the entrance of the structure. The three men went into the building. A night watchman sat at the receptionist's desk, which was just in front of the building switch board office.

Jack waved the Search Warrant and identified himself.

The night watchman, a former police officer, checked the warrant and nodded, "I'll let you gentlemen into that office if you wish."

Jack looked at Michael and shrugged, "Might as well, its early we can go through some of the stuff."

Tom shrugged, "I'm sort of intrigued, so I'll give you a hand."

The first room was a reception office fitted with a single desk and several chairs and immediately behind that desk were two doors that led to the rear offices. There were several small offices and then through two more doors there was a large room with telephones setting on a long table in the center, each telephone position was separated from the next by small partitions. Adjacent to each telephone was a desk and the phone person could either sit at the desk or spin about and work the telephone. It was obviously a well thought up set of arrangements. At the back of this large room were two larger offices, one on either side. They were clearly labeled one belonged to William Barber, General Manager and the other belonged to Robert Kaplan, President.

Jack went around and pulled all the shades down so that as little light as possible would leak out to the night. He pointed Michael to the office of the General Manager and then he went into the office of the President. He was wondering, who is this guy Robert Kaplan? Is this a family affair?

Tom started going through the boxes that had been placed adjacent to each of the desks.

Writing pads and pencils had thoughtfully been placed at each desk and the officers put them to use.

Jack went through Robert Kaplan's office very quickly. Michael called out to Jack that he had found something and Jack hurried over. Michael was smiling broadly and produced a fancy looking appointment book with the initials SK.

"This box may have been misdirected, but take a look at this." Michael fanned through the booklet. "Names and numbers, addresses, I think that we have just found the mother lode."

Jack took the book from Michael's hand and glanced through it. He found the name and phone number of Warren McGruder and as he did so he began to smile. "I think you're right, Mister Caine, you may have just broken the case."

At seven the next morning Jack and Michael returned and Tom and several uniformed officers were standing by as were several Federal Marshals. A large truck was backed up to the back door. Jack briefed the officers. They were to let everyone come in, but no one was to go out. Jack made the coffee and they waited for the crew to show up. The first person was a very attractive receptionist and she was taken into custody. As each successive worker made his appearance he was arrested.

Jack questioned the first few, but they were universally reluctant to say anything to a Federal Officer. In Jack's opinion Mister William Barber turned out to be the typical administrator. He ran the office, but all of the serious problems he turned over to Mister Robert Kaplan. Now this guy Kaplan was of a different breed entirely. He was the cousin, not the brother of Steven Kaplan. His cousin had hired him to provide the muscle and the determination that Mister Barber lacked.

"You are aware that someone killed your cousin Steve aren't you?"

Robert shrugged his indifference and avoided Jack's stare, "Yeah, which was a terrible thing. They killed his broad too, didn't they?"

"Yes they did. Now, what do you suppose old Stevie did to get three bullets in the gut?"

Robert looked up with a grin. "He pissed the wrong guys off."

Jack smiled in return, "Right! And who do you suppose those guys were?"

Robert gestured vaguely, "Even if I knew I wouldn't tell you. I have no desire to die."

Jack sat down casually on the couch. "I get the distinct feeling that you aren't going to tell me the things that I want you too. So what I'm going to do is take you and Mister Barber back to Chicago with me. Then I'm going to set up a little schedule to move you around the city, well away from the jail until you tell me what I want to know."

"I got my rights!" Robert protested. "You got to put me in jail with the rest of them."

"Wrong. Mister Kaplan, I'm going to give you some very special treatment."

"You can't do that to me. I'm an upright citizen."

"Right!" Jack agreed with a sarcastic laugh.

Tom came into the room. "I hate to interrupt. But the press guys are outside and they're raising hell. Can you go out and speak to them?"

Jack nodded and stood up. "Relax, Robert, I'll be back for you."

At about eight-fifty-five, A.M. Lisa Crowley, the secretary asked for permission to go to the ladies room. Michael was assigned to go with her. She went into one door and out a second door that led down the back stairs to a door to the parking lot. The officers that had been assigned were busy loading the male members of the organization into Paddy Wagons for transportation to the Police department for booking and paid no attention to the attractive woman that left the building. By this time the local Press had gotten wind of the operation and began showing up in substantial numbers. This was big news they clamored, and they wanted to see the Agent in Charge, which is why Michael was with the girl and Jack was outside trying to placate the press with as little information as possible.

It was a while before Michael came out and surreptitiously tugged at Jack's sleeve. "She's gone," he explained cryptically.

"Who's gone?" Jack asked.

"Lisa, the Secretary."

Jack didn't know what he was talking about at first. "How did she accomplish that?"

"Out the back door and then down the stairs. She's in the wind."

Jack looked at Michael in astonishment.

Michael blushed, "I didn't know that there were two doors to the Woman's room."

"For Christ's sake it's freezing out here. She couldn't go far without a coat."

Michael fidgeted a bit. "An officer saw her get into a car with some guy." Michael was chagrinned. "The cop noticed because she is so attractive."

"Did he get a make on the car?"

"He was watching her ass, not the car."

Jack was angry. "Why don't you call in and report to Walt, that we've just blown the deal!"

"Wait a minute," Michael protested. "We didn't blow any deal, we got lots of evidence."

"You lost her, you tell him about it."

"Who is the raccoon?" A reporter asked amid the laughter of the group.

Michael went back inside in a rage, as did Jack, but for a different reason.

"When in the hell are you going to learn to think like a cop? If some broad wants to take piss you go with her and watch her. You've seen women piss before there is no secret. They all squat and go. It's a normal body function."

"For Christ's sake Jack what to you want from me?"

Jack relented and smiled, "All I can get. There! The mission is clearly stated! Are you happy?"

"You do know that you are working for me don't you?" Michael said.

"Ah ha!" Jack shouted. "That's it. The Raccoon's feelings are hurt."

"Do not under any circumstances ever again refer to me as either Raccoon or as an Albatross."

"I'm just kidding you Mike; don't you have a sense of humor?"

"Don't refer to me as Mike either."

"Yes your Majesty."

"Goddamn it, I'm the boss."

"You are not the boss! May I remind you that your function in this partnership is merely to keep me out of trouble?"

Michael broke into unrestrained laughter. "You've got to be joking. That would be a Herculean task far beyond the capabilities of any mere human being! There is absolutely nobody in this whole Goddamn wide world that is capable of keeping you out of trouble. How you manage to stay employed, much less stay alive is beyond my imagination. You have killed two men in the space of a couple of weeks. There have been at least two attempts on your life. That is beyond my comprehension. No normal person ever gets involved in so many loony circumstances." Michael took several deep breaths as if to control himself. "I think that I have hit upon it. You are not now and never have been normal. Look at what you're doing here. You've managed to single handedly violate every goddamn protocol that the Bureau ever invented."

Jack grinned. "Are you going to go to back to work or just stand there and clown around?"

"You are not the boss!" Michael shouted.

"Neither are you and I'm going back to work." Jack stopped at the receptionist's desk and picked up a piece of note paper. It had a scribble in a feminine hand, 'McG at nine.' Jack looked up at Tom, who had just entered the room. "We just lost a chance to put this thing to bed. Your girl friend Lisa just went out to warn off McGruder."

"She is not my girl friend," Tom laughed. "Is this guy McGruder the villain?"

"He's the guy that we think killed four people."

"There was a call that came in about half hour ago. About the time you were going out side with the press. I thought that Michael had caught it, but it must have been the girl."

Jack slammed the desk with his fist, and then held up a thumb and forefinger just barely separated. "We were that close to catching a suspected multi-murderer."

Tom shrugged. "We've got her address, maybe we ought to go over there and hook her up?"

"Good idea, grab your coat." Jack shouted down the hall, "Hold down the fort Your Majesty, Tom and I are going to recapture the girl you lost."

Michael waved a hand and extended a fore finger, indicating that he understood. He was still angry at Jack. For lack of anything else to do Michael went to work. The data that he had worked here was different than that they had found at the Warner apartment. He believed that this material should be analyzed and processed into pertinent information at some point, but it wasn't particularly pertinent to solving the reason for the murders. He searched through the files looking for some clue as to the identity of the men who had led the immediate organization and to the men that had sponsored that operation. As far as Michael was concerned this was his element of expertise. Jack was all action and muscle, but in his opinion it was he that possessed the brains. An errant thought had eased into his mind. He refused to think of himself as a Mike. He irritably dropped some files back into their box as if trying to dismiss this Mike thing with action. He hesitated and looked down at the box again. He lifted out the files and laid them on the desk and then bent and picked up this stray piece of data. Was it of any particular use or just scrap?

Michael didn't know anything about Ju-Jitsu or weapons and certainly not much about women, but he did know about business and about business organizations. Every organization in the world, whether it was legal or illegal, had to possess some sort of organization. Mike glanced at the scrap of paper and found that it listed the names and telephone numbers of several very well known Chicago political figures. He got so excited that he almost fell off the chair.

"Jack, Jack, I think I found it." He stood up waving the paper about in the air. Then he remembered that Jack had left. He folded the piece of paper and put it in his pocket. This, he thought will make up for that stupid deal I pulled this morning. The more he thought about the woman's escape the more he realized that he should have checked out the ladies room before he allowed her to go in there. But he wasn't accustomed to checking out ladies rooms, no gentleman would ever consider invading a woman's privacy much less standing there watching her urinate.

He walked aimlessly about the various offices in the suite. The officers had captured the last of the workers and only this fellow Barber and Robert Kaplan remained. Michael went to the front office and locked the doors as the last of the boxes were taken down to the truck for shipment to Chicago. Then he went back and sat down with Mister Barber and Mister Kaplan.

"What are we waiting for?" Robert asked.

"We're going to take you to Chicago, with us."

"Suppose I tell you I ain't going? Come on Barber we can take this guy."

Michael grinned. "Then I should have to shoot both of you."

Mister Barber took a deep breath and moved as far away from Michael as he could.

"You're going to shoot me just because I won't go with you?" Robert asked in disbelief.

"I'm kind of new at this stuff and I'm not a very good shot. Now Jack could put one in your leg, which would disable you, but I just shoot and hope for the best. So for your sake and for my peace of mind, please don't try to torment me."

Robert was incredulous.

Barber was terrified, "Don't worry about me, brother I'm just going to sit right here."

"Chicken shit," Robert said angrily.

Across town Tom and Jack had pulled up in front of a small apartment building. They found Lisa's body in the kitchen. The knife wound across Lisa's throat was obvious and couldn't be disguised. The knife, a common kitchen instrument, lay on the floor just a few feet away. "We'll call homicide. There's no sense in our being here."

"Let's go see if anybody out there saw a stranger," Tom suggested, "some of those old broads spend their entire days looking out windows."

Much to Jack's surprise they found one lady to state that her new neighbor, Lisa Crowley, a beautiful young lady had arrived in a black car maybe a half hour ago and she had been with a stocky gentleman, who was perhaps six foot tall and another man. This second man had the girl by the arm and was almost dragging her into the apartment. The girl was crying and simultaneously pleading with the man. At one point the first man's hat had blown off and revealed what the lady described as very unusual and lovely silver white hair. It was the only description that he had thus far of the mysterious Mister Warren McGruder. This second man was much younger and wore a jacket similar to those worn by aviators. "You know," she said, "the ones with the big sheep skin collars." The lady didn't have that much more to contribute, but he was grateful to her. She had placed the man he believed to be McGruder at the scene and had described an adversarial relationship. If they could get McGruder into court that description of events might be enough for a conviction and particularly so if they could get any prints off the knife.

It was mid afternoon when all the details were finally smoothed out and Jack and Michael bundled Barber and Kaplan into the car and prepared to set out for Chicago. Jack cuffed both men with their hands behind them and then tied their ankles together with a length of rope.

"For Christ's sake I'm not a criminal," Barber complained.

"No, but your ugly friend is," Jack said, "and I don't like surprises. Michael, keep an eye on them and if they act up shoot both of them."

Barber squealed in anguish and Kaplan grunted in frustration. "You two assholes will pay for this."

"Nice talk, what with it being Christmas and all." Jack was laughing sardonically. Jack slammed the car door. Michael was standing on the curb waiting to get into the car. "Did you ever load that weapon again?"

"Certainly! I'm not going to be caught in that sort of situation ever again."

Jack grinned and threw the car keys to Michael, "You drive, because if anybody decides to follow us you'll drive them nuts."

"I beg your pardon? Did I hear you correctly?"

"Drive the car, Your Majesty. It's your Christmas present from me."

Michael shrugged and walked around the car.

"Why do you suppose they killed the girl?" Michael asked.

Jack shrugged, "Hard to tell. She probably knew all the regulars and some of the connections. If she wasn't too particular about her morals, a good looking broad like that could pick up a lot of gifts by being friendly to the right guys. She presumably knew McGruder; I think he's trying to eliminate all of the players that knew too much. The guys in this car might or might not be candidates for execution."

Barber sucked in his breath and began to fidget. Robert evidently hadn't considered the possibility that he might be on some one's hit list and began to turn a bit pale. Jack had the impression that he had might have hit the target with that last comment.

After a little, as they passed the city limits, Jack looked back and noticed a car that was pacing them. What caught his eye was that as with Michael's driving the other traffic was passing the laggard at the first opportunity, which meant that there were two cars for the normal traffic to pass and vehicles were backing up behind the second car.

"You're creating a traffic jam. Speed up."

"I'm driving the speed limit. There is absolutely no reason to drive faster than the posted limit. There are protocols you know."

"You're pissing a lot of people off."

"Screw em!" Michael said emphatically.

"Where in the hell is your Christmas spirit?"

"Don't start with me," Michael warned.

"Pull into that gas station up ahead I want to get some help."

"I've got to go to the bathroom," Barber whined.

"Jesus Christ, he's like a little kid," Jack complained.

Michael stopped in the middle of the road and waited for a chance to turn left into a station. Horns were beeping and people were making obscene gestures out of their windows as Michael finally managed to get through traffic.

"Might I remind you, that there is a large sign that clearly states that left turns are not allowed here?"

"I didn't see it." Michael said calmly.

"That cop over yonder saw it and you're going to get a ticket."

"It's your fault. You told me to turn."

"So I did, but I didn't tell you to turn left. That's okay, Mike, you just might have done the right thing by mistake."

"Goddamn it, don't take that patronizing tone with me. And don't call me Mike."

Jack watched as the Police car pulled up and as the car that had been following them sped by. He got out of the car and presented his ID to the Indiana State Police Officer. "We have two prisoners and that car," he pointed at the vehicle, "was following us. We thought that we had better get a little help."

"Are you serious?" The Officer asked.

"Deadly serious."

The Officer's eyes widened in surprise. "Do you want me to call it in?"

"Yeah. Can you contact the Illinois State Police?"

The Officer shook his head. "Not by radio, they were supposed to set a mutual frequency, but they haven't. I guess that would be too easy for us. But we can call in by phone, which is a pain in the ass."

Jack took the number and went to a phone booth and called. He reached a Sergeant with the Illinois State Police and identified the car that had been following them and asked if it were possible to get an escort. The answer was that there were two patrol units near the Indiana Illinois State line and that they would be waiting for Jack to come by.

In the meantime the car that had been following them had turned around and was pulling into the station. Jack hadn't seen it because he was on the phone. Michael was standing beside the car, but didn't recognize the other vehicle. Then the shooting started. Robert had evidently seen the whole thing going down and he opened the door on his side and was getting out. Barber was still tied to his leg. The killers were using shotguns and Kaplan, who was probably thinking that they were coming to get him away from the Feds, stepped out of the car until he caught a blast full in the chest. Barber was ducking down behind the seat, but his leg extended into the open. Michael was drawing his weapon and beginning to return fire. Jack dove out of the phone booth for the ground drawing his forty-five as he fell.

The State Police Officer had gotten back in his car to report and took the second blast into the side of his vehicle. Both Michael and Jack were firing at the suspect vehicle. But Michael was standing in the open trading shot for shot with the killers. Then Michael spun about and fell to the ground. Jack emptied his magazine and rolled behind another car to reload. Then the car was gone. Speeding back out into traffic and headed for Gary. The spraying of the shotgun shells had been indiscriminant and the windows of the station were smashed. The State Police Officer lay dead, sprawled across the seat of his car. Michael was down and bleeding badly. Jack got to his feet and went to the car. Robert was clearly dead. Barber was alive, but wounded in what had been the exposed leg and was bleeding badly. Jack went to the police unit and informed the dispatcher that they had two officers down, a dead civilian and one wounded civilian. They needed help instantly. Then he broadcast the description of the Killer's automobile. At that point he went to check on Michael.

There were several tears in Michael's coat, where rounds had passed through without touching the man, but the one that had done the damage was a round into his left side. The coat was torn and the blood was oozing out. Jack used his belt and his handkerchief to fashion a pressure bandage. Then he picked Michael up and carried him into the gas station. This was another scene of carnage. A middle aged woman lay dead upon the floor and the station manager had been wounded. A mechanic was on the telephone frantically calling for an ambulance. Jack went out to the car to see what he could do for Barber. The man was nowhere in sight. Jack finally found him in the bathroom sitting on the stool and trying awkwardly to clean him self. Jack was presented with a smelly and messy alternative and decided to take the cuffs off of the prisoner.

The wounds in the man's leg were bleeding and the blood and seeped into his socks, but he was more concerned with the fact that he had messed himself.

"You get yourself clean and come out here and we'll dress those wounds. Don't make me come after you because I'm in no mood for bullshit. If you try to run I'll kill you. If you play square I'll hide the fact that you're still alive and protect you. You got that?"

Barber nodded glumly and went back to work.

Jack went back to see what he could do for the officer, which was nothing other than to say a prayer. Then he went after Mike.

Michael was sitting against the wall. He smiled when Jack came in. "They put a hole in me Jack."

"It was probably some guy pissed about your driving."

"You never stop do you? I could be dying and you have to start your crap."

"You got shot in the side. It was probably a thirty-eight, from the looks of it. The damned thing probably didn't hit anything other than baby fat. Calm down, I got to see what I can do to help this guy over here."

"Wait a minute," Mike said. "In my shirt pocket, there's a list."

Jack retrieved the document and looked at wonderingly.

Mike explained. "When we got all those boxes from Werner's place, there was reference to payouts in the books, but just by numbers. Those are the names that correlate to the numbers."

Jack grinned and put the sheet of paper in his pocket. "God bless you Michael. This time you really did it, Mike my man, you have provided the answer." He patted his partner on the shoulder and then gestured towards the wounded man and Mike nodded.

Jack bent down over the proprietor of the station and removed some bloody rags that the Mechanic had applied. The man had suffered a stomach wound and was in bad shape. It might be possible that the man could live, but the odds were against it. The first ambulance arrived about the same time the cops descended upon the place.

As a precaution Jack had his car pushed over into the garage and had secured it. Then he briefed the officers as to what had occurred. By the time that he managed to secure a ride to the hospital Michael and Barber were in surgery as was the fellow with the stomach wounds. Senior Officers from the Indiana State Police wanted to know what in the hell was going on as did the Illinois Officers. Jack called Walt and reported the situation. Walt promised to send additional FBI personnel as soon as possible.

The Indiana State Police reported that they had found the suspect vehicle about three miles down the road. There was a body in the back with a thirty eight hole in the head. There was additional blood and the Police were hot on the trail of the Cop killers. Jack didn't think that there were going to be any prisoners to question and personally he didn't care.

Jack reported to Mike that he had scored a kill and was somewhat surprised at Michael's reaction. At first there was a smile of pleasure and then a look of dismay.

Jack patted his shoulder reassuringly. "Don't dwell on such things. They didn't give us much choice, partner, and I'd rather that it was them than us."

Mike nodded and seemed cheered a bit. "It was the first and hopefully it was the last."

Jack left the room to check on Mister Barber. Barber had taken ricochets into the legs and though he suffered bloody flesh wounds they had not done significant damage. Mister Barber was sitting up in bed with the covers huddled about him.

He looked up at Jack and shook his head. "I have never been so goddamned scared in my entire life."

"I told you they meant business. Are you going to cooperate?"

Barber shook his head in the negative and a tear rolled down his cheek. "I don't know what to do. They'll kill me."

"Look at it this way, Barber; they'll kill you for certain if they get a chance. We'll at least protect you as best we can. Those are your options. You saw what happened this afternoon. The way I see it your only chance at life is to cooperate with us."

Barber nodded reluctantly. "What do you want me to do?"

Jack produced a pen and paper. "Start writing your story. We'll be moving you to a safe house just outside of Chicago. The agents are on their way right now."

She was a tall, thin aristocratic looking woman dressed in furs and wearing a fur hat. She approached Jack, removed her gloves and held out her hand. "I'm Melinda Caine, you're Jack Kelly, and I would recognize you anywhere. I've heard so much about you."

Jack took her hand and relayed the news. "I'm pleased to meet you too, I have heard a little about you. If you would care to join me I'll take you to Michael's room. Allow me to give you the brief that the Doctor gave me. Mike was hit in the left side by a thirty-eight caliber revolver round. The projectile went through the body and missed all of the vital parts and to that extent, if one has to suffer a wound it was probably the best possible part of the body for that sort of thing to happen. The wound is closed. It took about twenty-eight stitches externally, but even more internally. He has lost a lot of blood, but the wound is clean and barring any unforeseen complications he will recover. They are planning to transport him to Chicago as soon as possible."

"I have my limousine outside. That should do won't it, Jack?"

"A Limo?" Jack asked with an incredulous grin.

"Oh yes, it's Michael's Dad's, his family is quite well off, you know?"

Jack smiled at her, "There are some things that we haven't discussed."

"Can I see Michael?"

Jack smiled and led the way to Mike's room. "He was very heroic, you know, he fought valiantly. I'm sure that he will receive a decoration for bravery."

"His father will be very proud of him and simultaneously very angry."

Jack shrugged, "Fathers are like that."

Melinda entered the room fully expecting the worst, but Michael was sitting up in the bed smiling broadly. "Michael," she exclaimed in surprise, "what in the world has happened to your eyes?"

Michael frowned momentarily, "Oh that," he explained, "Jack and I got into a fight with several hoodlums."

Melinda giggled, "You must excuse me, but you look ever so much like a Raccoon."

Michael grinned, "I know, that's what Jack has been telling me."

"Now what other surprises do you have for me?"

Jack grinned at Mike and closed the door.

Chapter Seven

Christmas Eve

Jack decided to spend the holiday at the Sheraton. It would be impossible to find a new place to stay on Christmas Day so he might as well sit back and relax and bite the financial bullet. Then, as if to make it worse they were playing Christmas Hymns in the lobby and in every bar in the building. There were a few lonely people sitting there trying to make the most of it and listening to those abominable Christmas hymns. Usually Jack really enjoyed the Christmas Carols, but tonight he just wasn't in the mood. What other time of the year do they play hymns in saloons? A couple of the drunks had grown maudlin and had begun to sing. Now the misty eyed lady at the end of the bar had begun to sing along with them. Sweet Jesus, it was pure torture. He bought a bottle of Scotch, Johnny Walker Green, which is a fifteen year old single malt whisky and paid an outrageous price for it. As he left the bar he tried avoid the envious look of the thirty-five year old that was sitting alone at the end of the bar.

Jack cracked the bottle and threw the cork away. Then he poured the whisky into a glass. It had been a hectic day cram full of contradictory clues and horrific events. He sipped the Scotch and then settled down in an easy chair and kicked off his shoes. He wanted to review those events in the silence of his room. He saw McGruder as having been a liaison between the politicians and the con men. They - those mysterious background people that McGruder worked for had presumably read about the murder of Myron Howard and the pursuit of the killer. It was probably about that time that "they" decided to cut the strings. McGruder might not even have known Myron Howard, but he recognized the fact that Kaplan's car was parked at the murder scene. Unlike the police, the bad guys don't need proof positive of guilt. The slightest indication that something was going wrong would be enough evidence for them. So it would appear that as the go between, McGruder had to clean up the problem, which in this case was the stupidity of Kaplan and Crouse. Perhaps that wasn't completely fair, if the murder had been successfully executed no one would have had a clue. If Hymie's body had laid on the snow covered sidewalk overnight someone would have pilfered the corpse thus disturbing the evidence at the scene. Then the ring, the money, the car and all of that would have been gone as would all evidence of the killer's identity. Simply put, Crouse blew it.

McGruder goes to Kaplan's house and the two men get into a fuss. Why? Well, obviously because the murder has caught the attention of the FBI and Police. Politicians don't like that sort of attention and the subsequent murders only intensified the situation. Killing Kaplan might not have been so bad, but the girl was there and the press would scream about the death of a woman. Jack could almost imagine McGruder's consternation when Werner and Crouse showed up. If Jack's surmise was correct it was Crouse and Werner that got into it. So in the end analysis, McGruder plan to cut the ties only exacerbated the issue. If they, the masters, whoever they were, were angry at Crouse they have to be furious with McGruder. The mental image that Jack begins to draw of McGruder is not that of an all seeing monster, but something of a jerk that had found himself in the middle of a bad situation presented with a terrible set of choices. The jerk then proceeded to complicate matters.

Of course, Jack thought, it doesn't change anything. McGruder is no less guilty, but somehow this shadowy character is far less intimidating and is something of a clown. Perhaps he is a dangerous clown, but a clown nevertheless.

Then Robert Kaplan was killed in a real shoot out conducted by a bunch of real killers. Obviously they didn't want Robert to get into an interrogation room and were ready to risk everything to take care of it. Had McGruder been in the car that had followed them? The only thing that they knew for certain was that he was at the scene of the girl's murder and though possibly not directly responsible for the girl's death he was at least a party too it. McGruder was only digging the hole deeper and deeper and sooner than later he would have to pay the ultimate price, Jack was determined that he personally would see to that.

The Mole in the Bureau was an entirely different problem. If it had been McGruder that had been responsible for the attempt on Jack's life and that seemed to be the case, then he didn't have anything on the Mole. The average agent was too busy with his own work to be looking over another guy's shoulder. So the Mole had to be a clerk or maybe even the Agent in Charge. All of this thinking could generate a thirst. It was time for another little sip of scotch. The one point that continued to bug him was that the man that had staged the attempt on his life had known about his change of address, but according to Marcy, Walt hadn't known. Walt didn't trouble himself with trivial matters. Well maybe he did and maybe he didn't, but somebody surely did. He couldn't forget that it had been the Mole that had lured Hymie to his death. In Jack's mind betrayal was a crime far worse than murder.

He took a sip and tasted the scotch rolling it around on his tongue. The snowflakes were being blown against the window and disappearing, evaporating into nothingness as they touched the relatively warm glass.

Tomorrow would be Christmas day. He would go to the office and take Marcy's typewriter and prepare a report to date. Now there was a nice decent girl. She had a great figure and a truly pleasing manner. A guy could take a girl like that home to Mom and Dad.

He wanted to type a list of the payoffs using the code that Michael had discovered. Should he give the finished document to Walt? He would have to think about that. Was there anything that he had missed in his haste to follow up on each murder? Well, he hadn't found Hymie's girl friend. Was there any point in doing so? What the hell they know all about the connections to the politicians. The killer of Myron Howard was dead. What could Myron's girlfriend possibly tell him? He remembered an old professor in a Criminology course telling the class that until they knew all of the answers to all the questions that had been raised; they really didn't know the answer to anything. He took another sip. One more drink. What the hell, he thought, maybe we'll stop thinking and have two more drinks and we can watch the snow flakes and just relax.

When he arrived at the office he was surprised to find two other agents there having coffee. It turned out that they weren't married either and had nothing else to do. They intended to listen to the football game on the radio and work on some of their cases. This was the first time that Jack had an opportunity to chat with the other agents. They were both about his age and one was an attorney and the other an accountant. They asked about Michael Caine and about the case in general. Jack had to describe the shoot out for them and to consider the lessons to be gleaned from such an event. Jack concentrated on the weaponry, "We were," he said bitterly, "outgunned with pistols against shotguns."

The attorney worried about the ramifications of killings in broad daylight and the reputation of the Bureau. The accountant thought about establishing better communications equipment and coordination procedures with the other police agencies. They all agreed that there were lessons to be learned and turned into procedures and not just forgotten.

Bill Davidson, the attorney, was the assigned duty officer and because Jack had never received the tour of the offices and because he was certain to catch this duty one day, Bill gave him the grand tour. The junior agents shared large offices that Bill referred to as bull pens. Senior Agents were assigned to private offices, which were across the corridor from the bull pens. It was the duty officer's responsibility to check all the offices, with the exception of Walt Albright's, to ensure that confidential materials hadn't been left out over night. As they strolled through the offices, Bill described the occupants. "This office," he said, "belongs to Charley Farrell. Charley is the next in line to Walt and is an old experienced agent. Charley predated Hoover's regime and was one of the few people that he retained in the Bureau. Charley had once been in the Marshall's service. The man was self educated and for all of that he was a very accomplished man. Bill went on to describe Charley. He's about five feet, ten inches tall, stocky build, silver grey hair. Usually he is very well dressed. They peeked into his office and Jack noticed an Army Engineers insignia on a cigar humidor.

"Cigars?" Jack said.

"Cubans, They say that they're the best available. I wouldn't know. I don't use them. They also say that he counts them and woe-be-tide the duty officer that thinks to share in Charley's private spoils. Some of the guys that know him say that he is really bitter about Hoover's policies and about the current promotion system. I can't say I blame him. He has been around for years and from what I hear he is an extremely competent agent."

Jack was half listening, Cigars, five-ten, silver hair. The man is displeased with the system and the director, perhaps looking for revenge of some sort. Hell, it can't be, this is too damned easy.

After the tour was completed Bill found out that Jack needed a place to stay and recommended the apartment building that housed several agents. Jack wrote down the address and the telephone number. He thanked Bill and then went to work on his project for the day. He wanted to compare the coded names that Michael had given him with the payouts listed by Werner. He was surprised that Werner had been so meticulous. It occurred to Jack that the Internal Revenue Service was going to love to get their hands on these files. The payoffs to the politicians would be enough to put them all in a Federal Penitentiary.

After he finished his work he carefully put his files away and set out to get his own house in order. Bill called his landlord and asked if Jack could drop by. After all it was Christmas Day, but the old man was Jewish and wasn't impressed with the sanctity of the day. First, Jack went over to his old apartment and dug his car out of the snow. He didn't think that it would start, but was pleasantly surprised when it did. Then he went and checked out of the Sheraton. Then he went to the apartment house and spoke with Mister Titlebaum, who was a friendly old gentleman. It seems that he enjoyed have so many Federal Agents living in his apartments. "Nobody, but nobody will screw around with Titlebaum, while all you guys are staying here."

Jack laughed and thought about his last apartment manager. He sincerely hoped that Mister Titlebaum would never be disappointed in his security. If anything the new digs were even better than the last place and not as expensive. Jack decided that it really was sort of a Christmas Day as far as he was concerned. As he moved about he kept a careful eye behind him and never once could he spot any tails. He visited the hospital and had a chat with Michael and explained what he had found and sort of propounded his new theory of events to see what Michael might say.

Michael listened and shrugged. "It certainly sounds reasonable. We do tend to demonize our enemies and attribute skills to them which no normal human possesses." Michael looked into Jack's eye with an unexpected ferocity. "Don't let your guard down, Jack. Don't think that's its over, less you end up on a slab." Then Michael looked away and seemed to be thinking. "Jack, you're a hell of Cop and tough as nails, but this accounting business is what I'm good at so please listen to me. The FBI typically has rarely pursued these cases when local political corruption is involved. Hoover believes that we operate at the discretion of the President and he also knows that administrations change just about every eight years or so. As a result he has no intention of antagonizing the party in or out of power."

"I feel certain that we will pursue the fraud end of this case, but I seriously doubt that the politicians will be harmed in anyway. I might amend that thought, if the evidence is so damning that the opposition press won't let go of it, then the guys in the smoke filled rooms may elect to sacrifice those that will suffer prosecution. Those victims will serve a couple of years and be back on the street and though they won't be in City Hall they will be doing business as usual. Think about what I'm saying Jack and don't press Hoover to hard."

Those thoughts were staying with him as he left Mike's room. As he was leaving, he encountered Melinda and she seemed to be sincerely pleased to see him.

"Michael is coming along nicely, he'll be out of here in a day or two," Jack predicted.

"He says that you saved his life."

"Michael was incredibly brave standing there exchanging shot for shot with the bad guys. He's exaggerating about my part in it. I was hiding under a car."

Melinda smiled, "He should have been hiding too."

Jack just smiled at her.

She grinned, "I think it is you that are down playing your part in preventing a disaster."

Jack demurred, "Take care of him, Melinda; he's a good man."

Jack was in the office early the next morning and hard at work when Walt came charging into the room.

"Go grab some gear, enough for three or four days. We catch the afternoon train for D.C. Hoover wants a thorough review of this case and he wants to meet you. Jack I can't emphasize how important this meeting could be to your career with the Bureau. Bring your best suit. Shine your shoes. Go out and get a fresh haircut. Jesus, get moving boy, we got things to do."

They met at the station and Marcy was with Walt. "She going to do the typing to get this report prepared in first class form."

Jack just smiled and said hello.

Once they were on the train Jack offered to do the typing of the first draft and took her typewriter into what ostensibly had been designated as Walt and Jack's compartment. They all stayed together for a while with Walt sorting out the evidence that had been gathered. When Jack had begun typing they were surprised at his speed and accuracy. After a while Walt announced that He and Marcy were going to go to the club car for a couple drinks. Jack just waved them away. He had plenty of work to do.

It was several hours later when Jack completed the report and laid it down on the small table. Time had flown by as far as he was concerned and now it was time to find the Club Car and get a sandwich. He assumed that he would find Walt and Marcy, but such was not the case. Jack had a drink and something to eat and sat there staring out at the night flashing by. It wasn't really late as yet, but the sun had long since gone down and out there in the darkness little squares of light flickered past. This was the express and it fairly rocketed through the small town stations along the way.

Then Walt and Marcy showed up. It was clear from their chatter and mannerisms that she and Walt had a thing going. They were sort of giggly and obviously pleased with one another. Evidently it was a new exciting thing for both of them. It was about this time that Walt identified the new sleeping arrangements. He and Marcy would be staying together. He winked broadly at Jack and Jack smiled in return. Marcy was no longer on his list of good girls. Not that her little adventure with Walt meant that she was really a bad girl it was just that he had lost interest in her and had stricken her from his take home to mom list.

The next day they brought all their gear to the hotel and then Walt and Jack took the report to Hoover's Office. It didn't take long for them to understand that this was not to be a friendly meeting. Walt went in first and Jack sat in the outer officer cooling his heels. Through the closed door he could hear Hoover just raising hell with Walt. Little phrases managed to escape the room, such as red haired oaf. Was the God like Director referring to Jack as a red haired oaf? Now that was a tad unfriendly and annoying, since Hoover didn't even know the specific red haired oaf that he was talking about. Another phrase that leaked out was Senator Caine. Could that be Michael's father? What in the hell does Senator Caine have to do with this case? Oh well, Jack thought, I'm sure to hear my share in a minute or two.

Jack was ushered into the room. Walt was sitting in a chair that was set so low to the floor that his knees were sticking up under his chin. Hoover was a diminutive man and Jack had been counseled not to stand as straight as was his usual habit. Bow down a tad and avoid looking directly into his eyes, was Walt's advice. Hoover stood behind his desk and did not offer to shake hands with his newest agent.

"Do you have your report?" Hoover asked.

"Yes sir," Jack replied and handed the report folder to Hoover.

"Sit down," Hoover commanded.

"Yes sir."

"You're dismissed Mister Albright, you may return to your hotel and prepare for the return trip."

Walt jumped up as though he had been shot out of the chair and nodding a farewell to Jack, left the office hurriedly.

"Normally, I interview all of my new agents, personally. I regret that I have missed that opportunity with you, because it would have saved us both some time. You have been employed with us for less than two weeks and I have had repeated complaints concerning your behavior." Hoover held up a restraining hand, "Hear me out, Mister Kelly. I have received letters from two Chicago Councilmen and a bill for damages and a complaint from the attorneys of a Mister Kowalski of South Chicago Trucking Company. The Attorneys for Security Financial Services are complaining that you have seized their company files without a warrant. There was a shooting in broad daylight at the Illinois State Line in which a Federal Officer was wounded and an Indiana State Trooper was killed. The Indiana authorities want to know why we didn't obtain an armed escort. This is not to mention the deaths of two innocent civilians and the families of both are suing the government for wrongful deaths."

Jack sat there looking at the director.

"Well!" Hoover roared.

"I beg your pardon, Sir. I didn't realize that your expected me to reply. First of all there is a copy of the warrant issued by a Federal Judge for the seizure of Security Financial Services in my report. Secondly, Mister Kowalski had some of his roughnecks assault Special Agent Caine and me for absolutely no reason. I will admit that I may have overreacted a tad, but I want to see Federal Officers treated with respect. As for the shooting at the border how could we possibly anticipate that a group of armed men would assault us in broad daylight? We weren't carting arch criminals. As far as we knew we were carrying a couple of cheap con man to jail."

Hoover seemed mollified for the moment.

Jack continued. "The reason that I was given for the precipitous hiring, was that Special Agent Albright believed that he had a Mole in his office, a person that was providing the local gangs with proprietary information. I was in fact going to be the lure to bring the traitor, if there is a traitor to bring to justice."

"A Mole?" Hoover thundered. "In one of my offices? How dare you!"

Jack got to his feet. "There is a Mole and we still don't know who it is! I've had three attempts on my life in the space of a week."

"Sit down!"

Jack sat down.

"Do you have anything else to say in your defense?"

"My defense?"

"Yes, your defense. I want to know why I should keep someone such as you in my employ."

Jack stood up. "Well, if you can't figure it out, let me make it easy for you, I quit!"

Hoover stood there for a moment and then sat down. He had been through this sort of thing before. All of these foolish young hot heads sought to protect their egos. It was the way he liked it. "Is there anything else?"

"Yes, here is a portion of the report that no one else has seen. Not Walt, no one, because I couldn't be sure who to give it to. I don't know who in that office I can trust with sensitive information." He laid the supplemental report on Hoover's desk.

As Hoover read it his face grew redder by the second. "Good lord man. You have accused nine high level Democrats from the Chicago area of receiving bribes from this gang of con men." Hoover threw the report down onto his desk. "The Democrats are in power. Are you asking me to anger the President of the United States with this uncalled for persecution of politicians?"

"I'm asking you to do your job and if you won't do it then I know damned well I don't belong here. Good day sir." Jack stalked out of the office and slammed the door behind him. As he rode down on the elevator he was mumbling to himself. "Dirty, arrogant, no good, conniving sonsabitches."

"I beg your pardon, sir?" A well dressed matron asked huffily.

Jack looked at her for a long minute and then stuck out his tongue at her.

Walt was waiting in the lobby. One look at Jack, confirmed his fears. "I gather that things did not go well?" He asked.

"The man is a goddamn bona fide lunatic."

"Jesus," Walt almost shouted, "Not here in front of God and everybody." In a quieter voice he asked, "What happened."

"I quit, but I think I was getting fired anyway."

"Jesus, what are we going to do about the Mole?"

"Feed him information until he chokes on it."

"Uh, Jack we leave at five."

"Okay, you leave at five, as for me, I'm going to go get drunk. I have worked like a slave for six and half years for this opportunity and then I blow it in about a week. Here is my badge and ID. Oh, and would you drop my weapon by the hotel desk and ask them to lock it up for me, seeing as how I'm not entitled to carry it any more. And tell them that I'll be here for at least a couple of days. Thanks for the opportunity Walt. I'm truly sorry that I didn't work out. I liked the job and the guys that I worked with. Good luck, Boss."

"Ah, Jesus, Jack, I feel bad about this."

Jack extended his hand. "Good luck, Walt and take good care of Marcy, she's a nice girl." He walked out of the office building and took a cab to the nearest bar. Jack had a couple of drinks there and then decided to go somewhere else. He took another cab to the Lincoln Memorial and sat down on the steps and sat there until the sun went down. He understood politics well enough to know that the indictment of high level politicians had to be handled with care. But to ignore the evidence was a betrayal of the oath of office of any law man, regardless of the level of authority. He had heard rumors that Hoover was something of a sycophant, but didn't really believe it. The image portrayed in the press was that of a hard charging dedicated law man, but what was the reality? I suppose, he thought nastily, that the reality is similar to Washington itself, a proud nation's capitol, built in a swamp. Maybe that was somehow appropriate reflecting the corruption that one encounters at every level of government, but it was contrary to everything that he had ever believed. He decided that he should have been an engineer instead of an attorney. It is the nature of the business, he thought, attorneys meet far too many flakes and then eventually by association they get a little flakey themselves. Take that jerk Hoover for instance, the man was pretending to be a hero and was in fact a sniveling, backbiting little flake.

Common sense told him that Mike was right, the Director's job was there at the discretion of the President and therefore, if the Director wanted to keep his job, no matter how high his ideals and how dedicated one might be, he couldn't afford to antagonize the political parties in power, but it was so damned contrary. To make matters worse Jack had personally handled that meeting as would a spoiled child. He had gone in into that room with a set of preconceived notions built on the second hand perceptions of young agents. Damn it, he had learned better than that in the Marine Corps. Here he was a trained attorney acting out his little tantrum as would a spoiled child. That Mister Hoover had lived up to every sorry expectation was no excuse for a rational person to reciprocate by throwing a fit. Obviously, he would never qualify for the diplomatic service. He sighed in exasperation and got up. It was time for another drink and maybe a chat with a friendly lady.

He walked into the bar and scanned the crowd. She was a lovely red head and a perfectly beautiful, well groomed lady with great charm. He fell in love with her instantly and took her dining and dancing. He was looking forward eagerly to an evening of wild unrestrained sex. Unfortunately, she was a nice girl! Goddamn it, of all the nights in his life, he had met a nice girl. The last thing that he needed on this particular night was a nice girl. Where in the hell were all of the girls that proudly sported their Scarlet "A's." For the first time in years he had needed some solid grubby erotic down and dirty sex and what did he get, a Goddamn Saint! Sweet Jesus, what a miserable day this had been!

Jack spent a fitful night and in the morning he stopped by the dining room for breakfast. Two men dressed in the usual obligatory dark suits approached him. He could see that they were packing weapons, but not back-ups. Amateurs, he assessed them in a single word.

"Mister Kelly?"

Jack looked up and nodded.

"The Director wants to see you."

Jack's first impulse was to tell them to go to hell. But instead he thought about his reply for a long minute. Then he said, "Go to hell."

"That's not an option, Mister Kelly. I hope we don't have to apply force."

Jack laughed at them. He was seriously tempted to take them apart, but they were just doing their jobs. Aw what the hell, he thought. "Okay, let's go see your boss," he replied.

As usual Hoover was standing behind his desk and looked to be taller than Jack remembered. "Sit down and shut up!" Hoover ordered.

Jack sat down and folded his hands in his lap.

"I am rescinding your dismissal. I have read your report and was surprised to find that you are quite proficient at using the written word."

"Not bad work, for a red headed oaf, eh?"

"Not another word from you, young man, lest I change my mind again and have you thrown out of here." Hoover glared at Jack and then started again. "We have encountered an extremely unusual situation. Special Agent Walter Albright and his secretary Marcy were shot last night. She is dead, he is barely surviving. I fear that it is the work of this mysterious Mole that you spoke of. Since you are the only able bodied man in the Bureau that has a grasp on this case I have decided to bring you back aboard."

Jack said nothing. His bland continence belied the turmoil that surged beneath the calm exterior.

"I want you to take a plane to Chicago this evening. I have arranged for your ticket, one of our agents will take you to the Hotel and to the airport. Do you have anything to say?"

Jack smiled, "Shall I be on my way, Sir?"

Hoover's face began to glow a bright red. "Be very careful, Mister Kelly." Hoover took a couple of deep breaths. "You will find the man that has killed my agents and are ordered to deal with them perfunctorily. Is that understood?"

"Perfectly. You are instructing me to kill the perpetrators."

"Only in self defense of course, are there any more questions?"

"What about my report concerning the graft in Illinois?"

"I have prepared an altered document, which you are to familiarize yourself with on the trip. A copy of this altered report will be submitted to the Attorney General for Illinois for consideration."

"Are you asking me to sign this amended document?"

"No! Are there any more questions?"

"None."

"Good day then and God speed. My secretary will return your credentials."

Jack was escorted to the secretary's desk and given his credentials and badge. He was also given plane tickets and an envelope containing Hoover's version of his report. The implication was clear, whatever conclusions Hoover had reached were to be the official version. The agents escorted him to his hotel, where he retrieved his weapon and then to the airport. He asked them what the circumstances of shooting may have been, but they claimed ignorance. Once safely ensconced on the aircraft Jack read the report.

The document was ostensibly identical with his report, but the names of four high ranking members of the Democrat Party had been omitted. So he would get five out of nine. What about the others? Jack had a hunch that Hoover would use the evidence to intimidate the others for future political accommodations. So to that extent they all may have just become FBI informants. Upon further consideration, Jack thought that maybe Hoover wasn't so dumb after all. The report wasn't what he had written, but conceivably there were political ramifications beyond his understanding. For all he knew the four may already have been FBI informants. Was he putting the best possible twist on this report business? Conceivably, he had just sold his soul to Hoover for a job. That thought annoyed him and he slammed the offending report back into the envelope.

An attractive young lady in a uniform asked if he would like a drink. Jack looked up and grinned. "What's your name?"

"Mary," was the reply.

Now Mary is a very nice name, he thought. "Scotch," he replied.

"Do you want anything in it?"

Jack smiled again and patted the seat next to his.

Mary laughed gaily and declined the offer.

Once Jack had his scotch he began staring out the window. This was the first time that he had ever flown and it was quite an interesting little adventure. The clouds were flat and at a bit of a slant downward toward the west. Then it began to rain. The water was sluicing across the wings and around the engine nacelles, but he could still see the ground. Evidently they were flying into bad weather. The thought occurred to him that before long he might need another scotch or two.

Mary sat down in the seat next to Jack and buckled her seat belt. She urged Jack to do the same thing and produced two small bottles of scotch. "We're running into bad weather. So get cozy."

Jack laughed and slid over closer to her. "Flying is great isn't it?"

"It is right now." She laughed, "But it might get bumpy here in a minute or two."

"There's nothing like a few bumps, to cement a friendship."

She looked at him and smiled. "Maybe that's true." Then the inevitable female questions began.

The rain had turned to snow as they neared Chicago. Despite the turbulence, Mary had to go to work, she thanked Jack for a very pleasant flight and promised to meet him this next Tuesday night for supper. She gave him her phone number and made him promise to call. He thought that she was really a very nice girl.

Charley Farrell was waiting on the parking mat with a car. Farrell was a stocky, well proportioned middle aged man leaning slightly against the wind and giving the impression of strength and determination. His silver grey hair was blowing in breeze, which he seemed to ignore. He motioned to Jack. "Please get into the car, Mister Kelly."

Farrell got in one side and Jack in the other. Another agent retrieved his bags and put them in the trunk. Farrell introduced himself and emphasized that it had been J. Edgar Hoover that had insisted that he meet Kelly at the airport. Jack gathered that the implication was that otherwise Jack could have taken care of himself. The Senior Agent was obviously annoyed that he had been placed in the position of welcoming committee for a junior agent. As Farrell began speaking the driver pulled away from the airport. "Walt Albright and Marcy Mason returned from D.C. by plane yesterday afternoon. They went to Marcy's house out in Oak Dale and were there when the shooting occurred. Chicago Homicide is handling the case at this moment. A Lieutenant Monaghan is the Officer in charge. You are to go directly to the PD and contact Monaghan." Farrell threw his hands up in the air as if to say there, it's over, I have done my duty.

Jack grinned, "Sorry to have been such a bother, Sir."

Farrell relented, "Aw it's not you, Kelly. It's that lunatic in Washington. The guy is so excitable it's unbelievable. By the way you might forget that little slip of the tongue."

Jack laughed again. "We are of the same opinion, Mister Farrell, but I shall forget as you suggest."

Farrell slapped a hand down on Kelly's knee. "Damn it, Jack, I heard that you were a cop for a while. It's good to have at least one other experienced officer in the outfit." Farrell leaned back against the seat. "Let me know what you find out about this business. Keep me posted. I'll be in the office, until you determine that no more can be done today. Hoover will be haunting me every thirty minutes." He took a deep breath. "Walt used to keep the man off my ass, but now I'm in the lime light and I don't like it." Farrell thought for a minute or two and then continued. "We'll stop by the office and you can pick up a car and be on your way."

Jack signed a car out and drove to the Homicide Squad and met with his old friend. Lieutenant Monaghan was delighted to see and Jack and they shared a cup of coffee as they discussed Monaghan's promotion. Then Monaghan mentioned that he had heard that Auggie was into some sort of strange relationship with Alice. Allegedly, the poor man was losing weight and was but a shadow of his former boisterous self. They were both laughing as Monaghan suggested that it was time to get back to work.

"We'll go out to Marcy Mason's house. That's where the shooting occurred."

Jack drove and as he did so they chatted about the findings in the Atlanta Financial Case. Jack mentioned that five big time politicians were involved and that the Attorney General would be pursuing the matter. "They're all Democrats," he said, "the President is a Democrat, the Attorney General is a Democrat, You're a Democrat and I'm a Democrat, so what in the hell happens next is not going to be a big surprise."

"Its hand slapping time," Monaghan agreed. "They might even send a few of them to that fun farm they laughingly refer to as a State Prison, but that will be as far as that goes. The real crime even in Hoover's opinion is not that they were guilty but that they got caught. In three years the whole damn bunch of them will be back in town working as political advisors."

Jack pulled up in front of the small old house and parked next to a Police Unit. The house was set away from its neighbors on a big lot. "The place looks as though it was a farm house at one time."

Monaghan nodded, "Yeah, the community probably grew up around the place. The family of this Marcy gal probably had a lot of loot years ago."

Jack chuckled, "She was kind of a fancy little chick."

"Did you ever tag her, Jack?"

"I never got the chance."

"That was an honest answer to an unreasonable question," Monaghan laughed.

The street lights were rather dim along this stretch of road and snow covered every house and driveway. Lights glowed in the windows of the other houses and the gaily colored lights of the Christmas trees added a false touch of peace. But the windows of the Mason house were boarded up. The Fire Department and almost literally destroyed the entire crime scene. The area around the house was littered with charred shingles and bits of furniture.

"I suppose that the Perp set fire to the house?"

"I don't know, but I don't think so," Monaghan shrugged. "The fire apparently started in the front room near the Christmas Tree. They had real candles on the tree.

Jack nodded, 'That happens from time to time, but it is a hell of a coincidence." Then he went back to considering the clues.

"Okay, Jack, this is a test. Tell me what you see?"

Jack grinned, "Now this is really a test, Lieutenant." He strolled ahead leading the way. "The door is still on its hinges so it was probably open or unlocked when the Fire department got here. Had it been locked the Fire Department would have taken it off its hinges."

"They said that it was closed, but unlocked."

Jack considered that information for a moment. "That is an interesting note. Consider that someone would be considerate enough to close the door after shooting two people." He walked around to the side. "All of the glass on the lawn was broken outward rather than inward. So the Fire Department was ventilating the scene. He continued around the structure. "The screen door on the back porch was knocked off its hinges, probably for more ventilation. There appear to be tracks leading away from the porch, but the water had washed them away."

Monaghan raised his eyebrows at that conclusion. "How do you know that?"

"The hook is still frozen into the eye screw. The entire unit was pushed outward, probably more of the work of the house demolishers, but perhaps someone exited the house."

Monaghan nodded at the logic as they continued around the structure. "Who do you suppose that might have been?"

Jack shrugged and dismissed the question. "So the killer came to the door. Walt would not normally have answered it if he didn't recognize the person."

Monaghan added another note. "Walt's body was on the floor near the front door. Five shots had struck him."

"Jesus," Jack said in awe. They walked up on the ice slick porch and through the door and into the dimly lit interior. A Police Officer got to his feet and met them.

"Stand easy, Officer. I'm Lieutenant Monaghan, Homicide; this is Special Agent Kelly of the FBI. Put the names down in your log."

The officer checked the Lieutenant's badge and backed away. "I got some fresh coffee in the kitchen." The Officer said.

The Officer led the way and poured coffee for both men.

Jack started to lean back against the counter.

The officer stopped him. "Careful, Sir, some of this stuff is still pretty dirty."

Jack grinned and silently toasted the officer. Then he went on with his analysis. "Walt wouldn't open the door for just anybody. He was still kind of antsy over the attempts on my life. So my guess is that he knew his killer."

Monaghan nodded his agreement.

"So the killer shoots Walt. Where was Marcy?"

"Her body was found in the bath tub. But allow us to back up a bit. We found five shell casings for a thirty-two caliber weapon scattered about the floor near the door. We figure that the Fire Department scene despoilers managed to scatter the rounds about."

Jack was impressed. "So the killer coolly jettisons the empty shells, reloads and all the while Marcy is probably wondering what in the hell is going on." Jack walked over to the door to the bathroom and looked at the door. "Two shots, the first one probably missed the lock so the killer fired again. Then he or she walked into the bathroom and," Jack paused.

Monaghan took the cue. "Put three rounds into Marcy at close range." With that Monaghan produced a set of photographs. "This is Walt."

The first photograph depicted a man in a hospital bed. He had a bandage on his left shoulder and one on a thigh. His stomach was covered with bandages and drains.

Monaghan handed Jack the second picture, which was that of a naked woman lying on her back in a bath tub. It was Marcy and she had three bullet holes in her. Two in her stomach and one in the lower stomach near her pubic hairs. "Which to you think was the last shot?" Monaghan asked with a grin.

"So this is a crime of passion, carried out by someone carrying a thirty-two caliber pistol, which is sort of a ladies gun. The shots into Walt indicate a lack of professional skill and a good deal of anger. The shots in to the door substantiate a lack of skill, and finally the shots into Marcy emphasize the anger again. So this is the work of an ex-boy friend, who Walt would never have allowed into the door, or that of a woman. Say a wife perhaps."

"Such as?" Monaghan prodded.

"Such as, Mrs. Albright."

"Bingo, Jack! That's how I got it figured. This business falls into the category of - she shoots him"

Jack turned to the Officer. "Is the phone working?"

The officer nodded.

Jack called Charley Farrell and explained the situation. "I figure that Walt checked in with someone when he arrived in town. Maybe it's in the log duty officers log book?"

Charley coughed loudly clearing his throat and said, "I have the book right here. The first entry mentions the fact that Walt is back in town and there is a telephone number where he can be reached. Then next entry references a call from Mrs. Maggie Albright about seven-thirty asking when he would be back in town. The duty officer explains that he was reluctant to divulge the number, but the lady was extremely insistent and highly agitated. So he gave her the telephone number. So what to you think Jack?"

"I think that she was smart enough to use her husband's police connections to get the operator to match an address up with that number."

Charley agreed. "Are you going out to her place?"

"Yeah," Jack looked at Monaghan and relayed the information concerning the log.

Monaghan took a document from his pocket, "I have a search warrant right here."

"We have a warrant," Jack relayed.

"I'll meet you there with the best attorney in town."

Jack shrugged, "She's probably going to need somebody."

The ride to the Albright house was silent at first. Neither Jack nor Monaghan were happy with what they were about to do. This was extended family as far as they were concerned and this wasn't the first cop to be shot by an angry wife. Then after a bit Jack changed the subject and explained his new theory of the murders and that McGruder had probably gone there to kill Kaplan.

"It sounds closer to normal than to the concept that this guy McGruder is a master criminal." Then Monaghan laughed, "Typically, every time we think that we think that we have encountered a master mind we eventually come to find out that the guy is really an idiot. It is just that the idiot's approach to crime is so different from the usual rum of the mill culprit."

When they pulled up in front of the big old home they could see the Christmas tree in the window.

As they walked up the cleared path to house they heard a single shot.

"Aw shit," Jack said sadly.

Charley's car slid to a stop next to the police unit and he and an attorney exited.

"I don't think there is any hurry," Monaghan said.

Jack knocked. Then he pushed the door open and went inside. Her body was there in an easy chair directly before the big tree. The gun, a thirty-two from the looks of it, lay on the floor. The presents had all been opened and were still lying under the tree. A small electric train whirled around the tracks, whistling, every so often. Tears had stained the cheeks of her shattered head. Jack didn't even know the poor woman, but he wanted to sit down and cry it was all so damned unnecessary. Jack had to leave the room to gain control of his emotions.

It was late when Jack got to the apartment that he had never inhabited. He carefully, silently unlocked the door to his apartment. Drawing his weapon he pushed it open.

"Are you expecting someone, Mister Kelly?"

Jack spun around resisting the temptation to lift his weapon. There in the gloom of the hallway was Mister Titlebaum, the super. "Aw no, Mister Titlebaum. I guess I'm just a little nervous."

Mister Titlebaum came silently down the hallway and approached Jack. "Let me tell you about my wife, Madeleine," he said. "The woman spends her whole day staring out the windows. She has arthritis now; once upon a time she was a great dancer. Well," he shrugged, "not in the truly great sense, but she was very good. We used to dance for hours." He grinned, "Forgive me I'm getting old and I wander off from time to time. My point is that she sees everything that goes on around this place. Regrettably, she has another characteristic, she snores. Not polite little feminine snores, but earth shakers, roaring steam engine snores. So she sleeps at night and keeps watch during the day. Unfortunately, I must remain awake at night and I usually sleep during the day. My point Mister Kelly is that no one comes around here without my knowing about it. There is no one in that room."

Jack walked into the room and holstered his weapon. "Would you care for a late night sip of Scotch Mister Titlebaum?"

"Call me Levi, Mister Kelly and yes I might enjoy a small drink."

"Please call me Jack. Levi do you want it with or without water?"

"Without, I prefer not to drink Chicago water." Levi said.

Jack took off his overcoat and then his suit coat and hung them in the closet and then poured a very liberal shot of Scotch for his guest and himself. He felt that he owed Levi an explanation.

Levi noticed the Forty-five. "I carried one of those in the Big War. I was a machine gunner. Can you imagine a nice gentle little Jewish kid from Chicago being a machine gunner?"

"I can imagine," Jack said. "Did you get to see any action?"

"More than I wanted," Levi said with a wry smile.

"My problem, Levi, is that I'm on the trail of a very competent killer. There have been three attempts on my life and I have tendency to get a little cautious about opening doors."

Levi lifted his glass and looked at the amber liquid. "A noble drink this Scotch. Fit for kings."

Jack grinned and touched Levi's glass.

"Sleep well tonight, Jack, I shall be on watch."

Jack smiled and lifted his glass in a silent toast. Then he slipped back into his mind. Levi went back to his apartment and settled down in his easy chair with a good book. It wasn't long before he dozed off. Levi wasn't accustomed to drinking Scotch at night.

Jack too went to sleep, but his rest was fitful and troubled.

Chapter Eight

Jack was sitting in Charley Farrell's office when a young woman came to the door. She started to speak and then noticed Jack.

"Oh my, I apologize, Sir. I thought that you were still alone."

Charley smiled, "Special Agent Jack Kelly, this Linda Manley. She is Marcy's replacement.

Jack stood up and shook the lady's hand. He noted that she wore her mousey looking hair drawn back in a tight bun. He large horn rimmed spectacles made her eyes appear owlish. Now here was a girl that constituted no apparent threat at all to her boss. "Welcome aboard, Miss Manley."

"Scrounge up some work for her, Jack. She'll be sitting at the receptionist's desk and doesn't have a lot to do as yet."

Jack laughed, "Boy, do I ever have work for you, Miss Manley. I'll be in there in a few minutes."

She smiled nervously and went away.

"Aren't you going to move into Walt's office?" he asked Charley.

"What for? Hoover will have someone new down here in a week or so. He's probably waiting until we clear this thing up so that the new guy will come in here clean."

Jack shrugged, "That's one way to look at things."

Charley smiled, "I know the man." He shifted in his chair. "Okay, Mister Kelly, my current line of thinking is that Maggie may have in fact committed the murders and that she subsequently committed suicide?"

Jack agreed. "Which brings up the question of how is Walt doing?"

"He's breathing, but he ain't talking. I went over to the hospital last night. I didn't say anything about Maggie taking one in the skull. I figured that this was hardly the time. But it didn't make any difference to Walt; he just looked up at me and started crying. I got the hell out of there and went over to see Michael Caine, who is doing well." Charley shook his head, "That's the Hospital Report. The Hoover Report is less than favorable. J. Edgar is having a shit fit. He's screaming and raising hell about you and about me and about the Attorney General and about Roosevelt and about everybody else in the galaxy that he doesn't like. According to the Director this is all a gigantic plot to get him."

"That seems perfectly paranoid to me."

Charley chuckled. "Okay, where do we go from here?"

Jack looked down at the floor for a moment as if gathering his thoughts. "We'll proceed with making the case for the prosecution of the political figures and of the people involved in the scam. You can leak it out to the newspapers that I am on the trail of several influential political figures in connection to a murder case and fraud scheme."

"And you'll be the lure to draw out the killer?"

"With any luck."

"Christ. What about the investigations into the murders."

"What investigations? Lieutenant Dekker of the Sheriff's Department has reached an impasse. We have a vague description of the man that we think is the killer. By the way, this guy looks a lot like you."

"Me? The Goddamn killer looks like me?"

Jack grinned, "I didn't say it was you, I said he looks a little like you."

"Sweet Jesus, J Edgar's going to love that one."

"He also smokes Cuban Cigars."

Charley grinned, "At least he has good taste."

"His preferred weapon is a thirty-eight."

"You aren't trying to set me up are you, asshole?"

It was Jack's turn to laugh. "I'm waiting for the analysis of the revolver that Maggie used and of the Christmas presents, to see whether there are any finger prints on them besides hers." He paused again. "I don't anticipate that we will find anything. However, I do think that we have our killer's fingerprints on the weapon at the Kaplan residence."

"How so?"

"He wiped the butt clean, but forgot about the prints that he left on the cylinder, when he reloaded. Maybe it was that he was getting hyper. He had just killed two people and then killed a third, which is reason enough to get nervous."

"Okay," Charley said, "We've got to get moving on this Atlanta Financial Case. I'm going to assign two more agents. Bill Davidson and Toby Warren will be assigned to assist you as you need them. Linda will be your typist. Toby, is a new guy, he will be your run around guy and back up." Charley pushed a buzzer on his desk and the two Agents came through the door.

Bill grinned and Jack shook hands with Toby.

"That's enough of the cordialities, gentlemen. Now get your asses engaged in some productive work!"

Jack led the way to his desk in the office across the hall and outlined the work that had been started by Michael Caine. "I want to marry up the amounts taken in from each customer with the totals dispersed to these five men. There are three years of files here and I want to tie this information down pat. We need the dates, the amounts and in the process you may search for any reference as to whom the go between might be." Jack produced the approved list. "Do not worry about these four names, but add their totals anyway."

Bill looked at the list questioningly.

"Don't ask," Jack said and meaningfully looked heavenward. "We must also compile a list of the suckers and what they lost, which, after the case is completed, we may or may not surreptitiously send it all to the Internal Revenue people. Mike Caine started this work before we went to Indiana. So get to it, there is literally tons of material that we have to process. I think that the best way to proceed is to start with the first year of the operation and work through. We want the names of the suckers, the amounts of the contracts, the actual amount collected, how much of it was turned into to the company and all the dates of course. If you come across any data that doesn't seem to apply set it to one side. We're putting a giant puzzle together, gentlemen." Jack looked at the pair questioningly and when satisfied that they understood, he outlined his responsibilities. "We have two agents in the hospital. I'm going over there and question Walt, if I can, that is. We'll be posting a twenty-four hour watch on his room. Gentlemen, the primary suspect in this case, at the moment, is a man named McGruder. We don't know anything about him, except that he is a cold blooded killer. Do not speak about this case to any one out side of this office. Do not leak anything to any of your associates in the press or in this office. We'll let Charley handle that end. Watch yourself and watch everything around you. I don't think that there is any real worry, but one never knows." Jack looked about for a moment. "When we get organized we'll put Linda to work, but don't jump the gun. I don't want her needlessly duplicating work."

Satisfied that his co-workers were hard on the trail, Jack left the office and went to the Hospital. He stopped in for moment and had a couple of laughs with Mike Caine and then went to see Walt. Both men had rooms on the fourth floor. The big man lay flat on his back in an oxygen tent. A nurse dressed Jack in a gown and mask and made him don rubber gloves and a mask. Walt's eyes were closed and he opened them as Jack walked into the room.

Jack heard what he thought was a murmur and Walt blinked his eyes. Reaching beneath the tent Jack touched Walt's hand. Walt smiled ever so faintly.

"Walt can you give me a minute?"

Walt blinked and winced in pain. Then he slowly nodded.

"We want to know who did this to you. Let me ask you a couple of questions and if the answer is yes blink twice, if it is no blink three times, I ask you to do that so that we can't make a mistake about what you are telling us.. Got that?"

Walt blinked twice.

"When you went to the door, did you recognize the person?"

Walt closed his eyes for a long while, and then he slowly opened them and blinked twice.

Christ! Jack thought, how in the hell do I ask the next one? How do you ask a guy if his wife nearly killed him? "There is no other way to ask this Walt, do you know who this McGruder character is?"

Walt closed his eyes and his face screwed up in pain. He nodded a yes.

"One last question, Walt. Was it McGruder at the door?"

Walt smiled faintly, just a mere movement of the lips. Walt blinked a smug no.

"Was it Maggie?" Jack asked.

Walt winced in pain and his face screwed up and a tear rolled down his cheek and he waved Jack away.

"Was it Maggie?" Jack persisted.

Walt nodded and began to cry. His entire body was shaking as if his heart was broken.

Jack gently patted the big man's hand and turned away. Case solved. McGruder cleared of three murders. "Rest easy, Walt. Everything will work out. I'll come back when you can talk."

"Sir, I think that you ought to leave," a nurse said.

Jack nodded and looked back at the big man in the bed. Walt was still crying uncontrollably. From rumors that Jack had heard around the office during his brief stays there this adultery was just a big game with Walt; he had always been very complementary of his wife. The significance of the conversation was that it was Maggie that had wounded him and killed herself, but where in the hell did McGruder fit it? Jack called Charley and reported the odd conversation.

"Then Walt was our Mole?"

Jack grimaced and thought about that. "That might be the case." Then it occurred to him that he hadn't heard anything from Barber since the shooting and asked Charley where he had been taken.

"We got him in a safe house out on the far south side. We couldn't very well stick him in with the general jail population since he promised to cooperate."

"Has he actually cooperated?" Jack asked.

"As far as I know he has. The interrogating agents report that he has given them a ton of material."

"The man is a con artist. It could all be bullshit! Ask someone to deliver that material to my desk by this afternoon if you will. I've got to go see the cops about the murder side of the investigation."

"Are you accustomed to giving orders to your boss, Kelly?"

"Forget it boss, I'll drive out to the south side. It shouldn't take me more than a couple of hours. Then I can talk to him myself. I'll be back in the office about six this evening."

"All right, all right, I get your not too subtle point. I'll have them deliver what they've collected. Oh, and Mister Kelly, if it won't hamper your schedule, you will check in with me from time to time won't you?"

"Yes sir!"

"That's better, Kelly. I'm just reaffirming the pecking order around here."

Jack was laughing when he hung up the phone.

The next stop was the meeting at the PD with Monaghan and Dekker. The two officers were still fighting little turf battles, but it was more of a game with them than it was a serious problem. To break the ice, Jack went first and reported that Walt had confessed that Maggie had been the killer. Monaghan confirmed that there were no prints on the weapon other than Maggie's. The big question, from Jack's perspective, was what in the hell was McGruder's part in this drama?

A thorough search of the Kaplan premises had turned up a black briefcase with the initials MH on it..

"Myron Howard," Jack said. "What was in it?"

"Nothing," Dekker responded.

The Sheriff's men had prowled the neighborhood with no luck in obtaining a better description of McGruder. They did find a postal employee that had seen McGruder leaving the house. He described McGruder as being a pleasant looking, nicely dressed older man, with white hair. This postman had seen the suspect get into a new model black Buick and drive away. A search of the Cab companies had turned up the fact that there were two cab deliveries that afternoon not one. Werner had arrived first from his apartment building and Crouse had arrived in the second cab, which had picked him up at an old rooming house in the downtown district. Crouse's room was subsequently searched, but there wasn't anything of any significance there. Mrs. Werner was still missing, but there was no reason to believe that she was part of the fraud conspiracy, or that she had been harmed. A search of the local Buick dealerships had failed to turn anything up. Everybody bought black Buicks.

"If she has half a brain in her head she's probably in California," Monaghan said.

"The Kaplan Brothers are dead and so are Crouse and Werner." Dekker added.

"The Kaplan cousins," Jack corrected Dekker. "They're both dead as are Crouse and Werner and so is the poor young woman, Lisa Crowley, who made the mistake of answering the telephone for these people."

"What was it that you got from that apartment?" Dekker asked.

"We actually retrieved it from the basement storage areas and it was the internal records of the company, which consisted of payroll records and check records."

"They weren't paying off the Politicians with checks were they?" Dekker asked.

"No. That was all cash, but they kept the money in their bank account and Werner wrote checks to Warren McGruder. He cashed them at the bank and identified the individual expenditure and whom it was to go to by number on the check. We found the code and were able to correlate the person with the payoff amounts."

Dekker and Monaghan exchanged glances. "There will be some guys leaving town," Dekker said.

"I got some information from the Indiana State Police," Dekker said.

"Such as?" Jack asked.

They found the stolen car that they had used about three miles away in an alleyway. There were holes all through it, particularly forty-five caliber holes. There was a body in the car with a thirty-eight caliber hole in his bean. This guy was wearing an aviator's jacket and there was blood in both the front and in the rear seat. A wounded man, with a forty five caliber chest wound, was dropped off in front of the hospital a night later, but he died on the operating table. They've identified both men as being former bootleggers, both of whom had violent records. They were tied to a specific gang, but all the rest of these people seem to have disappeared."

"The guy with the flight jacket was with McGruder when the receptionist was killed and he may have been the killer. If he had the thirty-eight hole in his head, it was probably Mike Caine that got him. Did he have a knife on him?"

"Yes."

Can you have it checked for human blood?"

"Sure," Dekker replied. Then Dekker lifted his coffee cup in a toast, "God bless the albatross he nailed one of them."

"Where does this guy McGruder fit in?" Monaghan asked.

Jack shrugged. "I don't think that he was the over all boss, but he is either the pay off guy, or the guy that collected the money from the company and delivered it to the gang and to the politicians. I think he is political go between, but I don't believe that he is a con man. He is far too violent a character for that profession. It occurs to me that he may be an enforcer. He is the sort of man that can deal with the lunacy of the politicians and yet still keep the Con artists in line."

"What portion went to the Chicago gang and who are they?" Dekker asked.

Jack paused again. "That isn't for certain as yet; we think that because the politicians were involved that the gang wasn't taking their usual portion."

Monaghan sipped his coffee. "That's really unusual."

Jack nodded. "Yeah, but they had nothing invested. It was all somebody else's money. As I understand it, the typical situation is that when the Cops put the heat on one of these operations is that they leave town owing everybody money. The difference here was that these guys had been making so damned much money for so long that they were actually paying the rent."

"Impressive," Monaghan said.

"Are they out of business?" Dekker asked.

Jack laughed, "Quite a few of them are permanently out of business. We were able to identify about forty employees. Some had outstanding warrants and we were able to keep them in jail. Federal agents are asking questions of those guys even as we speak. We were able to identify quite a few people who we hadn't known about and they now have records, but we don't think that they'll be in jail for very long, maybe a year or two." He shrugged philosophically, "If we meet them again we'll have the added force of a second conviction." Jack sipped his coffee. "This business is akin to prostitution, its easy money and far too enticing to ignore. The sucker thinks he's going to get this money back and doesn't realize that he has just made certain that he has no chance of recovery. The honest merchant may be desperate for the funds and so he goes to these guys, the dishonest merchant thinks that he is dealing with brothers in arms. We're not going to stop it, ever, the only thing that we can possibly do is to suppress it from time to time."

Monaghan sat smoking his cigar and gestured with it. "The difference from the normal routine is this character, McGruder."

"Yeah, good point," Jack agreed. "This guy McGruder is something else. One minute I'm thinking that he is something special. He shoots Kaplan in the stomach at close range. Then he buries the body in plain sight. Then he goes upstairs and kills the lady, with a single round to the head. You might think that the Kaplan kill in the basement could have been the result of spontaneous anger, but the killing of the woman was cold blooded murder. Then he kills Crouse, but who knows what the circumstances may have been in that case? That might properly be classified as self defense, or perhaps as a cold blooded spur of the moment impulse. Then he waits for me in my room and when that doesn't work he sends in a substitute. However, his assistant cuts Lisa Crowley's throat and then he engineers a shoot out that kills four people." Jack looked at his two friends. "What really bugs me is that you two guys have been in law enforcement for years and know most of the hoods in town and yet you have never heard of a distinguished looking, stone cold killer. How in the hell has this guy managed to move around with these characteristics and not have a reputation?"

"Good question Jack," Dekker said angrily, "How in the hell is it that you come out of nowhere and are suddenly the lead in a homicide investigation that will set records for bloodshed?"

Monaghan laughed at Dekker. "Cool down, Dutchman! Jack was walking a beat and talking orders less than three weeks ago."

"That's precisely why I'm asking?"

"Believe it or not Dekker," Jack said. "I've been in training for this job for ten years and I've had some damned good teachers, which includes you two gentlemen." Jack gestured with his hands, "I didn't mean to offend you guys, but it just doesn't stand to reason that this McGruder character comes out of nowhere and no one has ever heard a word about him."

"The answer has to be that he is either a stranger in town or comes from some other police discipline such as the Feds. Some of the things that he did were slick, some were amateurish."

Jack nodded, "Yes, by Walt's admission he knows this guy, but it will be a while before we can get Walt to talk. He's still very weak."

"Was Walt, your Mole? Was he the betrayer in your ranks?"

Jack shrugged, "We suspect that might be the case."

"Are you guys watching over Walt?" Dekker asked. "It occurs to me that if this McGruder guy finds out that Walt is implicating him that Walt ain't going to live too long."

Jack grinned, "A twenty four hour watch is in effect."

"School boys or real cops?" Dekker asked. "Maybe I can get some of my guys over there. Walt is important to our case."

Jack smiled, "The more the merrier. I would agree that some of our boys aren't all that smooth."

"They're smooth enough, but too trusting. My people have been through this sort of thing before and we have learned from our mistakes. You don't trust anybody."

Jack shrugged again. "Hell, Dekker, bring your guys on. I'll clear it with Charley Farrell."

Dekker grabbed the telephone, "Let's do it!" He said.

Jack went to another phone and called Farrell. Charley was apprehensive at first, but then agreed, but he wanted a sheriff's Officer and an FBI agent on duty. They were going to protect Walt at all costs. J. Edger wanted verification that an FBI agent had admitted to being in league with a killer.

"He didn't say he was in league," Jack protested, "he merely indicated that he was acquainted with the man."

"Do you suppose they went to school together, or that perhaps this McGruder is an attorney?"

"We've got to pursue every possible lead. We know that he drives a new black Buick. The Sheriff's have already checked with the Motor Vehicle Registration and the dealerships."

Farrell said that he would have the agency check nationwide for a Warren McGruder. "I think that Walt went to Princeton. We'll start there."

Jack returned to the office and checked on the work of the agents. The sucker list was arranged in the assembly room on three long tables by each month and by the year. The same was true of the records of each transaction and now the agents were compiling the lists. They had finished the first year and Jack looked it over and took it to Miss Manley for typing. He quickly composed a letter and got her started on the work. He watched as she reached into her desk drawers and produced the carbon paper and the typing paper. She made certain that everything was lined up and then rolled the sheets into the typewriter. The girl was extremely fast and accurate and Jack felt that the work would begin to take shape very shortly.

The material from Barber's interview was on his desk and he began to go through that material. It was detailed and to some degree was substantiated by the data that he had assembled. There wasn't anything new or startling, although there were dinners and lunches mentioned involving various local characters. Nowhere in the tales was there any mention of Mister McGruder. He edited this work and then took it to Miss Manley laying it down on her desk.

"This will be low priority, but please get to it when you can."

She laughed as she pulled a completed page from her typewriter. She took the carbon that she had used and dropped it into the waste paper basket. Then she laid the work down and went through it rapidly. "Mister Kelly, I shall get to it all in good time."

He smiled at the gentle rebuke. "I apologize, Miss Manley, I am used to doing my own typing and directing someone else at this kind of work is alien to me."

She smiled prettily and went back to work assembling another page. Placing new sheets of carbon between each sheet of paper she made certain it was square and rolled it into her machine. He watched her for a minute and then went back to his own work. Jack was revising his first impression of her; actually she had a very nice smile and was friendly enough. He decided that she was probably a very nice girl.

Getting this material into some sort of logical order and then writing the synopsis that the Attorneys preferred was time consuming. He couldn't help but feel that he was spinning his wheels doing work of this sort, but a moment's consideration led to the realization that it all had to be done and there was no one else to do it. As the report took form he was constantly plagued by the realization that four selected politicians were walking free. Had there been some logical reason to exclude them he would have felt better about it, but the fact was that they were involved in it right up to their dirty necks. In truth the exclusion of the few made the entire document suspect and moment-by-moment Jack was feeling greater levels of frustration. Logically, when you are given an illegal order you have every right to refuse taking part. From a personal perspective there was the crude balance of putting at least a few of them in jail, which was a very weak sop to one's conscience. He began to wonder how he might implicate all of them by making some sneaky little mistake. Perhaps he ought to tell J. Edgar to chuck it. The problem with making these exceptions was that in the long run they had you by the ass, because whether you liked it or not you were a party to their crime. Should they ever be brought into court they could claim that you were an accomplice. You could bet your bottom dollar that if they could sell you to save themselves they would do it in a heartbeat. Jack was determined that this would be his last piece of work for the FBI. He enjoyed the job and the men that he worked with, but he could not stand the thought of old J. Edgar crouching behind his desk as would some sort of evil gnome.

Then he tried to take the long view. Theoretically, you should be adult enough to understand that in politics there were always all manner of accommodations to take into consideration. It was an accepted way of life for these characters. That's how they made their money. They bargained and weaseled and screwed the public and became so accustomed to cheating that it became a way of life. If you didn't take part they looked upon you as a fool and as an enemy. As a prosecuting attorney you took what you could get and figured that they'd screw up again sooner or later, because they got more brazen by the day. Perhaps if you couldn't get them today you'd get them next tomorrow. Why sacrifice your life and well being to embarrass some thieving political moron? Jack sat there for a long while wondering how he could get around J. Edgar's instructions and indict all of them.

Toby and Bill came into the office and sat down. They were done for the day, Bill said. All that Jack needed to do was to correlate the data and have it typed. Tomorrow they would tackle the task of analyzing the books and perhaps by week's end they would wrap up the entire package. Jack was ready to ask what in the hell they thought they were doing when he glanced at the window. It was dark out there. He checked his watch. It was seven o'clock. The day had flown away and the office was empty. Jack thanked the men and apologized for the length of the day and shook hands with both of them. Then he went into the office where Miss Manley was still typing away. The pile of the paper on her desk was reaching an amazing height and the carbon paper was flowing over the edges of the waste basket. She stopped and slumped back into her chair.

"I didn't realize that it was so late," he said.

She smiled weakly, "Do you think we can stop? It's New Years Eve."

"Christ." He said. "Look I apologize. Can I take you to dinner or give you a ride home? I really feel so badly about this. I sort of lose track of time when I work." He fumbled about searching for the right words to express his dismay at having pressed her so hard. "Please let me take you to dinner. I've got to make up for this. You've worked so hard and done so well."

She looked up at him for a long minute. "I think that you are sincere. Yes sir, you may take me to dinner."

Jack went around carefully locking up his stuff and the room that they were using. He had grabbed his coat and was amazed to see the light on in the room that he had just locked. He went down the hall and encountered a colored man in a service uniform who was cleaning the room.

"Sir, do you have a key to this room?" Jack asked.

The man nodded and grinned, "Yes sir, we have keys to every room in the building."

Jack sat down a waited for the man to finish. Other people had gone through the offices and rooms and were emptying the waste baskets into a large container.

Miss Manley came looking for him. "Did you change your mind about dinner?"

"Ah no, no, I just wanted to be sure that all the doors were locked."

Miss Manley smiled and appeared to be waiting impatiently.

As Jack watched the cleaning man emptied the waste basket full of carbons into a bag that was smaller and different from that used by the other cleaning personnel.

"Mister Kelly? It's New Years Eve." Miss Manley urged.

Jack was smiling widely. "Yes Miss Manley, just one more little thing." He asked the man that he had spoken to earlier what time the cleaning crew finished their work. The answer was at about eleven or so and then they would check out through the back of the building.

Jack took Miss Manley to a sumptuous dinner. She allowed him to call her Linda and they talked cordially about the things that young men and women always talk about. She had been born and raised on a farm down in the southern end of the state. She had attended high school and two years of college. She had an AA degree and had studied office management. Linda was twenty-four years old. Looking at her youthful, unspoiled complexion Jack felt as though he was positively ancient. Perhaps it was her realization and comment that when he had gone into the Marine Corps she was but fourteen years old. He thought that an odd thing to say. Was he robbing the cradle? Was he in the same category as all the other elderly roué in the room that were courting the young females? Why in the hell was he so sensitive about this difference in age?

She rattled on about how delighted she was to have obtained a position with the FBI. One good thing about her was that she wolfed down her dinner. She was not a dainty eater, but she wasn't unmannerly either. He sat there in awe as he watched her eat and simultaneously carry on a non stop conversation. This girl was anything but shy. Farm girl, he thought. An image came to mind of burlap skivvies and hairy legs. Then she was off on a different tact. Her daddy owned a five thousand acre farm and she had grown up riding horses and driving tractors. Then she admitted that she wasn't supposed to be driving tractors, but she had intimidated some of the hands to allow her to learn. Her father had taken her to Switzerland to learn how to ski. Next she was off talking about her love of England. He sat there totally fascinated with this precocious young lady. She may have been born on a farm, but she was no hick. Jack revised his thought about the burlap skivvies; this girl was all lace and silk. He also sensed that if anything, she was far more sophisticated than he was.

Jack listened without saying a word. Then he noticed that the room was clearing out as the other diners left and that the waiters were circling impatiently. My God, he thought, it's almost ten o'clock. He had to get back to the Federal Building. He paid the bill, called a cab and put Linda in it and sent it to her apartment. She protested that it was an unnecessary expense and that she could take care of herself. Then she suggested that she could go with him and he politely refused. He kissed her lightly on the cheek and sent her off.

"Happy New Years," She laughed.

Jack had the distinct impression that she was pouting. As he got into his car he breathed a sigh of relief. Listening to that girl talk was positively exhausting.

Jack went back to the Federal Building and enlisted the aid of several Federal Security Officers. They waited out behind the service entrance as the cleaning crew left the structure. Then they rounded then all up and took them back into the lobby. The Supervisor of the clean up crew was an elderly colored man. He was dressed slightly better than his co workers and carried a brief case. There were several women in the crew and these ladies were quickly searched rather perfunctorily and sent into a separate room. The men were searched a bit more thoroughly and separated from one another. One man had a shopping bag that was filled to the brim with carbon paper. Jack looked over the material and then all of the workers were sent on their way. Jack took two of the Security Officers with him and got in his car and drove to the street car stop. The crew of colored workers left the downtown area and finally embarked on the State Street Car for the ride south. At Thirty-Fourth Street the man that had carried the shopping bag from the building got off the car and waved good bye to his fellow workers. He didn't have the bag with him. At Forty-Fifth the supervisor got off and he was carrying the shopping bag. That is when Jack picked him up and took him back to the Federal Building.

"What's your name?" Jack asked.

"Rodney Williams."

"You're in deep trouble, Rodney."

"You're damned right I am. My old lady is going to be very concerned, when I don't get home on time," Rodney said in a belligerent tone of voice. Evidently he was not awed by the federal badges.

"You can give her a call in about five years," Jack replied.

"For what?"

"For stealing government property."

The man almost went apoplectic, "What stealing? All I got is a bag full of trash."

"That's why you had your buddy carry it out of here. You figured that if we tumbled to what you were doing that he would take the heat."

Rodney fidgeted. "I don't know what you're talking about."

"I'm talking about copies of every report being prepared in our office." Jack leaned forward, "That infers collusion to defraud the government, obstruction of justice, and Christ knows what else, in addition to theft."

Rodney squirmed again. "Aw, it ain't like that."

"What's it like, Rodney?"

"A white dude gives me fifty bucks a month to bring all of that crap to him. Hell, I can't turn down fifty bucks; I got a wife and five kids."

"What's this guy's name?"

"I don't know," Rodney said as he slumped down in his chair.

"Aw Rodney, and we were getting along so well. I was almost beginning to believe you."

Rodney shrugged. "I take the stuff over to the Sears store on Sixty-third and Halstead. I take it to the tool department. I leave it there in the men's room at eleven o'clock. The money comes once a month, just like the guy promised."

"Describe the guy."

"White, maybe sixty years old or so, give or take five years. White hair, not fat but stocky, seems like a real nice guy. I met him once. He made the deal and gave me fifty bucks up front. I deliver everyday and I get the money just like he said."

"How does the money come?"

"Cash, every month."

Jack took the carbon copies from the bag and laid them out on the table. He sorted them out and put them to one side. Then he took dozens of blank sheets of carbon paper and crumpled them up and put them back in the bag. He gave the bag to Rodney and then asked the Federal Officers to deliver Rodney to the street corner where they picked him up.

"Rodney, this is your one and only chance to get out from under. If you blow this deal, I'll hunt you down and slam your ass in jail for a long, long time. I'm not asking you to do this I'm telling you. If I find out that you've warned off your friend you're dead meat and your wife and kids will be sending your mail to Alcatraz."

Rodney was impressed. "What do I do, sir?"

"Just deliver your package as you usually do. The store is closed tomorrow, so you make it Thursday. I'll take care of the rest."

Rodney considered what he had been told and nodded his assent.

Jack took the actual carbon copies back to the office and laid them on Charley Farrell's desk with a note. "Here is your Mole. The Cleaning Crew picks up the carbons, which by J. Edgar's edict are only used once. They are delivered to a mysterious man who resembles our Mister Warren McGruder. I'll tell you the rest a little later."

Jack went home. As he opened the door and entered the structure the door to Levi's apartment opened. "Your room is clear, and Happy New Years, Jack."

Jack grinned and patted Levi on the shoulder. "Thank you, brother. Would you care for a little more Scotch?"

Levi laughed, "My lady isn't over last night yet. Thank you anyway."

"Happy New Year, Levi."

Jack sat back and had a sip of Scotch and thought about the day. This Linda babe was something else. She certainly seemed to be a very nice girl.

In Jack's opinion holidays and Sundays were just so much wasted time. He woke up as early as usual, showered and shaved and dressed informally. He drove over to an old restaurant that he knew of and ate a leisurely breakfast as he browsed through the headlines. The world was heading for war just as surely as God made little angels. According to the business pages industrial orders were picking up for military aircraft and for armored vehicles.

The folks at home would be having a big get together at some one's house to celebrate the New Year, but he hadn't inquired as to where that might be and he really didn't want to intrude upon their happiness. It was only on days such as this that he felt the loneliness that had haunted his life for the last ten years. If he had an ounce of brains he counseled himself he would marry some nice girl and hang out his shingle. What the hell difference would it make if he didn't make a lot of money? Yeah, right, and then the world would go to war and he'd be serving on some far off battlefield, while his wife struggled with a couple of kids. In his opinion this was not going to be a happy new year.

After a bit he drove over to the office, maybe he could clean up a little work some where. Maybe he could visit Walt. There was one thing he could do and that was to arrange for tomorrow. He'd need to put people in the Sears Store that would be unobtrusive. Perhaps a lady with a couple of kids, or an old man sitting in a stall in the men's room, someone just to identify the drop off of the material and the guy that picked the stuff up. He would need a couple of cars and it would be great if they could get some of those new radio cars.

The guys sitting around the office were drinking coffee and telling lies. Jack fought the impulse to go to work, but he was soon typing up the specifications on the indictments for the five men that Hoover had allowed him. The case material was damned near air tight. Thanks to Werner they had the dates when the money was taken in and the dates when those various specific portions were paid to the politicians. Thanks to Mike they had the code and could marry up dates with the sums paid out. The problem was that if he followed Hoover's lead that there would be obvious gaps in the records. He couldn't very well delete evidence, or at least he had no intention of doing so. If Hoover's office crew wanted to eliminate some the data let them do that. He went back and retyped the entire mess just as he found the evidence.

Before long he noticed that the sun had gone down and his back was aching from sitting at the typewriter all day. Christ, he hadn't done that since he had left school. The office was empty but for the duty man. He had allowed himself to get so distracted that he really hadn't done anything that he had wanted too. Oh well time for supper and maybe a good radio program or two. That was another thing that he hadn't done for years. There should be some kind of special program on New Years.

Jack had left his car sitting at the curb in front of the building. For a couple of seconds he stood inside and took the time to button up his coat. He saw a young colored man open his car door slip inside. The son of a bitch is stealing my car, Jack thought, and he hurried through the revolving door. The man's head was down in the car. Hooking up the ignition wires, Jack surmised. Then the vehicle went up in a burst of flame. Jack ducked back into the doorway as showers of glass came raining down from the busted windows above him. The shock wave had shattered windows on both side of the street. He stood there for a long while and wondered who the poor bastard was that had decided to steal his car. Happy New Year, kid, you made a bad mistake. The Cops arrived first and then the Fire Department arrived. The fire was almost out, but for flames shooting out of the gas tank and the professionals made short work of smothering the fire. His first impulse was to walk out and identify himself and then he thought better of that. He decided that he would stroll out through the back door and go over to the streetcar line. It might be better if they thought that they were successful, at least for a while.

His hands were trembling slightly when he sat down on the streetcar. It had been a near thing. Far too near for comfort and far too surprising. He hadn't expected anything of the sort. Perhaps the single pertinent question was how did McGruder know that he would be working on a Sunday? It occurred to Jack that maybe it wasn't McGruder. Maybe the guy lying in the hospital bed wasn't the connection. Perhaps the real Mole was still out there and still trying to kill him.

Later that evening he grew bored of listening to the radio and went to bed early to get a good quiet night's sleep. As hard as he tried to put the bombing out of his mind he was haunted by the sight of the exploding vehicle and the burning man. Bad dreams kept him stirring for hours. In the morning Jack went down and got an FBI vehicle and picked up Bill Davidson and Toby, both of whom were very surprised to see him and as they headed for the south side they asked him about his car, but there wasn't much that he could tell them. They were waiting in the Tool Department of Sears and

Roebuck when Rodney arrived with his package. He dropped the bag off in the men's room and quickly left the store. Moments after Rodney had departed a pimply faced young man went into the room and came out with the bag. He walked out to the alley behind the store and stood there on the corner of the alley and Halstead Street. He was there for perhaps ten minutes. Seeing what was going on Jack had ran for his car and managed to get out of the lot just as a car came by and the kid threw the bag into the back seat through an open window. Jack paused long enough to pick up Bill Davidson as he hurried out to follow the car.

Traffic was picking up as the noon hour approached and Jack had a bit of trouble staying up with the old Ford in front of him due to traffic, but the driver of the car wasn't trying to avoid a tail. Jack surmised that this guy that he was following was nothing but another courier. The man pulled into the parking lot of an office building on the north side. Jack drove by the lot and Bill got out of the car to follow the man. Jack drove around to the front of the building and was looking for a parking space when the suspect came out the front door of the building with the bag still in his hand and hailed a cab. Jack watched the cab pull off and slid into that spot to allow Bill to climb into the car. In a moment they were back in the traffic stream.

"How did you figure that one out?" Bill asked.

"Luck," was Jacks reply.

At the corner of State and Madison the man got out of the cab and walked briskly into an office building. Bill got out rapidly and jogged up to the corner, he was able to spot the suspect entering an elevator. The elevator went up to the twelfth floor and stopped. By the time that Jack had joined him the suspect had come back down in a different elevator with the bag still in his hand, then the man walked across the street to a Candy Shop and came out without the bag. Jack had followed the suspect to the door of the Candy Shop and was looking in the window as the man handed over the bag. Then Jack went inside. Bill captured the suspect outside and led him discreetly into a nearby doorway.

Jack had watched as the guy gave the female shop keeper the bag
without so much as word and then leave the store. The female, a fifty
year old with graying hair, took the bag and with a bored expression
sat it down behind the counter. Jack went inside and pretended to
be examining the candies on display and he smiled at the woman.
Moments later a prosperous looking middle aged man came in and
the woman reached down for the bag. The man gestured a warning
to her and she let the bag drop back to the floor. Ignoring the man
she came to where Jack was standing.

"Oh well, you were first, what can I do for you, sir."

Jack smiled broadly, "Let me have your hand, please."

Smiling questioningly she extended her hand and Jack slipped a
set of handcuffs on her. Then he gestured to the middle aged man.
"Come over here and join your sister."

"She's not my sister."

"She is now, get over here."

The woman tugged at the cuffs, but Jack had them solidly in
his hand. He reached down and took the man's hand and slipped
on the other cuff.

"What the hell do you think you're doing, young man?"

"I'm arresting two people that are involved in a conspiracy to
defraud the United States Government."

Jack led them to the back of the store and sat both of them
down. Then he went out and got the bag and signaled to Bill to join
him. As Bill walked in with the first suspect the middle aged man
snarled at the younger man.

"You led them to us you damned fool."

"What? What?" The first suspect cried in surprise.

"Call for some assistance from the Marshals, Bill, we'll take
these people to the Federal holding facility."

The middle aged man was identified as Barney Bierman and he
had been separated from the other two. Jack walked into his room
and introduced himself.

At first the man cooperated. Barney's job was to take the bag to
his office and to copy the data onto clean white paper. He employed

several young women as secretaries who had performed that task day in and day out for the last two years.

"And what do you do with it, Barney?"

"I mail the typed documents to an address in Washington, D.C."

"Give me the address," Jack demanded.

"No."

"Okay, lock him up." Jack directed the Marshals. Jack got up as if to leave the room.

"That's it?" Barney asked incredulously.

"That's it. I haven't got the time or the inclination to screw around with you. You've made your bed, so sleep in it for the next ten years or so."

"Wait a Goddamn minute?" Barney shouted. "I know stuff."

Jack gestured to the Marshals and grabbed Barney by the shirt front. "Barney, if you ever want to get out of here you had better start talking and the information had damned well better be accurate." Then he dropped Barney back into the chair.

"They'll kill me." Barney whined.

"Yeah, they might at that," Jack laughed unsympathetically. "I'll tell you what; on second thought we'll let you out of here tomorrow right after we let the press know how much you have helped us."

"You've got to protect me. No shit, this is heavy stuff."

"So you realize how serious this is, that's a good sign Barney. Get it through your head Barney; we're the only people that can or are even remotely interested in trying to help you. But I haven't heard so much as a coherent word out of you as yet."

"The address is just a Post Office Box. You can't get much out of that."

"Let us worry about that."

"These guys are real careful."

"I noticed. That's why we caught you. Come on Barney, move it or get off the pot."

"The guy's name is McGruder."

"Yeah, Warren McGruder," Jack laughed again. "Tell me something I don't know."

"He works for somebody real big. And I mean really, really big."

"Who set up the system?"

"McGruder. Well, he told me how to handle it. I got the people, but he had already made arrangements with the kid driving the car to deliver the stuff."

"What's your background?"

"I was a stock broker. I was really doing well and then the entire world went sour. I was just getting back on my feet when this guy comes along and makes me a deal. He pays for the girls and the office and all I got to do is run it. I do whatever I can on the side. It's not a bad deal."

"Did you know where that information was coming from?"

"Yes I did. I read it. The girls just typed it. They probably know little pieces of the whole, because typists don't usually read what they type, but I read all of it."

"It didn't bother you that you were spying on the FBI?"

"Well we didn't do anything wrong. What the hell, it's really not secret or anything, they were throwing it out. Anyhow, most of it gets into the papers in a couple of days."

"Has anything changed in your routine lately?"

"Such as?"

"Such as Mister McGruder anxiously looking over your shoulder?"

Barney looked up in surprise. "How did you know that?"

"I'm psychic."

"Yeah, well. Mister McGruder has been calling me from time to time. He was really interested in what you were doing. It all started a couple of weeks ago when some guy named Howard got killed."

"Do you have McGruder's phone number?"

Barney's eyes went wide with fear. "Oh hell no."

"Barney you're not helping me."

"Christ, there's nothing I can say. Wait a minute! Wait just a minute. I got something you ain't got. I kept records. I got records of everything. What the hell, I had all the carbon paper I'd ever need. I kind of figured that maybe someday I might need it."

Jack was making arrangements for Barney to have a private cell when Charley Farrell walked in the door.

"I heard you were dead, Jack. I suspected that I may have been misinformed when this operation continued without a stutter. What have we got here, Mister Kelly?"

Jack described the connection.

"It's like having an ear in our office," Farrell said.

"Yeah and how many other of our offices are infiltrated?"

Farrell shook his head in disbelief, "Aw no, that can't be? Can it?"

"We have to have a search warrant to check out this guy Bierman's office."

"Hell, it's our carbon paper, they are our reports, let's just go and seize everything."

"If we do and if we find something other than our reports that is pertinent to some other investigation we risk having those materials declared inadmissible in a court of law."

Farrell grimaced and shrugged, "Call Toby and Bill Davidson get them to have Linda type up a form for Judge Callahan to sign."

Jack grabbed the telephone and made the call, providing the details and then he called the Federal Marshals requesting support for the seizure of the documents. He gave the officers the address and the approximate time of the raid.

"What next?" Charley asked.

It was Jack's turn to shrug off the question. "Charley, based upon what we know at this minute, I think that it had to be Walt that made the appointment with Myron Howard."

"So you're accusing Walt of being an accomplice in a murder? Christ, Hoover will love that."

Jack nodded, "It kind of looks that way, but maybe not, maybe it was an accident."

"A guy gets two forty-five rounds in the chest and that is no accident."

"But passing the word to the bad guys may have been an accident. In that Walt didn't know who he was talking too. I'm going over to the hospital and ask him."

Farrell shook his head no. "Ah no, Jack. We got to let the guy come around first. There's no hurry."

"I don't agree boss! There is every reason to push as hard as we can. This guy McGruder is getting desperate and after the bombing yesterday and the interruption of his Mole today he is really going to go nuts. His source has been discovered and his ties to someone in D.C. have been revealed. The next thing that is going to happen is that his bosses are going to cut his string. We are beginning to know too much about him now and he is a serious threat to their welfare. They will try to disassociate themselves from the man. These guys play rough, Charley, and this disassociation is going to be sudden and final." Jack leaned forward, "Look Charley, here's how I make it. We know that Walt knows who this McGruder guy is. They may have been buddies, which could have been part of Warren McGruder's plan to penetrate our security. Walt either contacted a known con man or the guy contacted him, how ever it happened, Walt persuaded him to turn states evidence. Perhaps through sheer coincidence he may have bragged about that to his friend McGruder, which is the worse thing that he could possibly have done. Or at least it was for Myron."

Farrell listened carefully and took a cigar from his pocket; he slowly went about the routine for lighting up and looked at Jack as he performed that ritual. "We got to get this guy and put his ass on ice. Not capture him, not arrest him, but kill him."

"I've heard that before," Jack said. Then he picked up the phone and gave instructions to Bill for collecting all of the data at Barney's office. Placing the phone on its cradle he turned to Charley. Want to go over to the Hospital with me?"

Charley shrugged, "Let's go to lunch. I know a place called Quincy Number Nine. The drinks are generous, the chow is decent and the girls are pretty."

Jack grinned, lunch was over due. "Ladies you say?"

"They are plentiful and particularly so at this time of day. All of the office ladies are getting out for forty minutes to grab a quick shooter and a sandwich for lunch." Charley led the way to the elevator. "Speaking of ladies, it didn't take you long to corral Miss Manley."

Jack actually blushed. "She's a nice friendly young lady. Very intelligent, clever really, I'd say that you picked the right girl from the pool."

"I didn't pick her from the pool. She's a new hire. None of the girls in the pool can type anywhere near as fast and accurately as Linda. And in addition to all that business stuff, she's got really nice legs."

Jack was laughing as they got into Charley's car. "Study all of her qualifications carefully and then if she's got nice tits hire her. Is that the way it works Charley?"

It was Charley's turn to laugh, "As if you didn't notice her legs right?"

Quincy's was a good place for a sandwich and there were plenty of girls. Jack noticed that everyone in the place seemed to know Charley. So this was one of the Boss's haunts. Even the girls from the other offices knew Charley which suggested that he had a reputation for hosting parties.

It was difficult to have a serious conversation and so Jack gave up and joined the frivolity. It had been at least a week or more since he had been able to laugh at jokes and have a quiet beer. He flirted with the girls and they all reciprocated. Jack decided that he would have to come back here someday. Finally the laughter subsided and Charley and Jack headed for the hospital. Jack checked his watch. The raid at Bierman's offices should just have gotten underway. He felt that he should have been there, but everybody has to eat once in a while.

When they walked into the hospital they immediately sensed that something was wrong. The security people were swarming about in frenzy. Charley asked what was going on and received a one word briefing.

"Shooting!" The guard said excitedly and then hurried off.

Charley and Jack exchanged glances and then hurried to the elevator. A guard stopped them and they both pulled their ID from their coat pockets.

"As I recall we had posted security?" Charlie asked.

"Yes." Jack replied. "There was supposedly an FBI agent and a Sheriff's Deputy."

When they arrived on the fourth floor the level of confusion and terror was reaching incredible levels. Jack led the way. A Sheriff's Deputy sat on a gurney with a bandage about his head. The FBI agent had a black eye and sat on a chair with a nurse in attendance. Jack brushed past them and headed for Walt's room. A Security Guard stood at the entrance and Jack identified himself and looked into the room. Walt still lay in the bed, his chest covered with blood. The oxygen tent was shattered and at least a dozen holes had penetrated the tent.

They had to have used a shotgun and double ought buckshot, Jack thought.

There was also blood on a nearby bed and blood at the foot of Walt's bed that was not associated with Walt's wounds.

"Who else was hurt?" Jack hesitantly asked the Guard.

The man shrugged, "Another patient took a couple of rounds in the gut and chest."

Jack experienced a sinking feeling. "Where is this other patient?"

"Surgery," was the brief explanation.

"Do you know who it was?"

The Guard shrugged again, "I'm not certain, Sir, but I think it was some guy named Caine."

Jack looked at the bed again. The bloody trail indicated that Mike had evidently tried to protect Walt."

Charley came up with his story. "There was an altercation in the waiting area. The Sheriff's Deputy went to take care of it. They assaulted him and knocked him down. When our guy saw the Deputy go down he charged in to help." Charley grimaced, "I know, I know, it was stupid. What happened here?"

"The shooters pushed in the door and Mike Caine tried to protect Walt. Caine is in surgery. From the looks of it Walt took a shotgun blast in the chest."

"Aw shit," was all that Charley could think of to say.

Chapter Nine

Jack began an investigation of the scene and it wasn't long before Monaghan and his crew showed up. Jack and Lieutenant Monaghan reconstructed the scene as best they could. The men that had created the diversionary scene had come up on the elevator; the two shooters had come up the stairs. Once the officers were distracted and lured away from their post the gunmen had invaded the room. The first man through the door had fired at Mike who had thrown himself in front of Walt. As the seriously wounded Michael had staggered over toward the other bed the second man had fired a shotgun at point blank range into the oxygen tent. Evidently they had left the way they had come. The two Officers assigned as security attempted pursuit, but were dissuaded by two more shot gun blasts that echoed through the stairwell as the killers emphatically convinced the Officers that they were outgunned. As the Officers had pursued the gunmen down the stairs, the men that had caused the diversion had left the floor via the elevator. It was over as quickly as it had started. Walt was dead and Mike was badly wounded. Two Federal Officers had been shot and Hoover was going to go berserk.

Melinda came to the hospital and sat quietly next to Charley as they waited patiently for word of Michael. These wounds were far more serious than the first one had been and blood for transfusions had been needed. Neither Jack nor Charley could qualify, but several officers were able to contribute. Bill Davidson came over and reported that the raid of Biermn's office had come off without a flaw and that the records were all committed to the security locker for safety. The analysis of the Atlanta Financial records was continuing and though nothing new had been uncovered the data was taking shape and should be ready for the Attorney General's Office within the week. Then Bill equivocated, "Well perhaps in ten days or so," he said. Then he announced that he was going back to the office, there was still work to do.

Jack indicated that for the moment he would be waiting for word of Michael's recovery and that he would join the team shortly.

The surgeon came out and one look at the man's expression was enough to tell Jack that things had not gone well. The Surgeon took Melinda's hand and announced that Michael had died bravely and in defense of another human being. No greater accolade could be offered. The staff had done all that could be done but the wounds were too severe. Melinda cried as if her heart was broken and Jack had to get up and walk over to the window and stare out at the black snow, lest he too begin tear up. His stomach was clutching up and releasing in spasms. Jack didn't want to think about Michael. He wanted to think about the man responsible. Mister McGruder was busy covering his ass and Jack was determined that he wasn't going to get away with it. A very brave young man had just died because of this cowardly bastard and Jack vowed that McGruder was going to pay dearly. Jack wasn't quite as touched by Walt's death. It had occurred to Jack that nothing good was coming Walt's way and maybe in a way he had lucked out.

If Jack could have, he would have avoided contact with Melinda, but he couldn't very well do that. He went over to her and offered to take her home. She hugged Jack to her and she cried and cried. "He so loved you, Jack." She whispered and as she did so the tears ran uncontrollably down Jack's stern countenance. It wasn't that he was ashamed to shed a tear for a friend, but it was an impulse that he usually suppressed. He had cried before. He had shed a tear when the Gunny had died due to a sniper's round over there in that far land. He had cried and then he had killed the sniper. There was no chance of controlling this impulse with this weeping woman clinging to his neck and in a sense he realized the instant relief that the tears offered, but even as the tears ran down his cheeks he vowed to apprehend the killers and to terminate their careers. The bastards that did this were never going to go to trial. There would be no slick uptown attorney explaining to a jury that the killers had experienced a terrible and abusive childhood. There were three guys on his list and he vowed that he was going to get all of three of them and to hell with law and order. Even as he had those thoughts he realized that it was all emotion and that there was very little common sense involved. She was still in his arms when he remembered his oath to preserve law and order and began to put the nonsense out of his mind. That didn't mean that they wouldn't die, but that he would follow the law.

Melinda had her chauffeured limo and so she didn't need Jack to drive her around. He did walk her down to the car and bade the tearful woman a fond farewell.

After she left Jack went back into the hospital and caught up with Dick Monaghan. The Officers had rather tentatively tracked the two killers out to a car. Three witnesses had been found that could describe the vehicle and the men that had excitedly clambered into it. The vehicle was a 1934 black Ford Model A. The three other men, those that had allegedly started the fight that served as a distraction for the sentries had ran down the street thus alerting the citizenry that something was going on. According to witnesses they had embarked upon an east bound streetcar. A quick check revealed that the men had gotten off the streetcar on State Street and had entered a bar. The conductor had been very suspicious of this group and had watched them as they left the car. He subsequently called the police. Within a half an hour the police knew where the three men had gone.

Jack had a hunch that the suspects wouldn't be able to contribute very much to the overall investigation, but somebody had hired them and had given them a little bit of money to carry off their charade. The charges against them were substantial, suspicion of conspiracy to commit the murders of two Federal Officers. There was more than sufficient evidence to justify their arrest. Even though he didn't expect much out of them Jack was in a very bad mood and was hoping that they would be foolish and drunk enough to resist arrest.

They stopped outside the bar and Jack took off his coat, overcoat and hat and handed them to Monaghan. "Why don't you call for back up, Dick? I'm going in there to interrogate the prisoners. Take your time, there's no real hurry."

Monaghan shook his head violently, "That's a mean assed place, Jack, they don't like cops in these places."

"That's a pity," Jack said as he pushed through the door.

The three men were standing in the center of the bar, buying drinks for the usual hangers on. To a man they were all scruffy, seedy looking, young street bums.

Jack started off the show by declaring that they were all under arrest. The men laughed and started after the lone officer. To make matters worse several other men crowded in as if to join in the fight. The first man swung a wild right and found himself sailing through the air and landing flat on his back on a table. The second man grappled at Jack and was instantly blinded by Jack's fingers. He backed away in horror screaming that he had been blinded. The third man hesitated and went for a knife. Jack put him in a quick arm lock and broke his arm thus disarming the man. Now the bystanders had backed away and Jack went methodically from victim to victim kicking and striking into kidneys and ribs. He wasn't asking questions or even speaking and then he stopped and looked at the bystanders as if seeing them for the first time. "Get the hell out of here!" He shouted and they all scrambled for the door.

Jack grabbed the neck of the largest of his victims and slammed his head against the bar. "Now I'm going to ask you one question, if you don't answer me I'm going to kill you. Do you understand?"

The man stared up at Jack with obvious fear.

"They killed two federal Officers and I want the names of the two killers?"

The man hesitated and Jack slammed his head back into the bar again. Then he dropped the body to the floor and kicked him violently in the side. One could almost hear the ribs cracking. Then Jack grabbed the second man and this person began screaming.

"Don't hurt me anymore! Please don't hurt me! We didn't know what they were going to do, honest. It was the Skelton brothers; they live over on Twenty-eighth and Union. Twenty-eight-forty-one, I think it is. Apartment B."

Jack dropped the body to the floor and stepped over him just as several uniformed officers hurried in.

"I hope I don't have to come back for you," Jack said softly.

"I want that mean son of a bitch arrested!" The bartender shouted.

Jack turned toward him.

"Don't let him touch me," the bartender squealed in terror.

"One more word from you and nobody will ever be able protect this place. Do you understand me?"

"Yes sir, yes sir, forget it officers, It was my mistake."

Lieutenant Monaghan handed Jack his hat and coat. "Did you get what we wanted?"

Jack nodded.

"Feel better?"

"I will in a few minutes."

"The do gooders will be raising hell about this." Monaghan said.

"Yeah I know."

"Where are we going?"

"Twenty-eight-forty-one Union. Apartment B."

Lieutenant Dekker of the Sheriff's Department came rushing in the door. "You guys weren't thinking of leaving me out of this were you?"

Jack grinned despite his mood, "I wouldn't think of it Dutchman."

"I'll get some help." Monaghan said.

"We won't need any help," Jack said. "But we'd better be certain. These guys aren't getting away."

The ride over to South Union Avenue was silent. Each man was buried in his own private thoughts. They were met at the address by three Police Units which were filled with armed officers.

"These guys that we're after just killed two Federal Agents. We'll take them alive if at all possible," Monaghan said. "Eight guys go

around back. We'll chase them out toward you. Be ready to shoot, they probably won't want to be captured."

"What's that bullshit about taking them alive?" Jack asked.

"That's for public consumption. It illustrates our good intentions. On the other hand we might consider the value of keeping them alive. Somebody paid them to do this."

"If they're alive after this is over it will be because I'm dead," Jack muttered.

Jack went up the stairs two at a time, but he was as silent as a big cat. Monaghan and Dekker followed close on his heels. They found apartment "B" and could hear the two suspects arguing. Jack burst through the door without hesitating. The first brother was cleaning a sawed off shotgun, he slammed the barrel down into the handle and began to raise the weapon. He was struck by three rounds from a forty-five and two from a thirty-eight. The second man lurched toward the back door and then turned as if to fight. Another quick volley of rounds and he staggered through the door and into a blast of gunfire from the alley. The Skelton Brothers were dead.

The three officers exchanged glances.

"Too bad they didn't want to cooperate," Monaghan said.

Dekker nodded and smiled grimly.

"Yeah," Jack agreed. "Too bad." He ejected the spent magazine, put it in his pocket and inserted a second magazine and holstered the weapon. "Beans, bullets and bandages." Jack said.

"What's that?" Asked Monaghan.

"Aw it's just something that I learned in the Corps."

Monaghan nodded.

Jack found a telephone hanging on the wall downstairs and called into Charley Farrell. "We found the guys that started the diversion and they led us to the killers."

"Did you take them alive?" Charley asked.

"No, unfortunately they chose to fight it out."

"That's too bad, I'd like to know who it is that was behind this."

"Is there some question in your mind?"

Charley equivocated, "Well, we can't be absolutely certain."

"I can. Before this is over he'll be laying on a slab too."

"Christ, Jack, don't let the press hear you say that."

"Right."

"Well I guess its over we have our Mole, or at least the system they used, and Walt is dead. So all the connections are broken?"

"I don't think so."

"What?" Charley asked.

"I'm hyper Charley, I can't slow down. I'm going out to the south side to conduct some unfinished business."

"Such as?" Charley asked.

"There are a couple of loose pieces that have to be cleared up. I'll be back later."

"Hold it. Hoover is on the other line."

Jack groaned impatiently, but held on.

"He wants to talk to you."

Hoover came on the line. "Special Agent Kelly, Senator Caine wants me to fire you. Did you capture the people that killed his son?"

"I killed both of them." Jack stated flatly and then added, "With a little help from our friends in the PD."

"That won't bring his son back, but it might ameliorate the situation and help him to know that they didn't get away with it."

"I find it odd that he allowed the young man to join the Bureau if he wanted him protected, knowing that there was some risk involved."

Hoover coughed, "We rarely have an officer even wounded much less have two of them killed. It has been years since we've had officers killed. I thought those wild days were over."

Jack remained silent he didn't know what the Director wanted.

"Are you there, Kelly?"

"Yes sir, I don't know what to say."

"I want the instigator. I want the man that started all this horror."

"So do I."

"Do we know anything more than we did?"

206

"We know that he works for some entity in Washington. Probably as a go between to funnel the graft to the right people and to protect his boss from discovery. The reports concerning our operations were forwarded to a P.O. Box in Washington so somebody in the Capitol was busy looking over your shoulder. I questioned Charlie Farrell as to how many other offices have been penetrated? Has our Washington headquarters been infected?"

Jack could hear the irritation in Hoover's voice as he ignored the question and replied "Have you the slightest idea who that person might be?"

"I'll find out. My mission, as I see it is to discover who the ultimate spy may be and then to eliminate his agent Mister McGruder."

"I concur. Do you have any leads?"

"I have the name of a woman out on the south side. She was involved in the Howard case. We put her on the back burner after we found Crouse, but I'm going to track her down and see what she knows."

"Good luck, Mister Kelly and keep me posted."

"Am I fired?'

"Not yet."

"Christ, pretty soon I'll have two whole weeks with the Bureau."

"Please keep your smart remarks to yourself."

The line went dead.

"Asshole," Jack muttered and he hung up the phone.

"Jack, I hate to slow you down, but you can't go anywhere," Monaghan said, "We have statements and reports to write. The D.A. will want to know about the circumstances of the shootings."

Jack nodded, he understood the demand for the paper work, but he was impatient and wanted to keep going. "Let's get it over with," he said with obvious reluctance. He would as soon go to a dentist for a root canal as try to sort out everything that had happened in the last few hours.

After an unpleasant session Jack went back to his office, he wanted to give himself some time to settle down and think. When he got there he was appalled to find that the outer hall was packed with reporters. Someone recognized him and asked for photos and a description of what happened at the home of the Skelton Brothers.

Jack replied that they would have to get the official version from the D.A. and begged off any personal interviews until he had a chance to clear it with his bosses, all of which was true. That didn't deter them in the least and they remained outside clamoring for attention. Jack went into the office and was surprised to see that Linda was still there. She still wore her hair drawn tightly back into a matronly bun and the thick horn rimmed glasses that so effectively hid her face. They chatted for a few minutes and she expressed her dismay and sorrow at the death of the two agents. She hadn't know either of them but admitted to feeling saddened by the thought that good men had to die at the hands of such evil thoughtless men.

Jack asked where Charley might be and she informed him the Charley had left the office shortly after the phone call from Mister Hoover. Jack decided to use Walt's old office for a few minutes of quiet and seclusion. He turned the chair around and stared out the window at the worsening weather.

Linda had followed him into the office and said that she understood that he needed a little privacy and that under the circumstances she would go out and see what she could do with the reporters.

Under any other circumstances Jack would have denied her that task, but he was convinced that Linda could more than hold her own with anybody. He settled back into Walt's old oversized armchair and racked back a bit. The destruction of Jack's car was an indication of just how frustrated McGruder must be getting. That was at least the third attempt on Jack's life and it had been so close to being successful that Jack was frightened. Not terrified, but frightened and he had been frightened before in his life. When some people grow frightened they stop thinking, but Jack's mind was accelerating. He had to do something to take the offensive. He had gain control of the situation. The question was what was it that he could do that would plague the enemy? Where had he missed out on nailing Mister McGruder? There was another question. How had the killer that had attempted the second assassination known where he lived? The Bierman business that he had uncovered didn't answer that question. He had given the address to Marcy and she had typed it down, but according to her testimony she had sent the correction downstairs and the attempt on his life occurred shortly thereafter. Bierman wouldn't have had that information for a week.

Some man within this office had informed the assassin of the new address or he had been followed when he left the office. That just didn't seem to make sense. For that matter the death of Myron Howard had presumably been the result of Howard making an offer to turn states evidence and there wouldn't have been any copies of that conversation. Whoever the controlling agent had been he was the one that had leaked the info to Kaplan. Allegedly that was Walt, but according to Marcy, Walt wouldn't have known Jack's address. Nowhere in any of the company files that Jack had seen, was there the slightest intimation that Howard was in any way associated with the Bureau. Jack knew that Walt wasn't really a hand's on kind of guy. Had Farrell been in charge? That was possible. Hell, anything was possible. Where in the hell was Farrell? Considering the weather he was probably down at Quincy having a drink or three.

The money! Damn it how had he missed it? The large sums of money that the company had accumulated had to be the answer. The only record was that which had been turned up by Michael indicating that these particular people were being paid off on specific dates, but paid in cash. Was there any way to correlate these payments to some specific bank account? Very few people had that sort of money. Would the bankers cooperate? He realized that he didn't have the correct answer as yet, but it was coming to him.

"Do you want the light on?" Linda asked.

"No, thank you," he replied calmly. "Why do you ask?"

"You seem to be relaxing."

"I'm thinking about today."

"May I ask you a question?" She asked.

"Okay, shoot."

"You killed two men today, yet you sit here calmly and at ease. How do you do that?"

"Do what?"

"Is life so meaningless to you?"

"On the contrary life means everything to me. I also lost a good friend today. Would it help me or Michael to break down in tears?"

"I'm asking you how you manage to control yourself."

"I can't tell you that. I don't know the answer."

She came around the desk and kissed him very gently on the lips. It was the first gentle thing that had happened to him this day. Despite his apparent calm his emotions were in turmoil.

He responded by cradling her face in his hands and returned the kiss.

Then she slid down and into his lap and wrapping her arms around his head kissed him passionately. He realized that she wasn't wearing her glasses and that her hair was hanging down over her shoulders. Then she stood up and lifted up her blouse. There in the darkness, she was outlined against the window and this didn't seem to be the awkward girl that he had seen at the desk. He stood up and took off his coat and tie. They had exchanged signals of willingness. She came to him again.

"Love me," she whispered. "I'm hungry for love."

Jack was aware that extreme violence and death often elicited strange passions within people.

He lifted her up and kissed her again, then he took her to the couch and they quickly disrobed. He kissed her breasts and was surprised to find that she was a full breasted woman. She pulled him close to her as she fell back onto the couch and she wrapped her legs about him and guided him into her. Then she just pulled him close and they lay there kissing and sensing and then she began to move. He matched her thrust for thrust, slowly at first and then pressing deeper and deeper into her. She brought her legs almost up to his shoulders and concentrated on taking every possible bit of him. They made love for at least an hour and then she rested, still straining against him and still holding him close atop her. After a bit her arms fell away from him, but she pushed her hips forward against his and softly said "Thank you. That was very, very good."

Jack turned on a desk lamp. Her hair hung down to her hips and her eyes were still flashing a deep dark blue. She struggled with her hair for a moment and then just knotted it and tossed it over her shoulder as she left the room. This ugly duckling had suddenly become a swan and he was really impressed. When she returned they grabbed their coats and hurriedly left the office. His official car was kept in the garage and he believed that it was secure here. Still he opened the door for her and then he went forward and opened the hood for a quick examination. Then he drove out into the storm. He didn't see anyone following him, but it was hard to tell in the storm.

When he approached her house he circled twice to make certain that no one was following. She didn't ask what he was doing, but sat there stoically as she watched the traffic. Her apartment was in an upscale neighborhood and was actually a pent house. A gift from her daddy, she said. Once in her apartment she rubbed his cheek and suggested that he shave for her. He went into the spacious bathroom and was standing there finishing up as she entered in the nude and started the shower. He disrobed and without a word he joined her. She rubbed her hands up and across his face, smiled and then ran her hands down his body and around to his buttocks and then she pulled him close and they embraced. Next she handed him the soap and turned around with her back to him and he began to wash her. As he explored every inch of her body she leaned languorously back against him. Then she took the soap and began to wash him. It was a pleasing erotic experience. There was no hurry, no rush to culminate the mating. This was the teasing, the preliminary. Then they kissed and the tempo began to increase.

Once they got to the bed room Jack discovered that she had an extra large bed and they had all the room to frolic and experiment that they would ever need. Their mating was both intense and playful and she rode him much as Alice had, but the rhythm wasn't as frenetic. When they finished he lay there next to her completely sated. Then he reached over and kissed her.

"You're leaving?"

"Would you prefer that I stay?"

"Yes, I would, why don't you just turn off the lights and open the blinds and we'll watch the storm."

He did as she asked and came back to the bed. She lay on his shoulder for a long while and they watched the snow coming down. Then she reached down and took him into her mouth and the play began again.

In the early morning he dressed hurriedly and kissed her goodbye as she cuddled back into the covers. He absolutely hated going out into that chill world that waited out there, but there was no way to stay in the warmth. The snow lying across the hood of the vehicle hadn't been disturbed and so he assumed that the car was clean. Fortunately, he was right and drove to his apartment. No one was following him and no one was there waiting for him. He showered and shaved again and drove downtown to the office. In the lobby he picked up the paper only to be confronted by a screaming headline, "South Side Woman Strangled," Miss Sylvia Goldberg, 46, was found strangled to death early this morning in an alleyway behind the Normal Tavern, which is located at Sixty-Third Street and Normal Avenue. Police are searching for witnesses. Anyone having any information concerning this tragedy is encouraged to call Lieutenant Monaghan of the Chicago Police Department."

Jack purchased a cup of coffee and two donuts and went up to his office. A bitter taste of gall surged up into his throat. He could have gone down there after the woman, as he had intended, and if he had found her she might still be alive, but the real issue was why did they wait to kill her? Why now all of a sudden? The only guy that he had told about the possibility of meeting that woman was Charley Farrell. Could Charley be the Mole? If not that was a hell of a coincidence. But then if Charley was the culprit why hadn't he killed her a long time ago? He certainly had the opportunity.

Linda was sitting at her desk looking all prim and proper. She wasn't wearing her glasses but her hair was all done up in a bun. How in the hell did she do that, he wondered? She smiled a knowing intimate impish smile. He nodded and went into Walt's office. Her glasses were there on the desk. He picked them up and looked through them. They were just plain glass there was no magnification.

He had to wonder why she had bothered to disguise her identity, and then he shrugged and grinned to himself and took the glasses out to her. "You may need these," he said.

She grinned impishly again and put them on and as she did so she announced, "Mister Hoover is on the telephone, for you. And Lieutenant Monaghan of the Chicago Police Department wants to talk to you as soon as possible. Here is his number."

Jack settled down at Walt's desk and picked up the telephone. "Special Agent Kelly, he announced.

There was no preamble. "We are coming to Chicago this afternoon, Mister Kelly. That is to say, Senator Caine and I are going to arrive there Via American Airlines at about five o'clock. We will attend Special Agent Caine's funeral tomorrow. You will be there at the airport with three vehicles to meet me and my staff. Senator Caine will arrange his own transportation. Please arrange for accommodations at the Sheraton on the Lake. I would like my usual suite. Now, is there any thing new on this case?"

"The Killers of Special Agent in Charge Walt Albright and Special Agent Caine were killed in a shootout with the Police." Jack wondered whether he should tell Hoover that he had seduced a great piece of ass last night and decided against that impulse. "A woman was murdered last night that may have been a material witness in the killing of Mister Howard."

"I suppose that you are going to tell me that as usual the enemy got too her first?"

"Regrettably that was the case."

"Bah! Goddamn it, when are you people going to start thinking?" The phone went dead the conversation was over.

Jack had to admit that Hoover had a point. The man wanted a Suite at the Sheraton, Jack thought. Hell, there's no reason to follow up on a murder, allow me to piss away my time making hotel reservations. Jack dialed Monaghan's number. "Good morning Dick, I hear that Sylvia Goldberg bought the farm?"

"Indeed," Monaghan responded. "You wouldn't know anything about this would you?"

"What make's you think that I would know anything?"

"A lady named Sadie Malone called me this morning she tells me that Sylvia was a friend of Mister Hymie Howard's." Monaghan chuckled. "This Sadie gal wants to see you. She tells me that she owes you one."

"Where do I find her?"

"You find me first, at my office, and then we go looking for Sadie."

"That's a deal," Jack said. "I'll be there in a minute or two."

"By the way, I hate to bring up these trifling little errors on your part, but why didn't you check in with me after they blew your car all to hell? For a while there I thought that you had left us."

"I figured that you'd noticed the difference in skin pigmentation."

"It was somewhat difficult in that the gentleman in question was thoroughly singed. But it did occur to us that he was of a different color. How did it happen that this poor sap was in your car?"

"I think he was trying to steal it."

"That was really a mistake."

"Yes," Jack responded, "it certainly was."

Jack gave the reservation information to Linda, kissed her on the cheek and then called Bill Davidson to arrange for the vehicles.

"May I ask where you're going Mister Kelly?" She asked politely.

"I'm going to catch a murderer." He responded.

"And what shall I tell the Director, should he call again?"

"Tell him precisely that. By the way have you seen Farrell?"

"Not yet this morning, which is unusual, he is usually in before I get here."

Women, Jack thought in awe. He was amazed by their flexibility and resilience. This was the passionate and almost aggressive female of the night before, and yet she looks to be so prim and proper this morning. It would appear that ice cream wouldn't melt in her mouth and yet he knew that she was a seething sexual animal inside. He wondered if he would be invited back again. Her manner seemed to indicate that was definite possibility.

Jack drove to the PD and picked up Lieutenant Monaghan and his new assistant Jake McCauley and they drove south. Jake drove the Lieutenant's car and later on silently followed Jack and Monaghan.

"Who is this Sadie character?" Monaghan asked.

"Sadie Malone was sort of a part time prostitute, when I knew her. The rumor was that she was very particular as to her clients. She drank a lot and was a regular at Pat's Depot Tavern. She allegedly has a regular job, but I don't know what it is that she does." Jack paused for a moment and then continued. "She's a good, well meaning sort of old girl. I don't know if she has ever scored a husband or not, but she is single now. Crouse slapped her around and took a chunk out of her face. I understand from Pat that it didn't heal all that well and that now she wears a heavy veil to disguise her deformity."

"That's a shame," Monaghan said. "These goddamn street animals don't care who they hurt. I have never understood why a guy would hit a woman without a good reason." Monaghan was watching traffic as they cruised slowly along the street. "What the hell is going on here, Jack?"

Jack sighed heavily. "If you recall, the guy that owned the house where Hymie was rooming claimed that he hadn't seen him in several days. I think that is because Hymie was staying at his girl friends apartment, which means that whoever it was that wanted to get a hold of Hymie knew him well enough to call that number. That was a significant clue to the identity of the Mole and I should have jumped on it, but I didn't. This is sort of a convoluted story, but if you follow me the logic is solid enough.

"Walt hired me to find the Mole. I later found that the janitors were taking the carbons from our offices and it occurred to me that this carbon paper leak was the Mole, but that didn't really make sense, because the timing was off. I am convinced that whoever, it was that set Hymie up, he had to be an insider. Walt claimed to be Hymie's handler, but there had to be someone else. Allow me to explain, when someone calls the office and reveals a potential case an officer is assigned to cover it. In this case Hymie had the bad luck to tell his story to the Mole that was working for Kaplan. Talk about shitty luck. When this Mole finally found out that Hymie intended to turn states evidence it was he that set up the meeting for an odd time and at an isolated place. Of course he couldn't have anticipated the storm. Then he notified Kaplan that Hymie intended to rat on the group. We surmise that it was a last minute sort of business. It was Kaplan that hired Crouse and even had to lend the moron his car. It may be that Crouse simply went into the Depot Bar to warm up. He was forced to wait outside in the freezing weather until Hymie showed up and he well may have needed a drink, not because he was a boozer, but because he was chilled to the bone.

The allegedly clumsy stupidity of that killing was what convinced the big cheese, whoever that might be, to cut his losses and eliminate the local management. So he sent his man, Mister McGruder to clean things up."

Then this business with Walt surfaced. I don't believe that Walt was the Mole. If he had been it stands to reason that he would have never hired me. Perhaps because the initial murders were so violent, I assumed that there was one man behind all of the associated events. In fact there were two men, McGruder was one of them; he was an older, silver haired, distinguished looking individual that was seen leaving the Kaplan house. Yet there is another person involved and this individual is almost a twin of McGruder's.

I don't think McGruder was in on the killing of Myron Howard. We know that McGruder was probably just covering his boss's political ass in killing Kaplan. McGruder was being paid by this mysterious someone else to keep an eye on the Bureau and upon the locals and to collect and distribute the bribe money. I think that for this mysterious someone, this big Leader is operating at the national political level. McGruder was keeping tabs on the office through Bierman and his set up, but there was someone even closer. Someone that McGruder may not have known about."

"The Mole was the insider who was working directly for Kaplan." Jack gestured again in an all enveloping manner. "I don't think that McGruder, knew about the Mole, or the Mole would have been on the list for extinction. By the same token I don't think that the Mole knew about McGruder. Though I suspect that over the run of the case that they have become aware of one another and are now deadly enemies."

'Why would that be true?" Monaghan asked.

"Because they have inadvertently created a danger for one another and are trying to avoid the blame for a series of murders. McGruder killed Kaplan and company and the girl in Gary, and engineered the shootout on the border. I don't think that he had anything to do with Walt's original shooting or his eventual death. I think that was the work of the Mole."

"Okay, maybe, but what the hell does this have to do with Sadie?"

"Sadie once told me that Hymie had a girl friend, named Sylvia that hung out at the Normal Avenue Tavern. I didn't pursue the matter for the PD because we found Crouse dead and then we found Kaplan dead. The case was solved. At that time it didn't matter to me who set up the original murder. It couldn't matter to our prosecution in the PD that someone had killed both of them, but it did matter to the FBI, because their case continued. When I got involved with the FBI it was because Walt wanted me to find the Mole. He didn't really care about the fraud case and he actually shied away from it. That was particularly true when I found out that various local politicians were involved in bribery.

"You're wandering off the subject again," Monaghan chided.

"I wanted to get back to Sadie, because I was beginning to believe in this second Mole theory, but things were happening too fast. The key had to be this broad Sylvia, who was shacking up with Hymie and who may have known who it was that called Mister Howard on that eventful night."

"You might have mentioned this theory to me at the time, Jack," Monaghan said petulantly.

"I'm the new guy remember? And this is my first case."

Monaghan shrugged. "Still, I would have listened."

Jack looked over at Monaghan as if he disbelieved his old boss and smiled.

Monaghan grinned and shrugged again. "Okay, maybe not."

Sadie's apartment was on the third floor and it was Jack that knocked discreetly.

"Who's there?" She asked.

"Jack Kelly."

"Oh Christ," she muttered and there was a fussing inside before she opened the door. There were three dead bolts attached. She glanced out and smiled and then began undoing the locks. She finally got them all undone and asked Jack to come in as she hurried away into the other room.

Jack, Monaghan and Jake McCauley entered the apartment and locked the door again. It was a clean, very neat little roomette apartment. A very tall, very pretty doll occupied the only chair other than Sadie's. A teddy bear sat in a corner and stared at the men with black button eyes. When Sadie reappeared she was wearing a veil across her face and a thick pleated wrap about her thin frame and she was obviously taken aback at the sight of Monaghan.

"Sadie this is Dick Monaghan and Jake McCauley of the Chicago PD Homicide unit."

"I don't trust cops," she said bitterly.

"We're homicide, not vice," Monaghan explained.

"As if that make a difference," She said accusingly.

Monaghan shrugged, "What the hell I tried. Would you prefer that we leave?"

She looked from Monaghan to Jack several times and then relented. "Okay, but no bullshit." She looked around in consternation when she realized that there was no place for them to sit down. "I got another chair in the kitchen," she explained.

Monaghan fetched the chair. Jake stood nonchalantly in a corner trying to be as inconspicuous as possible. After giving Sadie a hug Jack settled down upon the floor. "Okay, Sadie," Jack said, "Tell us about it."

Sadie sat down upon the bed and folded her hands in her lap. "After that bastard Crouse beat me up I lost my job," she moved the veil aside for a moment and then quickly replaced it. "No body wants a receptionist with a scarred up face." She gestured to the bed. "I do the only thing I know how to do." She looked into Jack's eyes as seeking some measure of understanding. "I got to eat and pay the rent," she began to cry and he got up and went over and sat down beside her, putting an arm around her shoulders.

"You know why I'm here Sadie, I'm looking for a killer, and I honestly wish I could offer you more than that, but I can't. I won't lie to you."

She buried her head in his shoulder and cried and cried.

Jack looked at Monaghan helplessly and sat there resigned to assist an old friend if only to offer a shoulder to cry upon.

She gathered herself after a bit and sniffling loudly she asked. "Would you guys like some coffee?"

They all declined the offer.

"I didn't like that bitch, Sylvia. I was down at my favorite table when this tough looking guy walks in the front door. He wore a hat that was pulled down over his eyes and he had his overcoat collar turned up. He looks a little like Dick here as far as size goes, but maybe a little older, a little thicker. Any way as he comes down towards her table, which is in the back, Sylvia sees him coming and says, "Hi Charley how are you?" I could tell she was scared. She looked over at me as if she was asking for my help as if she wanted to get away from this guy."

"She called him Charley?" Jack asked.

"Yeah, Charley, I'm sure of it. That was the name. He pulled his chair around and sat down at her table and ordered a drink. I could see that she wanted to get away from him, but he wouldn't let her. After a couple of drinks he took her outside. I mean he took her. There wasn't any refusing this guy. She kept hanging back as if she was dragging her feet, but he never let go of her." Sadie shrugged. "That's all I know. I never saw her again until I read the papers."

"What time was that?" Jack asked.

Sadie gestured vaguely, "Aw, hell, I don't know maybe nine or so." She looked around at Monaghan, "This guy didn't act like a John. If you know what I mean, he wasn't asking. He was demanding. He was a tough looking dude, and there wasn't any doubt about her going with him. Is that any help, Jack?"

"I might bring a picture of this guy to see whether you can identify him?"

"Forget it. I've gone as far as I'm going."

It appeared to Jack as though she was about to tear up again. "Now Sadie, take it easy. You did a great thing. We got to get this bastard before he kills any more girls."

She blinked and looked up at Jack, "Jesus, do you think he's that kind a guy?"

Jack nodded, "Could be. So I want you to be careful."

Sadie's shoulders slumped, "Hell, maybe he would be doing me a favor."

"Now Sadie," Jack exclaimed, "You're tougher than that. Cut that crap. Maybe we can get that little scar of yours fixed."

She looked up at him again. "Don't tease me about that Jack, it isn't fair."

Jack gave her a little hug and stood up, "Come on Dick, let's get out of here, we got to go see a guy."

"Do you think it's possible, Jack?" She asked anxiously.

Jack grinned. "Any thing is possible, Sadie, let me call around a little, until then hang tight and stay the hell out of that Bar."

"You shouldn't have made that kind of promise to her, Jack," Monaghan said as they got into the car.

"They're doing miraculous things at the University. I know a couple of guys that might break down and to it for practice."

"Aw Jack, I don't think so, not for some old whore?"

"She's not an old whore, Monaghan you were running the vice squad too long. Sadie is a good hearted old gal and she is just running into some rough times. Besides that, I didn't make her any promises."

"Jack you're a little young, believe me that broad is a whore whether you feel sorry for her or not."

"We're potentially all whores, Monaghan; it's just that some of us haven't been pushed to the edge as yet."

Monaghan waved that thought away. "Who is this guy Charley? You acted as though the name struck a bell."

"Charley Farrell."

Monaghan shook his head. "The Charley Farrell! Aw hell no, no I don't think so."

"Why not, because he's a cop?"

"No, because he has too much to lose. The guy has been in the Bureau for years. He wouldn't do anything to cross them."

Jack put the car in gear. They didn't have far to go to get to the murder scene. "The guy joined the Bureau BH, that's Before Hoover. That was when you didn't have to be an attorney or an accountant to get a job as an agent. Charley was a U.S. Marshal for a while and then came on the Bureau. When Hoover took over the rules changed. He has been quoted as saying that he wanted to develop a more professional law enforcement agency, but the end result was that a lot of the old guys got passed over for promotions. Charley was one of those and though he has done well because he is an exceptional law man, he could have done a lot better without the administration favoring the new college kids. So he has motive to sell his ass, just as an old whore might."

"What possible motive?" Monaghan laughed derisively.

"Money! As I say he's become a whore just like old Sadie. He's going out in a couple of years without much in the way of cash to pay for his old age."

Monaghan grunted his contempt for Jack's theory. "Farrell is too good, he's too smart. I've heard of some of his work. The guy is a legend."

It was Jack's turn to grunt. They pulled up into the alley behind the Normal Tavern. A police officer was on duty there and had been sitting in his car. He got out of his unit and stopped Jack's car. Then he recognized Jack and Monaghan and waved them through. They got out and waved a friendly hello to the officer. He came up to them and pointed to a snow bank. "She was lying there in the snow, Lieutenant. The coroner said that she had been strangled. The body is down at the County Coroner." He looked at Jack and grinned. "How ya doing Jack?"

Jack shook hands with the officer and gestured toward Jake, "Jake McCauley of homicide." Then he walked over to the scene. There wasn't much to see. No blood, well there was a little trickle of brown drops in the snow. The Coroner's guys had traipsed all over the place making any kind of analysis almost impossible. They had avoided a couple of spots as if they were somehow significant. This appeared to be where the killer had kneeled down to straddle the body.

"He brought out back in the dark alley and strangled her. No noise, no muss, no fuss." Jack surmised.

"Aw she would have to have screamed wouldn't she?" The Officer asked.

"Good question," Jack said. "Have you guys checked with the neighbors?"

"Yes sir, but nobody heard nothing."

"Where's her purse?" Monaghan asked.

The officer that was posted there shrugged. "I never saw one. Maybe the Coroner has it. Or maybe it's inside."

"Is the bar open?" Jack asked.

"Yeah, it just opened, it opens at ten, we let the Bartender open it and have the first five stools, but all the ladies tables and the back end are closed off. There's another officer inside watching the place so they don't screw around."

"Who else has been here?"

"Just the various service guys, delivering their morning supplies."

"What about a clean up crew?"

The Officer chuckled. "That I don't know, but I would bet they don't have one."

Monaghan asked. "What do you see, Jack?"

"We aren't too far off the side street and only sixty feet or so from a busy thoroughfare. Of course it had been dark and it had been snowing. He brought her back here and slapped her around a little. There are some traces of blood drops over here and some more over there. Then he knocked her down and straddled her and strangled her."

Monaghan glanced up at Jake and that officer nodded his agreement with Jack's theory.

"So there was a short period of time when he was interrogating her. He didn't hit her because he is a sadist. He wanted something from her."

It was the officer's turn to nod in agreement.

When the three officers walked into the bar the two regular customers got up and left. The Bartender was infuriated. "Damn it thing's are bad enough and now you guys chase off my customers."

"Change your tone of voice when you're talking to me or you'll never open up this shit hole again," Monaghan warned the man.

"No offense meant officer, absolutely no offense."

"Were you here last night?" Monaghan asked.

"Yes sir. We only stay open until ten or so during the week. So I work a long shift."

"Did you see what happened in here last night?"

"What?" The bartender asked his eyes were wide with surprise.

Monaghan sighed in exasperation, "Did you see the guy come in and drag a broad out of here?"

"Oh that, well yes sir. I certainly did."

"Would you care to describe what happened?"

The Bartender looked about and leaned across the bar and begins to whisper confidentially even though his customers had all left. "This guy comes in about nine or so. He's wearing a fedora pulled down over his eyes and his coat collar is pulled up, so I really didn't get a good look at him. He walked straight back to where Sylvia was sitting and he drags a chair around and then sits down close to her. They ordered a drink and talked for a short while and then the guy kind of like, jerks her up out of her chair, really forcefully and they go out the door."

Monaghan was less than impressed. "Can you give me an impression of this guy?"

The Bartenders eyes went wide again. "What do you mean impression? I mean I don't do impressions. I used to sing a little when I was a kid, but my voice went sour when I was twelve or so."

Monaghan grabbed the Bartender's shirt front and pulled him half across the bar. "I sincerely hope that you aren't fucking with me." Monahan said. "I asked you to give me some idea of what this guy looks like? How tall was he, was he crippled, was he hunched over, what in the hell did he look like?"

"He looked like you!" The Bartender squealed. "He looked like a cop! He was all authority and arrogance!" The Bartender smiled wanly, "No offense meant officer. Perhaps that was a bad choice of words?"

Monaghan just stared at the man. He was apparently losing his patience.

The Bartender began jabbering rapidly, "Like I said, he came in here with his fedora pulled down over his eyes and his overcoat collar turned up and he looks around for a minute sizing everything up and then he heads straight for the back of the room, Straight for Sylvia. A couple of guys took one look at him and got up and paid their bar bills and left. He was that kind of guy. Nobody in that crowd wanted any part of him. He looked to be very determined."

Monaghan lowered the Bartender back to the floor, "Thank you, now that wasn't too difficult was it?"

The man straightened his shirt front running his hands over it to smooth it out. Then he shook his head in the negative.

"Did he say anything to you?"

"Well he hollered at me ordering two drinks, but other than that no sir, he didn't say anything to anybody, but I heard Sylvia call him Charley."

"What did he order?"

"Scotch for him and a shot and beer for Sylvia. I took them over to them."

"And then," Monaghan prompted.

"And then they talked for a couple of minutes and then he drags her ass out of here."

"That's it?"

"That's it."

"Thank you. Who cleans this place up?"

"A guy named Salvatore, he usually comes in when we open, but he wasn't here this morning."

"Was he around last night?"

"No sir."

"Describe him."

"He's about seventy or so, he has a game leg. But he usually does a good job cleaning up. Shit, I hope nothing happened to him."

"He wouldn't be the kind of guy that would be interested in Sylvia would he?"

The bartender shrugged, "Hell, he might try to gum her to death, but she'd slap the shit out him if he tried anything."

"She was a tough girl, huh?"

"She could hold her own. Not many guys gave her any crap."

"But this guy that dragged her out of here didn't have any trouble from her?"

The man shook his head, "She looked as though she was terrified."

"You didn't see any reason to mention that earlier?"

The Bartender shrugged.

"And none of you heroes thought to ask him what the hell he was doing?"

"I tend bar, I ain't a cop. For all I know he could have been her husband. Nobody in his right mind gets between the married folks."

"Did you ever see her with anyone else?" Jack asked.

"Yeah, she used to come in with a little Jewish guy, that used to hang out down at the Depot. But somebody killed him a couple of weeks ago."

"Did she ask for help when this guy was dragging her out of here?" Monaghan asked.

"No sir."

"Did you ever see him before?"

"No sir."

"Did you touch anything back there when you opened?"

"No sir."

Monaghan gestured to the table section, "Shall we."

The two glasses still sat on the table. "How come you didn't pick up these glasses?" Monaghan shouted.

"I was in a hurry to get out of here."

"Why?"

"Cause it was snowing again and I didn't want to get stuck here. Sometimes the street cars don't stop so regular late at night."

"What do you think, Jack?"

"I think I found her purse," Jack bent down and pulled a purse out from behind a drape. He set it up on another table.

Monaghan was examining the glasses. "The one that I assume was in front of her has lipstick and prints on it the other appears to have been wiped clean."

"There's nothing in the purse, other than the usual crap. There's a little phone book, but the numbers are scribbled and there are first names only. No Charlies are listed there. How about the back of the chair that he grabbed, is there anything there as far as prints are concerned?"

"No," Monaghan said softly.

"Shall we go over to her apartment?" Jack asked

"Indeed we shall."

As with most of the other local patrons Sylvia lived nearby. Her house keys were in her purse. It was apparent that her apartment was usually clean and neat, but it had been tossed. They decided that Charley must have been looking for something. The question was whether he had found what he was looking for?

Jake went to find the building superintendent.

Jack went downstairs to a hall telephone call in to Linda. She was all happy and bubbly. "Mister Hoover called from Washington, he is on his way, and he said to tell you that he will be here around three thirty."

Jack glanced at his watch, it was just after noon. "Tell Bill Davidson to meet him, I'll probably be at the morgue when he gets here."

"Is there anything to report?" She asked.

"Not yet. Is Charley Farrell around there?"

"He didn't look very well when he came in. When I told him where you had gone and that you were asking for him he took one of those paper bags that we have and opened Walt's safe and took a bunch of stuff and he left the safe hanging open. Then he went to the elevator. I saw him pass by and went out to ask where he was going? I anticipated that Mister Hoover would want to know."

"And what did he say?"

"He told me it was none of my business. I hope I didn't upset him, but I had to ask."

"Get Bill Davidson on the phone, please."

"Did I do wrong, Jack?"

"No Linda, you're doing just fine, get Bill for me please."

"Special Agent Bill Davidson speaking."

"Bill, this is Jack Kelly, we've got a gigantic problem and I need your help. I want you to put out an all points bulletin for the local police to apprehend and hold Charley Farrell. Check with our vehicle dispatch people and find out what kind of car he's driving."

"You're kidding right, Jack? This is a joke of some sort on Charley right?"

"No joke and I'm not kidding. If I'm wrong, I'll apologize. In the mean time please do as I ask."

Bill didn't sound convinced. "Well okay, but where are you now?"

"I'm working the murder of what could have been one of our star witnesses."

"Jesus, things are happening fast. We've got those reports ready for the Attorney General."

"Hoover's going to be here soon, we can run them by him for approval. Christ, be sure and pick him up at the airport. Bring three cars."

"We only got two and the other agents are all busy."

"Rent one if you have to, a Cadillac. And tell those guys in the office that if they ain't with us today they just might find themselves out on their ass in the snow tomorrow."

"Yeah, that ought to work," Bill laughed. "Okay, alert the cops and rent a car. Got it."

Jack stood in the doorway with Jake behind him, "I think we found the killer of Sylvia Goldberg."

Monaghan looked up from his search. "Charley?"

"Yeah, and he's making it for places unknown."

"Well, I'll be a son of a bitch. It just goes to show you, you never know."

Chapter Ten

It didn't appear that there was anything in Sylvia's apartment until Jack remembered Hymie's penchant for hiding things taped to the underside of drawers. It was there on the bottom drawer that he found a letter. It was addressed To Whom It May Concern and it was written in the form of a statement. "I Myron Howard being of sound mind and body hereby testify that I have been involved in a factoring business in which we were bilking the clients out of thousands of dollars in cash. This list contains all of the people that were involved in this scam."

There followed a list of thirty people, starting with Steven Kaplan and including his cousin Robert and Martin Werner, Barber and various other people. There was no mention of the rake off for graft paid to the politicians. It was apparently because this scam had an amazing run of longevity that Myron was growing apprehensive that the ax was about to fall. So he sought to obtain immunity by divulging the operation to the Feds. He had met Charley Farrell at Quincy Number Nine where Myron and Steve Kaplan hung out. When he discovered that "Good Time Charley" was an FBI Agent. They had entered into an agreement that would lead to the downfall of the gang, which Myron assumed would be a feather in Charley Farrell's hat. Myron had taken the time to write this explanatory letter just in case any thing went wrong. He cited the time and place of several meetings that according to Charley would eventually lead to the arrest and imprisonment of all of the participants. The end of the letter was rather upbeat. Myron had no way of knowing that he had contacted the single worst person possible.

Both police officers sat down and listened as Jack read the letter.

"I'd have never believed it," Monaghan said. Jake just shrugged.

"I'm not going to the morgue. I'm going out to the airport, because his majesty Mr. Hoover is arriving shortly. There is a lot to do, but I've got to put everything on hold while I bow to protocol." Jack frowned, he was annoyed. "For your information Dick, I've already put out an all points bulletin on Charley."

"Even before you found the letter?"

"The receptionist told me that Charley came in late and that when he found out where I had gone he emptied the safe in Walt's office and left the building."

"Was there money in the safe?" Monaghan asked.

"You got me?" Jack said, "I never had access."

Monaghan stood up, "Well you've got the letter and that's the clincher and based upon the testimony of the witnesses we can pretty well nail his ass for this murder. Case closed. Christ this was easy."

"Why didn't he kill the girl sooner?" Jake asked.

Monaghan shrugged. "Maybe he didn't want to kill her at all. He didn't kill Hymie. Crouse did. He didn't kill Kaplan, McGruder did. I think that he might have hired the gunmen to kill Walt, but I can't prove that. In fact he hasn't killed anybody as yet other than Sylvia."

"I think that it was Charley that was trying to kill me," Jack said.

"That sure as hell wasn't self defense," Jake scoffed.

Jack gestured as if he was exasperated. "Maybe when he found out how much money was really going around he realized what a piker he was."

"It's a shitty world sometimes. He sold himself for pennies, when there were thousands floating around." Jake contributed.

"Yeah it is that," Jack agreed. "Well, I was going downtown, but I'd better get my ass over to the airport to meet the Boss."

Monaghan was intrigued. "What's Hoover doing here?"

"He's going to the funerals of Walt and Mike."

It was cold and the wind was whipping across Midway Airfield at a good twenty knots. The planes were all tied down and ground crews were carefully scraping snow off of the wings. Fine flakes of snow were blowing on the wind and the temperature was dropping down to below zero. Clouds were racing across the field at an incredible rate of speed. Bill Davidson and Toby were there with two cars. Bill was delighted to see Jack with the third car.

"God, I was really getting worried, Jack. I couldn't find another car anywhere and those bastards in Treasury wouldn't lend me one." Bill was standing next to the cars and beating his gloves together to produce some warmth. "Toby's been starting them up every few minutes, to keep the oil warm."

They went into the operations building next to where the passenger terminal stood. A DC-3, twin engine aircraft landed and taxied up to the Operations terminal.

"This has got to be the boss," Jack said. He was dismayed as he counted the number of follow on personnel following Hoover across the mat.

"Where's the fourth car?" Hoover asked. He addressed his questions directly to Jack Kelly, ignoring the presence of the other two officers.

"You requested three, Sir. I have provided three. I have a copy of your message right here."

"I requested four vehicles," Hoover snarled. "Goddamn it, can't you people do anything right?"

Davidson and Toby began to drift away from the conversation and left Jack face to face with the irate little man. Jack stood his ground. "You asked for three, I have provided three."

Hoover's face was rapidly turning a beet red hue. "Are you calling me a liar, Agent Kelly?"

"I'm saying that you are mistaken, sir. If you changed the number of vehicles in a subsequent message I did not receive the update."

Hoover put his hands on his hips and leaned forward putting his face close to Jack's. "What is it that you don't understand about the employer-employee relationship, Kelly? If I tell you that I requested four cars, your position is to say yes sir. Not to argue with me."

"Yes sir, But it was three cars."

Hoover stalked away in an outrage. "Arrange your own transportation, Mister Kelly. My people are taking the cars!"

Jack turned to his two friends, shrugged and grinned. "The little bastard is nuts."

They watched as Hoover and his men jumped into the vehicle and after some cramping and shuffling drove away.

Toby grinned, "You've got a lot balls, Kelly. Don't you like this job?"

Jack smiled again. "I love it, but I evidently won't have it very long. You two guys had better steer clear of me."

"What in the hell are we supposed to do now?" Bill Davidson asked.

"Let's go to lunch."

"Lunch?" The two men asked as one. Davidson smiled at Toby and then asked Jack, "You just pissed off one of the most powerful men in the country and you suggest going to lunch?"

"What the hell else is there to do?"

They all agreed that lunch was the one reasonable suggestion.

"We'll probably all be out of work tomorrow, so what the hell." Bill Davidson said.

Jack walked into the office a couple of hours later and went to his desk. He wanted to call Monaghan to see what they had found at the morgue. A visibly distraught Linda came in to the big room and gestured to Jack. Mr. Hoover wants to see you," she said.

"Has his mood improved?"

"Not the way I see it," Linda laughed. "When he saw Walt's office he about went nuts."

"The guy is really sort of temperamental," Jack explained.

Linda hesitatingly smiled and then shook her head at Jack's attitude. "He is very angry at you."

Jack grinned, "That's perfectly irrational."

"What the hell is going on here?" Hoover demanded when Jack entered the room.

"It appears that Special Agent Farrell has committed murder and has absconded with whatever sums were in the safe and has taken flight."

Hoover took a deep breath and his eyes narrowed. Even Jack could sense that the man's mood was approaching dangerous levels. "Why wasn't I told about this?"

"Your flight was in the air, when Farrell finally showed up. There was no way to communicate with you."

"Why didn't you tell me that at the airport?" Hoover fairly shouted.

Jack shouted back in the same tone of voice. "Because you wouldn't listen! Director Hoover, you were too God damned busy making a scene about a fourth vehicle."

Linda backed out and discreetly closed the office door.

Hoover settled back in the big chair. Jack's impression was that the man had somehow shrunk. "Sit down Agent Kelly and talk to me."

Jack shrugged, what the hell, he thought. "Last night, Special Agent Farrell strangled a lady named Sylvia Goldberg was the victim. She was Myron Howard's girl friend. We have obtained a statement written by this guy Myron Howard implicating Farrell." He passed the statement to Hoover.

Hoover read the statement. "Do you think that this is valid?"

Jack reluctantly nodded. "I'm afraid so."

"Where is Farrell headed?"

"Probably for the Canadian border, but I'm just guessing. I have an all points bulletin out; we're hoping that the local police will pick him up."

"Do you think that's likely?"

"Not without casualties."

"What was in the safe?"

"I have no idea."

"So Farrell was the Mole?" Hoover asked calmly.

"It would appear so and that explains the gaps that we have in our theories."

"Explain your theories at the moment."

Jack slouched back in his chair and brought the director up to date.

Hoover frowned. "We will apprehend Mister Farrell and if we place him in prison his trial will be a circus for the press. We will be made fools of everyday in the papers everyday for weeks. I would much prefer that he not have the opportunity to embarrass the agency."

There came another soft knock at the door.

"Enter!" Hoover barked impatiently.

Linda came in and announced that the Ladysmith Police Department had the suspect surrounded in a house, there were hostages and Farrell had promised to allow the hostages to go if Special Agent Kelly would come to the house. She was obviously upset and was nervously wringing her hands.

"Call the Airport and arrange for a flight to Ladysmith. Take another agent with you." He glanced at Linda, but continued, "Remember what I said about this man being an embarrassment to the Bureau."

Jack glanced out the window at the weather. It was grey and stormy and the sun would be down in a couple of hours. Jack dreaded a flight under those conditions. "I'll drive," he said.

"Then you had better get going," Hoover said. He was clutching at the edge of the desk with both hands. His knuckles were white under the strain.

"Yes sir." Jack replied and then he winked at Linda and hurried from the office.

Jack took Bill Davidson and Toby Crowell with him. They bundled rifles and ammunition in the trunk. They wore heavy winter gear. Davidson and Crowell's heavy jackets were brightly colored hunting jackets, Kelly's jacket and trousers were white.

Bill nudged Toby and pointed to Jack's white gear. "We will be clearly seen, he will be practically invisible, is here a message here?"

Toby grinned, "Christ I hope not."

They finally arrived at Ladysmith at close to ten p.m. They had to stop by the local PD to get a guide to take them out to the farm. The Police had spotted the car and were close on the trail of Farrell when he had turned down a gravel farm road in an attempt to elude the police. He had taken refuge in a house with a family of four, two adults, a male and a female and two children. The Police had surrounded the house and Farrell had made a bargain. If the Police would get Kelly, he would let the people go unharmed. The Chief of Police was a grizzled old gentleman named Grossman, had a group of six officers and had asked for and received assistance for the local Sheriff's Department. Fires had been built in old fifty-five gallon drums and these were positioned in front of and behind the house. The officers stationed in those positions gathered around the drums warming their hands and literally trying to stay live in the minus twenty degree weather.

Jack Kelly introduced himself to Chief Grossman and quickly assessed the situation.

"We've got to get those fire barrels behind some cover. This guy Farrell is an excellent shot with a rifle and the only reason your guys aren't dead is because he made a deal with you."

As the men struggled with getting their warming barrels behind some cover Jack walked around the house. Grossman went along and Jack pointed out the areas most likely to be used for any escape attempt.

Grossman shrugged helplessly. "I ain't got enough guys to cover all this space and the weather is closing in on us. It's damn near twenty-five degrees below zero and it's getting colder. When the storm hits, maybe it will warm up a little, but not much." Grossman gestured, "It won't be long before we won't even be able to see the house from our positions."

"Is there a good point, Chief?" Jack asked with a grin.

"The good point is that there ain't nowhere for him to go and even if there was a place to hide; there ain't no way for him to get there."

Jack laughed out loud. "Put my agents out back of the house. Tell them to load up and stay the hell away from those fire barrels for as long as they can."

"You're worried about their night vision?"

"That and their lives, should he decide to start shooting."

"What are you going to do?"

"I'm going to see what he wants."

"He'll kill you."

"I don't think so. He wants something or I wouldn't be here. He could have killed your officers and have sacrificed the family that lives there in order to achieve that goal. He wants something. I'm telling you Chief that this is a good guy gone wrong. We just don't know how far wrong he's gone. But he hasn't hurt anyone here as yet."

As the Chief headed back for the front of the house the way he had come, Jack approached the house from a blind angle. The sole gunman inside wouldn't be able to see him as he approached.

The big problem was that the snow had crusted over during the last few days and with each step he announced his progress. Even with the increasing wind the crunch, crunch of each successive step in the frozen snow crusts could clearly be heard. Then Jack heard the whispered voice.

"Is that you Jack?" It was Farrell.

"Yeah, I'm right here."

"Put that cannon away and come on in."

Jack holstered the forty-five and walked up on the front porch of the house. The door swung open and he walked inside. A fire roared in the living room fire place and the flickering light cast shadows across the room. Then a single lamp came on and Jack removed his jacket and gloves. The house was warm. Farrell gestured to the man of the house. "Alright, Smitty thanks for being so reasonable about this intrusion. Take your Suzy and the kids and get out of here."

"Please don't shoot up my house. I can't afford it."

"Don't worry, Smitty. I won't hurt it. I can't guarantee that the Sheriffs won't shoot it up though."

"I'll talk to the cops," Smitty replied. "Please be careful guys. This house is all I got." Then Mister Smith led his little family out the door and across the open space to the refuge of several trucks.

Farrell turned out the lamp. "Find a seat and sit down, Jack."

Jack did as he was bid and as he did so he asked, "Why in the hell did you try to kill me Charley?"

"I underestimated you, Jack. You were getting too close and I thought that I had better get you off my ass. I thought you would be an easy mark. I'm sort of glad that it didn't work, but I had to try."

"You blew hell out of the poor kid that was trying to steal my car."

Farrell laughed. "Yeah, that was funny; it served the thieving sonofabitch right."

"What do you want to talk about Charley?"

"Uh, not much. I wouldn't have killed that stupid bitch last night, but she wouldn't stop screaming and I sort of panicked. Jesus, I told her a half a dozen times that she had nothing to worry about."

"And she didn't believe you? Can you imagine that? You had her by the neck and she didn't believe you? Can you imagine such an attitude? What a surprise."

"Alright, alright, Kelly, can the sarcasm."

"Why did you contract the killing of Walt and Caine?"

"Aw for Christ's sake, come on Jack, I didn't know that Caine would be there. Once those two idiots started shooting there was no turning them around."

"Your timing was pretty good, at least for building an alibi, but why Walt?"

"He hung out at the Quincy. I figured that he'd be able to put it all together. Oddly enough he knew those guys too. I think that he was always a bit terrified that you'd find that out."

"Were you involved in the political pay off?"

"No, isn't that something? I was getting peanuts to look the other way and those crooked bastards are pulling down thousands for sitting on their asses."

"So what do you want from me?"

Farrell went to the window. The snow was beginning to fall. "Nothing, Jack, there's nothing that you could offer me. It's all over. Killing you now won't help and I always kind of liked you. You're free to go. I'll come out in a while, maybe in the morning. I just want to be free for a few more hours, maybe to enjoy the fireplace and storm and to drink a few last beers. I don't want to hurt anyone.

The game is up, what the hell is the point of continuing? They'll get me sooner or later. Tell them to just relax and I'll come out when I'm ready."

Jack got up and put on his coat and walked to the door. Farrell offered to shake hands, but Jack ignored him. "You killed a good friend of mine. If you don't come out I'll come in and get you." As Jack strolled across the intervening space between the trucks and the house he could almost feel the sights of Farrell's rifle burrowing into his spine.

"Okay, than what's all this bullshit about wanting you to come up here?" Grossman asked.

"He was stalling for time."

"You think that he's coming out peacefully?"

"No." Jack stated emphatically. "Where's the family?"

"They're in the bus getting ready to leave."

Jack ran to the bus and banged on the door until the driver opened it. He climbed inside and faced the family. It was stifling hot in there.

"I'm glad to see that you got out of there alive, buddy. I think that guy's nuts," Smitty said.

"What did he do all that time that you folks were in there?"

Suzy piped up. "I fixed him something to eat and he drank a beer. Then he made us all go in the other room. He was messing with my sewing machine. Later on I saw that he had cut up several of my best sheets."

"Do you folks have a radio?" Jack asked.

"Yeah sure, what farmer doesn't these days?"

"And you heard that heavy weather was coming in?"

"Sure. He was listening to the weather and to the news."

"Do you have snow shoes or skis?"

"Both. You got to have them up here."

"Thanks folks, get a good night's sleep. Your house should be okay unless he starts shooting and I don't think that he will."

Jack stepped off the bus and tapped the door to signify to the driver that he was clear.

"What's the verdict, Jack?" Grossman asked.

"He's been stalling for night to fall and for the weather to deteriorate. He's coming out of there at some point."

"Well, let's upset his plans and rush the house."

"Chief," one of the Officers shouted, "he wants to talk to you."

Grossman stood in the open area and called to the house.

Farrell answered. "Get all of your married men the hell out of here. I'll give you fifteen minutes and then I'm coming out."

A rifle shot cracked in the gloom and a round whistled over Grossman's head.

"I mean what I'm saying! Then next one will be between your fucking eyes." Farrell was shouting and moving through the dark house.

Grossman was pale as he lurched to cover behind the truck. "That round went right over my head. I could hear it going by."

Gunfire suddenly broke out and a couple of the deputies returned fire. A rifle round tore a headlight off of the truck and everyone ducked. Jack began running through the woods circling towards the back of the house. Toby and Bill Davidson had opened fire at the house and there was more gunfire erupting from inside.

"Cease fire!" Jack shouted. There at the edge of the woods he caught a glimpse of a pale shadow. When the firing stopped he could hear the noise of skis on snow and the white form moving swiftly toward the woods. Jack drew his forty-five and fired repeatedly emptying the weapon in the direction of the moving blur. Then he dropped to the ground to reload. Half dozen shots sang over head. They were coming from every direction and they were much too close for comfort. "Cease fire you idiots!" He shouted. Then having completed the reloading he tentatively regained his feet. "Chief he went that way! What's down there?"

The officers and deputies closed in around the house. There was another burst of gunfire from inside and the deputies returned fire. "What in the hell are you shooting at?" Jack shouted again.

Grossman shouted a reply. "There's a river down there that leads eventually to the lake."

"He isn't in the house; he is on skis and dressed in white camouflage. If he gets down to that frozen river he will be able to go like hell. Is there a bridge that crosses the river downstream?"

"Yeah, yeah, come on," Grossman shouted. "Jake take over and you and the boys follow him, keep him moving. Come on Jack, we'll head him off at the bridge."

"Who in the hell is shooting from inside?" Jake wanted to know.

"He probably threw some rounds in the fireplace," Jack explained.

They got into the Chief's car and the old boy spun the wheels trying to get on the road. Jack calmed him down a bit and the Chief laughed, "Hell, Jack this is the most fun I've ever had."

The snow was almost blinding in the headlights and the windshield wipers just couldn't cope with the amount of falling snow so try as they might they dare not go very fast. They made the main road and turned left. Grossman increased speed again and Jack cautioned him repeatedly. About three miles down the road and perhaps two hundred yards from the bridge Grossman lost control and they slid off into the snow filled ditch. The car lurched and spun about and then came to a sudden shocking stop. Snow and ice had erupted above the careening vehicle and Grossman lost all perspective of what was happening. The radiator was broken open and steaming hot water cascaded over the front of the vehicle. Grossman had impaled his chest on the steering wheel and fell back into the seat groaning in pain. Jack had a devil of a time forcing open the door against the snow and due to a stinging pain in his leg he was limping perceptively as he came around the car to help Grossman.

"Get him, go get that bastard, I'll be alright." Grossman pointed toward the distant bridge.

Reluctantly Jack left the old man in the car and hurried as best he could toward the bridge. He was in pain and limping and soon discovered that his leg was bleeding. He assumed that he had struck the handle, or the window knob. What ever in the hell it was it hurt. He was half walking half running with an awkward gait through the deep snow. He needed skis or snow shoes in this stuff and each

240

step was a struggle as he blundered into deep snow and had to back around it. He knew that if he didn't get there soon enough that Farrell would be gone and this opportunity would be for naught. Much to his surprise he heard something behind him and looked around to see Grossman holding his chest with his right hand and carrying a shotgun in his left.

"Jesus, Chief, you ought to take it easy you could have broken a rib."

"I started this and I'll finish it," Grossman said between coughing bouts. "Your leg is bleeding; you're a fine one to talk."

Somehow they made the bridge and with great effort they slid down to the river ice. They were beneath the shadow of the bridge walking through the dry reeds when Grossman held up his hand.

"Hold it, Jack. Hear that?"

It was the swish, swish sound of skis on snow. Jack nodded and took out his forty-five.

The shadowy form materialized in the darkness.

"Halt!" Jack shouted.

Grossman fired twice. The recoil of the shotgun caused him to moan in pain. The figure in the distance stopped and was taking a rifle off his shoulders. Jack took a stance much as he would on a pistol range and began firing. This was an extreme range for him. Farrell cried out in pain and fell backwards into the snow.

Jack could see that the man was struggling with his skis.

"You got him Jack, you got him," Grossman shouted gleefully as he reloaded the shotgun.

Suddenly Farrell was up on his feet again and firing the rifle from the hip as he moved forward. Jack dove into the snow and was searching frantically for the other magazine. Grossman lifted up at the last minute and fired both barrels of the shotgun. Farrell was literally thrown backwards and into the snow. When Jack stuck his head up he saw that Grossman was moaning and lying on his back writhing in pain.

"Were you hit, Chief?"

"No, it's my chest. God damn, but I hurt."

A car stopped above them on the bridge. Jack could hear Davidson and Toby chattering.

"Down here!" Jack shouted. He bent down for a fraction of second to check the Chief and then went cautiously to where Farrell's body lay in the snow. It had been close. A fraction of a second difference and Farrell would have been the winner of the race and clear of pursuit, at least temporarily. The Chief's shotgun blast had done the work. Farrell's chest had been ripped open. Hoover had his wish, there would be no one talking to the press. Jack was suddenly very cold and very tired.

Toby took Jack and the Chief to the town Doctor while Davidson waited on the lonely bridge at the scene of the crime for the rest of the deputies. Leaving Jack and Grossman off, Toby went back for Davidson they had all agreed that the weather could be deadly.

Grossman was unconscious now and the one most obviously in pain, he was taken into the Doctor's operating room, which smelled strongly of carbolic acid and alcohol. Jack stood nearby, watching as the doctor removed the Chief's shirt and unbuttoned the long underwear. A strong odor of a long unwashed body permeated the small room. Jack reminded himself that these folks out here took baths once a week or so and perhaps not that often in the winter. The Doctor, who was much older than Grossman didn't seem particularly repelled by the body odor. As the old man touched and probed the patient. Jack glanced at the certificates on the walls. Most of which applied to degrees in Veterinarian medicine.

"The sternum has been forced back into the chest cavity; I've seen this sort of thing due to being kicked by a horse."

"He jammed his chest into that large knob on the steering wheel of his car."

"How in the hell did he do that?"

"He ran the car off the road and into a ditch. He's lucky it's not worse."

"Well he ain't so lucky after all because it can't be a hell of a lot worse than it is and there ain't a hell of lot that I can do for him."

Jack wasn't all that surprised. "Can we take him to somewhere that they have better facilities?"

The Doctor glared at Jack and then noticed the leg. "Get your ass up on this table over here and let me look at that. Now how in the hell did you do that?"

"Same accident. I think that the window knob had come off and there was just a screw sticking out."

"You guys are always driving around like hell wouldn't have it. As if those damn sirens will protect you from harm." He cut open Jack's trousers and placed a gauze bandage over the bleeding wound. "A nasty long cut that. There'll be maybe fifteen or twenty stitches or so." He looked up from his work, "There isn't anything I can do for the Chief. There isn't a hell of a lot a surgeon in the finest hospital in the land could do for him. I can't tell how many ribs are cracked due to the force imposed by that wheel, everything is badly swollen. His lungs are intact and his heart is beating. He is suffering incredible pain and it is that pain that might kill him. I have given him morphine, but it may not be of sufficient strength.. Pretty soon the lungs will load up and we'll be fighting pneumonia." Doc shrugged, "If we move him that might kill him. As I say, there ain't a hell of a lot that we can do. If he lives he may never be quite the same man again." He cleaned Jack's wound and began preparing a pain shot.

"Are you a bona fide doctor or just a Veterinarian?"

"Are you being particular?"

"Just curious."

"I'm a vet, but I've been taking care of these folks and their animals and delivering their babies, calves and colts for forty years. There are no fully certified doctors dumb enough to come up to this neck of the woods. Do you want me to continue?"

"Shoot away Doc."

The old man smiled. "What were you guys doing out in that hellacious storm?"

"We were tracking down a killer. The Chief there killed him as he was shooting back at us."

The Doc was impressed and he gave Jack the shot. "Grossman was always a ballsy old bastard. It will take a minute for that shot to take effect and then we'll sew you up."

Bill and Toby walked into the clinic. Toby laid a back pack down on a counter. "It's got ten thousand dollars in small bills in it," He announced.

"How's the Chief?" Bill asked.

Jack extended his hand and made a shaky gesture.

Bill grimaced and shook his head. "He caught Farrell dead on with both barrels. It looked as though you hit him in the shoulder with the forty-five. There were also several tears in the guy's coat where rounds went through. The Sheriff's are preserving the scene, such as it is. Farrell's body is in the morgue. The snow has stopped, but it is still freezing cold out there."

"Call, the duty officer and have him notify the Director that Farrell was killed during a confrontation with Federal Agents and local Police Officers."

Bill nodded and asked the Doctor if he could use the phone.

"It'll cost you," The Doc said, as he began punching finger into Jack's leg to test the drug effect.

"Ouch!" Jack protested, "Jesus Doc, I'm not a horse."

"Careful what you're saying sonny."

Bill grinned and picked up the phone.

As Doc sewed the wound he glanced up at Jack. "There ain't no sense in trying to drive out of here tonight. We've got a small ward attached here. I keep it for contagious diseases. There's no heat out there, but we got plenty of blankets. And Mary will fix you fellows breakfast in the morning, for a small fee, of course."

"Of course," Jack said with a laugh.

Much to Bill's surprise he got through to Director Hoover. Bill repeated the situation and stated that Farrell had been killed by the local Police. He also reported that they had recovered ten thousand dollars from Farrell's pack.

"What happened to the paperwork?"

"Sir, I don't know what you're talking about," Bill said.

"Get Kelly on the phone."

"The Doctor is sewing him up."

"You didn't tell me that he was wounded. What the hell do I have to do to pry the information out of you?"

"He was injured in an automobile accident, sir."

"Good lord! Well then, have him call me in the morning."

"Yes sir." Bill hung up the phone and looked at Jack. "What's this about paperwork?"

Jack shrugged.

Chief Grossman expired during the night and even though there was an aura of sorrow in respect to an old law man, they ate a hearty breakfast.

"Life goes on," said the doctor philosophically, "rejoice that you knew him and if you can find time during a quiet moment, remember him, but don't dwell on his passing. It is a path that we all must follow."

Chapter Eleven

Jack Kelly had missed the funerals because he didn't get back until early evening that day. They had decided to drive and that had taken hours of cautious travel. Hoover was annoyed when Jack had called that morning. There were several documents missing, one of which was Jack's original report on the people involved with Atlanta Financial. Hoover was absolutely enraged and started to take it out on Jack.

"May I remind you sir, that I had nothing to do with determining the type of material to be stored in that safe. I didn't even know that it existed. Your anger is being misdirected."

Hoover was not to be corrected. "Did you know, Special Agent Kelly, that on the flight north yesterday that Senator Caine insisted several times that you be dismissed from our service?"

That question struck Jack as would a punch in the solar plexus. For whatever reason, the thought that this man that didn't even know him was insisting upon his dismissal was totally demoralizing. For the first time in this rather tumultuous relationship Jack was subdued. There was no argument that he could offer against such a demand. He understood that he was asking a lot of the Director to protect him from a Senator's wrath."

"Well?" Hoover demanded.

"Do whatever you must do," Jack said and hung up the phone.

When the radio newscasters on the car radio began to babble about the disgraceful situation in the Chicago FBI Office, Jack turned off the radio. Toby and Bill wanted to hear the latest news, but Jack was angry and adamant. He sat there in a deep depression staring out at the barren winter landscape. Jack was depressed, perhaps as a result of the pursuit and the death of Grossman. He was so annoyed that he insisted that they drop him off at his apartment. He refused to worry about making a report concerning their activities until the next morning. Jack watched as they drove off and then went into the building. The assassin was dead and so he wasn't worried about surprises.

Levi was waiting for him when he came. "Jack, Jack have you heard? Have you read the papers?"

Jack patted his friend on the shoulder and continued down the hallway. "If you don't mind, Levi, I'm very tired. I need a hot shower and some sleep."

Levi stood there in the hallway holding the paper. He wanted to say something, but instead, he shrugged and went back inside his apartment.

Jack took his shower and after redressing the wound in his thigh, he lounged in his comfortable chair with a glass of scotch. It had been a hectic two days liberally interspersed with the lunacy that was the Director. He was tired of Hoover and this asinine on again and off again relationship with the Bureau. The Farrell thing was over. The Mole was dead. He had accomplished his mission and could leave the Bureau with a clear conscience. Hoover might not be happy about that and have a different point of view, but Jack was satisfied. Since Hoover wouldn't allow him to pursue the case as it should be, it might be better to seek employment as an investigator for some other agency surely Hoover couldn't object to that.

Then he thought about Grossman. The tough old man had kept going despite a severe injury. He wouldn't stop until he finished his work and that dedication to duty had killed him. Grossman had lived as an average guy and had died a hero. Farrell had lived as a hero and had died as a disgraceful failure. Was there a moral there somewhere? Jack remembered Grossman telling him that he was having great fun. What a hell of a way to go.

Then he began to think about Linda Manley, now that was a different sort of critter. Linda had adopted protective camouflage. It takes a dangerously clever animal to do that sort of thing. The pertinent question was as to her motive for doing that? Was she attempting to protect herself or to deceive? Linda was an intelligent, self sufficient female, her only need for the male of the species was to mate occasionally and she had accomplished that coupling with an incredibly sensuous abandon. He thought that Linda was simultaneously the most dangerous and the most desirable woman that he had ever encountered.

He had to admit that it was she that had seduced him and not the other way around. It was she that had decided that he was to be the target for the night and she had pounced upon him as would a cat upon a mouse. Well, to be honest, he had reciprocated enthusiastically. What a hell of a woman she was and what a contrast to the other girls that he had met recently. Maybe that was the difference, the other two were still girls at heart and Linda was a full fledged woman. If he were to take that one home to mom, he would have to warn his mom that he had acquired a tigress. He finally put his glass aside and turned out the lights and crawled into bed. Maybe marriage to a tigress wouldn't be all that bad, he thought, she'd sure keep him on his toes.

The morning sun burst through the drapes and lit up the room. Levi had increased the temperature and the room was rapidly warming. He shaved, freshened up, changed the bandage on his leg again and went to work. He rode the streetcar, because Farrell had destroyed his vehicle. Jack wondered if he could get the Feds to pay for the replacement. After all it was indirectly their fault. This day had begun clear and cold, but not as cold as it had been. The temperature was up to almost twenty-five degrees. It was practically toasty, when compared to last week.

A copy of yesterday's newspaper lay on his desk. On page two there was an article about "Killer Kelly," an FBI officer that in the space of three weeks had been involved in five shootings. The article then went on to describe what a hard working, dedicated person that Special Agent Kelly was and how fortunate the local citizenry was to have such a fine noble gentleman guarding the gates against the barbarians. There were two pictures of the indomitable Jack Kelly. Jack glanced at the by line. It had been written a Linda Carlisle. He wondered who in the hell Linda Carlisle might be? Jack looked at the pictures again and reread the article. Then he laughed and laid it down on his desk.

"You guys didn't know that you were working with superman did you?"

There was some laughter and few mock groans.

Bill Davidson came in, he seemed a bit unhappy. "Mister Hoover wants to see you, Jack."

Aw shit, Jack thought, here we go again.

Hoover sat on the couch and a new guy was behind Walt's desk. "Well, well, if it isn't Special Agent Kelly, a true hero of the local press. It's so nice of you to come by today Mister Kelly." Hoover wasn't smiling. "Allow me to introduce Special Agent in Charge Tom Cartwright. Tom will be the man that will put this disaster of an office back to work. Tom this is the super hero, Jack Kelly."

Jack walked forward and extended his hand. Cartwright looked at the proffered hand and then ignored it. Jack looked at Hoover and shrugged. "This is the guy that's going to rebuild agent confidence and moral?" Kelly laughed sarcastically. "Okay boss, what do you want me to do now?"

"Sit down and shut up," Hoover growled.

Jack shrugged again and took the chair that had been positioned directly before the desk. He sat there staring straight ahead at the official seal that hung behind the desk. Jack appreciated the theatrical effect. Mister Cartwright, a short, slim built balding man, sat there between the flags of the country and the state and beneath the Federal Seal. Obviously he thought himself to be a very important man. The desk was cleared of everything. This was obviously to be a fresh, efficient regime, not like the slovenly management of that poor messy slob Walt Albright. Jack waited patiently. It was an old game to him. They wanted him to ask a question, or to fidget a bit, or to exhibit some degree of nervousness. He sat there stoically.

It was Cartwright that broke the silence and Hoover frowned at the man. "Have you seen today's paper Mister Kelly?"

"No sir."

"Don't you normally read the morning paper, Mister Kelly?"

"Rarely," Jack replied succinctly.

Cartwright was growing frustrated. "The morning paper contains a complete copy of what I have been told was your original confidential report to Mister Hoover. How do you suppose they managed to come by that document?"

Jack almost grinned, but he didn't. In his opinion the damned fool had just opened up Pandora's Box. "The assumption is that after Charley took the money he left the safe open and at that point Charley's former secretary took whatever she wanted, knowing that we would blame it on Charley. However, given the number of leaks in this office there may be some other leak, if which I'm not aware."

"It couldn't be that you gave it to them could it?"

"It could be, but it wasn't."

"Can you prove that?"

"Prove what?"

"Don't toy with the man, Kelly," Hoover almost shouted. "Can you prove that you didn't give that report to the newspapers?"

"No. Can you prove that I did?" Jack asked angrily. "You may have forgotten but the burden of proof lies with the accuser,"

"I don't have to prove anything," Hoover said angrily. "If I even thought that you did I would fire you right this very minute! Have you got that?"

"Obviously even you don't think that I did it. So what's the question?"

Hoover was obviously fuming. Cartwright stepped in, "We had to ask, Agent Kelly."

Jack relented somewhat. "Why in the hell would I give them a report that is of no use? We can't pursue the bad guys. I listed nine you gave me five. I don't know why you did that and I don't care. Maybe the others are already in your employ as informers, or soon will be. Those are decisions to be made at the executive level. I'm used to that sort of thing and while I find it annoying, I also understand that there are things that I don't need to know."

Hoover suddenly sat back in his couch and his expression changed as if by magic. In fact he even smiled slightly. Cartwright looked at the Director and then at Kelly as if he too had sensed that something had changed.

"That woman that was here as a secretary, Linda Manley was her name. She did not return today. I believe that she is the one that walked out of here with our reports, and I believe that those reports were taken from Walt's safe." Hoover gestured angrily. "I have contacted Colonel Murray at the Examiner and he has denied any knowledge of the theft. He did say quite a bit about the Goddamn thieving Democrats ruining the city, but I tend to ignore local politics."

Jack thought about Linda Manley and unconsciously looked over at the couch. Could she be the writer? Of course she could, but would she be this Linda Carlisle? Quite possibly, he thought.

"I wasn't aware that she had left permanently," Jack said. "I do know where she lives. I could check on her."

Hoover brightened up. "Her other address and phone numbers were all false. Give her address to Mister Cartwright and he will send agents to check on her. If she is the one, we can take her into custody."

"What would the charge be?" Jack asked.

"Theft of Government documents," Cartwright contributed.

"Thereby, giving complete authenticity to her reports, that's very clever," Jack laughed. "It would be difficult to deny the accuracy of her stories after dragging her ass off to jail."

Hoover frowned at Cartwright, but said nothing. Then Hoover handed the newspaper to Jack.

It was all there. The story about the band of swindlers and of the pay offs to the local politicians and about the murders that led the officers to the trail, unfortunately, there was no end to the story. There was nothing about Sylvia Goldberg dying face down in the snow, or about a Special Agent in Charge being the killer. She had missed the story of a good man dying as he did his job fighting for his little town. He could almost read Linda in that article. So she was a reporter and a liar and a betrayer, but somehow that wasn't a surprise. Linda Manley or Carlisle, or whatever her name might be, it was all about Linda and in Jack's opinion that was a shame and a waste. Of course there had been no pledge of love or devotion on her part. She hadn't pretended to be anything but hungry. Jack couldn't even remember the subject of love ever coming up. He decided that it was probably a very good thing that he didn't try to take her home to mom.

Jack dropped the paper on Cartwright's desk.

Hoover leaned forward. "I'm sending you over to the Attorney General's office as a liaison officer. It will be your duty to assist the Assistant Attorney General for this District in proving our case and resolving any issues remaining open." He looked at Cartwright and then continued. "At the moment this transfer should remove you from the lime light. I want to you to play it low key. I feel that I owe you one, because you did a good job up north. You will find that I am loyal to my agents."

Jack nodded and stood up. So Hoover was going to hide him from Senator Caine? Jack supposed that he ought to be grateful, but he was less than enthusiastic about this assignment. Frankly, he wanted out of this case, even though this murderous bastard McGruder was still out there somewhere. Special Agent Cartwright offered his hand and Jack just looked at it and then left the room. He felt that last bit was a cheap insignificant gesture and should have been beneath his dignity, but there was a flickering moment of satisfaction.

Jack gathered his gear, what little there was of it, and said goodbye to his few friends. He had a premonition that he would never return to this office and that he was on his way to his own personal Siberia. This assignment was just a temporary truce between him and Hoover. The two men clashed every time they met and Jack couldn't believe that it would ever go away between them. On the other hand there was an opportunity offered here. He was an attorney and maybe it was time that he grew up and went to work and stopped chasing bad guys.

The Federal Attorney's office was on the twelfth floor and so the change involved just an elevator ride. Even so Jack felt as though he had stepped into another world. When he introduced himself to the secretary she asked him to wait in the outer office while she found out how to direct him. Jack had the impression that they weren't ready for him and didn't know what the hell to do with an FBI Agent. After a bit the lady, a gal in her forties, came out and led him to a barren office on the eleventh floor. It was little more than a broom closet and Jack figured that this rousing welcome was to set his level of activities for the Attorney General.

An hour later another woman entered the room. "I'm Mildred," She announced. "I'm J. Townsend Ashman's secretary."

He watched her. "Am I supposed to bow or supplicate at the name?"

"You're supposed to come with me," she explained irritably. "Are you ready?"

"For what?" He asked.

"Why to come along."

"Sure. Well wait a minute; I have so much to do here. No, no it will be alright, let's go."

She looked at him askance and then realized he was teasing her. She grinned widely. "Okay follow me."

He decided that she had a very nice ass and was probably a nice girl. "Are you married?" He asked.

Mildred blushed and ignored him.

J. Townsend Ashman was lumpy. His suit looked as though he had been sleeping in it. Cigar ashes liberally decorated the vest that stretched tightly against a generous girth. He was partially bald. Strands of hair had been stretched across his beet red pate as if to fool the casual observer into thinking that J. Townsend had hair. It was not an effective camouflage. As with many of his ilk, J. Townsend was pretending to be busy. Jack assumed that it was trick learned early on by all Federal Employees.

Jack stood there hands folded behind him, politely waiting for the potentate to speak.

J. Townsend looked up as if in surprise. "Oh my, you're here, uh sit down make yourself comfortable young man. I have your personnel folder here."

Jack sat down. He classified J Townsend as a harmless idiot. Then he corrected himself, no bureaucrat is completely harmless.

J. Townsend looked up at Jack. "It says here that you are an attorney. You have passed the Illinois Bar and everything, well good, yes good indeed. The FBI usually sends accountants to us. Very useful in many of our cases, but some what limited in scope as it were. And you were a Marine, My, my, I'll bet that was exciting. You speak Chinese fluently, my how odd. We don't get many Chinese cases." He looked up again as if to verify that Jack was still sitting there. "Well Mister Kelly, uh may I call you Jack?"

Jack nodded his approval.

"You don't talk much do you? That's very unusual for an attorney."

Jack just smiled.

J. Townsend leaned across his desk indicating that this was to be confidential information. "I've been assigned the responsibility of prosecuting the five people that your report listed as being on the take from the ill gotten proceeds of the Atlanta Finance Company. Unfortunately, even before we start, our case has been dealt a heavy blow. The newspapers, uh the Examiner specifically, contends that there were actually nine suspects. Is that true Special Agent Kelly?"

Christ how do I field this one, Jack wondered. Then operating on the questionable theory that the truth can't hurt you, he nodded. "My original report listed nine people, all of whom are local politicians and who are said to have been the recipients of large amounts of cash as bribes from Atlanta Financial."

"Why were four people omitted from the list, wasn't the evidence as damning?"

"There was considerable evidence that all of these people were taking bribes from Atlanta Financial, but the paper work was rather one sided in that the only evidence that we have was a set of books prepared by one Martin Werner, now deceased. In fact he was murdered, by one of our suspects. We have no evidence that the money was actually paid out or that it ever actually reached the hands of the accused."

"Then it will be your job to make that connection, is that correct Mister Kelly?"

Jack stared into the eyes of J. Townsend. This guy has already got me confused, Jack thought, am I Special Agent Kelly, or Jack or Mister Kelly. "That seems to be the issue," Jack replied.

"And how do you intend to accomplish that grand objective?"

Jack cleared his throat and fidgeted for J Townsend's benefit. Two can play at this game, Jack thought. "There is a single person. Allegedly a Mister Warren McGruder, our primary suspect, I'm not certain that McGruder is his real name. Warren was the go between that took money from the thieves that they paid for protection from the law. They were stealing that money from some of our less than honest citizens and he was in charge of distributing money to the politicians. He was the pay off man. We must apprehend him and obtain his confession."

J. Townsend seemed dubious. "Do you think that's even remotely possible?"

"I'm an attorney, I like to think that anything is possible, but only if we can get to him first."

"First?"

"Before whoever else there is looking for him gets to him."

"How do we know that anyone else is looking?" J. Townsend wanted to know.

"It is inevitable. Mister McGruder is rapidly becoming a liability."

J. Townsend nodded and then asked, "What next?"

"We subpoena those nine culprits and threaten to drag them all in here one by one unless they cooperate by providing information on their relationship with our mystery man. We interview those that do cooperate and let the press know that they have refused to talk to us. Those that actually refuse to talk to us we drag in here and tell the press that they have cooperated fully."

"That's reminiscent of Alice in Wonderland and absurd and somewhat confusing."

"They are politicians. By the very nature of their work they are bribe takers. That's what they do for a living. Are you so naive as to believe that they can live in the style to which they are accustomed, on the money we citizens pay them?" Jack laughed sarcastically.

"Those that cooperate we must drag in so that they will appear to be recalcitrant, which will please their bosses and cohorts. Those that will not come in willingly we will identify as being cooperative with the investigation."

"That's a fine fantasy twist of the facts. And what do you suppose will be the effect of that lunacy?"

"Their friends will grow suspicious of those that we claim are cooperating. If they get too suspicious a few politicians just might disappear."

"Good lord man do you know what you're saying? We could be sending these men to their deaths."

"What I'm saying is that they had damned well better cooperate."

"And how do you get the press to cooperate with this lunatic scheme?"

"We have an exposé writer that owes us a great deal. Through our stupidity we have just made her career. However, if we want to get mean, we can destroy her just as quickly. The terms are simple; she will either cooperate or go to jail."

"Do you know this woman?"

"Intimately."

J. Townsend smiled for the first time during the interview. "I do believe that you will fit in perfectly here Special Agent Kelly. You seem to have a fine knack for the job."

Jack had also begun to develop a different appreciation of J. Townsend. The absurd costume that the man wore and the fumbling impression were lures to deceive the unsuspecting. J. Townsend had a sharp mind. The job might even be fun for a while.

"Mildred!" J. Townsend shouted. "Get Special Agent Kelly a nice office on this floor close to our office. We will require a close liaison."

"But sir the only office that could be made available is Basil Carter's."

"Yes, my dear, that's a pity. We shall miss Basil's smiling face in the morning. Please, get on with it as soon as possible." J. Townsend smiled again at Jack. "I shall prepare the subpoenas right now and you can begin delivering them this afternoon. How soon do you estimate that we will be able to identify and incarcerate this Warren fellow?"

"I'll go over to the paper this morning to confirm my suspicions concerning the reporter and have a little chat with her. Then we'll get started on the politicians."

"You should take some Marshals with you this afternoon. How many do you want?"

"None. I don't want any witnesses."

"You have some great ideas, Jack, but allow me to suggest that to impress politicians you must come in with power. That is what will get their attention and I would suggest that the more witnesses that we have the better it will be for us. You might even get your lady friend to come along."

"I'll bow to your experience."

"You say that your relationship with the girl was close?"

"It couldn't get any closer, but I doubt that relationship will prevail for long."

J. Townsend chuckled. "I dare say you are probably right about that. Oh well." he chuckled again, "There's always another streetcar."

Mildred was standing in the doorway frowning at both of them. "Your new office will be ready this afternoon, Agent Kelly."

Jack left the office at noon and headed for the Examiner in a government car that had been specifically assigned to him. As he drove along he decided that the one good thing about J. Townsend was that you couldn't trust him any farther than you could throw him. There is a value to knowing that your erstwhile business acquaintances can't be trusted. You'll never be surprised by what they do.

Jack was ushered into the newsroom and asked to take a seat in a small reception area. He stood there waiting patiently and enduring a good deal of finger pointing and whispering. Miss Linda Carlisle finally came out of her office and wordlessly led him back there. She casually indicated a chair and went behind her desk.

"Miss Carlisle you look suspiciously like someone I used to know."

"Don't you know me anymore, Jack?" She asked softly.

"It seems that I know you far too well, my dear."

"I never promised you anything." She was growing defensive.

"Nor I you, so we start even again."

"What is it that you want?" Now she was feigning impatience and righteous anger.

"I'm going to offer you another scoop. Are you interested?"

She looked at him for a long minute, "Why do I suspect that you are less than sincere?"

Jack smiled, "I'll be perfectly candid, you are going to do this for us or I'm going to have you arrested for betraying your oath to the government."

"You'll have a hell of a time proving it."

"Perhaps that's true, but we will pursue the case for the next several years and our platoons of lawyers will bleed your family fortune in the courts until it is no longer existent. The Federal Revenue Authorities will inquire into your family farm and other investments. I'm certain that they will be able to tie things up for years. And after all that, after months of trial, when your family has been reduced to penury and long after the newspapers lose interest, I will throw your ass in jail for theft of government property. We may lose our case in the end, Linda, but it will be your family that will be the real loser."

"You are a vindictive son of a bitch." She said bitterly.

"Precisely and I detest people that would betray their oath for a by line and a new office."

Linda grew defiant. "I'm a reporter. My job is to gather the news."

"Your job was to act as a secretary to the Agent in Charge of an FBI office. Your oath was to safe guard the evidence, not to flaunt it before the eyes of the curious."

"That's your version of events. I am protected by the First Amendment."

"It seems the ultimate irony to me, that your betrayal from prosecution is protected by the deaths of honorable men." He waved a hand to silence her. "I'm not going to arrest you for betraying your oath to the government. I am ultimately arresting you for thievery and that I can and will prove."

She stood there glaring at him and then she sat down behind her desk. "You mentioned an alternative. I will not print falsehoods."

He began laughing sarcastically. "You will print anything that I tell you to print. You have already proved that you are incapable of telling the truth, so what the hell is one more lie?"

"Why are you doing this to me?"

"Because, my dear, you are the only one that can do the job that needs done. You have the byline and this is your case. Let's face it Linda Carlisle or Miss Manley, or whatever in the hell your name is, you have made your bed and now you must lie in it."

She folded her hands on the desk and her knuckles were white with pressure. "What is it I must do?" She said resignedly.

He wasn't fooled for a minute. As far as he was concerned this girl's real name was treachery. "I am laying a trap for a murderer. In order to do that, I intend to intimidate the nine politicians on your list into cooperating with me. I need a good description of the killer and some viable back ground information. I'm going to get it from the politicians or their aides. I will protect the ones that cooperate. The ones that don't cooperate will go into the papers as being enthusiastically cooperating with the FBI."

"You're going to get someone killed."

Jack smiled and shrugged, "There has been a lot killing going around lately. A lot of maiming, mauling and killing, including two Federal Agents and a Chief of Police and I want it to end."

"Even if some innocent person might die for it?"

"We aren't dealing with innocents. We're dealing with a collection of blood suckers and as far as I'm concerned they've got it coming in spades."

"You're a goddamn Nazi," she accused him.

He smiled again, "Yeah, you might say that. I want a killer and I'm going to get him. Are you going to cooperate?"

"No! Hell no!" She jumped to her feet and her eyes were flashing with anger.

Jack stood up. "Have it your way. I'll see you in court," He said softly. "You'll be served this afternoon. Oh and do me one last favor, why don't you try to run. That will make it a lot more fun for the other papers and give the Marshals something to do."

She slumped back in her chair. "Wait, wait. Where do I meet you?"

"I don't think you're submissive enough my dear. I can almost see the little plots cooking up in your head. I think that I had better demonstrate my determination by throwing your ass in jail for a few days, or turning the Feds loose on your family."

Tears streaked down her cheeks.

He laughed crudely, "My mother once told me to never marry a girl that can cry on cue."

"You rotten bastard," She leaped to her feet and threw a dictionary at him.

He grinned again. "That's better, sweetie. Two o'clock at the office of the States Assistant Attorney General."

"Why him?" She asked calmly.

"Because he is going to want to fight the charges."

"What do you intend to do?"

"You can read about it in the papers."

"Asshole!" Linda shouted as he walked out of her office. Several of the other reporters had been watching him out of curiosity. Now they were all laughing and so was he. He winked at one gal and kept going. Then the reporters exchanged glances and shrugged they weren't quite sure of what had happened.

The local office of the State Attorney General was manned by an assistant named Buckminster Williams. Bucky was well known for playing fast and loose with the law and with the money of other people. Jack and seven United States Marshals and Miss Linda Carlisle and her photographer walked into Bucky's office and went right by his secretary. The esteemed Mister Williams was having a private lunch with two civilian contractors. Jack chased them out of there and closed the door. He laid the subpoena on Bucky's desk.

"Who are you and what the hell is that?" Bucky demanded.

"That is a subpoena for you and your records. I want to know all that you know about Atlanta Financial."

"Fuck you," Bucky grinned and pointed to the door.

"Now Bucky old boy, I don't want you to get me wrong. I'm after a murderer. His name is Warren McGruder. He is wanted for four counts of murder and I expect you or your aides to tell me all that you know about Mister McGruder and about the bribery."

"I already told you what you could do with yourself and with that asinine warrant."

Jack walked around the desk and grabbed Bucky by the back of the neck and hauled him around the desk to the door. He then opened the door and dismissed the Federal Marshals; He put an arm around Bucky and announced for the press that Mister Williams had promised his fullest cooperation with the investigation. Bucky tried to struggle for a moment, but Jack grabbed his arm in a vise like grip. "Have you anything you'd like to say Mister Williams?"

Bucky smiled, he always smiled when his picture was being taken it was a habit that he couldn't break. "Yes, yes," he said with the eternal smile. "I promise my fullest cooperation."

Then Jack closed the door and pushed Bucky back behind his desk. "Now Bucky, I want you to think about what just happened. Your picture will be in all the evening papers as promising to cooperate with the FBI in this murder investigation. Now I know that you don't have any problem with that, but you may have a problem with all of your contributors, because what you don't know is that you are listed as being part of a rake off of a fraud operation. The word the paper will publish is that you're giving states evidence, concerning the fraud and the skimming of funds." Jack gestured vaguely, "That may make some people very nervous." Jack walked over and calmly sat down. "Now I could change that to say that you refused to cooperate, and I will, if you will just give me what I need."

"Get the fuck out of here."

Jack grinned widely, "Somehow I thought that you'd say that. I wonder how your friends in Cicero will take this article." Jack gestured again, "What the hell, nobody believes the goddamn newspapers anyway."

Bucky sat down behind his desk, "Wait a minute, just wait just a minute." It was as if he was reasoning aloud with himself. "You're right nobody believes the goddamn papers, I'll call the Examiner and refute the claim that you just made"

"Fine and by refusing to cooperate with the law you will confirm the suspicions of the citizens and then all the people in the city will know what a useless bastard you are." Jack stood up, "Don't worry most of them already know that you're a lying shit anyway."

"What do you want?"

Jack leaned across the desk, "What I really want Bucky is a bad example. I want the mob boys to blast your ass so that my reception in the next office goes a lot easier. Don't worry, Bucky it won't be tonight, maybe not for a week or so, but one of these cold nights someone is going to come after you, because they can't trust you any more. And Bucky, you really deserve it."

"Are you insane?"

Jack shrugged, "Maybe a little."

"Stop this! Right now, right this minute! Stop this!"

"I haven't heard anything that I want to hear."

"For Christ's sake, I've got a wife and three kids. They're all in college. Do you know how much a college educations costs? Do you think I can make it on the shit salary they pay me?"

"I don't think it would make any difference what they pay you. You'd still have your paw in the till."

"You can't do this."

"The other night I held a dying Lawman in my arms. He fought until the very end; He was a game old bastard. One of your kind killed him and you expect mercy from me?"

"Get out of here! Get out! You can't scare me!"

Jack walked out of the office and met his crew out on the street.

"Did you get what you wanted?" Linda asked with a smirk. One look at his face gave the answer to her question. "I could have told you so!" She uttered a snide laugh, "Where next genius?"

Jack gave her the address of another North side Alderman and the force was off to their next target. This guy was awed by the intrusion as was his secretary and the few visitors that he had in the office. Jack laid down the subpoena and stared at the older man. He explained his theory and asked. "Mister Wiseman. I'm after a killer. Are you going to help me?"

Wiseman got up and closed the door. "Get those asshole reporters out of here and tell me what you want to know."

Jack went to the door. He addressed the Senior Marshal. "Mister Wiseman refuses to cooperate with us. Take the crew and the reporters and go back to the office. Turn the reporter loose when you get back downtown. I'll be here for a while."

The Marshal winked conspiratorially and left herding Miss Linda and her photographer out the door.

Jack sat down and asked about him Mister Warren McGruder.

Wiseman ordered some coffee and told his secretary to chase off the petitioners for the day. "I read about the killings of the Kaplans and wondered when you'd get to me? It's like waiting for the other shoe to drop. Frankly I'm glad you came, maybe I can sleep nights again. This guy McGruder is a very rough character. He pretends to be smooth and sophisticated, but he's a mean little bastard. I always thought that he was tough and smart, but when he killed Kaplan that bothered me. I began to wonder who would be next. He is about fifty-five maybe a little older. He is not muscular, but solid. He always dresses well. I never knew him to carry a gun. On the other hand I never doubted that he knew how to use one. He is reasonably well educated and once, a long time ago he served as a deputy sheriff down in Georgia or Alabama, or some such god-forsaken place. I forget where. He only spends some of his time here in Chicago. The rest of the time he lives in Washington. His real name is Arbuthnot and he works for some high up official. I saw the article in the Examiner the other day. We all got a little rake off from Kaplan to look the other way. So what's new? This guy McGruder would come up here about once a month or so and hand out the cash. It was a good deal. What the hell do I care about what they're doing? It was small time bullshit. Maybe not to McGruder or to them, but to me it was just a little spending money. Aw, I got a new car out of it, but it wasn't that big a deal. Frankly it wasn't enough for me to really worry about. I spill more on the bar than I ever got from them."

"You know more than you're telling me. Who does McGruder work for?"

Wiseman sat back and considered his options. "As I recall he was representing Senator Caine. McGruder has a house on the North side. He gave a party there one night about six months ago. Hey Cassie," He shouted. "Get me that address of that schmuck McGruder and there's another address where we sent his Missus a Christmas card." Mr. Wiseman sat back in his chair. "The only thing I want from you Mister Kelly is to get this murderous little bastard and put him away and after that you can stop looking."

Jack was shocked by the reply. "Do you want me to station a couple of Marshals around you until I put him down?"

"Goodness no! The locals see a couple of cops watching me and my whole business goes to shit. No, Mister Kelly, you take care of yourself and my advice to you is to be very careful, you got a lot people scared and when they get scared they get dangerous."

Cassie gave Wiseman the addresses and he passed them on to Kelly. "Is there anything else Mister Wiseman?" She asked.

"No, we'll be closing up for a week or so, Cassie. Why don't you go visit your sister? I'll call and tell you when to come back."

"Thank you, Mister Wiseman."

Jack smiled at the addresses. "Maybe we can do some good with these."

"I hope so," Wiseman said. "Take care Mister Kelly, I want you to take out this dangerous schmuck."

Jack didn't bother to offer to shake hands with Wiseman. They were on opposite sides of the law, but he still held the man in respect. "I'll tell the press what an uncooperative prick you are Mister Wiseman."

"Good! And goodbye to you Special Agent Kelly."

It was growing dark and colder as he left Wisemen's office. Jack called J. Townsend. I need a warrant for a house." Jack gave him the address. "Have somebody meet me there about six."

Then remembering a promise that he had made he called the number of a friend, "Bennie, I know a lady that needs a lot of help getting her face fixed and she ain't got any money."

"Not, hello Bennie, how are you and how's the kids? How's the wife? No, just, I need help for some broad. Call the Red Cross you Irish prick."

"Bennie, I'm working for the FBI now. You know they don't pay for shit."

"I see the newspapers. You're getting famous in an odd sort of way. What did you do bust some broad's jaw?"

"She's an old street girl and this moron hit her across the face with a forty-five. The front sight probably tore up her jaw. She told me that they said that they can't fix it. I know that you and Harry can fix anything."

"Oh shit, here it comes. Don't try to put me on a guilt trip. I still got to pay my bills."

"Think of the publicity, famous Chicago surgeon repairs lady's scarred face."

Bennie started laughing, "You just told me that she's a whore, what kind of glory do I get out of that? Okay, okay, send her around. I'll con Harry into doing it."

"Bless you my boy," Jack said mimicking a Priest's voice.

"Goniff!" Bennie said with a laugh. "Next time send me some rich broad."

Jack was smiling as he hung up. Maybe there were still a few good people left in the world.

Jack grabbed a quick supper and was waiting on the steps of the deserted mansion when Mildred showed up with the warrant.

"The house belongs to a guy Warren Arbuthnot," she said. "It's on the market."

He thanked her and watched as she drove away.

The Arbuthnot home was in a grand neighborhood and some of the Christmas decorations were still up as if the people were reluctant to let go of the cheery holiday. Taking a flashlight and a pocket full of batteries he went into the house. It was empty. Everything had been cleared out and had apparently cleared out in a hurry there were marks left on the walls as the furniture had been moved out. He checked the basement and found it cluttered with refuse, but with nothing of significance. Then Jack climbed to the attic and found a dress makers form which would be suitable for a rather matronly lady. Amongst the few things remaining was wicker sewing basket. Jack opened it and beneath a removable shelf he found some photographs. There was one of Mrs. Arbuthnot standing next to her husband. She had conveniently labeled all of the photos. There was another of Warren with his arms around Steve Kaplan and Senator Caine. Then there was one with Arbuthnot standing in the background as Senator Caine and the President shook hands. The Attorney General and the Speaker of the house were looking on and smiling. Jack put all the photographs in his pocket and left the house.

Chapter Twelve

Jack met J. Townsend Ashman at the airline counter. His boss had the tickets in his hand.

"Have you heard the news, Special Agent Kelly?"

Jack shook his head. "I have heard nothing other than the fact that Linda Carlisle and her boss Colonel Murray are more than mildly annoyed."

J. Townsend frowned, "Oh yes, there is that. The Colonel has called the White House, the Attorney General and the Director. He wants you fired." His boss smiled briefly, "The Director has spent damned near an hour asking me to explain how you were allowed to twist the dragon's tail."

Jack smiled at the odd simile. "What did you tell him?"

"That you were using that tactic to drum up some reaction and that we would not be doing that sort of thing again."

"And he said?"

"There was some rather vile invective, but he assured me that we would not transgress again or we would both be out on the street on our asses."

"He has fired me before."

J. Townsend looked over his glasses at the younger man, "so I have repeatedly heard."

"What other news did you have reference to?" Jack asked.

J Townsend smiled. "There was an attempt on Bucky Williams' life tonight."

Jack paled and his stomach churned. "The Mob?"

J. Townsend smiled. "No, it turned out to be a dissatisfied local that had been planning the assassination for quite sometime. We haven't informed Mister Williams as to the nature of the threat. We thought it better to keep that to ourselves."

"How did all this come about?"

J. Townsend smiled again. "To ah, well to be candid, and to cover our collective asses, I detailed two agents to keep track of Bucky. I didn't want the man actually hurt. He was coming out of his favorite bar at about six-thirty and this unkempt looking gentleman came at Bucky with a gun. He fired three shots and our boys returned fire. The culprit is currently recuperating at Chicago Lying In, which was the nearest hospital. Mister Williams, wasn't harmed, but is suffering under the impression that it was the mob exacting retribution for his allegedly making a deal with us and he is presently singing his little heart out at our office." J. Townsend paused for a minute, "Which, it so happens, is the only reason that we are both still employed. You do seem to have a facility for falling in excrement and coming up with a pleasing fragrance."

Jack informed J. Townsend that the house had belonged to a Mr. Arbuthnot who it was rumored worked for Senator Caine.

When, J. Townsend heard that remark he sucked in his breath and looked up at Jack with wide eyes. "Good Christ, Jack!"

Jack described his find and showed several pictures to J. Townsend. "We need an enlarged photograph of Warren Arbuthnot," Jack said. "And you might enhance Bucky's testimony with this photo of him with his arms wrapped around a four time murderer."

J. Townsend had recovered to some degree and nodded in appreciation. "I'll show this to him in the morning." He paused and then looked over his glasses again. "Look, Jack, about this photo of Senator Caine and the President..."

"I'll hold on to it, boss. It may or may not be of some future use."

"Yes, yes, you hold on to it, by all means. Let me know what you find in the morning."

"By the way, what has our friend revealed?"

"He has admitted to the bribery by Mister Arbuthnot and has implicated all of his friends. It seems that they were doing so well that they used to have monthly dinners where the bribes were passed out. Mister Arbuthnot paid for everything."

"They were probably being set up, by Arbuthnot. I suspect that whoever he was working for had them all by the ass, politically speaking of course. Arbuthnot took the payments from Kaplan and whoever else was contributing to the fund and made the payments to the politicians. He probably kept close track of who was getting what, and anticipated that someday they would all demonstrate their loyalty or obedience to him by voting the way the Senator wanted them too."

J. Townsend nodded. "Bucky was the exception. He was probably there to insure the others that the Justice Department was in on the scheme and that they were all as safe as babes in their mother's arms."

Jack nodded. "It sounds complex, but it would have been easy to set it up. But how in the hell does this guy Arbuthnot figure in?"

J. Townsend smiled. "We have been doing some checking. Allegedly, he was Senator Caine's political advisor during the last election campaign. He arrived in Chicago about two years ago. He is a registered Political Consultant in Washington and his original office was located in Atlanta Georgia."

"I wonder if that was a coincidence." Jack speculated.

"What was that?"

"The original name of the company was Atlanta Financial. We might check with the Georgia Attorney General to see if there was a connection."

"Here are your tickets Mister Kelly. You plane will be leaving shortly. Good luck and good hunting. Damn, I always wanted to say that." J. Townsend Ashman was laughing.

Jack rolled his eyes exaggeratedly, nodded and then he smiled, he shook hands with J. Townsend and headed for the door. As he strolled out to the plane he noted that the wind was rising again and that it was clouding up. He was a bit apprehensive as he climbed aboard. It seemed odd that airplanes would fly at night and in bad weather, but the Stewardess seemed quite composed and smiled prettily as each passenger came aboard.

There was the usual discomfort as Jack slid into his seat and fumbled with the straps. It was chill in the plane even though one engine was turning and the heater system was struggling against the cold. There was a slight delay and then the door was closed and the port engine was started. The lights dimmed as the generator came on line and then everything seemed to brighten up and it grew warm. Ice and snow lined the taxiways and blue lights outlined the route. They taxied to the end of the runway and Jack could sense that the pilots were fighting the wind as they moved along. One engine was revved up and then the other. Then they took the runway. The Stew hurried back and slid into the empty seat. Jack could see that the wind was pushing the plane ever closer to the eight foot high stacks of snow that lined the runway even though the left wing was almost down on the ground. Then they were in the air and the aircraft slewed into the wind. The impression that Jack received was that they were flying sideways down the runway. He realized that they had simply turned to compensate for the wind and were still following on the runway heading.

True to J Townsend's word four Marshals in two cars met him on the tarmac at Washington National. The other passengers and the Stew were impressed that these government cars had met one of the passengers. With great ostentation the men removed shotguns from the trunks of the vehicles and put them inside. Then Jack greeted them and they all got in a drove off.

A red sun was just coming up on a beautiful day as they turned into a small rustic community.

"Red at dawning," One Marshal began to quote.

Jack nodded. "It was blowing like hell in Chicago last night. I imagine it will all catch up with us later today."

"Who is this guy we're after?" The lead Marshal, Harry Moffett asked.

Jack looked up from his scribbled notes. It was time to get serious. "Warren McGruder, alias Arbuthnot, a political advisor, consultant, and murderer. He killed three people in cold blood and then watched as a henchman cut the throat of pretty girl." Jack passed the picture around. "He's the guy on the left."

"Ain't that the Senator on the right?" Harry asked.

"It is."

"Christ." Harry said in awe. 'What in the hell are we into?"

"The Senators presence may have no significance." Jack suggested.

"Then again, on the other hand it may, right?" The Marshal suggested.

"That's a fact." Jack replied.

"You Chicago guys always bring some serious crap to the table. What are we to do?"

"We have a search warrant correct?"

"That's correct."

"What are the restrictions?"

"We are specifically searching for Mister Arbuthnot or anything that will lead us to his whereabouts."

"That gives us a little slack, inferring that we can interpret what we are looking at, right?" Jack asked.

"That's the way I read it, but the court will second guess us if we over step our bounds."

"Big deal. They always do." Jack turned to the Marshal. "May I ask what your mission is today?"

"Today and everyday while you're here, I'm here to watch you."

"That was candid and to the point."

Harry laughed, "I think you kind of scare the AG." Then he looked at Kelly eye to eye. "You're not going to do anything really stupid are you?"

"I hope not," Jack responded.

Arbuthnot's home was set on the corner of a cul de sac. Trees and brush surrounded the house and flower gardens lined the walkways. Two Marshals went to the rear of the house and Jack and his team went to the front door. Jack had just raised his hand to knock when the door opened.

It was a matronly lady, who announced that she was Missus Arbuthnot and she asked what she might do to help these gentlemen?

"Is Mister Arbuthnot at home, Mam?" Jack asked politely.

"No, he was here earlier," She smiled impudently, "but he left very early."

"I have here a warrant that will entitle us to search the premises."

"Don't you believe me young man?"

"Yes, I do Madam, but I must make certain. Now while my friends search around would you care to give me a few minutes of your time?"

She smiled cordially, "I have made some coffee for you boys, but please don't disturb my gardens during your search. Oh and by the way, my attorney tells me not to answer any of your questions."

Jack smiled. "Then you are involved somehow?"

She just smiled and calmly led the way to the kitchen. "We've tied up the dogs, but please don't go into those storage areas."

Jack laughed. "If you don't want your dogs shot, you will see to it that they don't get in the way."

"I'm trying to be cordial young man. We southerners are accustomed to dealing with the excesses of northern soldiers."

Jack bowed courteously, "And we northern soldiers are accustomed to the subterfuges of southern women. Please comply with our instructions and everything will go smoothly. If you refuse to cooperate, I will make a disaster out of this place and your gardens will look as though a herd of horses have gone through them." Jack turned to Harry Moffett. "I wouldn't drink any of that coffee, Harry."

'I beg your pardon, sir; do you think I would be so crude as to poison my coffee?"

"Okay, you're right, you drink some of it."

She turned away. "I don't drink coffee."

"Don't drink any of the coffee, Harry."

She sat down on a kitchen chair and clenched her lips together.

"You evidently knew in advance that we were coming over here. Can you tell me who warned you?"

She smiled, but said nothing.

Jack looked into her eyes and wondered if J. Townsend was changing sides or just hedging his bets. "What do you know about the murderers of Steve Kaplan, Missus Kaplan and Martin Werner?"

She looked up at Jack and he thought that he caught a flicker of doubt.

"Perhaps you can tell us why your husband participated in the murder of a young lady named Lisa Crowley? Your husband allegedly watched as another man cut her throat."

Her lips were clenched more firmly than before.

"Watch her, Harry. I'm going upstairs and check out their living quarters."

"You northern bastards are just not gentlemen," she growled and then clenched her lips tightly again.

Jack positioned a marshal in the second floor hallway and then went through each room as thoroughly as possible. He checked the walls for size and proportion. The relics of the underground railway could still be found here in parts of Virginia. He eventually found a sliding panel in a closet that led to the attic. The area contained a bed and dresser, and an easy chair and lamps and had clearly been recently used for habitation. It was even comfortably heated and there were windows. He checked for dust on the sills and found that there was none and that the windows functioned. Then he went into the main bedroom and quickly checked through the dressers. Next he went down to the office and leafed through the mail. He hadn't really expected to find anything. McGruder had been given too much time to clean things up. One surprise was that there on the walls of the office were photographs of all of the important people that McGruder had hung around with. Jack took a large picture of McGruder by himself out of a frame and rolling it up he put it under his arm.

A Marshal announced that Missus Arbuthnot's attorney had arrived. Jack greeted the man at the door and introduced himself. He accepted the Attorney's business card and led the way into the kitchen. "Have some coffee," Jack suggested and as he did so he glanced at Missus Arbuthnot and placed a finger over his lips.

She frowned and started to object, but settled back and said nothing.

"We have a warrant," Jack said. "Specifically we are looking for Mister Arbuthnot, who is wanted in Illinois for three murders and in Indiana for arson and complicity in a murder."

"These are merely allegations, of course," The attorney said as he sipped the coffee. He moved the cup away from his lips and looked at inquisitively. Then he began to gag.

"That way," Jack suggested as he directed the attorney to the nearest bathroom. Then he looked at Missus Arbuthnot. "Shame on you," he said with a grin.

She smiled momentarily. "I don't like that son of a bitch either." Then she pursed her lips.

A Marshal came in the door. "The car is gone, but last years license plate is hanging on the wall. We should be able to identify it and get an alert out."

"Where is Mister Arbuthnot's office, Mabel?"

She was startled that he knew her first name, but said nothing.

He went back in to the office and found a business card for Washington, one for Chicago and one for Atlanta. He pocketed the cards and as he went by the bathroom the attorney was still gagging. As he passed a hallway door that presumably led to a closet he opened and leafed through the clothes hanging there. Then he noticed another sliding door and found it locked and opened it with a pick. It led to the basement. A lot of the houses in this area didn't have basements. This place was obviously the exception. Jack drew his weapon and went slowly down the stairs. A large dog growled and though chained it came to the bottom of the stairs. This one wasn't barking as the others had been, but was perhaps even more of a threat. Jack put the weapon away and approached the snarling animal. Now it was lunging at the end of its leash to get at him. Jack didn't want to hurt the animal but had no intention of getting bitten.

Mabel had come to the head of the stairs, "Leave him alone," she shouted. "He'll rip your heart out."

Jack fainted with his left hand and caught the dog's collar with his right. He lifted the struggling animal with one hand even though it weighed at least a hundred and twenty pounds. He shook the dog as one would shake a rug and then threw it to the floor. The animal whined and then went back to snarling, but it didn't get any closer. "If you can control him, you had better do that, Mabel, before I have to hurt him."

"He belongs to Warren. I don't dare get too close to him."

Jack went to the files in the back of the room and the dog followed him as if he was stalking the man. Then the dog leaped and Jack jumped to one side and struck the animal behind the head. As the dog reached the end of its chain it somersaulted onto its back and lay there stunned. When the animal came too it lay there watching the man warily.

Jack went through the files, there were personnel folders and they were filled with everything that Warren could have gathered on the person named on the label. Jack extracted a selection of files and placed them into the arms of a Marshal who had prudently waited on the stairs. "Put these in the car and come back for more."

The dog growled and Jack spun about and then the animal backed away and fell silent again. Jack went back to the files and gathered more data and delivered this to another Marshal. He made three more trips and went back upstairs and closed the door.

"Mabel if you hear from Warren, tell him we're going to have his ass. And for your information, you will be facing lawsuits from the various civil actions on the part of the families of the victims. Civil damages resulting from the shootings and throat cuttings will probably require that you sell this house and all of your precious gardens and anything else that you own.

"They can't do that," she said, but she obviously wasn't sure of her ground.

The attorney had tried to regain his poise, but looked like hell. "You can't take that material."

"That's your version, take us to court, but by the way you have puke on your shirt."

"That simple, dog ignorant, hick bitch," the man cursed.

Mabel slammed the door on all of them.

"What do we do with this stuff, Jack?" Harry asked as they drove away.

"I'll deliver a couple of folders to Hoover and then we'll probably destroy it."

"Probably?" Harry persisted.

Jack grinned and shrugged.

"Where are we going?" Harry asked.

"Take me to the FBI headquarters."

"We work for the Attorney General, I'm not sure that we want to give this stuff away."

"I'll tell you what I'll do. I'll give you all but five folders."

"Which ones?"

"You don't want to know, Harry."

Harry laughed and shrugged. "What the hell, what's fair is fair. But I think I've just been had."

Jack left the Marshals and went into the headquarters. He had the five selected folders under his arm. Much to everyone's surprise Jack was immediately allowed into Hoover's office, but before he went in he left two folders on the secretary's desk, explaining that he would retrieve them in a minute or two.

"Now what in the hell are you up to?" Hoover asked apprehensively.

Jack laid the three remaining folders on the Directors desk. The first was labeled Hoover and the Director glanced through the folder. His complexion went from normal to intensely red as he read through the document. He was in a complete rage when he threw it to the floor. "Did you read that shit?" He shouted.

Jack shook his head. "I noted the lead in and closed the folder. I don't know what's in it and I don't want to know."

"You're certain about that?"

"Scouts honor," Jack replied.

"Goddamn it, don't get flippant with me."

"What the hell do you want me to say?" Jack shouted in return. "You asked, I answered!"

Hoover leaned his elbows on his desk and shook his head. "Jesus H. Christ." After a bit he picked up the next folder. This one was labeled President Roosevelt. Hoover began reading with interest and chuckling from time to time. By the time he was finished he was in a much better mood. "Did you read this one?"

"Yes sir, I did."

"I'm sure that this gentleman would like to have this."

"Why don't you send it to him," Jack suggested.

Hoover seemed to consider that option and then thought about it. "It may be of some minor advantage at a later time."

Jack shrugged. "The next is some data that Warren has gathered on the Vice President and on the Speaker of the House."

"How many folders were there?"

"About fifty."

"Why do I get just three?"

"I thought these to be superfluous to our case. Many of the rest will apply. If we don't include them in our trial I will offer them back to the individuals involved rather than to Arbuthnot's Attorney."

Hoover changed that concept. "We'll keep those folders on file here despite what the court might think. Okay, I've heard about your antics with the newspaper and as a matter of fact Colonel Murray has bent my ear for an hour about violations of the First Amendment and various privacy issues. I also heard from the Attorney General about the Bucky Williams case." He paused and looked at Special Agent Kelly, "You have to be one of the luckiest men I've ever known. Had this guy Bucky not experienced a fear spasm, it very well might be that you would have landed in jail. You had better go check in with your new boss. I want this cretin Arbuthnot apprehended."

Jack got up to leave.

Hoover looked up from his work. "Thank you, Mister Kelly, thank you very much for this folder and for your work on the Farrell case."

Jack nodded his understanding of what had been said and then retrieved the folders from the secretary and took the elevator to the main floor. There in the lobby he called the Senator's office. "This is Special Agent Jack Kelly. I need an interview with the Senator as soon as possible. Tell him that we have retrieved some very personal data from Mr. Arbuthnot's files concerning the senator and many others. I am offering the Senator a chance to examine that data prior to handing it over to the Attorney General."

The secretary sounded very officious and very superior. She promised to advise the Senator of the agent's call when he came into the office. Was there somewhere that Agent Kelly could be reached?

"I'm a very busy man and I have but a very few minutes to spare. I'm trying to do the man a favor. I'll wait for a minute while you discuss this with him and if he isn't ready to chat informally then we'll forget about this offer. Talk to your boss right now and ask him if he's interested?"

Jack waited and was about to hang up when an excited voice came on the line. "Yes, Mister Kelly, the Senator can spare you a few minutes at three this afternoon, would that be satisfactory?"

Jack considered the time and then agreed.

"Sir, the Senator would prefer a meeting at a less official place such as the bar at the Congressional Golf Club. Would that be convenient?"

"Certainly," Jack responded and then hung up he didn't want to give her time to give him any more conditions. The meeting was to be informal, without significance and that suited Jack to a tee. He went to the Attorney General's office and rather than sitting with the visitors waiting impatiently for an audience he went to Harry Moffett's office.

Harry had divided the information into Chicago area and Washington area categories. The Chicago area included the folders of the original nine participants that were in on the scheme and several people in the Gary area. What surprised Jack was that most of the folders belonged to people in the Atlanta area and folks that lived around Washington. In terms of category the locals were all city or county politicians and in the Washington area they were all Feds.

"Where do you think our pigeon is, Kelly?" Moffett asked.

Jack shrugged. "Maybe Atlanta, he has friends down there."

Moffett nodded, "We have alerted all of our offices, particularly Chicago and Atlanta that a killer is on the loose."

"You know Harry, the incredible thing about this case and cases such as this one, is that we have very little idea of who this guy really is. I mean things such as his property holdings, his education, and his habits. All we get is second hand information and if the guy has never been in jail he is as good as invisible. Have you any idea of how easy it is for somebody to disappear in this country?"

Harry laughed. "Christ, Jack, there's a hundred and eighty million people in the country and there are a lot of them moving around. That's a bundle of folks to keep track of. I don't think we'll ever get a hand on it."

A young lady came in and looked around the room. Then she came directly to where Jack was seated. "The Attorney General will see you now, Special Agent Kelly. Please follow me."

Jack got up and smiled and shrugged at Harry.

Harry held a thumb up and grinned.

Jack was escorted into the Attorney General's office and stood in front of the man's desk. The Attorney General continued to work and then after a bit looked up and apparently noticed Jack. It was an absurd little act and the same one that Ashman had employed. That nonsense annoyed Jack, he hated phonies and this guy was clearly a phony.

"Oh yes, Special Agent Kelly. I suppose that you realize that you are the subject of literally dozens of telephone calls that are fairly rocketing back and forth across this country. The President himself has heard about you and wondered just what in the hell you were doing? Tell me Agent Kelly are you on some sort of personal crusade?"

"No crusade, sir. I am just doing what I have been told to do. Jack stepped forward and laid the folder on the man's desk. "You might be interested in reading this sir."

The Attorney General impatiently pushed the folder off onto the floor. "Do not presume to ever touch my desk again."

Jack stood there and made no effort to pick up the folder.

The Man seemed to be working himself up into some sort of anger. "Did you accomplish your mission this morning, Kelly?"

"No sir, Warren Arbuthnot wasn't there, although there was evidence that he had recently been there."

"What do you intend to do now?"

"I intend to go see Senator Caine this afternoon."

"My office has made no such arrangement."

"I made it myself. This is informal."

"You have no authority to make such requests. There is no such thing as an informal meeting with a member of Congress. Everything my agents do goes through this office. I will not have my people contacting Senators without my knowledge."

"I am not one of your people. I am supposed to assist your Chicago office in prosecuting the Atlanta Financial bribery case and tracking down a killer."

"You are not a free agent. You have obligations to my office and I will insist that those protocols are followed to the letter." The Man's voice went up in volume. "Do you understand what I am telling you young man?"

"Special Agent Kelly."

"What? What's that?" The Attorney General shouted.

"That is my name and rank. You seemed to have forgotten."

"Goddamn it, don't you presume to come up here and goad me. Get the hell out of here and go back to Chicago. They seem to tolerate cowboy behavior there."

Jack turned around and left the room.

The Attorney General was still shouting. 'The goddamn lack of discipline of these so-called Federal Agents is just appalling. Cancel that damned meeting this instance."

Jack was chatting amiably with Harry Moffett and killing time when the Attorney General's secretary appeared.

"Sir, the Attorney General would like to see you."

Jack followed her again and was introduced into the Man's office. Once again Jack stood at attention in front of the Man's desk.

"Ah, please sit down, Mister Kelly. Would you like some coffee?"

"No, thank you." Jack was waiting for the uproar to start again.

"Where did you get this folder?"

"From the files of Mister Warren Arbuthnot."

"Did you read it?"

"Only that portion relating to your relationship with Arbuthnot."

"This was nil." The Attorney General said defiantly.

Jack agreed. "It was practically nil and since it didn't pertain to the case I thought that I would deliver it to you personally. One doesn't want information of that sort lying around whether it is true or false."

The old man stared at Jack for a long minute, and then placed the folder in his desk drawer. "I owe you an apology."

Jack shrugged, but said nothing.

"Do you have a folder for the senator?"

"I do."

"Is he implicated in this series of crimes?"

"Not as far as I can ascertain. These folders appear to be accumulations of rumors and allegations most of which are not crimes or those that are crimes are without substantial supporting evidence. Such a collection of spurious insinuations is a reckless act. Should such material fall into the wrong hands, such as those of an unscrupulous reporter, the damage done to an innocent man could be severe."

The Attorney General nodded his agreement. "Such material could be used in a political campaign, where there are very few requirements for truth or for substantiating the allegations. I want to thank you for bringing that folder to me it was the act of a gentleman. I also must apologize for flying off the handle earlier, but this damned Arbuthnot thing has gotten completely out of hand." He leaned back in his chair. "Where in the hell do we go next?"

"Somebody knows where he is. We have to get the public concerned. The agencies are alerted and will soon have pictures of him. I figure that the more press we get the better the chance of finding a witness. The politicians may come out looking bad, but that is a temporary problem. Nobody is going to take a hard fall, we all know that. What concerns me is that this guy is dangerous to everyone that has ever known him."

"Do you think that the Senator may know something about him?"

Jack grimaced. "I served with his son as a fellow agent. No braver young man ever trod the earth. I would hate to think that his father could be a party to the horrors that have come to pass." Jack gestured vaguely, "I want to give the man every opportunity to do the right thing."

"And if he doesn't"

"Then we'll have to let the chips fall where they may. At the moment I have no proof of his involvement, but it wouldn't surprise me if we eventually found something."

The Attorney General stood up and came around his desk. The interview was over and He escorted Jack to the door. "Keep me advised," the old man said.

And Jack replied with a crisp, "Yes sir."

Harry Moffett drove Jack out to the Golf Club. They went out early and checked out the area. It was still very cold in Washington and there weren't many people out on the course. Both the parking lot and the bar were almost empty. Harry would wait out in the lobby, being as unobtrusive as possible. Jack went into the bar and ordered a beer.

The Senator was of short stature, a balding man with snowy white fringes of hair. He appeared to be robust in that he moved with a firm positive gait. The Senator walked straight up to Jack and asked what he wanted. There was no mincing of words, no introductory discussion. No courtesy at all. Just a rough "What is it that you want, Kelly?"

"I thought that you might want this folder that I found at Arbuthnot's office."

The Senator did not look inside the folder; he simply tucked the folder under his arm. "And what is it that you expect from me?"

Jack smiled at the officious little man. "Nothing, I'm doing one last favor for a friend."

"A last favor?" The Senator inquired emphasizing the word last."

"That's it." Jack said,

"I'll do you a favor, Kelly," Caine said. "Drop this investigation and forget about Arbuthnot."

"I have an alternate suggestion," Jack said, "You had better get out before everything goes to hell and falls on you."

The Senator uttered a snorting contemptuous laugh and turned his back on the agent and strolled purposefully away.

Jack pushed a dollar across the bar as a tip and got up off his stool. Then he too walked away. Harry met him at the door and they went out to their car. The Senator was getting into a rather ornate Packard Touring sedan. A chauffer held the door for the important man and two body guards looked menacingly at the officers.

"Is that what you expected?" Harry asked.

"To tell you the truth, Harry, I didn't know what to expect."

"Let's get out of here it looks like rain," Harry said.

The two men had just gotten back to their office when the phone began ringing. Harry answered and handed the phone to Jack. "It's for you."

A voice came on that Jack didn't recognize, "You'll find Arbuthnot staying at the Carlin Inn in Ocean City Maryland." Then the person hung up.

Jack lowered the phone and gave Harry the message. "I think the Senator is setting up his old buddy."

"What makes you think so?"

"It's obvious isn't it? Who else in Washington knows who I am and that I'm after this guy?"

Harry frowned. "That's a real long drive. It is out on the Maryland Peninsula. It's kind of a resort area in the summer time, but there isn't much going on during the winter. We'll have to drive over to Annapolis or somewhere where we can catch a ferry across the bay and then drive out to the ocean. The nearest Feds will be in Baltimore or maybe even in Philadelphia, which is still a couple of hours away."

"Let's get the locals to check it out," Jack suggested. "It just might be so much nonsense."

"I wouldn't want to send some hick cop up against this guy," Harry said. "That wouldn't be much of a contest."

"Yeah," Jack agreed, "but who is to say that this is a viable clue?" Jack muttered to himself for a minute. "Let's suggest that they don't try to apprehend the guy. Just check it out. If it's real we can hire a plane. Then we can fly over before the sun goes down and make the arrest."

Harry was reluctant. "You can fly over and meet somebody local. I prefer to stay on the ground. Let's call the Sheriff over there and emphasize just how dangerous this guy can be."

"I'll talk to them." Jack was remembering a cop down in Decatur who had made some sort of mistake with Crouse. He didn't want that to happen again. Jack spoke to Homer Cummings the local Sheriff. "We have this extremely dangerous man that is reported to be staying in Ocean City. He is suspected of killing four people and is a very intelligent man, which of course, makes him doubly dangerous. He is reported to be staying at the Carlin Inn and before we take off on a wild goose chase we would like some local verification that this guy is actually in town." Jack described Arbuthnot and then asked the Sheriff if he would send and man around to the Inn to see if such a man was residing there?

"Dangerous you say?" Cummings asked.

"Very dangerous," Jack replied.

"Hell, mister G-Man, we've handled our share of hard guys around here. Mister Kelly. Would you like us to apprehend this man?"

"Sheriff, I'm begging you to investigate very discreetly and if Arbuthnot is there post an officer outside to keep track of him and then call me. I'll fly over to the nearest airfield and make the arrest."

"Well sure, Special Agent Kelly, I'll look into this little matter for you. This would be a very important arrest would it not?"

"Yes sir, it would, but I must caution you. This man is very sharp and very dangerous. Please, for the sake of your men, stay the hell away from him."

"Well, no problem, pal. I'll look into this myself and we'll let you know. Are you going to wait for verification that we have him in custody?"

"Sheriff I'm begging you don't try to apprehend him. Leave it to us." Jack lowered the phone and looked at Harry. Jack was obviously worried.

"So you think this hick Sheriff is going to play hero?"

Jack nodded. "Yeah, I'm afraid so and right now I regret even calling this guy." Jack got up and began to pace about the room. "I can hear it in his voice, He thinks that this is a normal arrest, but this guy Arbuthnot is sharp and if he is pressed he will retaliate violently and in a hurry."

"Relax Jack; the Sheriff is probably an experienced law enforcement officer. He'll play it carefully."

"Christ I hope so. Let's anticipate a positive answer and make arrangement for a flight."

Harry threw his hands up in mock confusion. "We've never done such a thing before. Trains yes, but airplanes never, we're setting a precedence for this office. We can check the phone book for some service over at Washington National." Harry grabbed a phone book and leafed through it. "Ryan Air Service, aircraft for hire and flights arranged. Let's give them a call."

Jack called and made arrangements for a flight to Ocean City. It was only eighty air miles away and forty minutes of flight time would get him there. Jack made arrangements to meet the pilot and had Harry drive him over to the airport.

"You told the Sheriff that you would wait," Harry reminded him.

"How about calling him and asking him to meet me at the field? This is probably what I should have done even before calling that guy."

The aircraft was a Stinson Reliant, which was a big high wing monoplane with a large radial engine. The pilot was an older man and looked to be a calm and seasoned aviator.

"Have you ever been in an airplane before, Mister Kelly?"

"Big ones."

"Did you ever get sick?"

"No and we went through several rather violent storms."

"Here's a bag. Keep it in your lap. If you puke, puke in the bag. If you fuck up my airplane, you're going to clean it."

Jack grinned. "I think we'll be okay."

"Keep the bag," Gus said. The pilot strapped Jack into the aircraft. "It's going to get bumpy, the weather is coming in. Fortunately it will only take us about forty minutes. Getting back might be something of a problem. They're predicting icing at some low levels and I don't have anything to cope with that."

"One problem at a time," Jack laughed. "I got a guy I have to see." Jack watched the man with fascination. It wasn't long before they were in the air and Gus was right it was bumpy. The flight across the Maryland pine forests was executed in the pouring rain and it was difficult to see through the windshield due to the steady stream of water coursing over the engine nacelle. They were cruising along just below the base of the clouds and the damp forests were very close below. Then they went across Chesapeake Bay and headed southeast. Though the aircraft was tossing about violently Gus was sitting there as calmly as he would in an easy chair. Jack took his hint from Gus and began to relax and scan the water and terrain below. By the time they got to Ocean City the rain had stopped. The flight was over too soon as far as Jack was concerned. He asked Gus to stand by for an hour or so and ran to the nearest hanger to make a phone call.

Gus was shouting a protest. "If I wait, I'll never get out of here."

But Jack wasn't listening.

A Sheriff's car came around the hanger and slid to a stop in front of Jack. A grim faced Deputy asked if Jack was the FBI guy.

"Yeah, I'm him, what's going on?"

"The Sheriff's been shot and the culprit is gone."

Jack slammed a fist into the side of the car. "Goddamn it, I told that damned fool," Then he looked up and shrugged. "Okay, how bad is the Sheriff hurt?" He asked.

The Deputy was surprised by the reaction and stepped back a bit. "Uhh, he got hit twice and one of our Deputies was killed. The bad guy took off in the Sheriff's unmarked car."

"Have we alerted all of the surrounding towns? Our guy will probably be going north and trying to put as much distance as he can between him and us."

"We are calling all the nearest towns and the Maryland and New Jersey State Police have been alerted. We'll probably have this guy in the can in a few minutes."

Jack nodded his agreement, but he really wasn't as sure about that prediction as he walked back to the plane. "You might as well go home, Gus. I'll be here for a while."

"Can I ask you what happened?"

"The guy I was after shot two police officers and got away." Jack shrugged, "Now I got to do it the hard way."

Gus nodded and turned away. "Good luck, Jack"

Jack waved farewell and went over to the Deputy.

"Do you want to go to the scene?"

"No, I want to go to the Sheriff's Office. We've got a lot to do. By the way what kind of car is the Sheriff driving?"

The Deputy looked as though he was offended by Jack's decision to ignore the crime scene. "He drives a thirty-seven Cadillac Sedan."

In an effort to placate the man Jack asked about the events that took place. "Tell me about the scene, Deputy?"

The Deputy took a deep breath, "Well, the Sheriff and two of us went over to the Carlin Inn. There's a bar there right?"

Jack had no idea, but he nodded his agreement. Then he interrupted the Deputy. "Were you guys, all wearing uniforms?"

"Yeah, the Sheriff insists that we wear the proper gear. He likes uniforms. Anyway we were just going to have a couple of beers and talk to the bartender. So the Sheriff asks Herby whether he has seen this stranger. Herby is the Bartender. And then he describes the guy we're looking for. And it was at just that minute when this old guy gray haired guy comes walking into the bar. So suddenly Herby points to this guy and says, "Yeah, Sheriff, there he is."

"Then the guy started shooting right?"

"Yeah, how did you know that?"

"I'm psychic."

"Yeah? Oh hell, you're bull shitting me right?"

Jack smiled and prompted the Deputy to continue.

"Well, this guy starts shooting and Billy takes one right through the chest. Then the Sheriff falls. Hell, I'm brave enough, but this guy was shooting so I ran to the end of the bar to take cover and then when I turned to return fire the guy was gone. He went out the door and jumped into the Sheriffs car and hauls ass out of there."

"The Sheriff left his keys in the car right?"

"Well yeah," the Deputy said defensively, "Who in the hell is going to steal the Sheriff's car?"

"Probably somebody that doesn't know that it belongs to the Sheriff." Jack suggested.

The Deputy thought about that for a minute, "Well, there wasn't anything that I could do so I went over to the Sheriff to see if I could help him and he began raising hell for me to get outside and see which way the guy went."

"Did you?"

"Did I what?"

"Did you go outside?" Jack asked in exasperation.

"Well sure, hell, I always do what I'm told to do, but the guy was gone."

"Which way did he go?"

The Deputy frowned, "Well hell, I don't know he was gone."

"Did you ask anyone?"

"Well no, I was busy helping the Sheriff. We had to stop the bleeding. That's the first thing that you got to do, you know?"

"Did any of your rounds hit the subject?" Jack asked.

"Ahhh, no. I don't think so."

"How was this guy dressed?"

"Huh?"

"How was he dressed? What sort of clothes was he wearing?"

"Uhh, he had on sea boots and a black jacket."

"Let's go to the scene."

"Right, that's what I thought we ought to do to begin with," the Deputy said as if his opinion was vindicated.

Jack sat back and smiled, "Right," he said. When they arrived they went into the bar. The body had been removed and the Sheriff had been taken to the nearest hospital. The bartender was mopping up the mess on the floor. Jack wanted to ask if anyone had investigated the scene, but he refrained because the damage had already been done. Any evidence that may have remained in that room had been skillfully eradicated. "Did anyone find any shell casings?" He asked.

"Nope," answered the bartender.

"What happened here?" Jack asked

Herby shrugged and went back to mopping the floor.

Jack walked outside and stood under the porch to avoid the rain. On a hunch Jack stopped in at the Barbershop. He stuck his head in the door. "Did anyone see which way the bad guy went in the Sheriff's car?"

A vociferous discussion took place as differences in opinion surfaced. Finally, one old man shouted for all of them to shut up. "I used to be the Sheriff here, sonny, before that asshole car dealer got elected last year. The car went to the south."

As Jack closed the door the noisy argument over the direction of the vehicle resumed.

"He's trapped," Jack concluded. "There's nothing south of here but the Atlantic Ocean."

Jack walked over to the Sheriff's office and identified himself. The middle aged lady at the front counter smiled invitingly. "May I see the Assistant Sheriff," Jack asked.

The man that had picked him up at the airport came out of the office.

Jack groaned inwardly, but smiled. "The former Sheriff tells me that the car went south."

"Aw shit, that mean old bastard, don't know nothing. He's always trying to get his nose back in here."

"Can we alert the towns south of here?"

"There's no point," Mort said. "He'll have to turn around and go north. There ain't anything down to the south."

"Let's try it and see how it works, okay."

The Deputy frowned and then nodded at the woman. "Call around Maud and ask if anybody has seen this killing bastard."

Jack forced another smile, "I'm going over to check his room would you like to go along?"

The deputy pondered that offer for a moment. "Naw, I got too much to do here. You'all go right ahead."

Rain was coursing down now and it was turning cold. Jack hurried over to the hotel and checked in with the manager. She was a young woman and she looked as though her complexion was suffering from the effects of far too much sun.

"I'd like to see the room of the man that shot the Sheriff. By the way what name was he using?"

"Martin was his name." The young woman replied. "John Martin. He was a whisky drummer."

"Did Mister Martin own a car?"

She nodded at first and then found her voice. "Yeah, it's parked out yonder there across the street."

"What room number did he have?"

"Are you a cop or somethin?"

Jack produced his identification. "I'm Jack Kelly, Special Agent for the FBI."

She sidled up close to him and pretended to read his ID. "What makes you so special Jack?"

He smiled and backed away. "The room number please?"

She frumped about swaying her behind and found a key. "One twenty-two, it's the best room we got."

There wasn't much of Arbuthnot in the room. He apparently lived rather frugally. There were a few shirts and two pair of trousers. There were some socks and underclothes in the drawers, but the backs and bottoms of the dresser drawers were clean. On the top shelf in the closet laid a locked briefcase and an empty overnight bag. Jack opened the briefcase on the bed. There was a box of thirty-eight caliber ammunition and about a thousand dollars in small bills. There was another folder of data on the Senator, but this was much more definitive and damning. Based upon this data the Senator could be brought into a court of law and prosecuted for countless bona-fide crimes. For the first time in hours Jack could allow himself a sly smile.

He went through everything carefully and then went out to the car. It was a Thirty-one Ford and there wasn't much of anything in it. The man was a phantom. Jack went back over to the Sheriff's Office to make some phone calls. The word that the Sheriff had succumbed to his wounds had just come in as Jack had entered the door. Old Maud lapsed into hysterics and even the Sheriff's former assistant had shed a tear or two.

Jack called Harry back in Washington, but Harry had allegedly gone home for the day. The night shift went into action and the word that Arbuthnot had added two police officers to his list of kills went out over the wires. Every Federal Agency was alerted and Jack had added the description of what the man had been wearing at the time. There was no word from the State Police, but roadblocks had been established at every major intersection. The biggest problem was that no one had an adequate description of the suspect. One State Police Officer that Jack spoke to asked him if he had any idea of how many middle aged white males had silvery white hair? Jack in turn asked how many of those people had been wearing sea boots and black woolen coats.

The reply was that out here on the peninsula there were quite a few.

Jack borrowed a marked Sheriff's car and went back to the hotel. The Thirty-one Ford was gone.

Jack asked the manager about the vehicle.

"Oh hell, that old wreck belongs to the mean old guy that owns the Owensfield Boat Yard. He came and got it."

"You didn't think it prudent to tell me that earlier, huh?" Jack asked.

"What's to tell?" She asked with a startled expression. "Hell, everybody knows that."

Jack fought mightily to restrain his anger. "Can you please give me directions to the Boat Yard?"

He listened as she rattled off a series of road names and turning instructions. He took out a piece of paper. "Try again, please, but slower this time."

It was dark and the rain was still coming down as Jack drove out of town. He could have called for help from the Deputy, but was reluctant to place another local officer in jeopardy. It didn't take long for him to realize the error in his ways. He desperately needed some local help. Most of the road signs were down or were completely illegible as a result of sea salt drying out the paint. There was a radio in the car, but the only frequency available was apparently a State Police Station. Jack had no idea as to whether the County was tied into the communications net. Finally, after damned near an hour of frustration Jack found the Boatyard. The Sheriffs Cadillac was parked there outside the yard. Jack reluctantly got out in the pouring rain and walked up to a house located near the front gate to the yard. He decided that if the condition of the front steps and porch was any indication of the skill of the boat builders that he would much sooner fly than hire a boat. He knocked and waited. Then he knocked again and heard a commotion inside.

"Who's out there and what do you want?" A male voice shouted.

Evidently, Jack concluded, the custom here was to shout at one another through the locked door. "Special Agent Jack Kelly, Federal Bureau of Investigation."

"You got a warrant?"

"No, I just want to ask you a few questions?"

"I don't like Cops and I especially don't like Feds get the hell off my porch!"

"Okay, tough guy, I'll be back in an hour with a warrant and with the State Troopers and I'll tear this goddamn dump to the ground."

"A warrant for what?" The argumentative old man asked.

"For being an accessory to the murder of two Sheriff's officers. Don't go away asshole, we'll be right back."

The door opened, a scruffy looking old guy was peering out into the darkness. "Now wait a minute, Bud. Don't let's get excited. What's this about a murder?"

"The Sheriff and his Deputy Billy were shot just an hour or two ago."

"Too bad about Billy getting killed, but as for that goddamned used car dealer is concerned it's good riddance."

Jack pushed the door open and forced his way inside. The old man moved back toward a rifle rack in the corner. An old woman was peering around the corner of a door. "You touch one of those rifles," Jack said calmly, "and I'll blow your ass away!" Then Jack spoke to the woman. "If you have a shotgun back there, mother, and if you so much as move I'll kill your husband first and then I'll kill you."

The man's hand recoiled from the rack as if he had been stung. "She ain't got nothing. Go back inside, Ma. Close that door and stay the hell out of this, before you get me kilt."

"Where in the hell is the guy that was driving the Sheriff's car?"

"He's gone." The old man moved further away from the gun rack. "His name is Martin and he said he wanted to park his boat here for a couple of weeks."

"Where is he?" Jack asked through clenched teeth.

"He's been gone for a couple of hours. He came roaring in here in the Sheriff's car and then hot footed it out to his boat. He said the Sheriff would probably be by to pick up the car tomorrow. Then he took his boat and cast off. Paid me in full, he did."

"What kind of boat are we looking for?"

The old man shrugged, "It's a double ender, a rum runner. He told me that they use to use it for smuggling booze. Fifty feet long, it's got two big gasoline engines. The damned thing will do thirty-five knots. There's a picture of it. I always get shots of the big boats that stay here." The old man squinted out at the rain. "Well, maybe as rough as it is out there it would cut along at about fifteen knots or so. Hell, by now he's probably tied up at some dock in Virginia. It's faster than anything the Coast Guard has around here."

Jack took the picture of the boat. "I'll confiscate this. Where is his home base? You got a phone?"

"Yeah, but you ain't going to use it. You'll run up a big bill and I'll be the one paying it."

"Thank you for your cooperation. I'll mention you to the State Police and to the local Sheriffs, seeing as how two local officers were killed today maybe they can figure out some way to reciprocate."

"Don't threaten me you big asshole, this is still a free country and besides all that crap, the line is down. The damn thing never works in a heavy rain."

Jack was in a rage when he went out to the car. Then to increase his irritation he tried to retrace his steps through the maze that was the south county and find Ocean City. By he time he got back to town another forty minutes had elapsed and he was in a rage. Arbuthnot was surely in Virginia by this time. The Deputy was still in his office, doing nothing because his phone lines were down.

The Deputy was feeling grumpy. "Where in the hell did you get too? I had a dozen calls looking for you."

Jack slammed a fist down on the desk. "I was looking for the murderer you incompetent horse's ass. Your Sheriff was murdered and you sit on your ass down here to answer phone calls? What in the hell is the matter with you? What kind of police officer are you?"

"Don't holler at me," The Deputy fairly screamed out. "You're the guy that sent the Sheriff out to meet a killer!"

"I'm the guy that told the Sheriff not to do anything of the sort. How in the hell was I supposed to know that the man was an idiot?"

"You can't call the Sheriff an idiot. Don't you have any respect for the dead?"

The telephone rang and interrupted the shouting match. It was a telephone lineman announcing that the single line was clear and functioning.

Jack motioned to the deputy for the phone and the deputy cowered back and meekly offered it to furious man confronting him. Jack called the Marshals headquarters and notified them that Arbuthnot had escaped the peninsula and was somewhere in Virginia then he added the description again. He asked where an adequate landing might be situated that would facilitate a boat of that size. He was informed that there were literally thousands of possible landings and all of them would safe and suitable. Jack hung up and handed the deputy the phone. "Call the State Police. Tell them the hunt is off hereabouts and is moving to Virginia."

The Deputy obediently made the calls.

Jack apologized. "Sorry, if I got rough, Mort, I'm really upset. I begged the Sheriff not to go overtly after this killer, but he wouldn't listen. You guys really aren't set up for this sort of law enforcement." Jack smiled wanly, "By the way, the Sheriff's car is down by the Owensfield Boat Yard. I may point out that the guy that owns that place wasn't very cooperative."

"Where can I find you, sir?" The Deputy asked.

"I'm going over to the bar and have a stiff drink and try to figure out how in the hell I'm going to get out of here."

"Yes sir, I'll transfer any urgent calls to the bar."

Jack walked into the bar and was surprised to find his pilot Gus sitting there sucking on a bottle of beer. "So you decided to stay on the ground?"

"Discretion is the better part of valor," Gus laughed. "Have a beer."

Jack leaned against the bar and ordered a double shot of scotch. "Our boy escaped in a boat and ran across the bay."

Gus threw his hands up in the air. "Hell, he's gone, but that would take some balls in this weather. The bay can get damned rough. As to the other there are thousands of places that he could go."

Jack nodded glumly. "He's driving a fifty foot double ended rum runner."

"He has a fifty foot boat? Well that sort of changes things, most of these local boats are smaller than that. Have you got some sort of description?"

Jack reached into his pocket and pulled out the snap shot. "It's a good looking boat. It's an ocean going double ender, black with white trim and it's supposedly a way overpowered. The guy at the Boat Yard told me that it would do thirty-five knots."

Gus frowned, "Yeah, maybe in the open sea on a calm day, or up the Bay, but not up the waterways." He looked at Jack. "What would you do, if you were this guy?"

Jack shrugged. "I guess that I'd try to get as close to a major city as possible. Maybe he'll go as far as Baltimore."

Gus thought about that for a moment. "He could have gone up the Potomac to Washington. He couldn't do anything like forty knots at night, maybe a max of fifteen or so. Look, I got to fly back to the field as early as possible in the morning, if you want to come along and pay for it, we can go up the river and check out the various yacht clubs and docks."

Jack laughed, "When can we take off?"

Gus shrugged, "Let's grab a little chow and a few hours of shut eye and bust out of here early."

Gus pulled the Stinson off the deck and into a crystal clear dawn and allowed Jack to follow through on the controls during the take off. Once they were comfortably in the air he also allowed Jack to fly the aircraft and made a friend for life by doing so. It was a beautiful day and the only problem was that they were headed right into the dawning sun. They flew low across the bay and then followed the Potomac River up towards Washington National. As they passed each successive boat landing Gus circled while Jack checked out the boats. It was as they neared the Darlington Yacht Club just south of the City that Jack spotted a familiar looking boat. A white haired man dressed in a Navy pea coat and sea boots was tying the boat up to a dock. This man looked up at the circling aircraft and then strode rapidly up the dock toward the administration building. Gus got on the ground control frequency at Washington National and asked for a discrete frequency to transmit an urgent message to the Federal Marshals. Jack got on the radio with the Tower Operator who relayed that information to Harry Moffett on another line that a man resembling Arbuthnot had just landed a boat at the Darlington Yacht Club.

Jack wanted to land on a city street near the club, but Gus wouldn't have any part of it.

"Look at this philosophically, we're closer to catching this guy than we were an hour ago," Gus reasoned,

As frustrated as he was Jack had to agree. The local police were to be advised and Jack insisted that they circle the Yacht Club to see what the results might be. Gus didn't like the idea, circling a yacht club at seven in the morning was a good way to get a complaint, but he reluctantly agreed. The white haired man stood outside the Club for awhile and then finally got into a cab.

Jack was beginning to rant into the radio. "Where in the hell are the Cops? This guy killed two police officers. Goddamn it, he's getting away again!"

Then Jack insisted that they follow the suspect. Try as they might they soon lost the cab in traffic, but the general direction was relayed to the Marshals and hopefully to the local police.

Chapter Thirteen

When they landed at the airport a car was waiting for Jack.

Gus apologized profusely, "Sorry, Jack, the plane is just too damned fast to allow us to watch some guy in a cab. If we had a Piper Cub we just might have done it."

Jack laughed it off, "Hell, we just might have started something new," he said as he got into the vehicle. He still had the briefcase in his possession.

Harry was driving the car. "The Attorney General is having shit fits. The Director is in the same condition. The Senator is going nuts. I'll say this for you Jack; you're the greatest threat to a man's retirement that I ever came across."

Jack grinned. "The Senator senses a threat. This simple arrest didn't go the way he wanted it to. Now why do you suppose that might be the case?"

"He's naturally nervous?" Harry guessed.

"He was probably the only guy that knew where Mister Arbuthnot was staying. Were I him, I think I'd be a tad nervous too."

"So this guy Arbuthnot is going after the Senator?"

"I would if I was in his shoes. Evidently the Senator betrayed him. By the way where in the hell were the cops? That frigging city isn't that big. They should have been there in minutes."

Harry leaned back, "I called them and gave them the message that a killer was loose, but they seemed to be dragging their feet. I think the Chief was having his morning coffee or perhaps he was reluctant to face up to a Cop killer."

"Well let's go look at the boat. Then we'll impound it and take those distributor caps and disable it. We'll keep circling him in until he has no more places to go. Soon there will be nowhere for him to hide. In his briefcase here, there is a list of places that he felt safe. The Carlin Inn was one of those at the top of the list. We'll have the local police keep close tabs on all of the others. There will be no place to go, no place to hide. We'll send out another all points bulletin in the clear listing these places and pointing out that he has killed two officers. I want the heat on this bastard. When we get back to the office I want you to pick my brain. I want you to force me to remember anything that may have slipped my mind."

Harry drove along in silence for a long while and then blurted out, "Jack, I had to tell the Boss about those folders that you took."

Jack shrugged, "So? Hell that's what I would have done, if I were in your shoes."

"No hard feelings?"

"None whatsoever, I'm not in love with this job anyway."

"Aw shit, I'm sorry Jack."

"Don't be. I did what I thought was right and there was no harm."

Jack disabled the boat's engines and had just conducted a thorough search when Harry came down the ladder.

"They want you at headquarters at one o'clock. Big meeting! I think they're looking for an excuse to get you out of here."

"Good, let's go the hotel. I need a shave and a shower. It would probably help my case if I had on a clean shirt."

They stopped by the office and Harry went in to get the all points bulletin prepared for transmission and to find out what happened to the Darlington Police Department. Jack took the car and went to the hotel. His bags had been left in the room that he had never seen. He showered and shaved and then lay back on the bed to relax and gather his thoughts. It had been an early start and yesterday had been a very hectic day. Somehow he had forgotten to eat much yesterday and was starved. Supper had consisted of a cheeseburger, bar peanuts and two double scotches. Those were his thoughts as he dozed off. He slept soundly as if he didn't have a care in the world.

His automatic internal clock awoke him with a start at eleven-thirty. Great, he thought, time for a breakfast and then the big meeting. He didn't object to leaving the job, but he wanted to nail Arbuthnot, before they canned him. One the other hand he objected to getting sacked due to some bastard's political machinations. It occurred to him that if you were to work in D.C. that you'd have to get used to the political nonsense and spend every waking moment covering your ass. No wonder so little gets done in such an environment. Every time a police officer gave a speeding ticket to some idiot, he had to contend with the possibility of encountering some massive ego and connections to even more important connections.

Jack went into the meeting carrying the briefcase that Arbuthnot had left in the hotel room. There were three men in the room, the Director of the FBI, the Attorney General and a distinguished looking man that Jack had never met before. A chair had been arranged directly in front of a long table at which the three officials sat. The Attorney General introduced Jack to the members.

"You have met the Director, I know. To illustrate how important this case has become due to the alleged involvement of a United States Senator, this gentleman to my right is James Marley, who is a special advisor to the President of the United States. We are here to inquire into your actions yesterday involving the death of two police officers and into your meeting with Senator Caine. You may take note that even the President is concerned with the rampage that has followed your arrival. Now, I want you to bring Mister Marley up to date."

Jack leaned the briefcase against his chair leg and began to brief the President's right hand man. Jack ran through the situation quickly.

Mister Marley nodded his understanding of the situation. "Where are all those various files?"

"They are still in the possession of the Bureau."

Marley looked at Hoover, "And what do you intend to do with those records, Mister Hoover?"

'They will be turned over to the AG for criminal prosecution and then to the IRS."

Marley frowned and gestured for Jack to continue.

"Arbuthnot shot the two Sheriff's officers yesterday. This morning we tracked him to a Yacht Club in Darlington. We are presently closing in upon that man."

"Do you have an estimate of when he will be arrested?"

"No sir, not at the moment. The Darlington Police failed to respond in a timely manner and he is in the wind again."

"You say that you are closing in. How are you doing that?"

"I have a list of possible hiding places that he has chosen and we are limiting access to those places. We have also stationed Marshals at his home and at his boat. We will close his bank accounts and due to his hurried departure from Ocean City we have retrieved approximately one thousand dollars of his running money. It well may be the death of the two Sheriff's officers in Maryland that has sealed his fate. Every Police Department in the land has a vested interest in running down cop killers."

The Attorney General frowned, "I understand that you captured fifty personnel folders from the Arbuthnot home and subsequently withheld five of these folders from the evidence locker. Where are they?"

"Three went to the Director, one went to you and one went to Senator Caine."

The AG blushed evidently he hadn't considered that he had received a folder. "Ah yes, well thank you, that answers that question."

Mister Marley fixed his gaze on the AG and then asked Jack, "What did these folders contain?"

"They contained allegations, insinuations, and assorted material that while somewhat incriminating and embarrassing were totally without substantiating evidence that I could see and the material was without any leads as how to obtain that evidence. It was the sort of material that would be a windfall to an unscrupulous newspaper reporter and would be a burden to a prosecuting attorney. It was, by and large, filthy trash."

"Why did you keep five of them?" Marley asked. "Do you have some personal plans for these documents? Were you planning a little blackmail campaign of your own, Mister Kelly?"

"No sir. I gave the Attorney General his folder, I gave three folders to the Director, One was his personal folder, and the other two applied to the President and to the Vice President and I gave one to Senator Caine."

"Did you read the information they contained?" Marly asked.

"Yes sir I did. I wanted to see if there was any real evidence attached to the accusations or whether it was all innuendo and insinuation."

"What happened to the President's and Vice President's folders, Mister Director?" Marley asked fixing a hard stare on the Director.

"Uh, sir, I haven't had time to forward them to your office."

Marley smiled thinly, "You will see to it that you do as soon as possible, Mister Director."

"Yes sir."

"Now, Mister Kelly lets talk about Senator Caine. Where is his folder?"

"I gave it to him yesterday."

"Why? What I mean to say is that I can understand your taking such material out of circulation for the President and your bosses, but why Caine? Perhaps another way of asking that question is what did Caine ever do for you?"

'Nothing. Is the answer to that question, but his son and I served together in the Bureau and the young man died defending his supervisor. He died for his duty and I guess I figured that we owed the old man one break."

"What the hell is that Kelly's Law?" Marley asked.

Jack slowly shook his head. "There was nothing of any use there. Not for the AG, not for the Director and presumably not for a United States Senator."

The Attorney General had something to pounce upon. "You don't have the prerogative of deciding how to dispose of evidence, Agent Kelly."

"You didn't complain, when I gave you your copy," Jack replied.

Marley laughed uproariously. "Okay, okay, boys calm down. Mister Kelly are you aware that Senator Caine is a leading Democrat? He is a very important man in this administration."

Jack looked into Marley's eyes. "I'm a Democrat, you're a Democrat, but Senator Caine is a thief. He maybe a successful thief, but he is still a thief."

The Director groaned and the Attorney General looked as though he had been goosed.

The blood rushed to Marley's cheeks, but his voice remained even. "You are accusing the Senator of criminal activity and you had damn well better make it good."

Jack picked up the brief case. "This is Arbuthnot's. I found it in his room at the Carlin Inn. He had some money, and a list of places he intended to hide. He also had a private folder on Senator Caine, which delineates their relationship and his connections to the gang of fraud artists, plus a lot of things that we didn't know about. There are also some more names. I suspect that this was Arbuthnot's ticket to the gravy train."

The Attorney General stood up and started around the table. He was about to grab the briefcase when Marley's command stopped him. "Don't touch that damned thing." Marley settled back in his chair. "You say that there is hard evidence in that briefcase that would indict the Senator?"

"Precisely."

"What makes you think so?"

"I'm a trained attorney. I know evidence when I see it."

"Give me that brief case. Please."

Jack looked at the other men at the table and then shrugged. He stood up and laid the briefcase before Marley.

Marley continued. "There is an allegation that you were responsible for the death of two police officers. The Governor of Maryland is beside himself that such a thing could happen in his state."

"I have several witnesses to the fact that I cautioned the Sheriff not to approach Arbuthnot. In fact I practically begged the man to allow me to take the risk."

"What makes you so different, so much more efficient than the Sheriff?"

The Director piped up, "Special Agent Kelly has killed five or six men in the past two months."

Marley's eyes went wide.

"Five is more like it," Jack said.

Marley smiled.

"It was a matter of extremely odd circumstances," Jack attempted to explain. "Perhaps you are aware that most police officers have never drawn their weapons. I spent six years on the force before I encountered a homicidal maniac in a diner. Then I ran into an assassin, employed by Farrell, who attempted to kill me. I later participated in the shooting of two men that had killed two Federal Agents. I don't know that I was any more accurate than the other officers. Then there was a shoot out on the border during which I returned the fire of a car load of killers that were intent upon killing my prisoners. Finally there was the killing of the person that had been the Mole in our Chicago office, Charley Farrell. Actually, I had only wounded the man. The Chief of police of Ladysmith killed him. I want to point out that it sounds a hell of lot worse than it really was."

"Still, despite you're disclaimers, I'm impressed," Marley said. "Would you please wait outside for a few minutes?"

Jack nodded and obediently went outside. He sat down in the waiting area and watched the secretary. She certainly seemed to be a very nice sort of girl. She had pretty legs and auburn hair she was a very lovely young woman.

Marley watched the Attorney General and the Director for a long time and they both sat there waiting rather impatiently for him to speak. "We have a major problem. Senator Caine has long been a stalwart of the party. He is the sort of man that we can depend upon for his vote. I don't know the extent of his legal transgressions, but would really hate to see him embarrassed in any way whatsoever." He held up a halting hand. "Not that I am, for even a moment suggesting in any way, that we overlook illegal activity on the Senator's part." He waited, but the two men sat there waiting his lead. "I am very concerned that this fellow Arbuthnot should be captured by the police and subsequently be allowed to spill his guts to the press. It would be far better that he perish in the process of apprehension." He gestured in an odd way. "It would advantageous for us, if Arbuthnot died in a shoot out with police." Marley paused again. "Do you think that we might suggest such a thing to our Special Agent?"

Hoover began shaking his head in a negative manner. Then he looked up. "I once suggested that it would be good for the Bureau if our Mole, a man named Farrell, met summary justice during the arresting procedure and though that is what happened, I am not sure that it was due to Kelly's hand. He maintains that it was the deceased Chief that did it."

"The Chief died in the process. Not due to a gunshot, but due to a chest injury." The AG pointed out. "But I don't know that we can suggest such a thing and expect him to keep it secret and particularly so if he comes to understand that we want to defend Senator Caine."

Marley smiled slyly, "If I were instructed to kill a man. I would be most reluctant to admit that I had followed orders. Perhaps, Mister Kelly is smarter than we might believe."

"Then we must be very circumspect." The AG said. "Perhaps Mister Hoover might issue the instructions."

"I have no such authority. I don't mind discussing hypothetical situations with you gentlemen, but I would steer well clear of issuing any such order."

Marley sighed in an exasperated fashion. "Perhaps you two gentlemen will excuse me if I choose to have a private conversation with the Officer."

The AG and Hoover almost leapt to their feet to be the first to get out the door.

Jack was ushered back inside the meeting room. Marley gestured to a chair next to his. "I will give this briefcase to the Attorney General. He will have the responsibility to determine whether we have valid charges against the Senator." Marly offered Jack a cigar and Jack politely declined. "We have a giant problem, Special Agent Kelly. It might be very embarrassing to the administration if this Arbuthnot fellow was able to find his way into a court of law. He would spray accusations of complicity about in an effort to minimize his guilt. The upper echelons of the Party might well be unjustly accused of participating in various crimes and conspiracies. It would be well if this evil bastard died where he was found."

Jack smiled wryly, "That would be my sentiment, but for a slightly different reason."

Marly pulled on his cigar and waited for an explanation.

"The guy killed two cops. I don't want to see some slick attorney get him a life sentence, or what might be worse I don't want to see some politician pardon the bastard after a couple of years in jail."

Marley and Jack both knew that the only politicians that possessed that sort of power would be the Governor or the President.

Marley gestured with his cigar. "Point well taken, I don't want it to come to that. In fact, just between you and I. I would encourage you to see to it that the man never reaches a court house."

This all sounded very familiar to Jack. Hoover had once suggested such a thing to him. These bastards sat on the fat asses far removed from the street and couched their directions as being suggestions. If the agent found himself in trouble for following their suggestions they would deny that any such conversation ever took place. "I may not be in on the final chapter of Mister Arbuthnot's life, but considering how aggressive he is I can almost guarantee that he won't survive the arrest."

"About the briefcase," Marley said vaguely.

Jack looked directly into Marley eyes. "I work for the government. I am neither judge nor jury. My job is too obtain the evidence, not to determine how it is too be used. Having outlined my position, I might point out that I would be very unhappy should that evidence go to waste. Arbuthnot is a killer, Caine is worse. He is a traitor to his oath of office."

Marley slowly nodded. "I can sympathize with that position, Jack, but need I remind you that the woods are full of such men and weeding them out is a very delicate task. We may have but a few years left to accomplish that goal. Maybe we can let the damned Republicans handle the problem."

"This is probably the best time to get rid of him, Mister Marley. I think if I were you I would distrust a man that would sell his soul to the highest bidder. You had better never take your eyes off of him for long."

Marley grinned, "You definitely have a point Jack. Go about your work young man and good luck in your effort to rid the world of Mister Arbuthnot." He pulled the briefcase closer to him and the message was obvious.

Jack nodded a good day and left the room. Both the AG and the Director almost pushed past him to get into the room. As he got into the elevator he glanced at his watch. It was almost three p.m. he wondered how in the hell anybody got anything done with all of these meetings.

Harry was waiting and as Jack entered he gestured with his hand, as thumbs up or down.

Jack just grinned, "We've got work to do, Harry."

Harry matched the grin.

Jack smiled at the irony. Maybe the press wouldn't need the briefcase after all. "Where are we with Arbuthnot?"

"He ended up stealing the cab and drove to the nearest train station. The ticket guy remembers seeing a man dressed as a seaman buying a ticket and getting on a train for the District of Columbia. We had officers waiting at the central station and figure that he got off somewhere along the line. Everybody along that line is looking for him."

"He'll have to change clothes and get some money somewhere."

"Probably a robbery or perhaps a friend," Harry agreed. "We have news broadcasts on the radio. He'll be running out of friends in a hurry."

Jack sat down next to the desk and began to fidget. "I think the key is going to be Senator Caine. This guy has to know that Caine ratted on him. I think that if we watch Caine then sooner of later we'll find Arbuthnot."

"Caine has turned down any offer of additional body guards."

"Where does Caine live?"

"He has an apartment in town and a little fourteen room country place out in Forest Falls."

"What kind of security does he have in town?"

"He has a private chauffer and one or two body guards. These guys are former Secret Service Officers and they are damned good. Nobody is going to get close to Caine with these guys around."

"How about the Farm?"

Harry shrugged. "No idea. It would be a Secret Service function, but they don't have people with each Senator unless they are specifically requested."

"Let's go out to the country."

"What for?" Harry asked.

"For something to do, I can't just sit here."

"Come on, Jack, what are you thinking?"

"I'm thinking that Arbuthnot has got to get to Caine where it hurts. He just might try to do something to the family to lure the old man out from under the protection of his men."

Harry nodded slowly and then said, "Let's go protect the Senator whether he expects it from us or not."

It was growing dark as they drove up to the gates of the Caine Estate. Harry stopped the car at the entrance and stared for a minute at the formidable obstacle. It was a huge wrought iron double gate with sharp spikes protecting the top of it. An eight-foot high block wall fence, shielded by shrubbery extended for several hundred feet in both directions. A small gatehouse was positioned unobtrusively amongst heavy shrubbery at the left side of the gate. There was no guard and no apparent way to signal the house.

The two men looked to left and right seeking a way around the obstacle. Across the street and backed in some trees on that side sat a Buick Sedan. Jack walked over and checked it out. The keys were in the ignition. He pulled them out and laid them on the left front tire. Then he walked back across the road and stared for a moment at the gate.

"That's an odd arrangement," Jack said as he approached the gate. Then he grabbed the wrought Iron gate and scaled it with all the grace of an acrobat. He dropped lightly to the other side and went to the gate house.

Harry sat there in the car marveling at the fluid grace of the big man. He remarked to himself that anyone else would have struggled for several minutes to get over it and yet Jack had made it look easy. "What have you got over there, Jack?"

"The gate guard is jammed down in the gate house and has a bullet hole squarely between the eyes. It looks to be about a thirty-eight-caliber wound. We definitely have trouble here. I think you had better call on your radio and notify the local cops"

Harry struggled with the radio as Jack went jogging up the driveway toward the house. "Wait Jack, open the gate." Harry grabbed the radio, but the reception in this hilly area was not very good. "Wait, Jack, I can't get them! Jack hold up! Goddamn it," He shouted as he put the car in gear. He had to find a telephone and the nearest house was at least a mile away.

Jack stayed along the right edge of the drive and he jogged easily along. As he neared the house he removed the forty-five from its holster and jacked a round into the chamber. The Packard Touring car was parked in the garage facing outward toward the street. Rather than approaching the house directly Jack skirted along the wooded area and then when he was in a blind area he ran across the open grassy field to the garage. He found the body of the uniformed chauffer sitting upright in the driver's seat with a slashed throat. He rather futilely checked the man's pulse more out of habit than hope. Sighing in exasperation he headed for the kitchen door. Then he heard a sound behind him. He spun about leveling the weapon. There it was again? Jack back tracked to the garage. He had half expected to see the remains of the Senator's entire family strung out as lifeless crumbs leading to the body of the Senator. Much to his surprise he found a maid, a butler and the woman of the house and Melinda all gagged and tied up snuggly in a back room off of the garage. Their eyes went wide at the sight of the pistol in his hand and Mrs. Caine began struggling violently with her bounds. Melinda was lying there. She was slightly disheveled but as lovely as ever. Her skirt was hiked up well above her hips. He pulled her skirt down, smiled, and left them all lying there.

As Jack entered through the kitchen and found the body of the first body guard lying in a pool of blood. Then he went forward to the front of the house. It was there that he found the other guard lying in the foyer. There was obviously no hope for either of these two. It would have taken some time for them to bleed out in such a fashion so they must have lain there for some time. Where in the hell were Arbuthnot and Caine?

That was when he heard the first sirens. Christ, he thought, that should do it.

Voices were raised in violent argument and then three shots rang out in the library off of foyer to the right. Then Arbuthnot appeared in the doorway struggling with a heavy satchel. He was momentarily as surprised as Jack was and they exchanged fire. Even as the first rounds left the weapons, Jack was knocked to his knees with a hammer like blow to the left hip. Arbuthnot took a round through the chest and staggered backwards. His second shot went wild and Jack's second shot caught him between the eyes and about tore his head off. Arbuthnot's body fell back into the library. Jack fell to the floor in the foyer. After a moment or two he could hear the police cars coming up the drive. The pain in his hip was excruciating. He wanted to see what he could do for the Senator, but there wasn't much likelihood of doing any good in there.

Then as things began to go blurry the police were forcing the front door and Harry Moffett came running in. Moffett kneeled down next to Jack. He had a worried expression on his face.

"Behind the garage, servants quarters, there's four of them," Jack managed and then he passed out.

Jack woke up in the hospital. The surgery had required several hours. The prognosis, offered by a properly subdued doctor was that they had saved his leg, but that he would forever walk with a heavy limp and might have to employ a cane. He was in pain, severe pain.

When he next awoke the room was empty and barren. Just his bed was there. He remembered patches, little incidents, perhaps a part of this and a part of that. Perhaps they were dreams then again maybe they were reality he couldn't tell one from the other. It was close, the Doctor said at some meeting.

At some point he heard a nurse speaking to another woman. "He has no friends that care? How sad. He is a very handsome young man in a rough sort of way."

When next he awoke his mother was there and she was crying.

"Why all the tears?" He croaked."

"Oh Jack," She shouted, "Dad, Jack's coming around. Oh Jack, I'm so glad."

His father had the usual kind words. "Let's get that kid home, before these incompetent bastards kill him."

Jack remembered the train ride back to Chicago through patches of drug induced fog. By the time he could reasonably understand everything that was going on two weeks had elapsed. His hip was bad, so bad in fact, the doctor explained, that someday they may have to do some more exploratory surgery.

"In a pig's ass," Jack murmured.

Jack was up on crutches and it was tough at first, but he caught the hang of it. The pain was slowly subsiding as the February days went by.

J. Townsend came by the house and congratulated Jack on getting Arbuthnot. "Too bad you couldn't have stopped him before he killed the Senator. Bucky Williams was to be given a pass for turning states evidence. The other gentlemen were scheduled to be tried some time next year. The courts are so overcrowded," J. Townsend explained. "Well," He said as he got up to leave, "Some how the Administration is coming out smelling like a rose. The newspapers are lying off of the bribe stuff. Thankfully there are always so many other things to keep the presses turning these days. The truth is that we have exceeded the public's attention span. Surprisingly, you are being regarded as something of a hero."

"How gratifying," Jack said with a sardonic smile.

One has to be very careful when walking on crutches in the snow. The slightest little imperfection in the pavement can send you tumbling. Jack always took care to land on his right hip, which would impart heavy shooting pains through to the left, but he soon learned to endure the pain. After a bit somewhere in mid March he graduated to a cane. The black snow had gotten ever darker by the week and then one day it was all gone. A spring rain had washed the filth down the gutters.

By April it looked as though it would be a while longer before he could walk without a cane, but he was well on his way to mending.

Jack was summoned to the Chicago Bureau Office to chat with the Director. He could just about imagine what this would be about. Thank you for you service, Mister Kelly. Don't let the door hit you in the ass. In this case he expected to be cashiered, and expected very little in return, perhaps there might be some little pension offer, wounded in service and all that crap. He had discussed law with his father, who in effect told him that it was about time he grew up and went into real work. Still he went to the meeting.

The new secretary was really a very attractive woman. She had nice legs. With all that time in bed to consider such things Jack had decided that he was an ass man. He really preferred women with pert little derrieres although one had to admit that there were other enticements. This lady looked to be a very nice girl.

Someone in the office had found Hoover a chair that would bring him almost up to a head level with a normal sized man. They sat there staring at one another for a full minute, until Hoover grimaced.

"I have considered your future assignment. The Doctors tell me that you have done remarkably well. Some didn't think that you would ever walk again, to be doing so without even a cane for support so soon is, they say, something of a miracle. Frankly, I would have expected something of the sort from you. By the way Mister Marley sends his best regards. He had great faith in you, but he sort of regretted your killing the Senator."

Jack gulped, "Killing the Senator, where in the hell did he get that idea?"

"Mister Marley is of the opinion that you are a very accomplished killer. That, coming from him, is something of a complement. It turns out that the President agreed with you that the Senator was a very dangerous ally. And so in an odd sort of way everyone was pleased when it worked out so well." Hoover smiled urbanely, "I might add that you and the Bureau were the subjects of considerable praise at the Cabinet meetings." Then he frowned, "There were of course a few bad points. Mrs. Caine is incensed that you didn't untie her and that you allegedly messed with her daughters skirt."

Jack decided that he almost couldn't take any more of this crap and started to rise.

"Wait, Mister Kelly, I haven't given you your assignment as yet. I first considered some far off distant post. Puerto Rico and Panama came to mind and then I realized that being a product to the eastern seaboard, I wasn't looking at a broad enough picture. Alaska came to mind. There is a small military detachment at Dutch Harbor, which I am told is out on the Aleutian Island chain."

Jack glanced up at Hoover and it was obvious the man was enjoying this immensely.

"Considering your present acclaim in the oval office, I ran this assignment by the President and it was Mister Marley that reminded me that we owed you something better than that. Nevertheless, I insisted that it be as far away from Washington as possible. I have settled on Hawaii. Out of a feeling of gratitude I am sending you to Honolulu."

Jack sat there astounded. He had heard that they were some really beautiful women in Hawaii. No more black snow. It was far enough away from Washington that one could breathe in the fresh air. Well now, things were looking up again. "May I ask one question Mister Hoover?"

Hoover frowned, but reluctantly nodded.

"What was in the valise that Arbuthnot took from Caine's office?"

"What valise? We didn't find a valise." Hoover asked with a smirk and then he smiled a superior self satisfied smile. "There never was a valise, Mister Kelly it was probably a figment of your imagination, perhaps some drug induced specter of a dream." Hoover held up the halting hand, "Please don't try to correct me, at the moment I am still in somewhat of a benevolent mood and Dutch Harbor remains a possibility. As soon as we get a green light from your physicians you are on your way Mister Kelly, on your way to far off places."

Jack didn't know whether to laugh or cry. The dirty bastards, he thought, and then he started to laugh. What the hell times were tough and he still had a job.

The End.